MURRAY SMITH

Legacy

MICHAEL JOSEPH
LONDON

MICHAEL JOSEPH LTD

Published by the Penguin Group
27 Wrights Lane, London W8 5TZ, England
Viking Putnam Inc., 375 Hudson Street, New York, New York 10014, USA
Penguin Books Australia Ltd, Ringwood, Victoria, Australia
Penguin Books Canada Ltd, 10 Alcorn Avenue, Toronto, Ontario, Canada M4V 3B2
Penguin Books (NZ) Ltd, 182–190 Wairau Road, Auckland 10, New Zealand

Penguin Books Ltd, Registered Offices: Harmondsworth, Middlesex, England

First published 1998

Copyright © Murray Smith, 1998
10 9 8 7 6 5 4 3 2 1

The moral right of the author has been asserted

Set in 12/14.5pt Monotype Bembo
Typeset by Rowland Phototypesetting Ltd,
Bury St Edmunds, Suffolk
Printed in England by Clays Ltd, St Ives plc

A CIP catalogue record for this book is available from the British Library

Hardback ISBN 0-7181-4335-3
Paperback ISBN 0-7181-4176-8

for Christian and Kiaran

Acknowledgements

The author would like to thank the Boston Police Department for its unstinting assistance in researching this book. Among the several detectives who went out of their way, special thanks are due to James Fitzgerald, Thomas Boyle and Larry Robicheau. Also the Dublin Records Office for easing my investigation of the adoption, legal and otherwise, of illegitimate infants.

And special thanks to Kiaran for his tireless research and wise comments, to Christian for sharing his knowledge of Byzantine Sicily and to Roz for her help and encouragement during the writing of the manuscript.

Jack never knew he was dead. One second he was on top of the world, flashing that glance of his that had won for him so much of his own way for so many years, his cool, intelligent eyes meeting those of Tom Hanrahan, spinning the wheel to keep Zeralda's prancing bowsprit exactly on 53°, so alive, so vital. Then the big ketch surged on a forty-foot wave and the close-hauled boom, 1,134 pounds of solid teak, swung faster than a bullet, to smash his head and propel his already lifeless corpse off the yacht and into the dark, green, thundering sea.

That's how quick it was.

It's how Jack would have liked it.

1

It had been snowing. Not that feathery, gentle cascade, the stuff of Christmas cards. And not the driving, hostile, silent attack that sent explorers to their doom. More a half-hearted, in-between sort of snow, cold and falling in a relentless curtain on Dublin's grey pavements, still warm from the false thaw, to settle into a thick, grimy slush.

And the light was a silent, cold, cadmium yellow, hanging all over the city, pale and ominous, like a shroud.

Two days earlier, about a hundred miles to the south-west, the cemetery at Crough Bay had been white as a Vermont winter landscape. Unheard of, Joe O'Shea the handyman and supplier of potheen from his still in the hills of Glen Carr had declared, it being so close to the Atlantic coast and the warming waters of the Gulf Stream.

Half the Irish cabinet had been there, along with Jean Kennedy Smith, the American ambassador, William Gates, from Silicon Valley on the West Coast of the USA, the mayor of Boston and representatives from Harvard University, the Massachusetts Institute of Technology, the New York Yacht Club, the Americas Cup Committee and the US and Irish horse-racing world, for Jack had been a keen man for the Turf.

As the mourners had walked back to the big house, the scrape and dull clunk of gravediggers' spades against iron-hard earth had accompanied them, muffled by the drifts, like funeral drums, their steady rhythm just as final.

It was hard to think of Jack being dead, and squelching along the grimy Dublin pavements on her way to Fitzwilliam Square, Alison Clancy remembered the last time she had seen him, just two weeks before. Exhilarated and exhausted, at four in the morning in the Boston board room, the big Irish-American had just survived a hostile raid by the Katakura Corporation and in the process, like a pike snatching a passing trout, had swiped from under their noses a four-year deal to supply Zeralda micro-electronics to McDonnell Douglas, a deal worth over two hundred million dollars in finder's fees alone.

Always courteous, the corporation's president had thanked his colleagues and had personally shown them off the premises and by the time he came back upstairs, Alison had stowed away the champagne – Jack couldn't stand the stuff but he knew his colleagues had appreciated the gesture, to toast a new beginning – and she was pouring him a glass of thick black Irish stout, and an apple soda for herself.

Jack had tugged off his necktie and flopped into one of the eleven leather and steel chairs, imported from Finland, which surrounded the long, iroko table.

'Ali,' he said, 'we beat the bastards, gloves off and up against the wall, but we did it.' There was perspiration on his face, still tanned from a Christmas cruising the Leeward Islands. And his chest heaved with an excitement he could at last reveal, now that they had all gone.

'This is what you live for, isn't it?' Alison smiled, watching him. 'Keeping Zeralda all for yourself.'

His eyes had glinted, amused. He drank down half the pint tumbler in one go, then wiped his mouth with the back of his hand and smiled that quiet smile she had come to look forward to.

'Not to the exclusion of all else,' he had replied softly. 'Lock the door.'

But Alison had already been turning the key, heart pounding, and now, trudging through the slush on her way to the family lawyer's Dublin office, feet damp and chilled, she remembered every detail of the last time she and Jack Fitzrowan, self-made captain of industry, and she, Alison Clancy, attorney at law, had made love. It had been . . . nice.

But all that was gone, and her letter of resignation from Zeralda nestled in her purse, like a paper time bomb. For once out of that dynasty, there was no way back.

'Jesus, Mary and Joseph,' said Bridget O'Callaghan as she waddled her ample behind, encased in a few yards of Moriarty's tweed, up the stairs towards the offices of Stevenson, Stevenson & Malahide, Solicitors and Notaries Public. 'I'll be dead meself before I get to the top of these.'

Alison, who was following Bridget, smiled. From somewhere below the voice of Paul drifted up, along with a waft of Dublin street sounds, traffic and a fellow calling Dan, Dan, you forgot your . . . the rest was indistinct, it sounded like goldfish. Or maybe galoshes.

'. . . the five o'clock shuttle,' Paul's soft, educated brogue was saying, 'for I have an early start in the morning.'

'Don't tell me you have a job after all this time, Paul Fitzrowan, for I just won't believe you.' This was a more familiar voice, for Grace Hanrahan, Paul's sister, had a place on the board of Zeralda and Alison had briefed her just the week before, in Boston, over the firm's commitments and plans. Jack's plans. Grace's ongoing crusade was to persuade her husband, Tom, to leave the Homicide Division and join Zeralda's board, then go into politics. Stranger things had happened.

'Markus and I have a recording studio booked,' said Paul. 'We're making a demo and Mick Jagger's lawyer said he would play it to him.' Paul wrote occasional lyrics for unsuccessful rock bands and was a part-time session guitarist.

'Playing? That's what you're doing all right. And who's paying for the recording studio, as if I need to ask . . . ?'

'In the name of the merciful Virgin would you listen to them? It was the same when I used to wipe their noses at the big house: argue, argue, argue.' Bridget angled her considerable girth on the landing outside one of those frosted-glass doors like in old Bogart movies, with STEVENSON, STEVENSON & MALAHIDE painted on it in gold. She lowered her voice. 'He was a lovely child you know. The way his eyes lit up when you gave him lemonade in the summer you'd have thought it was holy water.'

Daft old biddy, thought Alison Clancy to herself as she murmured politely and followed Bridget into the lawyer's office to join the assembled company.

'Well now,' said Pronsias Stevenson, glancing at the assembled relations, close colleagues and family servants, sitting quietly on chairs brought in from his partners' offices, 'we are thus convened, to learn the last will and testament of John Pearce Dunmill Fitzrowan, fourteenth baronet Fitzrowan, President of Zeralda Electronics Incorporated of Boston, Massachusetts and Chairman of its wholly owned subsidiary, Zeralda Electronic Industries of Dublin, Ireland.'

A coal and turf fire flickered comfortingly in the small grate. The room smelled of polished wood, leather and old volumes. Open on the eighteenth-century desk was a leather-bound folder bedecked with red and pink seals and ribbons. The Will. This, Stevenson reflected, was what they had all gathered here for, flying across the Atlantic from Boston, driving into town from their country estates, or by the railway, the retainers among them. Jack's younger daughter Grace had travelled by personal Lear Jet from California, where she had been on Zeralda's business, and Paul, from London, on the shuttle. The dynasty was thus convened.

The dynasty, Fitzrowan had chuckled when his lawyer teased him he was after rivalling the Kennedys. But looking around the room, and with such considerable wealth to disburse, the makings were all there.

Jack had not been born rich. His father was an Irish aristocrat with twelve generations of the same behind him. But what money there had once been had long since gone and a rambling, tumble-down country house, its first stones laid in 1589, and three hundred stony acres of County Kerry were his inheritance. That and a brain that was to confound many adversaries before Takahashi Katakura met his match.

From those penurious if not exactly humble beginnings, and despite his reputation for sailing close to the wind in his financial affairs, Jack Fitzrowan had amassed an impressive private fortune. Not to mention the Zeralda Corporation.

It was rare, Pronsias Stevenson considered, for a minor member of the landed gentry, no matter how hard up, to take the plunge, first renting out, then selling up his acres to put himself through Trinity College Dublin and MIT, followed by an MBA from Harvard.

You couldn't help thinking about Jack without fond memories. Sure he was a tyrant, sure he rode roughshod over every man (and not a few women) who got in his path, but Jack Fitzrowan had also been most generous and stoutly courageous, whether sailing his beloved *Zeralda of Erin* off the Connecticut coast or presiding in the board room, and strangely forgiving – traits which, coupled with his almost feline perception, made the dead electronics million-aire a most complicated human being.

Dead. Stevenson felt a coldness in the room. If he were to get maudlin about it, he supposed Fitzrowan had been as close to a best friend as any attorney would prudently allow.

The lawyer put on his reading glasses. The room was silent, apart from the gentle hissing of the turf fire in the grate. He cleared his throat and, gazing over his half-moon spectacles, studied the assembled beneficiaries. Their expressions varied from studied non-chalance among the immediate family to apprehensive expectancy from the lower orders.

'Sir Jack was both an American and an Irish citizen, having dual nationality. Just plain Jack, in Boston, as he used to say . . .' Just plain Jack in Kerry too, thought the lawyer. The 'sir' came from an old Anglo-Irish baronetcy, going back to the twelfth century. And Jack Fitzrowan had never been slow to use the old title, either to further his business, or to annoy people – that was the Irish in him. '. . . but he chose to have his family affairs handled in Dublin and his will is in accordance with Irish law.

'Sir Jack hated official jargon and red tape, as I am sure you all know, so you will not, I trust, find this at all hard to follow.' He picked up the Will and began to read. '"I John Pearce Dunmill Fitzrowan, being of sound mind and body, do hereby declare this document dated fourteenth July nineteen hundred and ninety-five, to be my last will and testament . . ."'

As Stevenson dispensed with the legal preliminaries Grace Hanrahan crossed her elegant legs and contemplated what differences to her life this imminent inheritance would make. She wondered just how much was involved. Zeralda, while a solid enterprise, was repaying a massive investment loan from the First National Bank and share prices had dipped following the Katakura take-over bid. But Jack was nobody's fool and Grace had seen and heard enough over the years to know his properties in Kerry, Boston and Connecticut were unencumbered and his art collection was his own. With shrewd investments, she calculated her father would have left around eighteen million dollars: about five million each for herself, Darcy and Paul.

Surely now Tom would get out of the police force and take a seat on the board. At forty-one, there was still plenty of time for him to reach the Senate. And with five million in the bank, there would be enough of the folding green stuff to ease his path.

' "To Daniel Shaughnessy, the gardener at Crough Lake House, I leave and bequeath the sum of three thousand pounds," ' Stevenson read out.

Shaughnessy, a man in his early sixties, nodded. What he was thinking, he never, as usual, revealed.

' "To Bridget Deirdre O'Callaghan, cook, jam-maker and nursemaid to the entire household, if not to the County of Kerry, I leave seven thousand pounds." ' Stevenson removed his spectacles and peered at the others. 'Where pounds are mentioned we are talking sterling. Other parts will mention US dollars.'

He replaced the reading glasses and continued. ' "To Joseph O'Shea, my chauffeur-handyman and to his wife Margaret Anunciata O'Shea, peerless housekeeper at Crough Lake, I leave and bequeath each the sum of ten thousand pounds, for they have been with me the longest. Also they are to enjoy a free life tenancy of the cottage in Glenbeigh, on the road to Kilorglin, known as Dook's Cottage, so that they might end their days among their kin. Thereafter, the cottage to return to the estate and the administration of the Executor." '

The O'Sheas exchanged glances of relief and delight. Pronsias

Stevenson marvelled at the way Jack had always managed to bring pleasure to those loyal to him. And pleasure took various forms, he reflected, as he gazed around the room.

Lauren Styvesant, once Jack's social organizer, now a fashion editor, still fine featured and svelte at forty-five; Mary-Anne Radleigh, something important with the US State Department; and the Boston Corporation's legal eagle, Alison Clancy – all very attractive and intelligent women. And all, to be fair, looking as if they would rather have Jack alive and dominating the assembled company than all the dollars or pounds in creation.

There were other peripheral beneficiaries: Jack's Americas Cup skipper, his horse trainer from Lexington, Kentucky, the farrier from Crough Lake, where a dozen Arab thoroughbreds were reared for bloodstock, along with several charities and institutions, a library in Cambridge, Massachusetts, and an orphanage in Louisiana.

While Pronsias Stevenson waded through this with his customary diligence, Grace Hanrahan, sitting near the back next to a bookcase pregnant with legal tomes, took in the others in the room. Her brother Paul, taller than their father, with the same good looks but lacking Jack's essential, restless, afraid-of-nothing attitude, what their sister Darcy had called Dad's fuck-you mouth and quadruple fuck-you eyes. It had become a family code, shortened to 'FYM and E to the power four'.

Had they been scared of him? Maybe. Maybe sometimes. He had always made time for each of them. No favourites. But those eyes – you knew when he was pissed off with you.

Darcy, at thirty-two three years older than Grace, sat a little to the right and further forward. Next to her was Edward, her husband, the only Englishman in the room. Edward was a nice guy. An English don at Oxford, Edward had been orphaned at the age of six and brought up by his mother's brother and his wife. The uncle was a missionary and the boy had been educated at mission schools in north-west India, Ceylon and South America. He had graduated from Oxford and Trinity College Dublin, and had sailed the South China seas on a tramp steamer before returning to the academic world.

Jack Fitzrowan had liked Ed Bailey. He had liked the man's quiet intellect and his easy-going ability to handle Darcy, whose convent school reports had not infrequently included the words 'wilful' and 'headstrong'. Grace wondered what her sister and Edward would do with around five million dollars.

' ". . . and to the Metropolitan Museum of Modern Art, I leave my collection of Van Gogh sketches which, apart from ensuring for them a good and caring home where they can be enjoyed by many, is part of a settlement I reached in 1993 with the I R S." '

Pronsias Stevenson glanced over his half-moon glasses as the assembled beneficiaries laughed gently, if, on the part of his children, somewhat ruefully, for the sketches had been valued at over three million dollars. We're getting near, the lawyer thought, we are getting close to the big surprises. He straightened and waited for silence.

' "To my good friend and social assistant, Lauren Styvesant, of 525 Park Avenue, New York City, the sum of one hundred and seventy thousand dollars . . ." '

The fashion editor nodded. Social assistant, thought Alison Clancy, well that's one name for it.

' "To my infallible secretary and companion on those otherwise lonely days at the Boston office, from 1984 to 1987, now a member of the United States State Department, Mary-Anne Radleigh, the sum of three hundred thousand dollars . . ." '

Mary-Anne Radleigh glanced at her hands, holding her gloves on her knees, then gazed quietly at the attorney. Grace and her husband exchanged discreet glances. It was common knowledge that Jack had been a man of considerable energies, as his obituary in the *New York Times* and London *Telegraph* had diplomatically put it. It was a tribute to her father's considerable tact and grace that his two favourite mistresses sat there among them, without embarrassment on their part, or overt rancour on the part of the more legitimate family and retainers. She wondered which of Mary-Anne's talents merited a bequest nearly double that to Miss Styvesant.

' "To Miss Alison Clancy, of Cambridge, Massachusetts, my

Legal Affairs Executive who in three short years with Zeralda Electronics USA has become indispensable, the sum of three hundred and twelve thousand dollars, which is the bonus she would have received if you were not all sitting here listening to my last will and testament . . ."'

Subdued smiles. If that's what he left his fancy women, thought Darcy to herself, seven hundred and eighty-two thousand dollars, half a million pounds sterling, it augured well for the three heirs. She did not begrudge her father's generosity.

Pronsias Stevenson took a deep breath. 'That covers the . . . um, those outside the immediate family. After due settlement of death duties and outstanding accounts, and following the extraordinary success of his most recent financial dealings, the balance of Sir Jack's financial estate is . . .' Here the lawyer paused, like a striptease artist, down to the final veil. He studied the figures written in copperplate on the ledger in front of him. 'Two hundred and twenty-six million, four hundred and eighteen thousand, four hundred and one dollars. And thirteen cents.'

Holy shit, thought Grace. Tom could make the White House with that kind of money. Seventy-five million each for Darcy, Paul and me, give or take a few dollars.

Pronsias Stevenson would have been offended by any suggestion that he was enjoying himself, but this was a milestone occasion in his life as a lawyer and enjoying himself he certainly was. In his own repressed, tight-sphinctered way. 'Now then,' he went on, 'it was the wish of the deceased, that every beneficiary present should hear the whole of his testament.' Stevenson pushed his glasses down on his nose and looked over them at his rapt audience. 'But we are now into private affairs and I will be guided by the principal family on this matter.'

Darcy turned to Grace. Paul leaned back in his seat and turned to them both. They put their heads together and conferred.

'I have no problem with the others staying,' said Paul.

Darcy frowned, then agreed. 'Why not? There can't be much more, just dividing the balance of the estate . . .'

I love this bit, reflected Stevenson.

Grace contemplated, then relaxed. 'It's all right, Pronsias,' she said to the lawyer. 'Please continue.'

Stevenson nodded. 'Thank you,' he said, and, clearing his throat, returned his attention to the Will.

' "My beloved first wife, Scarlet, having died so tragically while hunting with the Galway Blazers when Darcy was just an infant, and my discerning second wife, Elizabeth, having had the taste and good judgement to divorce me and remarry, choosing a gentleman whom *Forbes* magazine tells me is the sixth wealthiest man in America, and therefore having no need of another few million dollars, I will divide the remainder of my fortune among my children . . ." '

Glory be, thought Grace, who would never have put it past him to leave it all to some floozy.

' "First, my ninety-five per cent holding in Zeralda Electronics Incorporated to be divided in three equal parts between my beloved children, Darcy, Grace and Paul, who will thus each be entitled to an equal place on the board." '

Darcy glanced to her sister. Only Grace had taken an active part in the electronics firm, but knowing how their father often raised huge bank loans as he forced the corporation further into the international big league, Darcy knew that a third of the firm's worth could be a treat, or just plain tricky.

Grace, meanwhile, was calculating that Zeralda shares would on paper make them very rich indeed, say about seven million dollars each. But she also knew Jack Fitzrowan had so tied up the firm's capital in banking collateral that nobody was going to be able to cash in their chips and walk away with real money. Not yet. Maybe in four or five years' time.

' "To my daughter Darcy Patricia," ' Stevenson announced, reading from the pink-ribboned document, ' "I leave and bequeath the sum of two million, six hundred and eighty-four thousand dollars." '

Darcy blinked slightly, her back ramrod straight, the way she rode her three-day eventer in the Dublin and Badminton horse trials. The first pricks of adrenalin jolting into her bloodstream. It's a tax thing, of course, she rationalized, and felt immediately calmer.

Dear old Daddy was a wizard when it came to off-shore funds. This is a death-duty scam. How very clever of him. She wondered how he had sheltered the remaining two hundred and eighteen million. And how it would be made available to the three of them. It would be interesting to hear. Stevenson glanced at her and seemed to read her mind. She smiled, relieved. And Pronsias Stevenson smiled back.

'"And to her fine husband, Edward Alexander Bailey, as good a sailing companion as you could find, in an Englishman"' – Smiles and chuckles and friendly glances towards the man in question – '"the sum of eighty thousand dollars and my yacht, *Zeralda of Erin*, to enjoy and use as he wishes. Unless, of course, *Zeralda* and I have both gone down together and that's why you are sitting in my good friend Pronsias Stevenson's office."'

In the silence which followed, there was not a person in the room who did not feel the cold breath of Jack Fitzrowan's prescience. Tom Hanrahan, who had been looking straight into Jack's eyes when the boom smashed his skull and swept him overboard, sat motionless, his face as grey as a gravestone.

Trust Dad to predict with near accuracy the manner of his own death, thought Paul. Right again, you big windbag, he could hear himself saying – they always called each other daft names – and blinked in annoyance, ambushed by a tremble of the lip and a sudden moistness in the corner of his right eye. Christ, I'll miss you. He swallowed, and the moment passed.

The lawyer continued, '"To my daughter Grace Antonia, I leave and bequeath the sum of two million, six hundred and eighty-four thousand dollars."'

There, Darcy met her sister's eye and smiled a comforting smile, in case Grace had not cottoned on to the cleverness of their father's fiscal mind. But Grace was cool and unperturbed. She too had worked out that these paltry sums were part of some death-duties scheme and that the main millions were being shielded against punitive taxation. Say they finished up with about sixty million each. Grace felt she could get by with that.

'"And to Grace's upstanding husband, Thomas Patrick

Hanrahan, Lieutenant of Detectives in Boston's finest, the sum of eighty thousand dollars, my golf clubs, the signed photograph of John F. Kennedy – did I not threaten to do this, Tom? I'll be chuckling wherever the good Lord has sent me, for every time she sets eyes on it, my beloved daughter Grace will start on at you again to quit the force and run for the Senate."'

Laughter, during which Grace had the grace to blush.

Pronsias Stevenson smiled, and returned to the business in hand. '"And also to you, Tom, my Aston Martin motor car. Try explaining that to Internal Affairs . . ."'

Tom grinned. He and Jack had spent many a weekend driving out to the Lincoln country club in that car to play a round of golf.

Stevenson sipped from a tumbler of water and continued. '"To my dear son Paul. *Sir* Paul now . . ."'

My God thought Alison, of course he is. It had never occurred to her. Sir Paul Fitzrowan. She supposed he would now be described in the media as a twenty-four-year-old titled millionaire rock groupie. There was, indeed, no justice.

'"To my son Paul, who has no interest in worldly wealth and who is content writing his songs and playing his music, I leave and bequeath Crough Lake and all the land and property therein, together with my house in Boston and my Dublin flat, to enjoy during his lifetime, thereafter to be inherited in equal shares by my daughters Darcy and Grace, or their heirs and successors. Also to Paul, the sum of two million, six hundred and eighty-four thousand dollars. To be held in a trust, administered by my good friend Pronsias Stevenson, of Stevenson, Stevenson & Malahide, so that you will never go short, Paul, but you will not be able to blow the lot in some hare-brained scheme."'

Eyes were on Paul. Bloody Dad, he was thinking, how can you make me so choked one instant and so fucking angry the next? Of course I can look after my own bloody affairs. Stevenson was looking at him with barely concealed distaste. And Paul looked right back. Oh, this is going to be fun, having to crawl to you every time I need a few quid.

Come on, come on. Darcy was watching the attorney intently.

Tell us about the big bucks. That's what we're all doing here. And she realized, with something approaching physical arousal, that with all these millions, this would be a perfect time to grasp the nettle and divorce good old, boring old, Edward.

At the time, Darcy had felt that, by marrying someone so very different from her father, she was asserting her independence. She probably had assumed Jack would be annoyed at his elder, hell-raising daughter, never out of the gossip columns of *Vanity Fair* and the *Irish Times*, settling for a dull, safe, Oxford don whose idea of risk-taking would be to split an infinitive or invent an oxymoron.

But Jack Fitzrowan had taken to Edward Bailey with such a huge and disconcerting generosity of spirit that Darcy sometimes wondered if the whole thing was a piece of play-acting, just to tease her. Edward, on the other hand, was impressed (*quietly* of course) by the electronics millionaire's sharp intelligence, and the breadth of Fitzrowan's interests. So Darcy had been stuck with him. For Daddy, though divorced himself, would not have countenanced such behaviour from his own daughter. Well, no longer. There was a New York trader with Merrill Lynch she had been seeing discreetly for the last two years. And the skipper of Daddy's Americas Cup yacht, lean and muscled, with a taste for Jack Daniel's and certain things polite ladies did not mention. Time to break free and live a little. Darcy felt warm at the thought.

Her husband glanced at her and smiled gently, as if to reassure her. She smiled back, her green eyes pools of mystery, her thoughts far away.

Pronsias Stevenson lifted the ribbon-bedecked vellum testament to reveal a slimmer document, replete with red and green wax seals and more pink tape. 'There are certain instructions,' he said, 'concerning the disbursement of any residue of funds, but as we shall see, these have been overtaken by events.'

Excellent, thought Grace, we're getting close to the nitty gritty. Close to learning how Daddy sheltered his real wealth. It was comforting, how he had always been thinking of his heirs. Being so busy and all.

The attorney read on. 'Sir Jack closes the main will and testament by indicating he would like to be buried in the small family cemetery at Crough Lake, and he mentions how satisfied he is to have bought back the big house and estate from Herr von Schlader. Well, we buried our friend there two days ago, of course, so that concludes the business of the original will.'

The turf fire hissed comfortably in the hearth. Somewhere outside a Dublin bus sounded its horn, a faint, remote sound, light years from this cramped, Dickensian room which seemed suspended in time and space. It was like being at a seance.

Time for the big surprise, the *pièce de résistance*. Stevenson seemed to be reading the slim document before conveying its contents. He glanced at a couple of pages, nodding to himself, as if making sure he understood its every nuance. Then he leaned back in his chair and spoke.

'There is a codicil.'

He turned to the lower orders, to Bridget and Dan, to Joe and Anunciata. 'A codicil is something which the deceased added to his will at a later date. It has been witnessed and properly attested by a notary. It is completely in order and such things are not entirely unusual.' Stevenson held the codicil at arm's length and said, 'I'll read it, just as Sir Jack wrote it down.'

The lawyer took a breath, then, ' "Over forty years ago, being just nineteen, I met the love of my life. Three years younger than I, she felt the same way. We were fierce and elated lovers, head over heels, brushing fingers in the corridors, to consummate our secret. You know, I would find my breath catching as she scurried from the kitchen to clear the table, or out in the back courts, hanging out calico bags of apple and ginger jelly. For my Helen Costello was a kitchen maid.

' "Of course I should have been more cautious, more responsible, but we were both young and she became with child." '

Stevenson's eyes met Darcy's once more. Her smile had gone. He continued, ' "My father, the thirteenth baronet, and my stepmother, Lady Caroline had, as they say in Galway, a severe sense of humour failure. Being good Catholics, abortion was out of the question.

Within the week, Helen was packed off to confinement with discreet people – where she was sent I could not, despite every effort, discover.'"

Bridget sat whey-faced, kneading her handbag as if it were a lump of dough. She could hear the laughter and the whispers from young Helen's tiny cell, along the passage from her own, in the servants' quarters at Crough Lake. Cold and draughty the big house had been then, before Sir Jack had sold it to a German with delusions of grandeur and the Kraut, as the locals had called him, had installed central heating, fresh copper-pipe plumbing and all kinds of things such as washing machines, deep freezers and enormous fridges from the USA.

And in that cold and draughty servants' wing Bridget, then just twenty-three herself, second cook and jam-maker, used to lie in the dark, listening to the gasps of delight and the energetic pounding of Helen Costello's bedsprings. God, they were all so young then. She remembered too the sounds of the little kitchen maid's sobbing, and going to her room, and the sixteen-year-old's terror at being three weeks late.

There had been an old woman, a traveller, in a trailer up in Glen Carr, who, it was said, could resolve such disasters; but Bridget had also heard of a Glenbeigh girl who had died of infection afterwards. She had kept her counsel, half because she did not want to endanger Helen's life, and half because she needed the work and could not risk getting the sack.

One night there had been the muffled sound of a motor car in the back courtyard, as if it was reversing. And some whispers, from the master's wife, Lady Caroline (a right bitch, with a smarmy smile and fake words of concern to trap the unwary), and two others, one a woman, the other a man. And in the morning Helen's room was empty, bed stripped and her few things gone.

'"As soon as the baby was born,"' the lawyer continued, '"it was handed over to adoptive parents who took it, I believe, to America. And Helen was dispatched to Australia, with money for a few weeks' keep and a letter of introduction to help her gain employment as a kitchen servant. I never heard from her again."'

Grace noticed her husband and Edward Bailey exchange looks and felt an irrational spasm of hatred for their insouciance. Jesus, did they not realize this meant the money was likely going to be split four ways now, for this codicil heralded something momentous, she could feel it.

Pronsias Stevenson had paused. Bridget was fumbling in her handbag for a hanky. Then he went on, '"But even through two marriages, with two attractive and educated women, and through all the gratifying success of Zeralda Electronics there was not a day which went by without me thinking of Helen. And missing her. After years of trying to trace her, I had given up all hope until, in February last year, word reached me in Boston, by a circuitous route, that Helen was in hospital in Zurich. She had been knocked down by a tram and had asked for me. She was badly injured and not likely to survive.

'"Of course I flew immediately to her bedside, where Helen had by great effort of will clung to life so that she could be held by me just once more. She told me that, over all those years, she had never stopped loving me, she had been so proud of my so-called success. A success I would have surrendered for just the touch of her hand, for the sound of her laughter. I was so relieved to be able to kiss her and tell her she had never been out of my thoughts.

'"Helen told me she had been looked after by two unmarried women in the west, and had been treated with kindness but never permitted to leave the house, which was in a remote part of the country, not far from the sea, for there were gulls sometimes, wheeling around, before a storm. The baby was a boy, delivered on the fourteenth of June nineteen hundred and fifty-four. She had called our son Oliver, although she doubted if his adoptive parents, whoever they were, would have respected that.

'"Although I assembled the finest doctors in Europe to do everything they could to save her, the following day my beloved Helen passed away, holding my hand. And just before she died, I swore that I would move heaven and earth to find Oliver, or die in the attempt.

'"Well, since my good friend Pronsias Stevenson is reading this aloud, my promise remains unfulfilled. And so without more ado, I bequeath the balance of my fortune to my first-born son, in legally specific terms the male child born to one Helen Theresa Costello on or about the fourteenth of June nineteen hundred and fifty-four, and my solicitors Stevenson, Stevenson & Malahide are to use every means to find him and furnish him with his legacy.

'"If Oliver is proven to be dead, the money will be distributed equally among the three principal beneficiaries, Paul, Darcy and Grace, and Oliver's surviving offspring, if any.

'"In order to encourage my friends and family to assist in the search for Oliver, twelve and one half per cent of the balance of this legacy will be deducted and paid to any of the principal beneficiaries today assembled who finds him.

'"Should a period of eighty-nine years elapse since the date of Oliver's birth without him having been traced, the legacy will be divided equally among the heirs and successors of the principal beneficiaries.

'"Any attempt to circumvent or dispute the terms of this codicil will result in immediate forfeiture of that individual's personal bequest. And should any beneficiary harm or commission the harming of Oliver, they will forfeit any inheritance provided by this last will and testament.

'"In all matters concerning this, the decision of my good friend Pronsias Stevenson will be final. If Pronsias is no longer available, then the most senior of his legal partners will substitute. Pronsias Stevenson also has my authority to release disbursements, at his discretion, to any person or group with a realistic proposal aimed at finding my lost son and principal heir, who in order to receive his inheritance has only to change his surname to mine."'

Pronsias Stevenson removed his reading glasses and closed the file with the Will and codicil. Every eye was upon him, the three Fitzrowan offspring each had a kind of a searching intensity written on their faces, as if they hoped to hear more, as if they needed to learn that the finality of that codicil could somehow be overridden.

You could have heard the snow falling outside.

To Alison Clancy, sitting to one side of the room, it seemed as if the moment had been frozen in time. It was like the profound stillness immediately after a car crash. Just before the screams. The expressionless faces of Grace and her sister gave way first to confusion, then to cold fury. Only Paul seemed relaxed about the bombshell.

It was Darcy, sitting there primed like a grenade, who failed to contain her emotions.

'A bastard . . .' she intoned, almost to herself.

'Darcy,' murmured Edward, mildly, his essential Englishness setting him apart from the others.

'A bastard son.' Darcy had never been renowned for her self-possession. 'And how much is it that this bastard Oliver is to inherit?' This last directly to Pronsias Stevenson.

'Two hundred and eighteen million dollars,' replied Grace, before the lawyer could answer.

Stevenson nodded. 'Give or take a few hundred thousand,' he confirmed.

'Well that cannot be right.' Darcy had never been angrier. Nor her husband Edward, the Oxford don, more embarrassed. 'Daddy and the rest of us were tight.' She looked around for support. Grace nodded, as did Dan the gardener and Anunciata O'Shea, although her husband Joe remained impassive. 'He would never have . . .' here she nearly burst into tears – of rage or hurt, sensed Alison – and faltered for a moment, '*humiliated* us like that. Under three million to his real children and . . . how much?'

She can't believe this is happening, reflected the attorney to himself. There had been a time when Darcy, an incredible flirt in her twenties, like so many well-born, convent-educated girls, had seemed almost . . . available, and to be honest, she was still an attractive young woman. Even more attractive, he mused, than the fairly stunning Lauren Styvesant, whose elegantly crossed legs had not escaped his notice, even while reading the driest parts of the Will.

But when he had dared, just the once and so very casually, at the 1983 Kentucky Derby (when one of Jack's horses had overhauled the favourite at the last furlong and Darcy, high on adrenalin, had hugged him), to suggest dinner together, her response had been laughingly scathing. As if the very idea was too absurd to take seriously. Well now she was hurting. And Stevenson felt a certain mild satisfaction at her discomfiture.

'About two hundred and eighteen million dollars,' he repeated, meeting her confused, outraged, gaze.

'And where did it come from?' Darcy's eyes had narrowed. Confused and outraged she might be, but she had just formulated the question on everyone's mind. 'What, precisely, was the sudden, overnight if you like, source of this . . . king's ransom?'

Stevenson nodded, and pushed the beribboned documents around, pensively, like a minor deity performing an august version of the three-card trick. 'Well, you know your father. The entire thing was a bit of a mystery. Some kind of a coup. Cryptic words on the phone. I recall "dawn raid", and "personal piggy bank" were mentioned. Along with a fax detailing where the funds are being held. US Treasury Bonds and bankers' drafts. All off-shore and tax-sheltered of course. And all in your father's name. Very simple to release,' the lawyer appeared to have rearranged the papers to his satisfaction, and he met Darcy's hostile gaze, 'since I have full power of attorney, as executor of Sir Jack's estate.'

Stevenson tapped the codicil. 'There is no question of the amount involved. Or that the residue is indeed payable to his son born out of wedlock, to the late Helen Costello.'

'Well I just do not believe it! The bloody thing must be a forgery!'

'Darcy. Darling . . .' protested Edward gently.

'I witnessed it myself, Mrs Bailey,' said the lawyer quietly, 'in the presence of my partner, Justice Malahide.'

Heart thumping, Darcy subsided, tight-lipped, face flushed. She shrugged her husband's comforting hand from her arm.

Disbelief sat like Venetian masks on the faces of Grace and Paul. Stevenson felt a bit like a hanging judge pronouncing the ultimate sanction. 'Please let me know,' he went on, 'where you would like your money to be paid or if you would prefer a cheque, which of course you can have immediately. You may wish to confer and decide if and how you might assist in the search for Oliver, who could be anywhere on the globe. If indeed, he is still alive.'

Silence.

'I think,' said Paul, with a quiet authority – Sir Paul, the new head of the family, albeit on a financial leash, 'that Mr and Mrs O'Shea, Dan Shaughnessy and Mrs O'Callaghan, Bridget, should have their cheques now.' He turned to the servants. 'Will that be all right with you?'

Joe O'Shea looked to his wife for guidance. Anunciata nodded briefly. 'Yes, sir,' said Joe. 'If you please.'

Bridget was putting her hanky back into her handbag. 'I, um wouldn't be minding at all if you posted it to me.' Then she went scarlet with confusion. 'That is, if . . .'

Paul smiled. 'Don't you worry, Bridget,' he said, and Alison was surprised to see this kindly and courteous side to Jack's son. 'Where would we be without you to look after us? You will always have a place at Crough as long as you wish it.'

Bridget nodded, upset by the entire business, from the shock of Sir Jack's death, the funeral and this appallingly embarrassing episode with all that talk of more money than she had ever heard of, and by the sudden memories of Helen and life at the big house and bygone times, when the world was young. When she herself was just a slender cook's helper of twenty-three summers.

'Thank you,' she replied, almost in a whisper.

'Dan?' enquired Paul. 'Will you stay on too, please?'

'Yes,' answered Dan Shaughnessy, a man of few words, with the unfathomable expression of a cigar-store Indian.

'And Mr Stevenson should post your cheque there?'

'Thank you, sir. That will be fine.'

Paul turned to his father's chauffeur-handyman and Anunciata, the housekeeper. 'Joe? Anunciata?'

'I think, Sir Paul,' said Joe, 'if we were able to work on for another year, give you time to get sorted, then it would be fine to retire. If that was all right with you.'

Paul nodded, he had never really liked Joe and he felt the feeling was mutual. 'Good.' He addressed himself to the group of servants, all seated together. 'Thank you very much for coming here. I'm grateful for everything you have done over this painful time, to look after the family and our guests at the funeral.' Bridget was weeping now, the handkerchief back in action. 'I will be back at the big house in a few days, and we can talk about the future more fully then.'

There was a slight pause, then Paul rose, crossed to the door and opened it. 'Thanks.'

Taking their cue, the lower orders rose and filed from the room, muttering goodbyes and condolences to the family as they went.

Well, fancy that, thought Pronsias Stevenson, the boy has matured overnight, like Prince Hal in *Henry IV*. Well I have no intentions of being his Falstaff. He waited until Paul had returned to his seat.

'I know this will have come as a bit of a shock to you all,' he said. 'Is there anything you would like to ask?'

'When Father made this codicil . . .' began Grace.

'Yes, Grace?' Stevenson could guess what was coming. He had known Grace Fitzrowan since she was about eleven.

'Did he know – How can I put this? – Did he know he would be worth so much?'

'What you are asking, if I am correct,' replied the lawyer, 'is, did your father intend that Oliver would inherit such a vastly greater sum than the three of you, Sir Jack's legitimate heirs?'

'It's a fair question,' said Edward Bailey, levelly.

'The answer is no,' replied Stevenson. 'At the time of the codicil, your father was worth, all found, about sixteen million pounds. He was due to come over from Boston the week after he died, to redress the disproportionate amount of money Oliver stands to inherit.'

'So if Daddy hadn't died,' remarked Darcy, 'we would have inherited many more millions each.'

'If Dad hadn't died,' commented Paul drily, 'we would have inherited bugger all. And you know him, he could just as easily have been back in the red six months later.'

'So surely we can contest this codicil,' said Grace. 'I mean, this was never his intention.'

Pronsias Stevenson was ready for this. After all, he would have asked the same question. 'It is a legal and binding document, as I am sure Miss Clancy will confirm.' He looked towards Alison.

Alison felt the hostility of the assembled Fitzrowan heirs. 'Mr Stevenson is right,' she said. 'Such anomalies are not unusual and there are a hundred case precedents to confirm that your father's codicil is the last word on the subject.'

'Is that so?' Grace was suddenly angry, her husband's opportunity for political advancement back to square one. 'We'll see about that. I, for one, will fight this piece of bloody whimsy all the way. Come on, Tom.' Her face tight with fury, she rose and left the room. Tom Hanrahan followed, pausing at the door to look at the others, then he too went out.

'I think I should leave,' said Alison, who was quickly followed by Lauren Styvesant and Mary-Anne Radleigh.

Paul and Darcy exchanged glances. Edward Bailey rose and crossed to the door. 'I'll be just outside,' he said. Pronsias Stevenson tidied up his documents in silence.

'Pronsias,' asked Darcy, 'what would sort out this awful mess?'

Stevenson reflected for a moment. 'If Oliver were proved to be dead,' he replied, 'and without children. That would mean you, Paul and Grace would each share equally in the entire legacy.'

A clock ticked on the mantelpiece, above the flickering turf fire.

'Well now,' said Darcy, 'is that a fact . . . ?'

And Paul saw in her face a look he had not seen since they were children. It was a cold, unsettling look, a look which meant don't cross me, for sometime, someplace, you will pay most dearly. It was that look which masked a deadly unforgiving, which had been both the strength and the terrible weakness of the Irish down the centuries.

2

'Nothing?'

'Zilch.'

'Nothing at all?'

'How many ways do I have to tell you?'

Senior Jail Officer Max Logan scratched his neck, perplexed. This was a new one.

'Look,' he said, 'I'm just looking at the F-Prop list. One Rolex, gold and platinum. One ivory pen, Mont Blanc. One identity bracelet, platinum, with two emeralds. Man, twenty-four hundred dollars cash . . . Driver's licence – you're sure as hell going to need that, mister.'

Peter Girolo gazed back into Logan's pink, Celtic, piggy eyes. You didn't get eyes like that in Sicily. And yet, he had met some tough and ruthless Micks in his time.

'Nothing.'

Officer Logan tapped his pen on the desk. Girolo had never been any trouble, the whole four years. There had been that bit of excitement, but nothing proved. And if a Teamster boss had ordered him, Max Logan, to be gang raped in the showers, Logan had no doubt he too would have killed the man, if he could have gotten away with it.

Apart from that, Girolo had been no trouble.

'I don't know if there's a procedure. Why don't you just sign for it and throw it away, outside?'

'I'm not signing, I don't want it.'

'I don't know . . .'

'OK. I sign a disclaimer. Gimme that . . .' and Girolo pulled the Felons' Property sheet towards him, turned it around and scribbled his signature and in big letters, NOT WANTED BY RELEASED PRISONER.

Logan shrugged. 'What about your driver's licence? The car keys? The small key, what's that? Safety deposit box?'

'Mr Logan, I'm leaving now. See you around . . .'

Logan stared at the Sicilian. He shrugged, scribbled on his box on the release form. 'There's a hat.'

'No, thank you.'

Logan watched Girolo's back as the tall gangster headed towards the outer skin door. 'Mind telling me why?' he called.

Peter Girolo turned round, raised his shoulders. 'Ask the Fed standing behind the one-way glass,' he said, and walked on, pushing open the third-last door between himself and freedom.

Max Logan kept his smile to himself. All that time and trouble the Feds had gone to, illegally appropriating Girolo's personal possessions and returning them just the day before. The mafia boss was probably right. Electronics these days. Inserting minuscule bugs and even trackers in Rolexes, pens and car keys was definitely possible. If it was worth going to that much trouble.

And Peter Girolo, who had graduated, it was said, from trained contract man to one of seven eastern seaboard *capos*, with law and commerce degrees from Harvard and Europe, was worth a whole raft of inconvenience and taxpayers' money.

The two Feds came out from the back office. One gazed at Girolo's signature without comment. The other lifted the heavy-duty plastic property bag, its contents opaquely visible, and turned to leave.

'Hey,' said Logan, 'you can't take that.'

'Officer Logan, you just watch,' replied the one with eyes like a dead crocodile. And they left.

What a fuckin day, thought Logan, as he contemplated the paperwork those few moments had spawned.

Nobody waited to exchange pleasantries after the bombshell of the Will. Paul Fitzrowan took the evening shuttle from Dublin to London's Heathrow Airport for his recording session the following day. And as the coast of Ireland dropped below the climbing airliner, he could not get the words of the codicil out of his mind. *The baby was a boy, delivered on the fourteenth of June nineteen fifty-four . . .*

Twenty years before his own arrival, puking and squalling he had no doubt. Paul hated babies and he contemplated even his own nativity with an involuntary shiver.

She had called our son Oliver.

Oliver would be forty-three, if he were still alive, and there was no reason why he should not be. Except, adopted by Americans, he would have been eligible for the tail-end of the draft and the final years of the Vietnam War. And wasn't America full of muggers? And dope-crazed gunmen, some just fresh into their teens? Come to think of it, there were plenty of reasons why the Oliver child might not have survived into his forties.

The real question was, did Paul (Sir Paul now) want this half-sibling to be alive?

On balance, yes. As much from curiosity as filial instinct, for Paul was intrigued at the prospect of suddenly acquiring an older brother. What would Oliver be like? Would he have that Jack Fitzrowan way of glancing at you, amused, warm, yet with a heart of pure tungsten? That look which said, I aim to get what I want, so don't stand in my fucking way.

Darcy had those Jack Fitzrowan eyes. Grace did not. And neither had he. Maybe Oliver would be a mess, a disappointment. Like himself.

The new, fifteenth baronet Fitzrowan gazed idly at wisps of mist drifting past the window as the airliner punched remorselessly upwards. It had been a hectic nine days since the thunderbolt of that dreadful phone call from Boston, at ten minutes after midnight, two Saturdays before.

'Paul . . . ?' He had recognized his sister's voice at once.

For a moment there had been silence, that profound silence of an empty line, connected half-way across the world, with someone tangibly there. But no words.

'Grace? Are you there . . . ?'

'Oh, Paulie . . .' She hadn't called him that since they were about ten.

Then, the desolate sound of weeping. Had Tom left her? They were so tight together. Such an item. Or worse? Boston Homicide was no picnic. Maybe Tom had been shot. Shot dead. This was about death, abrupt bereavement, that much was sure.

'Is it Tom?' he asked gently.

Gradually his sister got her sobbing under control. A couple of sniffs. A long, choking sigh, then, 'It's Daddy.'

Paul's heart had banged against his chest. For a man who had spent so much of his brief life exasperated and outraged by his father, this was one of mother nature's bonded, welded imperatives taking over. Fear, panic, absolute – and instant – desolation.

'They were beating against a stiff breeze. The boom hit his head. Knocked him overboard. They took him to Massachusetts General, Paulie. He looks asleep. And peaceful. Not a mark on his poor face . . .' At which point Grace had broken down completely, and Paul had stood there in the darkened room, suddenly as lost as Major Tom, floating out there in hyperspace . . . And he had wept.

The seat-belt lights went out, accompanied by a little electronic 'ping'. Trust Dad, thought Paul, smiling grimly to himself, eyes moist from the memory of that terrible midnight. Trust you, you old bastard, not to quit us completely, but to leave a little surprise. A grown man, made in your likeness.

Paul Fitzrowan found himself smiling. He hoped Oliver was around somewhere. And as he hoped, he felt a warm assurance that it was so. Up there in the clouds, as a steward came round with the drinks trolley, he knew with complete clarity that his brother, his half-brother, was still alive. And he resolved to use his place, as head of the family, to find him.

The lot was almost deserted. It was five before eight and the staff of Zeralda Electronics (Boston) generally started to arrive about quarter to nine. The night security men's cars were there, and the cleaners' Dodge van. Also the silver Porsche 911 Turbo convertible belonging to Zeralda's Accountant and Chief Executive, Sebastian Tree.

Alison switched off the engine. She unclipped her safety belt and relaxed into the leather seat of her BMW, contemplating the day ahead. She had been unable to sleep and on impulse had decided to drive to the office, download her confidential files, complete some briefing documents for her successor, and hand Sebastian her letter of resignation.

The Zeralda Corporation was housed in a modern eight-storey E-shaped building a few blocks from MIT. It comprised research facilities, workshops and production lines, along with administrative offices, executive and conference suites, a commissary, a gymnasium, a presentation theatre and a medical centre.

The two hundred and fifty-seven workers employed there turned out state-of-the-art electronic components for hi-tech computerized equipment world-wide. Clients included McDonnell Douglas, the Ford Motor Company, NASA and two Japanese communications giants who were household names.

Zeralda left the hardware to Silicon Valley geniuses like Andy Grove of Intel, who had been at Jack's funeral, Fitzrowan having made his corporation's reputation by supplying essential microchips and microscopically miniaturized platinum trace boards, and by producing them better, faster and more reliably than his competitors.

As she swiped her plastic to gain access to the secure admin-floor elevator, Alison Clancy marvelled for the hundredth time at Jack Fitzrowan's foresight. In 1956 he had been just twenty-one years old, studying literature and politics at Dublin's Trinity College, when his father, Sir James Fitzrowan, had finally run out of cash and Crough Lake had been rented to a wealthy German, Dieter Christian von Schlader.

Schlader was a cultured and amusing man, with a taste for fine art and an authority on bloodstock. He was also richer than anyone Jack Fitzrowan had ever met. Jack had told Alison of the Easter he had arrived back from university to do some secretarial work for the German – a sinecure he did not doubt, but von Schlader knew how tight things were and it suited him to have a familiar face to deal with the locals – to find an army of gardeners, chauffeurs, grooms and indentured hands from nearby farms, heaving and pushing bloody great rollers up and down a hundred and fifty yard lane of more or less level turf, rolling it flatter, smoothing it more even, than God or nature had ever intended.

With the number of men, strangers in work, and the enormity of the rollers, borrowed from the golf course at Dook's, it was like a scene from *Gulliver's Travels*.

'And what in the name of Saint Theresa of the Little Fishes is this all about?' Jack had enquired of Colm O'Brady, brother of Anunciata who was at that time newly engaged to Joseph O'Shea, then a bartender in the Towers Hotel at Glenbeigh.

'An aerodrome he is making, for his Messerschmitt to land on and take off I don't doubt it at all,' Colm had replied, sucking on his clarty clay pipe stuffed, it was rumoured, with goat manure.

'A landing strip.' Jack nodded.

'Ah, well, you are the scholar, I stand corrected,' O'Brady answered, spitting on the flattened grass.

And sure enough, Dieter Christian von Schlader had a small aeroplane, not a Messerschmitt but a Beachcraft, a dilly of a little four-seater. And he took Jack Fitzrowan up in it and for the first time Jack saw the whole beauty of Crough Lake and the old house, with its winding driveway, its parkland and the lake and the gallops leading down to the miles of curving white sand abutting the Atlantic Ocean with America next stop, way beyond the horizon.

'What is it you do, exactly?' young Jack had enquired casually of the man who had just been re-christened 'the Kraut Tycoon' in local bars.

'Computers,' responded von Schlader. 'They are going to be very big. Very small actually, young Master Fitzrowan. Today they fill rooms and hum and whine and use mile upon mile of expensive magnetic tape. But one day . . .' and here, according to Jack, the German had poured him a glass of Trockendeerer Ausliesen, whatever the hell that was, '. . . one fine day, when somebody gets it right, the same equipment will fit into a matchbox, and later, something the size and thickness of a thumbnail.'

The Lilliputian concept of reducing something that filled rooms to the size of a thumbnail had thrilled Jack Fitzrowan and he had returned to Dublin and gone through the Electrical Engineering

Department's library and files like a termite in a lumber store. He befriended professors of electronics. He flattered them, he listened to their every notion on the subject and he bought them whiskey and stout he could ill afford in the taverns and bars around Dublin's university.

'MIT is the place, if you really want to know. If you are really after the last word on the subject of computers.' This not from some learned professor of electronics, for in 1956 there was no such animal in the whole of Dublin, but in fact from a playwright and tutor of dramatic literature called Sam Beckett, who had been sitting quietly in the corner of Slattery's upstairs bar those last few nights, listening to young Fitzrowan's relentless, sometimes inebriated, but always subtle grilling of teams of scientific academics.

'And what is MIT when it's at home?' Jack had asked.

Samuel Beckett had told him and the very next September, John Pearce Dunmill Fitzrowan, former literature and politics under-graduate, had won himself a place, by dint of charm and unrelenting persistence and transparent intellect, at Massachusetts Institute of Technology, in Cambridge, just across the river from, and to all intents and purposes part of, the fair city of Boston, to study electronics. In particular, micro-electronics, for Jack never needed to be told something twice.

He had thought every day of that white and curving sand, just a few thousand miles to the east, with nothing but the relentless waves between. Jack had sworn that one day Crough Lake would be his again, that he would find Helen Costello and the child of their love, and they would bring him up well, and live the life of Reilly.

Later, in the way of things, he had married the beautiful Scarlet Hennessy and the memory of Helen had gradually receded, though never entirely. And later than that, with a degree in micro-electronics and another, *cum laude*, from Harvard Business School, round about 1967, employed by a research company in Los Angeles, Jack had decided it was time to go into business for himself. He would concentrate on creating the best damn components corporation in the micro-electronics industry.

Which is how Zeralda came to be born.

It had started in a loft of La Cienga, a rough neighbourhood in downtown LA, then moved east to Boston, to be closer to MIT (from where Fitzrowan poached some top computer brains), working out of an old warehouse not far from where they had thrown all that tea into the harbour and started the War of Independence a couple of hundred years earlier.

But now they were in the custom-built Zeralda compound, set back from Memorial Drive, and in 1983 an aerial photo had been on the front cover of *Newsweek*, with a feature inside on the rise and rise of Jack Fitzrowan. It was the same year his horse had won the Kentucky Derby, and the same year Spiros Kulardis, the Greek shipping and airline magnate, had named Jack as co-respondent in his messy and expensive divorce from opera diva Carmen Takodopola.

The admin unit was on the fourth floor, protected by all manner of electronic security, for here were kept patented designs, technical data awaiting patents, plans and records of negotiations for the future, financial records and the Zeralda Corporation's other secrets.

As the brushed steel elevator doors sighed open, Alison paused for a second, breathing in the familiar and unique smell of that fourth floor. Leather, waxed wood, the warm aroma from a score of computer main-frames, plastic, and . . . something was missing. She stepped out into the corridor, head tilted slightly, almost sniffing, like a diffident hound dog. Surprising how long it had lingered, actually. The scent of Jack.

Bay Rum aftershave, Stuart's of Barbados Lime Deodorant. And just . . . Jack. His scent had hung in those corridors for days after the tragedy. Perhaps just in her imagination. But now it was gone.

At that moment, Alison Clancy realized she could hear, very faintly, the voice of Sebastian Tree, speaking on the phone. As she understood just what she was listening to, the Zeralda Corporation's lawyer felt a blip of adrenalin, and wished the elevator doors had not slid shut, the cabin behind descending noiselessly.

Sebastian was deep in conversation – easy, confidential, relaxed conversation – with the enemy; Takahashi Katakura, President of the Katakura Corporation of Japan, the electronics multinational that had tried to swallow up Zeralda and put Jack Fitzrowan out of business.

Alison was not used to danger, not these days. Sure, when she had been working in criminal law, when her ambition had been directed towards the DA's office, she had visited police precinct houses and prison interview rooms, and there had been some alarming moments. But she had switched to corporate law, and those memories were a thing of the past. Until now.

Standing alone, vulnerable, in that hushed, fourth-floor corridor, so redolent of money, success, and discretion, Alison Clancy was suddenly reminded of one awful evening six years before in the Boston Correction Center, in a cold concrete room, alone with her client, a convicted murderer and rapist manacled but still taut with menace, to whom she had to break the news of his doomed appeal.

'Yeah, sure thing, Tak.' Tree's voice was, as ever, confident, but tinged with diffidence. '*Wakarimaska*. With the daughter in the hot seat it should only take a couple of months. I've put together some thoughts on how to help things along . . .'

Fascinated, Alison stood rock still, ears straining.

'If a high-turnover client, for example, held up on payment, that would be . . . embarrassing.'

Zeralda had a number of contracts with a monthly gross income of many millions of dollars. The Rockaway Project, for instance, produced around twenty-one million dollars each month which went straight into servicing corporate loan reductions with Chase Manhattan, First Boston and the Bank of Scotland, New York office. Any hold-up in the regular flow would indeed be embarrassing. And with fast fluid credit transactions, quickly raised and quickly settled – the like of which had made Jack Fitzrowan a giant in his field – any major glitch would be like a boulder hitting a millpond. The ripples of stopped credit would affect payment of wages, which would damage production schedules, which would lead to cancelled orders, which would hurt cash flow and collateral and so on and like that. Zeralda was healthy and bankable. Just as long as none of the major components got out of kilter. And Rockaway was a most major component.

'Listen, Tak, I have to sign off now. I hear the cleaners packing up. That means staff arrives in twenty minutes.'

Shit. Alison stretched out and pressed the elevator button. A light above the door informed her the cabin was on hold. Doubtless to let the cleaners load up their industrial vacuum machines.

Tree's voice lightened. They were talking golf. Tak Katakura was an eight handicap fanatic who had bought his own golfing club a half-hour outside Phoenix City.

Come on, come on.

The elevator light remained obstinately static. She could hear muffled noises of heavy equipment filtering down the shaft.

And of course, Alison Clancy suddenly needed to pee.

'Three under par but a birdie on the fifteenth . . .' Tree could have been talking Amharic as far as Alison was concerned.

She jumped as the brushed steel doors slid open. Inside, two stocky Mexicans wearing dust masks and boiler suits stood among several orange metal cylinders, with black hosing and stubby wheels, like two cybernetic shepherds in some far-flung space station.

One shuffled reluctantly to make a space for Alison. She smiled and stepped inside. The Mexican nearest the panel pressed a button and the cabin re-commenced its upward journey to the sixth floor.

Up, down, Alison Clancy did not give a damn. She had escaped from a potentially unpleasant, possibly dangerous environment. And what she had overheard was dynamite. Sebastian Tree was plotting with Katakura to weaken confidence in Zeralda, thus preparing the way for a second take-over raid. And this time, without Jack Fitzrowan's prodigious ability, it would surely succeed.

At the sixth floor, the Mexicans held the door open while a colleague squashed in with his own orange and black vacuum and a bucket and mop. Even with so much on her mind, Alison wondered why the two cleaners had taken the elevator up, just to collect their compadre. Solidarity? Habit? Who could say?

The new arrival pressed the button for the basement. Alison rode all the way down with them, then took the stairs to the first-floor commissary where staff were preparing for the influx of early morning staff. After a stop at the rest room, she joined the small queue and took a mug of black coffee and a plate of toast and honey with a tumbler of orange juice, to a corner table and sat deep in thought.

Damn.

Alison wished she had never heard the Chief Executive's indiscreet conversation with Katakura. It did not feel right to resign so precipitately just when Tree was plotting the downfall of everything Jack had worked for. For now she owed it to Jack Fitzrowan to tough it out, and find some way of stopping the bastard in his tracks.

As that word passed through her mind, Alison Clancy was transported back to Pronsias Stevenson's Dublin office. *A bastard*, Darcy had snarled. A love child, more accurately, mused Alison. A man now, wherever he is, who would have been Sir Oliver Fitzrowan if he had been born on the right side of the blanket.

She had been close to Jack, closer than she had ever intended, for the big Irishman had a sneaky skill of seducing totally those few he chose to allow into his private space. He could be so open and unsecretive that the recipient of such trust felt both flattered and included. With such closeness went obligation and thus, like a medieval king, Fitzrowan created his own inner court.

But Alison had never had an inkling of the existence of Helen Costello, Jack's great love, or of Oliver. Or indeed of any codicil. Deep indeed.

What other secrets had he kept to himself, she wondered.

All the time he had been in Marion, Peter Girolo had retained his place at the top of the major league, in the business of the USA's seven syndicate families. He had kept the honorific of *capo*, and he had been informed and consulted on matters of importance during his four years in prison.

But this absence had created a void, a vacuum, no doubt about it. And nature abhors vacuums, so by the time he came out, somebody had been sitting in his chair. A career mobster from the

Gambino family, Charlie Bagarella. And Girolo had always known, in the seclusion of his prison cell, two floors under ground, that upon his release he would have to whack the guy.

However, fate is fickle, as the saying goes, and two months before Girolo walked out into the clean air, Charlie Bagarella is hauled in front of a Grand Jury on a false accounting and racketeering indictment. Charlie sings like a bird and within days is under witness protection and out of the way of the mob.

'Nature still abhors a vacuum . . .' said Girolo to Albert Genovese, *consiglieri* to the Boss of Bosses, who himself was trying to exert control of the eastern seaboard organized crime business from a cell in Florence prison, Colorado, where he was doing life to eternity on account of another squealer, Joe the Peach.

'I wish it was that easy.'

'Meaning?'

Genovese glanced away. There was something about Girolo's gaze that had been known to paralyse the intestine.

'Meaning Charlie kinda let things slide.'

'Slide, what do you mean slide?' Girolo's voice had dropped low. They were on the roof of a car park in Atlantic City. An American Airlines DC9 whined over their heads, about six hundred feet up and climbing.

Genovese waited till the noise abated. He met Girolo's gaze. Best get it over with. 'Peter, you left a twenty-four carat organization. A Cadillac body over a Ferrari engine. The vacuum you left was gold lined, with diamonds floating in the space.' Genovese talked like that.

Girolo nodded. 'And each month you sent somebody to check the books.'

Genovese sighed. He looked about as worried as if his chauffeur was a few minutes late, but inside he was concerned, for if Peter Girolo took this badly, anything could happen. Girolo had been a real steady *capo*, for the guy was from the old country, from Corleone. Trained from the age of seven in the ways of the *cosa*, educated in Palermo, Rome and the Sorbonne in Paris, then a law degree from Harvard, Peter Girolo was a jewel in the mafia crown, a *mana morte*, in the patois of Sicily – an assassin. The best. Low key, white collar. Every international crime syndicate needs a couple or three.

It is not every day a *mana morte* makes it into the families' boss echelon. But the Girolos were a wealthy and respected Corleone family. Well travelled and with powerful friends in Naples and at the Vatican. The story of how they agreed to let young Peter be brought up by the Dons is so Sicilian that nobody outside the *cosa* would understand, and anyone inside, no matter how well travelled, no matter how many friends at the Vatican, would comprehend only too well. Suffice it to say that fear, love, common sense and human weakness all played their part.

The entire programme of educating the child, not only in the arts of murder, but in sophisticated stuff, like history, music and mathematics, that entire, Jesuitical programme to place a made man right among the professional classes of New York and the East Coast, was not only ambitious and imaginative – it created a ruthless killer, loyal to the old country *mafiosi*, who inevitably grew into an able and ambitious businessman, in the mob sense of the word.

And Albert Genovese was now required to explain about the monthly accounts.

'They were a fairy story,' he took the plunge. 'Charlie was at it from the word go. Not only did he cook the books, he was no fuckin good at running the family business. So in just four short years, you come out to a real *stronza. Esta stuccevole . . .*'

Peter Girolo lit a cigarette. Gazed around the rooftops. Two workmen were painting an elevator housing a couple of blocks away, near the railroad station. And somewhere a pneumatic drill was at work, its faint, lazy-busy chatter somehow reassuring; he had not heard anything so normal during his four years in the slammer.

Eventually he said, 'Tell me about it.'

Genovese described how, after the big arrests and stoolpigeon trials of the past few years, many of the men of respect, Girolo and the Boss of Bosses John Gotti among them, had been put behind bars. Young *mafiosi* had taken over and some had handled their business OK, but many of them had gone apeshit. Maybe they had seen too many Al Pacino movies – who knew – but they all ran around in flash automobiles, Porsches and Mercedes SLs, with greased-back gangsters' hairstyles, chains and medallions worn like bullion, carrying pieces, something the old-style *capos* never did, never needed to, and behaving like cheap hoodlums, shooting down men on the slightest pretext, just for the buzz, strutting their stuff, seeking reputations as bad guys, harder than hard. Screwing each other's women, causing more gunfights, drive-bys and general mayhem. And worse, selling dope to each other, to the made men and their relations.

'It was never like this before,' sighed Genovese. 'And Peter, I gotta tell you. Boston and around, it's as bad as here in Atlantic City. All that shit goin down. And more. Sonny Bragazzo took a chainsaw to some punk who vandalized his big-wheel Dodge.'

'His what?'

'You know, these four-wheel drive wagons with giant wheels,' Genovese lifted his hand above his head, 'so high.'

Girolo pondered this.

'Jesus . . .' he breathed.

'So that's what you come out to, *paisano*.' Genovese paused. 'Eastern seaboard is up for grabs. The Russians are moving in. Word is, it's yours if you want it.'

Peter Girolo nodded. The Russian mafia were hell-bent on taking over international organized crime. They made the Jamaican Yardies look like a gang of teenagers. And the vacuum was far bigger than he had imagined. He dropped his Marlboro and stepped on it. 'I should get to work . . .'

As he strolled away across the rooftop, Albert Genovese, who had seen many bad things go down, shivered involuntarily.

Two thousand, eight hundred and forty miles to the west, grey clouds scudded low and fast over Crough Lake House on the shores of County Kerry.

Paul Fitzrowan was building a fire, kneeling at the sixteenth-century chimney breast. He sat, fascinated by the inevitability of the tiny flame igniting crumpled balls of paper in the hearth, the slow flaring as it spread, catching thin twigs, the crackling and blossoming of red, yellow, blue and orange caressing the bark of slender, parched branches, until a gradual heat touched his face.

Methodically, patiently, he placed larger pieces of old apple wood in a wigwam around the burning branches and taller flames reached upwards, swaying like glowing cobras. Behind him, Darcy poured whiskey from a square, crystal decanter into two tumblers and handed one to Grace.

'You came back pretty quick from London,' she said to Paul's back. But Paul was engrossed in his reverie, his face lit by the flickering pyre.

'The boy is an arsonist at heart,' commented Grace, taking her whiskey and shivering slightly. The central heating had been off since a big beech tree, its branches laden with snow, had fallen across the main power lines. The generator the Kraut had installed in 1969 had proved impossible to start.

'Just watch you don't set the chimney alight.' Darcy sat on the edge of a couch and sniffed at her drink.

'Bridget's making one of her lamb stews, on the old turf burner stove, is that all right for everybody?' asked Grace.

'Paul . . . ?' Darcy said, her tone suggesting she had not come all the way from Boston to talk to her brother's back.

After a moment, Paul sat on his heels and glanced round, his face reflecting the flickering flames. 'Lamb stew sounds fine,' he replied.

A silence ensued, more awkward than comfortable.

He looks lost, thought Grace. 'We should talk about Zeralda,' she said, more to break the moment than anything else, 'while the three of us are in the one room.'

'We have more than Zeralda to talk about,' replied Darcy, staring darkly into the blazing hearth.

'For instance,' Grace pressed on, 'we have to elect a president.'

'No contest,' Paul replied. 'You're the active board member. You know how Zeralda works. Who better?'

Well that's nice, thought Darcy. Cut and dried. Don't mind me,

I only own thirty-one point six per cent of the Corporation. 'I think I'll come over with you,' she remarked. 'Take a look at the balance sheets. Get an overview on our . . . inheritance. Such as it is.'

It'll be my turn now, thought Paul. And sure enough Darcy turned to him, that look in her eyes. 'I suppose you'll be too busy with your damn pop music and long-haired pals, smoking dope and too laid back, man, to take any interest in the business our father built up from zero.'

'Why, God bless you, Darcy,' he responded, 'but I'm of a mind to take my seat on the board. The title might lend a touch of class to the letterhead, if nothing else. However, I do not promise to remove my pony tail and wear a tie.'

Darcy rounded on him, her anger and confusion boiling over. 'Smart answers, smart bloody answers, that's all we ever get from you! Try growing up, sonny boy. Try the real world. Try doing an honest day's work for a change.'

Grace sighed. She started to say something, then sat down abruptly, as if whacked in the stomach.

'What is it?' asked Paul, concerned.

Grace just sat there, tears streaming down her cheeks, chest heaving.

Darcy, so fierce a moment before, went over and sat on the arm of the chair, cradling her little sister and soothing her grief.

'There, there . . .' she said. 'There, there, there . . .'

Later, when the fire had settled to a cosy flickering glow and Bridget was clearing away the remains of her famous lamb stew, to compliments from the three heirs and Tom Hanrahan, who had been out earlier with the three wolfhounds and the Rat, as Rumple, a diminutive Tipperary terrier was called, Darcy said softly, 'We're not going to stand for this Oliver nonsense, are we?'

Bridget swept out, laden with her tray, and flicked the door shut behind her with a surprisingly dainty movement of her ample ankle.

'You heard Pronsias Stevenson.' Paul pushed the bowl of fruit towards Tom. 'There is not a whole lot we can do.'

'The family lawyer?' snorted Darcy. 'He seems to be acting more for the bastard child than for any of us.'

She's right, thought Grace, and added, 'Don't forget,' she said, 'the fellow is sitting pretty with this absurd codicil. He holds the purse strings, and he is the final arbiter.'

'Pronsias is the man Dad chose for the job,' Paul commented. 'He's only carrying out our father's wishes.'

'It's none of my business . . .' began Tom Hanrahan, Boston Homicide Lieutenant and Grace's husband.

'Quite correct.' With eyes of ice, Darcy held her empty glass at him, while addressing the other two. 'Daddy had no idea he was going to be worth hundreds of millions when he wrote that codicil. The little shit lawyer admitted that himself.'

Tom shrugged and poured more claret – Pichon-Longueville '83, La Comtesse – into Darcy's glass, one of five survivors of a set of twenty-four eighteenth-century French crystal, a wedding gift to Sir Jack and Scarlet Hennessy, Darcy's mother.

'I think we may have a case for contesting it,' Grace continued. 'Why don't I get Alison Clancy to find us a top Boston attorney?'

'An inheritance lawyer, that's what we need,' agreed Darcy.

Paul shook his head. 'Our father knew what he was doing. We each have enough to live more than comfortably. We should find somebody professional to find Oliver. That's what the codicil says and that's what I'm going to do. Listen, twelve and a half per cent of all that money is nearly thirty million. That's another ten million each. I don't believe we have the option.'

'We're not really so very far apart,' suggested Grace, who had learned her negotiating skills from her father, 'Say we take legal advice, very discreetly, in Boston and in Dublin. After all, the deal which earned those two hundred million dollars was made from Daddy's American base.'

'So what?' asked Darcy, toying morosely with her empty wineglass.

'So a US judge could well decide that an Irish solicitor has no jurisdiction over those funds. Off-shore or not.'

It had become so quiet; the faint sounds of a radio could be heard coming from the servants' kitchen. Here was a ray of hope.

'And to accommodate Paul's wishes, and Daddy's,' Grace continued, 'let's agree that, if we manage to persuade a court, either here or in the USA, to annul the codicil . . . Then, if we do find Oliver, we split the money four ways instead of three.' She sat back and smoothed her white linen napkin. 'Thus honour would be satisfied, and Daddy's real intention would be met. Only more fairly.'

'Judgment of Solomon.' Tom Hanrahan smiled at his wife. 'Jack would approve of that.'

Darcy ignored Paul's attempt to offer her sugar from its silver bowl. 'If you all feel that strongly, give him some of your damn share.'

Paul lit a cigarette and exhaled slowly. In the silence, a Louis Quatorze mantel clock ticked and the fire hissed comfortably. The kid is more mature by the day, reflected Tom, who was wisely keeping out of this family discussion.

Finally Paul spoke. 'If we can agree, all three of us, to seek out Oliver, or establish he is dead. And if we each agree, and mean it' – here he glanced at Darcy – 'to share the legacy with him, four equal parts . . . then I do not object to taking legal advice.'

Grace glanced at Darcy. Irresistible force and immovable object, combined in one human being. Primed for the next outburst. But Darcy merely nodded, her expression softening.

'OK,' she said, the very voice of sweet reason, 'I can go along with that.' She gazed at Paul gently, benignly, with no trace of her previous rage, and smiled. 'Sure. Why not? There would be more than enough to go around . . . And you're quite right, the important thing is to find Daddy's long lost, ah . . . love child.'

Tom Hanrahan felt a chill deep inside him. It occurred to him right then – and this was his professional opinion – that this woman was capable of murder.

Paul examined his sister's face, all open and honest now, the clouds of avarice, jealousy and hurt quite gone. 'We will have to be discreet,' he said. 'Pronsias Stevenson would have a fit.'

Darcy folded her napkin and rolled it into a solid silver napkin ring, with her own initials on it – they each had one and they never left the big house. 'Grace, I don't think I shall come to Boston, it's not decent so soon after Daddy's death. If we all flew off to America so soon after the reading of the Will, the little shit might smell a rat.'

'How elegantly put,' said Paul softly. He turned to Grace. 'That's it then. We take counsel's advice.'

Down in the kitchen, a faint radio audience laughed and applauded.

Grace nodded. 'I'll get the best money can buy.'

'So how was the family?' Sebastian leaned against the frame of Alison Clancy's office door, fixing his frank, cool smile on her. The smile, his tall, lean frame, and that superficially sincere approach probably accounted for the string of attractive, if a trifle preppie, girls he always had in tow. These plus the silver Porsche convertible and a sleek cruiser with, it was rumoured, a water bed in the main cabin.

'You mean how was the funeral?'

'I read about it in the *Boston Globe*. I mean, how are they taking it?'

'They are Jack's children, Sebastian. With their father's courage, is the answer.'

'Maybe I should have gone.'

'Maybe you should.'

'Only, Jack would appreciate somebody had to stay back and mind the store.'

'He certainly would.'

'Why don't you like me?'

'I don't not like you, Sebastian. I'm sure you are a swell guy, outside the office.'

'You feel you can't work with me?' Tree's eyes glinted. It was common knowledge that he and Alison Clancy could not stand each other. Divide and rule was something Jack had learned from his Jesuit teachers in Saint Francis Xavier's, County Meath's slightly run-down but exclusive, old-money school for boys.

Alison waited before replying. She knew Sebastian Tree was half expecting her resignation. But her reasons for resigning, when that was what she had intended – just an hour or so before – had had nothing to do with Tree or their personal antipathy.

Truth was, Alison could not bear to be in the building with Jack gone. What had started as a pleasantly surprising, no-strings, mutual satisfying of basic instincts had gradually developed from raw, animal attraction into affection, even tenderness.

Goddam it, she realized, she, Alison Clancy, the original independent woman, had been starting to fall in love with the ruthless, charming, selfish bastard. And as she thought that, she could hear his gentle laughter.

'Do you always do that? Afterwards,' she had once enquired, sprawled naked, damp and languid across his perspiring, solid frame.

Jack had stroked her hair and after thinking about it for a while, he had replied, 'Only with people I feel close to.'

And the way he had said it, she knew he meant it.

Alison looked Tree straight in the eye. 'I have no problem working here, Sebastian. With you or without you, I don't give a damn.'

Tree held her gaze, then he nodded. 'Things will be different around here. Without big Jack to, uh, hold your hand . . .'

In the silence, Alison was tempted to take her letter of resignation out of her purse and throw it at him. But that would have smacked of surrender.

'I'm sure I will make the adjustment,' she replied evenly.

He shrugged. 'Fine. Zeralda is what matters.'

'You bet.' Alison returned her attention to the VDU screen on her desk, fingers racing over the keys. After a moment, Sebastian Tree turned and walked away.

OK, Jack, she promised, I will stay until we nail that asshole. And she could have sworn she felt his firm hand on her shoulder.

Tom and Grace arrived back in Boston three days later, in the Zeralda Lear Jet, with the President of McDonnell Douglas and two of the minor Kennedys who had been at the funeral. Grace had contemplated inviting Lauren Styvesant, *Vogue* fashion editor and one of her late father's mistresses, to join them but decided the strumpet's one hundred and seventy thousand inheritance, just for spreading her legs for God's sake, was generous enough.

Edwin, the firm's chauffeur, six foot three and black as the Earl of Hell's waistcoat, was waiting beside the midnight blue Bentley, Zeralda's car for collecting VIP clients from the airport or train terminals.

Tom Hanrahan felt a mixture of relief and disappointment, for he had half-expected the Aston Martin, his Aston Martin now, to be there on the runway apron. But maybe that would have been kind of gross. Spoils of tragedy.

'Hi, Edwin, thanks for coming to meet us.' Grace had inherited her father's ability to treat everyone on the same level. There was nothing patronizing about it. People are people, Jack used to tell his kids, and they each deserve respect and courtesy. Until they prove otherwise.

'How did it go?' asked the driver, glancing at her with a degree of sympathy as he loaded the two valises into the trunk.

'Sad, but nice to see so many folk at the funeral. From the Kennedys to the cooks and the handyman.'

'Mister Gates?' Edwin closed the trunk and held the rear door open for her.

'He was there.'

'You sing "Rock of Ages"?'

'Yes we did.'

'And "The Old Town I Love So Well"?'

'The cook sang it.' Grace smiled at Edwin's slightly confused reaction, as she slid into the far corner and Tom followed.

'Pardon me?'

'Bridget, the cook at our house in Ireland. She sings like an angel.'

And as she said it, Grace recalled the crystal silence while Bridget's astoundingly pure soprano, unaccompanied, had held the assembled mourners in thrall for the full rendition of Jack Fitzrowan's favourite Irish song.

'I have not heard anything so perfect. It was like a Stradivarius violin,' one of the Rothschilds had remarked to her as they filed out from the tiny family chapel.

Edwin met her eye and nodded, understanding her emotions. 'God rest his soul.'

'Amen,' said Tom, glancing at his watch.

As the sleek Bentley nosed towards a traffic jam edging into the Callahan Tunnel, Edwin said, 'Oh, Lieutenant, a Mr Rendel called me on the car phone. Said he needs you to interview Sammy and would you call him.'

'Sammy?' Grace turned to her husband. 'Who's Sammy?'

'He's an axe murderer, dear,' replied Tom, and caught Edwin's grin in the rear-view mirror as he lifted the car phone and tapped out the number of Boston PD's Homicide boss.

'Rendel.' Bill Rendel's laconic voice was a welcome sound after a whole week of high society mourning and explosive family politics.

'Bill, what's up?'

'Tom, just the guy. We picked up Sammy Jade last night. Fibres in the trunk of his Oldsmobile match the sweater Lee-Anne Kopecnick was wearing when they found the body. Well the upper part.'

'Sounds like the case has solved itself.' Tom had been hoping for more of a challenge. Homicide was his forte and the more difficult a case, the better.

'Only,' continued Rendel, 'he reported the car stolen day before the murder and he says he found it abandoned after a tip-off.'

'Tip-off? From who?'

'You gonna come in?'

Tom glanced at his wife. 'Grace, I have to bail out when we hit the Waterfront.'

Grace was not surprised. 'That's OK. I might just take a shower and go into the office. Dinner at seven?'

Tom glanced at his watch. 'I'll try.'

'I'm thinking pasta, with clams.'

'You sure know how to close a deal.'

★

Alison Clancy selected the files she needed, in order to brief Grace Fitzrowan Hanrahan, and walked along the corridor to Jack's office.

Diana Prentice, Jack's PA for the past eight years, smiled as Alison came in to the outer office. 'Hi Alison, Grace is expecting you.'

And there was Grace, sitting behind Jack's desk, gold-rimmed reading glasses perched on the end of her nose. The ebony-wood block with JOHN FITZROWAN - PRESIDENT was still on the desk.

Alison was almost exactly the same age as Jack's younger daughter, and they got on well. She was aware that, until the reading of the Will, neither Grace nor anyone else had an inkling about the intimacy of her relationship with Jack. Now, to her surprise, she felt slightly embarrassed, even apprehensive, standing there in the room where she and Grace's father had made love.

'You left Dublin pretty fast,' said Alison.

Grace did not immediately look up from the documents she was signing. When she finally glanced over the rim of her spectacles, her eyes were friendly. 'I was going to offer a seat on the Lear Jet. But you had . . . skedaddled.'

'I was embarrassed.'

'The codicil?'

'The money your father left to me.'

Grace smiled. She removed her reading glasses and pushed the chair away from the desk, just like Jack used to do. She tugged open the lower left-hand drawer, just like Jack used to do, and tugged out a bottle of Wild Turkey. Just like Jack used to do.

If she asks me to lock the door, I'm out of here, thought Alison.

Grace found two chunky tooth glasses and poured two good shots of Bourbon. 'How many women do you imagine Daddy had, in his lifetime?' she asked, pushing one tumbler across the iroko desk towards the attorney.

Alison could not figure if this question was a put-down or not. 'I guess more than a few.'

'I guess so too. Would two or three hundred shock – no, pardon me – surprise, you?'

Alison contemplated. 'Not really. He was, as the *New York Times* put it, a man of considerable energies.'

Grace held Alison's gaze. 'Daddy was in love with life. Mom left him because she couldn't handle his complete dedication to his work, not the women. Every time Jack pleasures a new woman, my mother used to say, he is celebrating being alive, celebrating life itself. How could I grudge him that?'

'That's kind of rare,' remarked Alison. 'You don't get many wives that broad minded.'

'She was born into wealth, old money,' said Grace, 'with a ton of style and real class. Jealousy is for the insecure, that was another thing she used to say. Still does, I dare say, not that we ever see her these days.'

In the silence, Grace raised her glass. 'Celebrating life, that's how I will always remember him . . .'

Alison smiled. 'Me, too.'

They touched tumblers and drank the Bourbon in a couple of swallows, setting the glasses back on the desk, firmly, like cow-punchers in an old western movie. Their eyes met, and they both smiled. It was a spontaneous thing, unexpected.

'But he only included three of his lovers in the legacy,' said Grace. 'You three must have brought him great happiness, so you should feel proud, Alison. Not embarrassed.'

Alison glanced down. 'You are very generous,' she said.

Grace poured two, more modest shots, and put the bottle back in its drawer. 'We aim to fight the codicil.'

'I thought maybe you would. All three of you, or just you and Darcy?'

'Paul too. The deal is, we get the codicil annulled, but obey Daddy's wishes and do everything possible to find Oliver – private investigators, local searches, maybe even a media campaign. And when, if, Oliver turns up, he gets a fourth, an equal share with Darcy, Paul and me.'

'Judgment of Solomon,' remarked Alison.

'That's exactly what Tom said.'

'I like Tom.' Alison smiled, she had not eaten much and the

second Wild Turkey had brought a warm glow to her neck and face. 'Listen, he's a detective. Can't he take some leave and organize the, um, hunt?'

'Tom is cosying up to an axe murderer right now. He is not interested in Oliver, one way or the other.'

'He must feel awful,' said Alison.

'Why?'

'Well, being on the yacht when Jack was killed.'

Grace glanced at the lawyer, the memory of that awful day ambushing her. She sat silent until the moment passed. Then she nodded. 'He'll never get over it. Will you help us find an attorney, here in Boston?'

Zeralda's Legal Executive frowned, considering. 'I don't think you'll succeed. That codicil is a legal and binding document.'

'Listen, you're a good company lawyer, but forgive me, Alison, I want to hear that from the best in the USA.'

Alison thought for a moment. 'OK, that will be Michael Medevik, he's the top guy when it comes to wills and codicil law. Retained by the man in the White House, author of several books on the subject, professor at Harvard Law School.'

'You know him?' enquired Grace.

Alison Clancy smiled, it had indeed been a long day. 'He used to be my husband.'

Boston PD's Homicide Unit is in a brownstone building straight out of a 1950s cop movie. You expect to find Richard Widmark or Pat O'Brien emerging from one of the grey-white rooms talking out of one side of his mouth, with a half-smoked cigarette in the other.

Tom Hanrahan nodded to the big plainclothes cop on the ground-floor desk, Sergeant Detective Luther MacDonald, close to retirement age, a stubble of white on his long chin.

'Yo, Luther. What's up?' said Tom as he walked past towards the back stairs.

'Sure thing,' replied MacDonald, whose hearing used to be better.

Sammy Jade Spencer was a skinny, self-pitying apology for a man, which perchance went some way to explaining his small foible of chopping up female victims with a fake antique battle-axe he had obtained by mail order from American Legend Artifacts Inc. of Basin Street, New Orleans. He had paid by Amex, which had been something of a help in identifying the perp to Boston Homicide.

The lugubrious strains of ZZ Top sounded tinnily from Sammy Jade's personal stereo, interspersed with the voice of Bill Silver, DJ with Boston's ZLX Classic Rock station. Tom sat on the other side of the interview table and, reaching forward, unplugged the earphone jack. Sammy looked crestfallen.

'So, Sammy,' said Tom, 'you got an alibi for the time of death?'

Sammy Jade smiled. He raised his eyebrows. Something about him reminded Tom of Groucho Marx.

'Nobody ain't told me the time of death, Mr Hanrahan.'

Tom relaxed. After the flights by executive jet, across the Atlantic to the aul' sod, the funeral and the reading of the Will, and the reaction of three previously normal, comfortably off people – Grace, Darcy and Paul – to the prospect of several hundred million dollars slipping through their fingers, this was like therapy.

'They found the girl's fingerprints on the side of your bath, Sammy. And blood where the rubber tiles meet the wall matches the deceased's DNA.'

'OK, no more questions without my lawyer.'

'Listen, this is not even my case. It's just a conversation, man. I mean, how many times have I pulled you in now?'

Sammy Jade grinned. 'Your forensics guys able to put a date to fingerprints?'

'Maybe. Why?' Tom was lying. Of course they couldn't and Sammy knew that.

'Because a test like that would prove I ain't been home for four days. So if the girl was killed in my bathroom, it ain't me that done it. Plus I reported my Oldsmobile stolen three days before. Then I get this tip, where I can find it. Then I get pulled over by some patrolmen. Man, how was I to know there was a body in the trunk?'

Tom nodded. 'And how were you to know that four days ago the girl was still alive?'

Sammy contemplated this. He smiled, dreamily. 'Man, if she had just been done, I woulda smelled the fresh gore. If she had been more than two days gone, I woulda smelled the cadaver.'

'You sound like an expert.'

'Thanks for the conversation. Charge me, let me go, or we speak with a lawyer present . . .'

Tom fished around for his pack of Winstons. 'Oh, we're going to charge you, Sammy,' he said. And as he lit up and inhaled deeply he gazed at the creep almost fondly. For this was home.

3

Pronsias Stevenson lived in a neat, three-storey house of grey sandstone, with a spick-and-span little front garden and a tidy back lawn, with rose and rhododendron bushes clipped and spaced apart like prickly, leafy chess-men.

The seventy-foot lawn was surrounded by a newish brick wall, eight feet high. A tall, wrought-iron gate at the far end of the lawn led directly on to one of Dublin's most exclusive, and expensive, golf courses. Stevenson and Martina, his wife, were both members. They kept the gate locked, for security reasons, as Dublin had a high crime rate, and since the bombings you could not be too careful.

That evening, Martina had cooked sole bonne femme, from a recipe out of the latest cookery book to sweep Irish middle-class cuisines. It was *Sister Marietta's Culinary Journal* and was in the form of a diary, with recipes in copperplate penmanship, which the publishers claimed had been discovered in the Bishop of Sligo's house, in the attic, and had been written by the good sister, who had cooked for an earlier cleric, at the turn of the century.

A mock Georgian carriage clock ticked gently on the immaculate, dust-free mantelpiece, as the Dublin solicitor and his wife ate in silence off the bone-china plates Martina had sent away for in response to an advert in *The Connoisseur*, a monthly journal for gentlefolk.

It was a silent repast, for Martina believed gourmet meals should be eaten without conversation interrupting the palate's senses. It was at times like these when Pronsias Stevenson guiltily wondered if his wife had perhaps been discharged from the Mother Theresa Home just a mite too early.

It was not that Martina disliked conversation, in fact she had one entire shelf of her Wolfe Tone replica bookcase devoted to works on the social graces, and in three of the volumes were well-thumbed chapters on the art of conversation. But not at mealtimes. Martina believed it was bad manners to talk while eating, end of story.

The fish was exquisite and Pronsias made approving signals with his face and eyes, and with his fork, like a conductor's baton. Martina nodded demurely, and concentrated on her sole and the tiny assortment of perfectly cooked vegetables.

As he ate, the Fitzrowan family's lawyer pondered the bombshell Jack Fitzrowan had left behind. He remembered the phone call that Thursday, at nine twenty in the morning, which meant Jack was wide awake at four twenty a.m., Boston time.

'Pronsias me boy, I have made a bit of a killing. There will be an awful lot more in the kitty when I eventually fall off my perch than I ever imagined. It will be kept safe in an off-shore fund, the details of which will be sent to you by secure digital fax. And I will have to re-write the codicil to my will, else young you-know-who would inherit zillions more than the other three.' Jack had laughed softly. 'Can you imagine the almighty confusion that would cause? Outrage, hurt, scheming . . .'

Oh yes, Pronsias could certainly imagine it. For just two weeks later, he had witnessed that very confusion in his own office. And he did not doubt that, even as he munched his sole bonne femme, much scheming would be taking place. In Boston, to where Grace had returned; in Oxford, where the stunning Darcy Fitzrowan Bailey had gone with her husband, Edward, the Magdalen College don; and in his own, more reticent way, wherever young Sir Paul Fitzrowan had repaired to. They would all be scheming, either separately or together. You could put money on that.

Just that afternoon, Pronsias Stevenson had overseen the electronic transfer of eight million and fifty-two thousand dollars from the Banque Credit Suisse's Cayman Islands branch into a holding account with the Bank of Ireland in Dublin. This was to be divided in three equal shares, two million six hundred and eighty-four thousand each to Sir Paul, Darcy and Grace.

Because Jack Fitzrowan had made it a condition of the legacy that no senior beneficiary should contest or otherwise block the codicil, Stevenson had discussed the matter with his partner, Frank Malahide. They debated whether, by the very act of accepting the funds bequeathed, each beneficiary would *de facto* be waiving his or her right to contest the codicil.

'Well, yes and no . . .' Justice Malahide had decided, after due deliberation. 'Maybe, Pronsias, it would be prudent to keep the funds in our holding account until you obtain written confirmation from each of the legatees that they formally accept the codicil.'

So that is what Pronsias Stevenson had done. And even as he contemplated his silent repast, documents were being delivered by couriers to Jack Fitzrowan's three heirs and successors. In the meantime, of course, interest in eight million dollars was accruing to the benefit of the partnership's holding account. All perfectly legal. And profitable.

He dabbed at a corner of his mouth with the snow white linen napkin, and his eyes met Martina's. He made a circle with his forefinger and middle finger. 'Perfect,' he said, quite forgetting the rules. Without a word, Martina Stevenson folded her napkin, laid it precisely two inches to the right of her half-finished plate, rose and walked out of the room.

Pronsias sighed, and continued to eat.

Mike Medevik got straight to the point. 'With dual nationality, the law of the country of principal residence generally takes precedence. But if a contract or other legally binding document is signed by the individual in the country of secondary residence, it would fall under the law of that country. Any monies earned by Jack Fitzrowan in either country, and deposited off-shore, would be at his disposal.'

'So we can't contest the codicil.' Grace gazed past Mike. Beyond the window, with its panes of slightly purple glass, she could see Boston Common and a gaggle of children playing around Frog Pond.

Medevik smiled. 'I didn't say that . . .'

He put on his reading glasses and opened a slim folder on his desk. Grace let her gaze wander around the room. Medevik's office was spacious, with simple, tasteful furnishings and two tall windows facing west.

Medevik himself was of average height, dark hair cut short on top, fuller at the sides. Sallow complexion, good teeth. Slender hands. He seemed a nice enough guy, able and competent. But she could not quite visualize Alison having been his wife. In fact, she could not quite imagine Alison being anyone's wife. The woman was an item of one. Approachable, likeable, but quietly independent.

Medevik glanced up, meeting her gaze. It was as if he knew precisely what she was thinking. He smiled. 'Jack Fitzrowan, like a number of rich men who generate their wealth using a corporate entity wholly or almost wholly owned by them, tended to treat Zeralda as his private piggy bank.'

Grace had, on two occasions, asked her father about the legality of his transferring funds from the Corporation's banks to off-shore accounts in other names. Fitzrowan had explained how it was necessary to generate the right paperwork: fees, consultancy contracts, bonuses and so on, even though Zeralda was, to all intents and purposes Jack Fitzrowan and Jack Fitzrowan was Zeralda. And Sebastian Tree, C E O and Chief Accountant, had agreed, and he had always ensured the records were in order.

'There was nothing underhand about it. Daddy was simply using his own money. He always kept scrupulous records. The I R S would have jumped down his throat, otherwise.'

Medevik nodded. 'And if I were representing Jack, that is the line I would take. However, today I am here to advise you, Mrs Fitzrowan.'

'Hanrahan. Mrs Tom Hanrahan.'

'I'm sorry, Mrs Hanrahan. And today I am seeking a way to exclude, from what is described in the codicil as the "residue", of your late father's estate, the proceeds of his deal with McDonnell Douglas. That one deal netted him around two hundred and seven million dollars in finder's fees, presently being held off-shore. And it is that single sum which has made the Oliver codicil so . . . unfair.'

So simple. Grace felt a glimmer of hope.

Medevik went on, 'You see, as long as Jack Fitzrowan *was* Zeralda Electronics Inc., no one at Zeralda was going to dispute his allocation of funds as fees or bonuses, or whatever.'

Grace Hanrahan felt vindicated in insisting on obtaining the very best counsel. Her daddy would have been proud of her. Except, Jack would have thought of this angle all by himself, for his brain was as sharp as any attorney's, as several had found to their cost.

'But now . . .' she said.

'But now that you and your brother and sister own ninety-five per cent of Zeralda's stock, you could take the view that the late president of the corporation had been over-generous to himself.' Medevik removed his glasses and laid them on the table. Way across the common, two mounted cops were trying to control their horses, while three small terriers snapped around their hooves.

'And if we did take that view . . . ?'

'You could obtain an international injunction, freezing the account, pending a hearing. And the case would be tried here in Boston, being the registered address of Zeralda Electronics Inc., Zeralda Holdings and the Zeralda Corporation Pension Fund.'

'And what would be our case?' asked Grace, suddenly able to taste the big bucks once more, just as strongly as in Pronsias Stevenson's Dublin office.

'That Jack Fitzrowan had wrongly appropriated funds belonging to Zeralda.'

Grace frowned. 'Even if we were successful, that would merely put the two hundred million back into the company.'

Medevik stretched back in his leather chair. Grace noticed a framed photo of a smiling Alison Clancy on the desk. The lawyer made a steeple of his fingers, the way lawyers do. 'There would be nothing to stop you from paying yourselves fees and bonuses . . . Even setting aside an equal sum for Oliver, should he be traced and his identity confirmed.'

Brilliant, thought Grace. But it would mean a messy court case, for she was certain that tight-assed little Irishman, Pronsias Stevenson, would fight tooth and nail to retain the power to administer her daddy's millions. Without his control of the legacy, he would be just another lawyer.

And of course, she was right.

Searching a colleague's office was not something Alison Clancy had ever contemplated before. However, now that she had decided to stay with Zeralda, until she had proof of Sebastian Tree's complicity in the Katakura take-over bid, there was no point in pussy-footing around.

So when Tree left the office, at five eighteen that evening, she went to the top-floor stockroom, overlooking the back yard, from where she watched him climb into his silver Porsche 911 Turbo convertible and, after putting on sun-glasses, drive away.

A quick walk from the stockroom to a lobby window on the north side of the building and Alison had a clear view of Longfellow Bridge over the Charles River. Sure enough, two minutes and twenty seconds later, the silver bullet, as Jack used to call it, appeared on the bridge and turned right, speeding west along James J. Storrow Drive on the way to Route 90.

Amy Schofield, Sebastian Tree's PA, left every evening promptly at five thirty-five. She had a routine which involved taking the food she purchased from Tarantola's deli each lunchtime to her mother's apartment in Charlestown, where she would cook supper and generally be home by nine. Amy was a perfect secretary for an accountant. You could set your watch by her.

Amy Schofield emerged from the Chief Executive's outer office, paused, turned on one heel, gazed thoughtfully around the room, eyes flicking over desk and work surfaces, voice mail on, printer off, filing cabinets locked, safe locked, window locked, Sebastian's door open, Sebastian's overhead light on . . . Finally she nodded, closed the door, and walked to the elevator. It was, of course, precisely five thirty-five.

In the security office, on the second floor, Alison Clancy was talking to Arthur, the senior guard on duty. Arthur was in his mid thirties, a former White House cop, and it was his daughter's sixth birthday the next day.

'Why it's terrific. Just dandy . . .' He examined the Osh B'gosh dungarees in grey and white striped denim. 'Just like a train driver's. How did you remember?'

'Big Jack never forgot things like that,' replied Alison, smiling. 'I knew Tracey's birthday was tomorrow, so I cheated.'

Arthur grinned. 'The boss kept a book.'

Alison nodded. 'Jack liked to keep in touch with the work force. To him, everyone at Zeralda is family.'

Arthur smiled. 'Tracey still wants to be a train driver, tell Mr Fitzrowan –' He stopped. 'Oh, hell. I'm sorry . . .'

'So,' smiled Alison, 'happy birthday Tracey from all at Zeralda.' On the eight-part close-circuit TV monitor were two shots from different angles of Amy Schofield walking with a couple of girl-friends to one of the small Zeralda buses which worked a shuttle to and from Boston and kept the company logo and name in the public consciousness at the same time. Alison went on, 'Is she having a party?'

'Sure thing. A buddy at Amtrak has arranged a ride to Cleveland and back on a brand new locomotive, just the engine and one carriage. We got a surprise birthday cake and funny hats. Soda–pop and the whole works. It's another kid's birthday too, one of the Amtrak security guys'. It'll be quite a party.'

Alison watched the company bus leave the front lot and lumber on to the Memorial Drive feeder. 'What are you and her mom giving Tracey?' she asked.

Arthur smiled. 'A kitten.'

'Lucky girl. Well you have a great time.'

'Thanks, Alison.' Arthur Jamieson felt really pleased, with all the business of Big Jack dying and so on, here was the firm's hot-shot legal eagle taking time to remember his kid's birthday. Who said it was jungle out here? The Zeralda Corporation was a good place to work.

'I'm working late, Arthur, so don't worry about the fourth floor for another half-hour, I'll buzz you when I'm about to leave.'

'Sure thing, Miss Clancy. And thanks again.'

Alison Clancy left the security control room and went back to the fourth floor. She suddenly had an awful thought that Jack had given Arthur's kid a set of engine driver's dungarees last year too.

Sebastian Tree's office was always a model of neatness. Because the office cleaners and security guards had the run of the building, it was a strict rule that nobody left any documentation lying around when they left work. Each main office and workshop had its own safes and heavy-duty filing cabinets.

There was a bonus for any Zeralda guard who found confidential documents, disks, tapes, etc., and every employee's contract clearly stated that a first lapse carried a financial penalty, the second a fine plus loss of leave and the third, immediate dismissal.

It was an efficient system.

But unknown to Sebastian Tree, Jack had furnished Alison with the combinations of his safes and duplicate keys to his cabinets. Jack had also arranged for Tree to have the same access to Alison's secure equipment, which Alison Clancy had long since figured, and which is why she stored the most highly confidential data on floppy disks, which were kept in a secret place.

The Corporation's lawyer closed the door to Amy Schofield's outer office and leaned against it. Her heart was beating hard and her head was unnaturally clear, which she knew was thanks to the adrenalin of fear pumping around her veins.

But frightened or not, she had to know exactly how Sebastian Tree was planning to give Katakura an edge in his next take-over raid.

The ketch *Zeralda of Erin* was still moored opposite Commercial Wharf. She looked somehow desolate, forlorn, robbed of the many happy memories which had brought Tom Hanrahan back here, seeking some solace, some comfort from the last place he had seen Jack Fitzrowan alive.

A breeze rattled steel and aluminium rigging lines. Faint music drifted across the flat water from the direction of the Aquarium. Tom Hanrahan recognized it as an old number by Led Zeppelin. He could not remember the name but it was the track they had used in the movie *Apocalypse Now*, when a Special Forces patrol boat was edging up the Mekong River in the dusk. An eerie, ominous sound then. And somehow still ominous now.

Tom frowned, slightly puzzled, at the blue and white plastic POLICE — CRIME SCENE tapes surrounding the moored sailing boat and stepped up the gangplank. He paused before setting foot on the deck, nostrils assailed by that salty, pungent, tarry, oily, sea-fishy smell which would always mean *Zeralda* to him.

Mingling with the fading ambulance siren, the noise of traffic and faint strains of Led Zeppelin, he became aware of the putt-puttering of a small tugboat making its way across the harbour towards the wharf.

The detective stepped down on to *Zeralda*'s solid teak deck and all those sounds faded abruptly, bushwhacked by memory. And there he was, hauling on the wheel to keep the ketch's bowsprit lined up on Nantucket Lighthouse, whenever he could glimpse it in the heaving seas. And there was big Jack's grinning face, wet with spray, blue and yellow oilskins massive on his broad chest and shoulders, like a medieval knight's armour.

It had been, as so often with Jack, a merry, happy moment. And in the next instant, the suddenness of that boom, hurtling like an Exocet missile, sweeping the tycoon from the solid security of his small sailing ship into oblivion, a tumbling, bloody corpus, even before he went beneath the surging spume. Jesus and Mary. Was Tom to be for ever haunted by that moment?

He had paused by the steering wheel, and as the noise of the approaching tugboat became very close, the Homicide cop realized he was gripping its spokes, white-knuckled, his heart pounding. Post-traumatic stress syndrome? Fuck that, boyo, he thought to himself. This is one hardnosed Boston cop. You have no idea the shit I've seen.

He delved into his coat pocket and tugged out a pack of Winstons and his Homicide Zippo, watching a tugboat crewman climb aboard *Zeralda*'s bows, and make fast a mooring line. Behind the crewman, a familiar face appeared. Sergeant Dan Tarantola, fellow Homicide detective and grandson of Maria Tarantola, founder of Tarantola's Magnificent Deli, a breath of the old country.

Tarantola was a couple of years older than Tom Hanrahan. He had multiple citations for valour, and the unenviable reputation of being the most-times shot police officer in Boston's finest. The Department had assigned him away from the rackets, dope syndicates and whorehouses of the North End, to the milder rackets, dope syndicates and whorehouses of the Waterfront in order to give Mrs Tarantola an improved chance of seeing her husband reach retirement age. It was no big surprise therefore to see Dan stepping off a harbour tug. This was his patch. Hanrahan imagined his colleague had come to chew the fat.

'Yo, Thomas, what's up?' Tarantola made his way aft, approaching Tom.

'Memories, my man. Bad ones . . .'

Tarantola seemed less than moved to tears. He paused at the foot of the mainmast, peering at the halyard ropes and cleats.

'I hear you got Sammy Jade downtown.'

'Yeah, he's doing a soft shoe shuffle but it's just a matter of time. Fuckin war axe is missing but we got another from the mail order company. Pathologist says that's what made the head wounds, and the back and thigh.'

But Tarantola was only half listening. 'Sure,' he said, and paused, turning to squint at the towering mast, running his hands along the boom cover. 'Where were you when it happened?'

Still no alarm bells sounded.

'Right here.'

'You were driving.'

'Helmsman, Dan. I was at the wheel.

'Yeah yeah. *Exactly* there . . . ?'

'Yep.'

Tarantola stuck his fists in his raincoat pocket and eyed Tom as the Lieutenant held the flickering Zippo and lit up. 'I thought you'd given up.'

'I started again.'

'Man, I been off it for eight months now. Mrs T says I been so bad tempered. So where was the victim?'

Tom smiled to himself. Even with an accidental death, here was

Danny the Wop – no term of obloquy this, no racial slur, it was just that there was only one Italian-American Dan, Daniel or Danny in the Boston PD Homicide Department, and nine Irish-Americans with the same moniker – here was Danny discussing it like a murder case.

Victim. In the squad the world was divided into victims, perps, stoolies, civilians and suspects.

'Jack was sitting on the port edge of the saloon hatch cover.'

'In English, *per favore* . . .'

'There.'

'Which side?'

'Left. The left side.'

Tarantola moved for'ard, round the mainmast, and came back aft to sit on the spot where Tom Hanrahan had last seen his father-in-law alive.

'About here?'

'Yes.'

Tarantola sat down. He met Tom's gaze. 'Facing which way?'

There was something about the professional attitude in the cop's approach which sounded the faintest of tocsins.

'His body was facing for'ard . . . ahead,' Tom pointed towards the bow, 'but he had twisted round to look at me.'

'Why?'

'He was enjoying himself.'

'Look at you how?'

'He was smiling. Grinning.'

'Then, ker-whack . . . ?'

'Exactly like that. Dan, it's all in my accidental death statement, downtown, with the Coroner's office.'

'I've seen it.'

A seagull settled delicately, but with a degree of confidence, on the lowered gaff, a slim spar, lighter than the boom and which, when raised, held the top of the mainsail out from the mast.

'How many a day?' Tarantola gazed wistfully at the smoke drifting out of Tom's nostrils.

'About six. Five or six.'

60

'Boy, I couldn't stick at that. Anyone else on board, when it happened?'

'Jack's Chief Exec. Sebastian Tree.'

'And where was he?'

'Being seasick. The guy is a landlubber. Drives a Porsche.'

'Where?'

'Down below. In the after cabin.'

The tugboat crew were now making fast a pair of heavy towing hawsers, to the fo'c's'le winch.

'What's going on?' asked Tom, suddenly remembering that *Zeralda* had become his brother-in-law's yacht. The property of Edward Bailey, Darcy's husband and Oxford don.

'It's being towed, is that the correct term, Lieutenant? Across the harbour to the Customs and Coastguard forensics dry-dock.'

'What the hell for? And they can't do that. This ketch belongs to the deceased's family. A member of the family.'

'For comprehensive forensic tests. And they can. I have a warrant.'

'Warrant? Warrant for what?'

'This is no longer an accidental death formality. The death of John Pearce Dunmill Fitzrowan is being treated as suspected murder.'

Alison lived in a neat little mews off Willow Street, on Beacon Hill. The terraced house had on the ground floor a front room and a back kitchen and previous owners had knocked down the dividing wall to make the two small rooms into a more spacious reception and eating area. A narrow staircase rose to the main bedroom with bathroom en suite and up to a third floor which had been two minuscule bedrooms before Alison had knocked down the wall between them to create a study.

The whole house was a delight to her. Original wooden floors, exposed brick and plaster, Navajo rugs and cedarwood bookshelves, fabrics from Connecticut and a practical kitchen which combined the most modern equipment with a quintessentially New England look.

She sat at her desk in the study listening to the unhurried ticking of the old Wells Fargo clock on the wall beside her and gazing at the computer screen in front of her, reading Sebastian Tree's most confidential files, on disks copied from those in his safe which were now safely back where they belonged.

Zeralda's CEO was no fool, and there was nothing in the files that immediately shouted 'foul!'. No evidence of collusion with the Katakura Corporation, no breath of impropriety.

There were, however, certain directory paths which Alison felt were blind alleys. Certain passwords into files which, without them, were denied to her. But passwords are not impossible to decode, given a comprehensive knowledge of the author. Alison Clancy had also taken home Tree's personal file from Jack's own safe. There was little about Sebastian which was not included, from his grade school details to dates of his several sports car acquisitions, food and wine preferences and a string of names and birthdays of his most serious amours. Somewhere in all that, given patience, Alison knew she would find at least a couple of passwords. It was going to take many hours, or just a few moments, depending on luck. And perseverance.

And Zeralda Electronics' Boston attorney certainly had that. She started with the name of her target's first dog, a fox terrier called Elvis. It was two in the morning before she thought of Blue Suede Shoes. And nothing would be the same thereafter . . .

Tom Hanrahan watched as water drained out from the Customs and Coastguard dry-dock. He noted that *Zeralda*'s bilge keels were in sound condition, and her new propeller might just need some tightening. New props often loosened slightly after they had been running for a couple of weeks.

Once the dock was empty, the wooden ketch looked like a toy, abandoned and vulnerable. A couple of workmen fixed a gangplank from the dockside to *Zeralda*'s port deck. Dan Tarantola stepped across, and Tom followed. Several attempts on the brief voyage across Boston harbour to learn what had prompted suspicions of murder had been ignored.

'First thing I ask myself, when a violent, unexpected death occurs to a man such as this Jack Fitzrowan,' Tarantola scratched his neck, just behind his right ear, 'is . . . who stands to benefit?'

'Dan, this is crazy. I was on the yacht, it was a force eight wind. The seas were like . . . houses. The fucking boom hits him . . . Blam!' Tom pushed the flat of his hand at the side of his head, to illustrate. 'Like Mickey Mantle's baseball bat. The guy was dead before he hit the water, who the fuck could have arranged that? It was bad luck. One of those things. I wake up asking myself could I have saved him? Seen the thing coming, shouted a warning?'

In the silence, Sergeant Tarantola took a stick of chewing gum from his pocket and started to unwrap it.

'And what do you answer? What do you reply, to yourself?' His eyes met Hanrahan's.

Tom shrugged, gazing at the spot where Jack had been, at the wheel, where he himself had stood. He shook his head. 'It was an act of God, Danny. It happened in a . . . a split second. A tenth of a second. It was his time. Nothing could have helped him, the moment he sat there. He should have known the risk.'

Tarantola digested this.

'How often did you sail with him?'

'Uh, regularly.'

'Ten times a year? Forty? Five . . . ?'

'About once a month. When he was here. When *Zeralda* was in Boston. Say, seven or eight times in a year.'

'And he never sat on that hatch cover before?'

Tom lit another Winston. He shook his head. 'That's the strange thing . . . he did. He did sit there, always when we were on the port tack, wind on the beam. When we were on a long reach, with a steady wind.'

Tarantola's eyes rolled. 'Please. Lieutenant. What the fuck are you talking about?'

'When it was safe, no chance of the boom suddenly swinging. Jack would sit there.'

'And nothing like this . . .' Tarantola nodded towards the smashed guard rail and twisted cable.

'No. Yes. Once, last September. The boom swung round, we

63

were running into the wind, too close, wind changed, boom flipped from starboard to port. Right to left. Grace screamed.'

'Your wife.'

'Yeah. But he just grinned. Boom missed him on that occasion.'

'Why?'

Tom shrugged. 'Maybe he ducked.'

'You are a trained detective, Lieutenant. Observant, is the word. Mister Memory. So did he or didn't he duck?'

Tom cast his mind back to a happier day's sailing, 'No.'

'And he grinned.'

'That's right.'

'And why did he grin, that time, why did he grin?'

'Jack was the kind of guy who enjoyed life. He smiled a lot. Laughed. Grinned . . . How should I know?'

Tarantola put the stick of gum in his mouth and chewed on it, pointed the empty wrapper at Hanrahan. 'He grinned, Thomas, because he knew the boom would miss. He grinned, Lieutenant, because he personally had overseen the sweating of the mainsail gaff close to the peak.' The cop's neck arced as he leaned back to gaze at the top of the mainmast. 'And he personally had tied off the boom, at a height which ensured the safety of anyone, uh, sitting on this hatch cover. He grinned, because he knew he was in no danger.'

'I thought sailing jargon was Greek to you.'

The detective shrugged. 'I been boning up recently.'

Tom held Tarantola's searching gaze. His mind racing over the preparations for that fateful voyage. Who had hoisted the mainsail? Had anyone inadvertently lowered the height of the boom?

'I been asking around,' went on Tarantola. 'I been asking around, reading up on Zeralda Electronics, some Jap take-over raid. Getting up to speed on the victim. His private life. Jesus, Tom, the guy was something of a master cocksman.'

'Maybe you should start smoking again . . .'

'So. I have to ask, Who wanted revenge? Who stands to benefit?'

Tom Hanrahan stared at the other detective.

'His immediate family stands to benefit. Which includes me.

Grace is a wealthy woman in her own right. Jack left me his golf clubs and a car. An Aston, DB7. Neat vehicle.'

'Yeah, Tom, I don't see you helping the man overboard for a set of wheels and a five iron. But my theory is, somebody fixed that boom. Knowing that Jack liked to risk sitting right there. Coming about, jibbing, head on into the wind, larboard wind goes dead, big seas . . . any number of events made it a fair bet the guy could get hurt in the resulting "accident".'

'Why have you brought the boat here?'

'I figure, Lieutenant, if the murder theory is correct, that nobody cunning enough, experienced enough at this yachting malarkey, would just leave it at the boom thing. There have to be a dozen other ways of rigging fatal accidents at sea. And I have a couple of Coastguard bosuns coming over with Tommy Boyle to snoop around, see what else might have been . . . adjusted.'

Tom shrugged. 'I need a receipt for the boat.'

'Sure thing.' Tarantola turned sideways and spat his wad of gum into the dock. 'One other thing . . .'

'What's that?'

'Don't go too far away, Lieutenant. In the immediate future.'

In the Dublin offices of Stevenson, Stevenson & Malahide, Pronsias Stevenson watched Jack Fitzrowan's son and heir sign a heap of documents concerning land registry, tenants' cottages, and all manner of things relating to the new baronet's role as landowner and the solicitor's appointment as trustee of Paul's two and a half million inheritance.

'How much will we deposit to set you up, young fella? You do have a bank account, don't you?'

Paul glanced across the table at Stevenson and smiled to himself. Here was somebody who was unsure if men of twenty-four with pony tails and an earring could handle anything so bourgeois as a cheque account.

He nodded, allowing a ghost of that smile to appear on his lips. 'Yes, Mr Stevenson, I do. Several, in fact.'

Stevenson nodded. *Mr Stevenson*, is it to be? Not Pronsias, he thought to himself. So the young fellow's new-found gravitas is not about to slip.

'I was thinking of an initial sum of around ten thousand pounds. With more as and when. Where should that be paid?' he enquired.

Paul's smile remained just as thin. 'Let's get a couple of things straight. The money being held in trust for me, how is it going to be invested?'

Stevenson frowned. 'Invested? It is being held off-shore. There are no instructions as to investment.' He thought to himself that Paul had a bit of a nerve, querying his judgement as trustee.

'Then I will put that another way. In the case of *Eire* versus *MacMonagle*, what was the final ruling on appeal?'

Eire versus *MacMonagle*? Bells rang in the back of Stevenson's mind. 'I am sure you will refresh my memory,' he replied silkily.

'It is incumbent upon a solicitor or law firm when acting not solely as executors but also as trustees of an estate, to manage available funds and property with a view to prudent growth, as if they were advising clients in the same respect.'

Pronsias Stevenson sighed and polished his half-moon glasses on his tie. Why did everyone think they could become a lawyer after two afternoons at Dublin Public Library?

'We are content that your late father's fiscal arrangements for growth are competent.' He replaced his spectacles and looked Paul in the eye.

'Indeed. And what sort of interest are we talking about?'

Stevenson consulted his neatly arranged volume of files and documents, an unnecessary piece of pedantry since he clearly knew such an elementary detail.

'Here we are, um . . . aggregate return of eight point six per cent, per annum.'

Paul considered this. 'OK. That's two hundred and thirty thousand dollars a year, a hundred and fifty thousand Irish pounds, a hundred and sixty thousand English. Enough after tax to keep me going. So tell you what, Mr Stevenson, I'll have the equivalent of a year's interest in advance.'

Stevenson looked shocked. 'Two hundred thousand dollars?'

'Two hundred and thirty. Please make out two cheques for one hundred thousand and one for the balance.'

Pronsias Stevenson remained silent, turning pages in his file holder and making little pencil marks. A charade this, he was taking time to think. For this was not the feckless long-haired loon Big Jack had been so – unhappy? disappointed? – no, saddened, saddened by.

This Paul Fitzrowan, while lacking his father's steel and surging personality, had a certain quiet determination and clarity of purpose about him. Stevenson remembered the reading of the Will, and his likening the new Paul to Prince Hal in *Henry IV* who, upon the death of his father the king, became a changed man, casting off the carousing playboy for a stately crown and mighty responsibility.

This was a watershed day. For the very first time it sunk in to Pronsias Stevenson that Jack was indeed gone. And his own magic strength, the latent power of being the Dublin voice of Sir John Fitzrowan Bt., millionaire President of Zeralda Electronics, confederate of international statesmen and the world's major players, was suddenly under threat. From this whippersnapper of a youth.

And in the wings, the fiercely unforgiving (and desirable) Darcy Fitzrowan and the able and shrewd Grace, herself a considerably attractive woman. Both with those legs and firm but shapely buttocks . . . The outwardly prim lawyer shook himself from his lustful reverie.

'One hundred thousand now. That's it. And I am obliged to know into which account or accounts the money is being placed.' He met Paul's relaxed gaze. God how he hated the confidence of the Kerry rich. '*Eire* versus *Kavenagh*, 1962.'

Paul smiled. 'That'll be fine, Pronsias. When I need more, I know you will be here.' He rose and laid a scrap of paper on the table. 'That's the account. First National Bank of Boston. O'Connell Street. And don't forget to let me have a statement of your firm's expenses per month.'

'Statement? May I enquire why?'

Paul paused at the door, and smiled coolly. 'Why? So that I can pass them to my accountant for approval of course.'

★

Darcy and her husband Edward Bailey had stayed at Crough Lake in Kerry for a few days, walking with the dogs, riding out along the miles of Atlantic beach, eating old-fashioned dinners cooked by Bridget and entertaining one or two of the local gentry who called in to pay their condolences.

She had noticed the sea change in Paul, somewhat to her disquiet. Darcy and Edward had been comfortable enough before Big Jack's death, for her mother, the noted beauty Scarlet Hennessy, had left her a quarter of a million pounds which Darcy had inherited when she was four years old, at the time of Scarlet's untimely death, hunting with the Galway Blazers.

That had been nearly thirty years ago. The money had been held in trust until her eighteenth birthday, by which time it had more than doubled.

But by the time Darcy had married Edward, at the age of twenty-five, when the trust if it had remained untouched would have stood at nearly a million pounds, there was just £376,000 in the kitty. What had she spent over half a million on in the intervening seven years?

It was easy, she told her father, when Jack, on the eve of her big wedding at the Kennedys' place in Hyannisport, had enquired after her financial situation. Easy, and fun. And Jack Fitzrowan had stared deep into his daughter's beautiful, defiant green eyes for a long, long moment. Then he had held her tight, the way he had used to cuddle her when she was a child, and laughed gently. A sort of low chuckle.

'I'm glad you had fun,' he said, tenderly. And when they returned from a honeymoon sailing and diving in the Caribbean, Mr and Mrs Edward Bailey learned they had become the owners of a small Tudor manor house on the road to Weston-on-the-Green, a few miles from Oxford University, where Edward taught English and had a research fellowship with Magdalen College.

It was in this manor house, known as Hedge's Hall, that the slender, elegant Darcy Bailey, née Fitzrowan, now sat, naked but for a short, silk shift, running a brush through her long, fair hair, her lover's juice still damp on her thighs and the aroma of Calvin Klein mingling with more pungent, vital scents.

In the marble bathroom – not in keeping with the period of the house, but luxurious and practical, a bit like herself – the lean, muscled skipper of Jack's Americas Cup challenger stood under the power shower, humming to himself.

And as the pleasure of the past hour and fifteen minutes passed, Darcy's thoughts returned to the subject which dominated almost all else. The bastard Oliver and his two hundred and eighteen million dollars, which would be increasing daily, like her own small inheritance, and out of reach until the love child could be traced and proven to be alive. Or not.

Where was Edward while all this trysting had been going on?

In his room at Magdalen, picking at the entrails of *Beowulf*, or discoursing to his students on iambics and trochaics. For it was four in the afternoon, Darcy's favourite time of day for such sport.

But now, as she brushed her hair with slow, thoughtful strokes, like some chatelaine of old, recent lust and heights of pleasure had gone from her mind and Darcy was formulating a plan. In order to trace Oliver, without putting advertisements in the media – she could imagine the chaos that would engender – it would be necessary to find out where the girl Helen Costello, the kitchen maid, Daddy's one great love among hundreds, had been taken. And who had arranged the adoption, for Darcy had little doubt the infant was handed over illegally to its new, apparently American parents.

There had always been a black market in illegitimate babies, unwanted embarrassments, in a land where the Church's rule was law and contraception forbidden. And the first place to start looking, Darcy decided, was among the Kerry nuns and their nursing homes.

Rich Calhoun, her seafaring lover of the moment, appeared at the bathroom entrance, covered in suds, his manhood risen proud, a knowing grin on his face.

'No thank you, baby,' said Darcy. 'Playtime's over.'

Grace and Tom Hanrahan lived in a roomy, pale green and white clapperboard house on Farragut Road, South Boston, between Broadway and Swallow Street. It was set back from the street on a slight rise and had a carport and a decent size grass yard at the back, with a couple of apple trees and a cherry tree in bloom.

Farragut was on the western tip of South Boston and the houses on the east side of the road looked over the grass and scattered trees of Marine Park across the bay to Castle Island, a favourite place for young families to stroll and relax, picnic and play with Frisbees on fine spring evenings and at weekends.

The house and location had been chosen by Grace and Tom to provide her with some comfort and space, where she could entertain colleagues and those of Zeralda's customers who had become friends, without making the Lieutenant of Detectives look like the kept man of some rich bitch, for South Boston, while not cheap, was very much a regular neighbourhood and Tom, too, could bring his Police Department buddies round for a casual beer and on Sundays they had barbecues for all comers.

It was a happy house and a comfortable arrangement. Grace and Tom had been married for four and a half years and had recently been planning to start a family. This was what they were discussing the evening of Tom's encounter with Dan Tarantola, an encounter the detective did not want to worry his wife with.

'Thing is,' said Grace, 'there could always be some damn good reason not to get pregnant. You OK with tacos tonight?'

'I love your tacos.'

'So taking on Zeralda, full time, is not a good excuse is it?'

'I would like to be a daddy. You want to, tell me when, I'll be there. We ain't getting any younger.'

'Tommy don't say ain't.'

'I ain't gonna, no more.' Tom ducked as Grace threw a wet dish rag at him.

'I know your detectives, Tom Hanrahan. They don't all say ain't and gonna, for God's sake.'

'Maybe nobody talked like that till the *Die Hard* movies come out.'

'Came out.'

'Whatever . . .'

Grace shook her head and they embraced, at first in fun, then tenderly.

'Baby,' said Tom, 'I'll talk any way you want. The rain in Spain falls mainly and like that. And Zeralda? I think we should have babies now. Now is the time, I love you, kid . . .'

'I saw Michael Medevik today,' said Grace.

'Who's that?'

She told him about the inheritance lawyer's advice that the Zeralda Corporation should sue the Fitzrowan estate for the return of Jack's McDonnell Douglas windfall, the two hundred and seven million dollars that was the root of the family's outrage over the Oliver codicil.

'That way, we do not contest the codicil, or any part of the Will. It would be a Zeralda lawsuit and there is nothing Pronsias Stevenson can do about it.' She smiled with the exact certainty of someone who has just received the sort of legal advice they want to hear.

'Pronsias Stevenson won't take that lying down,' predicted Tom.

'Too much is at stake to get excited about his sensibilities.'

'I didn't think money mattered that much to you.' Hanrahan gazed into her eyes, faded blue, so very Celtic, and as attractive as the first time he had seen her.

'It's not just the money . . . look what it's doing to Darcy, she feels betrayed and hurt. And it is not what Daddy wanted, even Pronsias admits Big Jack intended to fly over to Dublin after that weekend and re-write the Will. And over fifty million dollars each, to Darcy, Paul, Oliver – the bastard as Darcy calls him – and me, us . . .' She pressed her pelvis against his. 'Don't tell me you would turn it away.'

Tom examined her face. This was not the Grace he knew so well. 'Just don't mention the Senate. I'm happy doing what I do.'

'Of course you are, honey . . . Did you get your axe murderer?'

Silence, he nuzzled her ear. God she smelled fine. 'Oh, yes. D A says we have a case.'

'Well, I'm pleased for you. Mmmm . . . What about the tacos?'

'Later.'

And after they had made love, lying on the kitchen rug, warm and relaxed in each other's arms, Tom wondered if Grace would still be smiling if she knew of the Department's suspicion that her father's death was no accident. And that he himself seemed to be prime suspect.

But she had been through a tough time already, and he kept his own counsel.

The Marriott Long Wharf Hotel is on Boston's Waterfront, overlooking the harbour and next to the Aquarium. From his suite on the eighteenth floor. Peter Girolo had a panoramic view of the wharfs and, beyond Commercial Wharf, Black Falcon Terminal, where a tiny wooden ketch sat high and dry in its cradle in the Coastguard dry-dock. A number of men in blue coveralls were examining the rigging and rails.

Girolo gazed down at the harbour, deep in thought.

There was a knock at the door. A knock he knew well. The man who came in was aged about fifty, swarthy and wearing a brown leather coat and a black leather cap with a leather button on the top. His face too could have been made of leather. Once hard as granite, the features had slipped with age and the kind of experiences most people could do without. Giuseppe 'Joey' Buscetta, an enforcer from New York City.

'So, how are things?' enquired Girolo, pouring two club sodas from the mini-bar.

Buscetta settled into a comfortable sofa, unbuttoning his coat and putting his cap on a glass and chrome side table.

'Things is OK. *Grazie . . .*' He took the tumbler of soda and sipped, as if it were the finest Marsala.

They sat there for some time, sipping in silence, with Girolo making a few moves with his hands, touching an ear, rubbing a forearm, things like that. Joey Buscetta watched this closely and finally he nodded slowly, connecting his little finger to his thumb, palm upwards, which meant he understood. For just as racetrack bookies have their hand and arm signals, and the mute has his sign language, so is there such a way of communicating among certain *mafiosi*, from the old country.

'Good,' said Girolo. 'That's good.' And he rose and handed Buscetta his leather cap, as the older man headed for the door. At the door, Girolo embraced Buscetta, Sicilian style, and breathed into his ear just one word: 'Paolo . . .'

Joey Buscetta inclined his head gravely, put on the leather cap, and walked out into the corridor, his left leg stiff from where he took three nine-millimetre slugs in '87, courtesy of an FBI ambush. He had beaten that rap, and the *famiglia*'s lawyers had sued the Feds for six million dollars for unlawful wounding. Settled out of court for a hundred grand, but the point was theirs and it put some petty cash in the family's pocket. No chance of it reaching Joey Buscetta's pocket, naturally, but they gave him a party in that room with the check table cloths, back of the Gottis' spaghetti shop in Little Italy.

It made Joey feel good, marked him as *un uomo rispettare* – a man of respect, an accolade in the ranks of made men. And he became an enforcer of good order and discipline, ruthless and without mercy, discreet and reliable, feared in the ranks of the *cosa*.

And now?

And now Tom Hanrahan was going to have a busy night.

Ten after three in the morning, Alison Clancy sat staring at her computer screen, flicking through page after page, file after file of highly confidential insider information on Zeralda's innermost dealings, undeclared contracts, banking arrangements and classified government projects, all of which Sebastian Tree had squirrelled away in his Blue Suede Shoes protected path.

By themselves, the documents did not prove that Tree had been betraying his employer. Except for a secret file buried within that secret file, accessed by a password of the numbers 142170, which was 071241 backwards, and 071241 was 7 December 1941, the date of the Japanese attack on Pearl Harbor.

Which Alison thought was kind of cheeky.

And in the Pearl Harbor file was a series of communications by secure e.mail from Tree to Tak Katakura in his home outside Tokyo. The communications were in some form of cipher and that very fact was damning enough, for here was proof that the Chief Exec of the Zeralda Corporation had been talking in secret with the President of its greatest rival, before, during and after a hostile take-over bid.

Good for seven years in a correction centre as the Wall Street insider-dealing trials of '88 had proved, causing many a trader and broker to contemplate stepping out of the twenty-second floor.

Alison stretched and glanced at her wristwatch, a Patek Phillipe with a classic, plain white face and black numerals – a gift from Jack.

Jesus, look at the time. She copied the telltale directories on to her hard drive, switched off, hid the disks in a cornflakes packet and ran the shower. As she stepped out of her clothes, Alison Clancy reflected she had been this late before, but only after returning from Jack's mansion, not far from Willow Street, half-way up Mount Vernon Drive, following a night of . . . she smiled; passion, she supposed.

She stood naked under the hot, comforting water, soaping her lithe, slender body. Shoulders, flanks, flat belly and those almost juvenile tits she had always felt to be so inadequate until Jack had demonstrated such fondness for them with his special combination of tenderness and gently increasing arousal.

At the same moment, just a couple of miles away on the edge of a tough Boston neighbourhood known as Mattapan, Joey Buscetta and five *cosa* soldiers, made men from Atlantic City, got out from two unremarkable automobiles and walked quietly towards the Club Flamingo, whose pale pink and mint green neon sign had just been switched off for the night.

Dancers gone, gamblers departed, only the cashiers, the manager and the local *capo*, young Paolo Pecerone, with his stripper mistress, a beautiful mulatto kid called Bonnie Slater, and his two bodyguards Pizzuti and Calcara, remained in the building. And a cook, John di Falco, with no criminal record, who only wanted to save enough for his own small pasta place.

Tom Hanrahan was in a deep sleep, snoring gently, like a baby as Grace would say, when the jangling buzz of his bedside phone jerked him out of his slumber. He groped for the receiver, knocked

74

over a glass of water that Grace had warned him was too near the edge, said fuck a couple of times and caught the whole phone set as it tumbled off the bedside table.

'Yup?'

'Paolo Pecerone's just been whacked, nine cadavers, place is a fuckin charnel house. Nobody saw nothing, of course.' This was the voice of Dan Tarantola, the Homicide detective who suspected him of murdering his own father-in-law.

'Where?'

'That place of theirs in Mattapan. Flamingo.'

'Be right there. You wanna meet me?'

'You're the boss, Lieutenant.'

That's what Tom Hanrahan liked about the Police Department. Tarantola was not about to let a small thing like a domestic homicide investigation get in the way of a major-case gang war. Neither, of course, would he set it to one side. Homicide investigation was not a vocation, it was a disease . . .

Some murders were neat and tidy, a bruise here and there, small dark entry hole of a slug, or a broken neck. And some were messy. The Flamingo had surrendered its claim to be a place of fun and music, dope deals and booze, hookers and marks. It was now an abattoir. Corpses lay in pools of blood, like desserts in some classy joint where they put sponge cake or meringue in miniature ponds of raspberry coulis.

The walls were slashed and spattered with gore and worse. And at his usual table in a small alcove, Paolo Pecerone and his once-beautiful mulatto sat stone dead, no dignity in their horrific departure.

The two bodyguards had died as they headed towards the kitchen, their weapons still in their hands. The cashiers' bodies lay jammed around the front door, which they had been frantically trying to unlock. And John di Falco, the cook with ambitions, had been first to die, crumpled at the open door to a big, walk-in freezer.

Dan Tarantola was lighting one of the cheap cigars he kept in his inside pocket for moments like these. Crime scene forensics detectives in green coveralls were examining the cadavers and the room. Some were collecting spent shell cases and making chalk marks where they found them.

Tom Hanrahan gazed around, flicking a Winston out from its pack. 'Son of a bitch . . .' he said.

'Cook gets it first,' said Tarantola, then by way of involving the big, uniformed cop who had been first on the scene – Officer Joe Daly, a man in his fifties with more experience of sudden and deliberate death in Boston than most of the detectives in Homicide – he continued, 'Joe, you figure? Cook gets it first?'

Daly nodded. 'Cook, then the two foot soldiers, then Paolo, who has to be target one. Then the guys trying to get out.'

Another detective, checking those four, volunteered that every one had pissed himself. So would I, thought Tom to himself, and as his eyes met Daly's he knew the big cop agreed.

'So, Lieutenant, who does this?' enquired Dan Tarantola.

Tom shook his head, allowing smoke to drift out of his nostrils. 'Somebody who got the drop on Paolo, he's been acting like Al fuckin Capone these days. If any man had it coming to him . . .'

'So who?'

'Carmine,' stated Officer Joe Daly with authority. 'Word is Paolo ordered that drive-by last month. Carmine's old lady was breast feeding the baby. It was a Sunday. Three whole Uzi clips and eight pump-gun shells firing ball-bearings. Sheer miracle nobody got hurt. Glass all over the table and the baby's shawl.'

Tom shook his head. In the old days, before the big boys went away, the Italian mobs had something approaching class. They were discreet, caused no trouble in night-clubs and restaurants, and ran their illegal affairs prudently, respecting each other's territory and above all, each other's families. But now they were behaving like Mexican bandits. No discipline. No morals. No sense of survival. Sure, he could see Carmine losing his sense of humour over Paolo shooting up his Sunday joint. His bleeper sounded.

'Hanrahan,' he said into his personal radio.

'Luther here, Tom. You having a busy night?'

'Nothing two hundred and four years of paperwork won't cure.'

'Well you gonna get busier, Lieutenant. Somebody's just

whacked Carmine Genovese and his uncle Giuseppe. And his German shepherd.'

Carmine played pinochle Thursday nights with an old uncle, his mother's brother, who had the reputation of being kind of simple. Sometimes they played till dawn.

Tom glanced at his wristwatch; it was four thirty-two in the morning. Maybe this was a conspiracy to stop him making babies. He lifted his radio and spoke into it, 'I'll be right there.'

4

'Sure now it's a terrible thing, taking newborn babies straight from their poor, frightened mothers' bosoms. But it has been happening since before Cromwell burned down Wexford and Drogheda and it is still happening today.' The speaker was an owl-faced library clerk in the Church Records Office beside Dublin's St Stephen's Green. She had her hair drawn back and tied in a bun, and wore a long, sensible tweed skirt and fussy high-necked blouse. The whole effect reminded Darcy of Olive Oyl in the *Popeye* cartoons.

'And is there any kind of a record?' she enquired.

Maybe Olive Oyl had not heard Darcy, for she seemed to have gone off at a tangent, attending to some other business, walking between the rows of musty wooden filing cabinets and shelves. But then she ambled back, armed with a leather-bound ledger and put it on the table where Darcy was standing.

'This is known as the diocesan ledger.' Olive Oyl glanced over her reading glasses at the woman in the designer suit. 'It was started in 1887, by Father Thomas Fahey, and it records diocese by diocese those births that took place out of wedlock and whether or not the infant was taken into care by the parish or city authority, or kept by the mother or her family.'

'What about adoptions?'

Olive Oyl said adoptions were arranged by the civil authorities, and they kept such records along with the Register of Births, Deaths and Marriages at Dublin Castle. Although some church dioceses did note if an illegitimate child had been adopted during the first year of its birth.

Darcy considered this. 'Tell me about those babies that were taken from their mothers' bosoms and handed over, um . . . informally, to foster parents. Babies whose birth was not recorded formally, anywhere. Tell me how that works.'

The librarian seemed taken aback. 'Not recorded? Well not recording, not registering, a birth – quite apart from being against the law of the land – would mean there would be no record.' She tilted her bird-like head to one side and looked at Darcy as one would a slightly backward child. 'Unrecorded means there *is* no record . . .'

Darcy smiled back. 'Of course it does, how silly of me. Is there someplace I could sit down and look through this?' She had told Olive that she was researching for a thesis her husband was working on at Oxford University, and she had an open letter from Edward on a Magdalen letterhead confirming her credentials and requesting assistance in fairly general terms.

'Sure, why don't you use that table in the corner. I'll just get you a chair . . .'

And so Darcy sat down with the great tome and her notebook and started to trawl through the records of every parish from Kerry to Donegal, looking for a birth of a male child to an unmarried mother by the name of Helen Costello, on or about 14 June 1954.

At half past four the librarian came over, her flat, sensible shoes making flat, sensible footsteps on the polished (occasionally) wooden floor.

'Mrs Fitzrowan Bailey,' she said, for that was how Darcy liked to be styled. 'We are closing now. We'll be open again at nine thirty tomorrow morning.' She glanced at Darcy's notebook, with its few names and dates and places. 'If it's something in particular you are looking for, maybe I can help you.'

Darcy smiled. 'I'm really looking for local gossip, I suppose. My husband is working on the theory that, on occasion, parish registrars in the more remote regions might not have entered every illegitimate birth.'

Olive Oyl, in reality Sister Mary Ignatius MacMurrough, sighed, and Darcy braced herself for another homily on how unrecorded births would not be in the records, for reasons which were blindingly obvious. Instead, the librarian said, 'Oh, they are notorious for that. In the place where I come from, the registrar was a drunk. He got all those details of births piling up in his office and he would enter them as and when the mood took him. Why, in any one year there would be as many as seven or eight unrecorded births, for he had lost or thrown away the papers. Or written his shopping lists on them – one loaf of bread and three bottles of Jameson, usually.'

Darcy's mind reeled. 'So there are scores of people going around who do not exist, in rural areas?'

Olive nodded primly as she held the door open for Darcy to leave. 'I myself, he got my birth date a week out. And my sister Niamh is a whole year younger than she really is. My cousin Brendan did not exist at all till he joined the Garda and they fiddled the books.'

Darcy must have looked as crestfallen as she felt, for the librarian put a hand on her arm, comfortingly. 'Forgive me for asking, but is this perhaps more of a personal thing?'

Darcy shook her head. 'No, no. I was just thinking of all those poor lost children, never known their fathers, and not even known to church or state.'

'Ah, well, they'll be known to God, though,' smiled Olive Oyl, who held Darcy's gaze with a look of understanding.

Darcy smiled back. 'You're right, of course. I shouldn't take my researches so seriously.' And she left, and walked across St Stephen's Green to the Shelbourne Hotel, where she ordered a pot of tea and some scones with clotted cream and strawberry jam. It was a point of some amusement among the family, how much Darcy could stack away without ever gaining a pound. She had been a size twelve since the age of nineteen and some attributed it to the range of exercise she took, from show-jumping to sailing, to tennis and aerobics. But Darcy herself put it down to a hereditary keenness for a less public form of sport.

Sitting there, delicately spreading clotted cream and jam on her sliced scone, Darcy heard a familiar and not particularly welcome voice as a slender man in his mid forties approached, thinning black hair falling over his forehead and beaky nose red from the brisk chill outside, where General Winter was fighting a brisk, March, rearguard action.

'Why Darcy Fitzrowan, as I live and breathe. I heard you had gone back to Oxford,' said Pronsias Stevenson, MA LLD, as he weaved among the coffee tables in the lounge.

Darcy smiled to herself. Trust the Dickensian little snob to let the scattering of other customers hear the word Oxford and not England, for Stevenson's snobbery, like that of many of the Dublin professional classes, was hinged on intellect and connections rather than anything so vulgar as money.

'Hello, Pronsias.' She glanced up at him and raised a scone knife by way of greeting. He hovered for a moment, holding his Donegal tweed cap in both hands, like a suitor, until she relented. 'Will you ever sit down and take the weight off?'

The Dublin solicitor lowered himself into a chair, thanking her and glancing at her in that usual way he had. Darcy could never work out if he was short sighted or just plain lecherous. It had occasionally made her feel uncomfortable. She supposed he had long forgotten the day at Churchill Downs when her daddy's horse had won and she all of eighteen years old, had hugged the nearest person – him, by chance – in natural delight and ebullience. She supposed he had forgotten breathing an invitation to dinner into her ear – he must have been about thirty-six then – and she remembered, memory being such a subjective thing, turning him down with a gentle excuse, so as not to make him feel awkward, just as they had taught her and her débutante classmates at Miss Hilda's Academy for Young Ladies in Connecticut.

She recalled the feeling of high amusement at the very idea of seeing the creep socially, and an incipient hysterical giggle at the connotation of anything remotely physical. Yeugh!

She smiled encouragingly into Stevenson's eyes, for it had dawned on her as she walked across the green from the Church Records Office that scouring every parish register, and visiting every remotely likely parish church, could take the rest of her days and still not get her anywhere nearer to the bastard Oliver.

But perhaps God had delivered a sign, in this dark-suited figure with the Trinity College necktie and a way of looking at her. It was a sign that said, this man must know far more about the circumstances of Oliver's birth and adoption than he has let on. This man could be a key, or even *the* key, to locating Oliver and accessing over two hundred million dollars.

And there was nothing Darcy would not stop at, no move she would hesitate to make, for the freedom such a fortune would bring.

She let her head angle to one side and pushed the hair off her brow, holding Stevenson's gaze. 'So how are you, Pronsias? Dear Pronsias, you have had so much to shoulder, since Daddy's . . . accident.'

A few days later, Alison Clancy was wading through a raft of draft letters of agreement ratifying new deals with clients in Houston who provided electronic hardware to the big three oil and transportation multinationals. Over the next three years, gross turnover in the region of nine hundred million dollars was involved.

'It's a pity,' she remarked to Sebastian Tree, who had irritatingly taken to breezing into her office on the smallest of pretexts, to chew the fat. It was as if he had made a conscious decision to unfreeze the antipathy between them. In fact, Sebastian charming was more unsettling than Sebastian hostile. 'It's a pity,' she said, 'that we couldn't lock them into a five-year contract.'

Sebastian smiled. 'Nobody smart in electronics makes big financial commitments more than three years ahead. Two is more regular. I hear you ask why.'

Alison waited for the words from the mountain. In fact, she knew perfectly well why.

'Because an essential concomitant of the electronics industry,' pronounced Tree, 'is its ever-evolving state. Systems and hardware bought tomorrow will be obsolete in five months' time.'

Alison gazed at her keyboard in disbelief. Surely the Chief Executive knew she had been at the very same seminar when Jack Fitzrowan had first spoken that thought, words which were repeated verbatim in the *Wall Street Journal* and the *Boston Globe* the next day. And on his *60 Minutes* interview with Dan Rather.

'Really?' was all she replied. 'Well, that explains it.' Alison concentrated on her work. But Sebastian lingered.

'Hey, Alison,' he said, in his confidential, we're really good friends voice, 'I'm having brunch Saturday with the Kennedys, at Pocasset. Why don't we bury the hatchet and drive on down there in the Porsche?'

Only one place I'd like to bury the hatchet where you're concerned, mused Alison. She smiled brightly. 'Saturday is spoken for. But thanks.'

'No kidding. What are you doing?'

Alison stared at him. He looked really interested. 'I have things to do.'

'Like what? These people have *access*, they can be good for the company.'

Alison concentrated on her work, fingers racing over the keys. Sebastian glanced over her shoulder at the screen.

'Jack said it first,' he murmured. 'Obsolete in five months' time, hardware bought tomorrow.'

'I know, Sebastian. I was there,' replied Alison, without looking up.

Sebastian moved to the door, glanced back. 'Can't we try?'

I would not be surprised, thought Alison, if he now says, 'just for the good of the firm', but even that ratfink could not be so crass –

'Just for the good of the firm?' continued Tree. And Alison Clancy grinned to herself. It was only a matter of time before she would have him by the balls.

Ten fifty-eight a.m. Lieutenant Detective Tom Hanrahan sat in the back of the unmarked blue Ford saloon, talking with one Alberto Sanzo, a middle-aged second generation Neapolitan greengrocer and pool hall owner from Mattapan, who was encyclopaedic about local mob business, mixing gossip with overheard indiscretions and the occasional nugget of hard fact.

He was the seventeenth stoolie, snitch, informant, Tom and Dan Tarantola had spoken to about the Flamingo and Carmine Genovese slayings, which had occupied Boston's radio and TV stations since the early hours. And this guy had incontinence of the mouth. He just talked and talked and talked, going over the same stuff more than twice. But Tom Hanrahan just sat and listened. This was what made a good detective. Patience and memory. And intuition, without which you may as well hand an investigation over to a speak–your–weight machine.

'. . . the entire Genovese clan,' Sanzo was saying. 'But why the old man, I hear you ask. You know before he got the rep for being so goddam simple, old Giuseppe was considered somewhat of a smart potato. Why, he used to be driver and made man with the *capo* NNY.' He meant the rackets syndicate north of New York City.

'Who was that?' enquired Tom. And Dan Tarantola, sitting in the driver's seat, glanced in the rear mirror.

'Aw . . . lemme see. Peter G. Sicilian born. Law degree. Serious man. One of the first of the dons to go down. Rotting in some supermax. Thrown the key away. Charlie Bagarella moved in, took over the syndicate. That was the start of the big *sporcizia*.' The big mess; the big, obscene mess. Tom knew what he meant. All those kids running around playing gangsters.

'No serious men left,' continued Sanzo. 'No men of respect.'

The car phone rang. Unlike in the TV cop shows, with radios and coded numbers, Boston PD detectives often communicated by the mark-one portable phone. The caller was Luther MacDonald, the Homicide Desk Sergeant. 'Tom, you got Sammy Jade and his lawyer waiting. You want to kick it on for a few days?'

Damn. Hanrahan remembered this was the day he had arranged to charge Sammy Jade Spencer with the murder of one Lee-Anne Kopecnick, waitress at King's Creole Gumbo off Harvard Square, in Cambridge.

'No. I'll be right there,' he told MacDonald, and shutting off the phone he turned to Sanzo. 'Alberto, take a hike, we got work to do.'

'Ain't that worth a few bucks, Mr Hanrahan?' complained the stoolie.

'Dan?' enquired Tom, of his partner.

Tarantola shook his head. 'We don't need a history lesson, Alberto. You ain't told us nothing we don't know.'

'Unless . . .' said Tom Hanrahan, as if it had just occurred to him. Sanzo's head went to one side, like a hound dog, eager to please. 'Unless you know who wants to take over the family business, here in Boston.'

'It ain't local. That's all I know, Lieutenant.' Sanzo was at least not dumb enough to make up shit.

'OK.' Hanrahan pulled three tens out from a roll. 'Go buy some toothpaste. The fuckin car's full of garlic. Lucky my partner isn't a vampire.'

Sanzo took the money, less than thrilled, and got out of the car. On the way back to Homicide, Dan Tarantola noticed Tom was looking thoughtful.

'What you thinking, Tom?' he enquired, in that egalitarian way of Boston cops.

'I'm wondering, Danny,' replied Hanrahan, 'I am asking myself, just what in hell makes you think Big Jack Fitzrowan was murdered, and number two, how you could imagine I did it?'

Tarantola drove on in silence. Finally, just as they turned into the dead-end at the side of the run-down brownstone Homicide office he said, 'You would do the same, Lieutenant.'

And Tom nodded. Of course he would.

Upstairs, in an interview room with Luther MacDonald standing by the door, Sammy Jade sat with his lawyer, a fat, wheezing, diminutive guy somewhere between thirty-five and sixty, wispy tobacco-stained hair, sideburns and dandruff on the shoulders and lapels of his brown chalk-stripe double-breasted jacket. If anything, the lawyer was the more disreputable looking of the two, though it was a close decision.

'So you finally made it,' the lawyer said, in a nasal voice so startlingly like Woody Allen's that Hanrahan instinctively glanced to see if the movie actor was in the room.

'Yeah, I'm here, so let's get to business.' He sat down, putting a battered cardboard file holder on the table between them.

Audrey Caspian from the D A's office slipped in and sat behind Tom.

'You have been holding my client . . .' the Dandruff Dwarf wheezed, leaning forward, pausing for effect and examining, ostentatiously, his Taipan Rolex, 'right up to the limit that the law permits. So now, Lieutenant, charge him or I hit you with a habeas corpus.' He sat back, breathing laboured but triumphant, flashing a knowing glance to his axe-murdering client who smiled thinly, as relaxed and calm as ever.

'Well, this won't take long.' Tom Hanrahan turned his cool gaze on Sammy Jade. 'Samuel Jade Spencer, I am charging you with the premeditated murder of one Lee-Anne Kopecnick, between March first and second of this year. You are not obliged to say anything at this time. You are entitled to the services of a lawyer and if you cannot afford one, the City of Boston will provide one. I am now placing you under arrest and you will be held in custody until a hearing can be arranged. This is a capital offence and in this state, death by electrocution has not been removed from the statute book. Thank you kindly.'

Tom collected his files, rose and walked out of the room, as Luther and another detective, Jimmy Fitz, handcuffed the prisoner.

When Tom reached his office on the floor above, his secretary Marge Connery looked round from the filing cabinet, where she was pulling out folders with notes on homicides related to what the Department called Major Cases, which included organized crime.

'Commissioner wants you over at Headquarters,' she said.

'Yeah, tell Pete to get the car.' Tom realized the Commissioner, Gerry O'Brady, would need his senior investigator at his side when the D A's office and the mayor's troubleshooter and press-relations people descended. Nevertheless, it was a real brake on his investigation.

As he passed Dan Tarantola in the corridor, Marge hurrying after him stuffing relevant Intel and case histories into his beat-up attaché case, Tom Hanrahan said, 'Dan, you have command till I get back. Concentrate on outta town. I smell something more deliberate than our Boston punks could dream up.'

'Sure thing,' agreed Tarantola, the Jack Fitzrowan investigation consigned of necessity to the back burner for, apart from the appalling magnitude of the Flamingo and Carmine Genovese slayings, he too understood City Hall and the press, *and* the Commissioner, would be all over Homicide looking for results.

By the time Tom reached the Commissioner's office television vans from the local news stations, newspaper reporters and the plain curious were milling around the entrance to Police Headquarters, so he got Pete Mally to stop at a side entrance and took the fire stairs all the way to the fifth floor.

'OK, Tom. Gentlemen, Patsy,' announced Commissioner O'Brady, relieved to see his investigating officer. 'You all know Tom Hanrahan from Homicide. This is his case.'

The assembled civic servants nodded greetings. Gerry O'Brady's office was big, as befits the Commissioner of Boston PD, but even so it was kind of a crush.

'So, Tom,' said O'Brady, 'who did this?'

'Chief,' replied Tom Hanrahan, 'I got no fuckin idea.'

Peter Girolo was not, of course, staying in the Marriott Long Wharf. That was where he had taken a suite to conduct his business meetings, such as they were. He had rented for cash a comfortable apartment on Beaver Place, at the foot of Beacon Hill. It was on the upper two floors of a three-storey carriage house which had been converted, with plenty of light, armoured glass windows, pastel colours, cedarwood bookshelves and furnished in simple but expensive French-Italian style by a gay antiques dealer who was doing three to five for tax evasion.

The ground floor was occupied by a writer who seemed to spend most of his time sailing in the Caribbean. It suited Girolo. Only his incarcerated landlord knew of the arrangement, and Prisoner 81344 owed the Sicilian his very life and creature comforts during his time in the slammer, a debt the antique dealer appreciated could be collected at any time.

Bodyguards? Security?

Bodyguards were not the way the serious *mafioso* worked. They only drew attention. When he needed muscle, Atlantic City was a short flight away. And security was best availed by discretion and anonymity.

In his Beaver Place apartment, Peter Girolo considered the situation, now that he had initiated events in his stratagem to recover the Boston Syndicate, and all *cosa* territory north of New York City. It was a tragedy how Charlie Bagarella had let a solid family business slide into such a mess of hoodlum bad behaviour.

He sat watching television news coverage of the Flamingo and Carmine Genovese murders. He knew that the surviving Italian *capos* in what was soon to become his territory would be doing the same. And he tried to figure what would be going on in their inflated, egotistical apologies for brains.

Confusion? Fear? Anger?

Whichever of these emotions, he decided that a period of inactivity, for reflection on their part, would help. Soon enough they would pretend it had never happened. Then he would whack the emerging leader.

Then, and only then, would it be time to bring them into line. For Peter Girolo, this was merely business. Compared with survival in Marion, at the top of the tree, without the authorities being aware, this was child's play. The man was a professional. This was simple surgery, with a degree in psychology thrown in.

Grace made a point of dropping in on each floor of Zeralda Electronics and keeping up to scratch on new processes, observing the timbre, the mood of the work force, ironing out problems and quietly spotting the occasional malcontent that any big corporation is bound to acquire.

In the course of this, she remained on the lookout for workers who had earned an increase in pay, or promotion. Then she sat tight to see if the various managers had formed the same conclusions. If someone seemed to her to have been overlooked or unrecognized she would, with all the diplomacy Big Jack had taught her, raise the subject, often in such a way that the person's superior would think it was his or her idea in the first place.

Thus she found herself in conversation with Arthur Jamieson, grade one security guard and former White House cop. And Arthur had just said how grand it was to work for such a caring company as Zeralda, and how impressed he had been by Miss Clancy taking the trouble to remember his daughter Tracey's birthday.

This was a facet of Alison that Grace Hanrahan had not been aware of and she was pleasantly surprised that her late father's mistress had such a human side to her. 'Well, we're all family here, Arthur,' she remarked. 'Did you have a birthday party and balloons and stuff?'

Arthur told Grace about the special Amtrak railroad ride and the party on board, and had Grace laughing with his account of the effect of too much Jell-O and ice cream on hyper-excited kids in a swaying Pullman car at eighty miles per hour. 'Tracey was so thrilled with the train driver's overalls, Mrs Hanrahan,' grinned the guard. 'It was so thoughtful of Miss Clancy to remember she would have grown too big for the ones Big Jack, begging your pardon, your late father, gave to her last year.'

Grace continued to smile, and after a few more words bade Arthur a pleasant day and returned to her office, mildly thoughtful. Why on earth would Alison Clancy have taken the trouble to go out and buy a set of train driver's dungarees for the six-year-old daughter of a corporation employee?

Not for the first time, Grace felt her daddy's presence, as she settled into his chair, in his office. She stroked the primitive, carved Pawnee cedarwood recumbent wild pig, polished with many years of touching, a present to Big Jack from Scarlet Hennessy, his first wife and Darcy's mother. And as she sat there, missing him terribly, she could just hear him say, in that gentle, perceptive way of his, 'And what job, young Gracelet, does this particular Corporation employee perform? What is his special responsibility . . . ?' Well Arthur Jamieson's special responsibility was security. He was in charge of the control room, in direct contact with the men on the gate, the patrolling guards and the video surveillance system.

Her hand still resting on the recumbent carving, whittled into shape by some Pawnee hunter more than a hundred years before,

Grace tried to picture Zeralda's Legal Executive down there in Arthur's control room, chewing the fat with him, giving him the dungarees for his daughter's birthday. But why . . . ?

At which moment, Sebastian Tree knocked and entered, carrying a sheaf of computer printouts.

'Is this a good time?' he enquired.

Grace smiled. 'Sure. What's on your mind?'

'I'm a tad concerned about the Rockaway Project. They were due to make their usual electronic transfer of funds last Friday noon our time. It's almost a week overdue.'

Grace shrugged. 'It's got to have a simple explanation, Seb. Change of program, you know how easy it is. Fax Tod Santez at NASA, he'll sort it out.'

Sebastian looked uneasy. He shuffled through the sheaf of print-outs in his hands, scanning them carefully. 'I phoned NASA this morning, Grace. Tod seemed, how can I put it . . . ? Evasive.'

'Nonsense. He's just overworked. I'll give him a call.'

Grace's fingers moved briskly over her keyboard, summoning up the Rockaway Project, using Zeralda's most secret classification to get into the file paths.

'How much is involved?' she asked casually.

'Twenty-one million dollars. Just over, by a few pennies.'

Grace glanced up. The Chief Exec did appear to be a smidgen worried.

'Do we,' she asked, 'need this money badly?'

Tree shrugged. 'Uh, not this month. But if some computer error has kicked the Rockaway payments into hyperspace, it's a matter of twenty, twenty-five days before we become . . . embarrassed, in our loan reductions to, um,' he consulted his bundle of documents, 'Chase Manhattan, First Boston and Bank of Scotland, New York.'

'I didn't realize we sailed that close to the wind,' said Grace, mildly disconcerted.

'Rockaway is a seriously profitable project.' Sebastian Tree met her gaze. 'It's a major item in our portfolio, as you know.'

Grace Hanrahan nodded, reaching for the phone. 'Diana,' she

said, calmly, 'get me Tod Santez at NASA. If he's on the golf course, get him there. If he's in bed with his wife, get him there.'

Her PA's voice replied she had got the message, loud and clear. Grace sat quite still for a moment, her heart beating strong in her chest.

'I'm sure it's nothing,' said Sebastian, comfortingly.

'Thanks, Seb.' Grace waved a hand. 'Leave me alone for this one, would you?'

Paul Fitzrowan had driven to Dublin in his 1983 5-litre Mustang convertible. Petrol blue with a broad, cream strip running fore and aft. Wide wheels, wide tyres and alloy cylinder head. It was his baby. Now that he had inherited a couple of million, he was resolved to have the car stripped to the chassis and rebuilt, with a bare metal sand-blasting and respray.

He left the car at Quigley's Specialist Autos, off Lower New Street, and strolled towards Grafton Street and Trinity College, where he had arranged to play bass guitar with Subterfuge, an up-and-coming Dublin band he had met at the Abbey Road recording studios in London, and had stood in for two tracks while the regular bassist was treated for hyperventilation – hyper-something, anyway.

The band's manager had phoned him a couple of days before and asked Paul if he would stand in again, for the Trinity College live gig. Paul was delighted. Finally somebody had recognized his talents.

There are one or two smart restaurants and brasseries around the Grafton Street, Shelbourne Hotel, Fitzwilliam Square area, and as Paul ambled past, lost in reveries of rebuilt, gleaming Mustangs, and a possible career with Subterfuge, who did he see sitting *tête-à-tête* in Malone's Buttery, at a table for two near the window?

None other than his sister Darcy and Pronsias Stevenson.

At first glance they seemed far too cosy for a pair who had never liked each other, and who had been at daggers drawn the last time he had seen them together, at the reading of the Will.

Amused at the tricks first glances can play, he paused (loitering was maybe too harsh a word) just out of their eyelines, and took a casual but closer look. It would not have mattered if he had walked in and stood right beside them, so engrossed were they in conversation. And nothing in their body language suggested it was a hostile, or even a business, discussion.

In fact, if Paul Fitzrowan had not known better, he would have thought his sister was leading the little creep on. For the solicitor was slightly flushed, chuckling and moving his hands expressively, for all the world like a deluded Malvolio in one of the less-subtle performances of *Twelfth Night*.

And Darcy, of course, as usual, was clearly in control.

Paul resisted the inclination to walk into Malone's and bid them good morning, not merely because he had inherited his mother's impeccable, natural good manners, but for another, more subtle reason. He felt instinctively that this had something to do with the codicil, and the Oliver legacy of over two hundred million dollars. There was absolutely no other reason why his stunningly attractive half-sister would pass the time of day with that little shit.

Paul felt no need for such vast wealth for himself, but now that he was aware of the considerable cost involved in running Crough Lake, supporting his late father's Kentucky Stud and the thorough-bred stable in Kerry, along with a sympathy for his sisters, both of them married and presumably hoping to have children, he had come to understand the unfairness of someone who was a total outsider, if he were ever found, inheriting such a disproportionate treasure trove of hard-earned Fitzrowan money.

With every passing day, Paul was taking more seriously his new and unlooked-for responsibility as head of the Fitzrowan family. And the young baronet was now firmly intent on backing Grace's plan for the Zeralda Corporation to sue the Fitzrowan estate for the return of Big Jack's two hundred million. Always provided Oliver would receive an equal share.

. He turned and walked on, wondering if his beautiful half-sister was leading Pronsias Stevenson on, on behalf of the three of them, or if Darcy was pursuing her own agenda.

He knew Darcy too well to wonder for long.

★

Lieutenant Tom Hanrahan rubbed his fists against his eyes. Ten after ten at night, three days after the Flamingo–Genovese massacre and not a step further forward.

The Commissioner's assistant, Larry Shauseau was on line three, with the Commissioner himself waiting to speak. Marge had told him that Tom was on the phone, following up a lead from NYPD, just to give her boss time to clear his head and get ready for what, according to Larry, could prove to be a difficult conversation.

She stood watching, like a mother hen, as Tom stretched, flexed his aching neck and nodded, glancing appreciatively at the mug of hot, strong coffee she had just laid on his desk.

'OK,' he said, and lifted the handset. 'Hi, Larry.'

Shauseau grunted a greeting, the line went silent, then Gerry O'Brady came on. 'Tom, how's it going?'

'We're getting nothing from the street. If you ask me, there is not a *cosa* man in Boston knows what the fuck happened that night.'

'You're a good man with hunches, Tom,' said O'Brady. 'What's your gut feeling?'

This was no casual query. O'Brady was asking a seasoned detective, who had learned how to survive inside his office as well as among the worst hoodlums around, to put his reputation on the line.

Tom waited before answering. And Gerry O'Brady understood why. Finally Tom said, 'Has to be out of town.'

'Is that why you are speaking in New York?' enquired the Commissioner, believing Marge's white lie. And why shouldn't he?

'Yeah, something like that.'

Silence.

'Listen, Tom, don't take this personal . . .' Wait for it, thought Tom, this will be damned personal. 'People in the DA's office are talking about a task force.'

'Cosmetic bullshit,' retorted the detective, the essential Irish in him getting the better of diplomacy.

'Well, you yourself said out of town. If that means you think it's from another state, that involves the Feds.'

Thank you, Tommy, thought Tom to himself. Shoulda kept your big mouth shut.

'We can't involve the Feds on a hunch,' he replied. 'In any case, we have a task force in all but name. I already have detectives on attachment to the Feds, Customs, DEA and Major Cases. Boston is one of the few places where we are not castrated by dumb rivalry.' This was patent flim-flam, but all Tom Hanrahan was doing was throwing the Commissioner's favourite lullaby right back in his face, for inter-agency and inter-department liaison assignments had been Gerry O'Brady's very own brainchild. And he liked to remind his officers of it at every opportunity. No need, he would say – only last week – for task forces. In fact, Tom recalled, it had been Commissioner O'Brady who had used the term cosmetic bullshit first.

There was a quiet chuckle on the other end of the line, and right on the end of it came the barbed comment, 'One or two dumbskulls are saying you lost your edge, Tommy. Since you became a fuckin millionaire.'

Tom held his tongue. Eventually he said, 'You want to take me off this case?'

'Now, what would that look like? It would look, Lieutenant, as if I had made the wrong appointment in the first place. Just get us some results. I need it, City Hall needs it. And you sure as fuck need it.'

The line went dead.

Then the phone rang. Tom whipped up the receiver and snarled, 'Yeah?'

'Tommy, are you OK?' It was Grace. She sounded very down.

'Baby . . . What's the matter . . . ?'

'Oh, just the office. We've got some serious problems. I just got in. You be long?'

Tom Hanrahan looked at the clock on the peeling grey-green wall. 'Forty minutes,' he said.

And it would have been forty minutes, if the stoolie Alberto Sanzo had not called in, on one of Homicide's snitch lines, and asked for Lieutenant Hanrahan. He said he had something important.

And he had.

★

94

Midnight in Mattapan. Nobody walks the dog. Tom Hanrahan sat in the back of an undercover Pontiac, watching the pimps and dealers work their turf. Alberto Sanzo had asked for a high-profile meet, which meant Tom would arrange for him to be hassled, in full view of anyone watching, as Sanzo walked to his beat-up Dodge van after locking up the pool hall, near the Morton–Gallivan intersection.

'Here he comes,' said Detective Jimmy Fitz, the Lieutenant's partner for the occasion. Across the street, Sanzo locked the door with four separate keys, fastened a big chain and padlock and walked, businesslike, edgy, shoulders hunched, towards his van.

As Sanzo passed the Pontiac, Fitz opened his driver's door and stopped him. 'Hold it, Alberto,' said Fitz. 'My boss wants a word.'

'Man, it's late. I gotta get back.'

'You want to do it here or downtown?' replied Fitz, playing out this charade for the benefit of one or two hookers and dope runners in the general area.

By the time Jimmy Fitz shoved Sanzo into the back of the car and pushed the door shut, the small audience had lost interest. They were just happy it had been some other sucker's bad fortune to get lifted.

'This better be good, Alberto,' said Tom Hanrahan. 'I'm having a bad fuckin day.'

'Can he take a walk?' Sanzo indicated the wiry, dark-haired detective.

'Sure, and let the whole street know you're singing out loud?' Tom turned to Fitz. 'Jimmy, leave us alone.'

As Jimmy Fitz moved to open his door, the stoolpigeon changed his mind. 'No no. It's cool. I guess he can stay.'

'He can stay?'

'Sure. I said it. He can stay.'

Tom Hanrahan spoke to his partner's back. 'You can stay.' He tugged out a Winston from its pack and lit it. 'So, Alberto, what's up?'

Sanzo hunched further down in the back seat. 'You know we spoke about Carmine's uncle? Giuseppe.'

'Sure. You said he was once not so dumb. Made man. Drove some big *capo* around. Guy is now in the slammer.'

'You remember the name of the *capo*?'

'What is this, *Double Your Money*? Peter G, you said. Peter G, rotting in the slammer.'

'You check that out?'

Hanrahan glanced at the rear-view mirror, meeting Fitz's eyes. 'Yeah. Girolo. Peter Girolo.'

'And what?'

'Sanzo, I did not come here to answer your fuckin questions. That is not the nature of our relationship.'

'He walked out of Marion two weeks ago.'

Tom studied his cigarette, glowing in the shadow. 'He walked? He escaped from Marion?'

Sanzo shook his head. 'He did his time, Lieutenant. He was released on the eighth of this month. At ten in the morning.'

Tom Hanrahan frowned. 'How did you hear?'

Sanzo shrunk his head into his shoulders, like a tortoise. 'Well, after you asked about the Flamingo stuff, and Carmine and Giuseppe. And I told you about Peter G . . .' he shrugged, 'it just made sense to check that Girolo was still doing time.'

After Sanzo had gotten out, two hundred dollars richer, and Tom had moved into the front seat, and the Pontiac was cruising back towards South Boston on Columbia Road, the Homicide Lieutenant finally uttered one word. It was the F-word.

It was not until Jimmy Fitz turned into Farragut Road, on Dorchester Bay, and slowed to stop at the Hanrahans' house, that he spoke again. 'What kinda cop is it, Jim, who needs a low-life stoolpigeon to teach him his fuckin job?'

Grace was not asleep. She was turned on her side, back to Tom's side of the bed, quite still and silent. But she was not asleep. Tom Hanrahan felt bad. Three hours was not forty minutes. And she had needed him, she had sounded subdued. He laid his pistol and holster on the beside table, undressed, brushed his teeth, and climbed in under the bedclothes. Moonlight filtered through a chink in the curtains. The Homicide Lieutenant lay on his back, hands clasped behind his head, his earlier exhaustion and tension gone. Wide awake.

'Are you awake?' he whispered.

She nodded.

Tom went to slip an arm under her head, to cuddle her. At first she stiffened, then relaxed and turned round, wrapping her legs round him. He kissed her gently, on the forehead. 'What was the problem?'

'You don't care,' she murmured. 'It has nothing to do with murder, or guns. Or cop stuff.'

'Tell me, hon.' He nuzzled his mouth against her earlobe.

'Oh . . . somebody is late making a huge payment. They are avoiding my calls. Sebastian is worried, I've never seen him like that before.'

'How much?' enquired Tom, soothing her hair, still angry with himself for failing to check out the Girolo angle.

'Twenty-one million dollars,' she whispered.

Tom's eyes opened wide. 'Holy shit!'

'And it's like a house of cards, Tom. NASA pays us that every month. We need it to service three major bank loans. We are talking huge. We are talking loss of confidence. Zeralda could go under. And there is a rival, far bigger, Japanese corporation just waiting to swallow us up, in one gulp.'

In the silence, Tom stroked her hair a little more, and nuzzled her earlobe a little more, and moved his body against her.

'This is serious . . .' she murmured.

'Oh, yes,' he touched her neck with his tongue, 'this is really serious . . .' His wife's back arched, and she made that little moan. He held her more tightly, and they kissed, like teenagers.

Alison Clancy had been handed the urgent and delicate task of approaching the Rockaway Project's legal office and making discreet enquiries about the delay in transferring monthly funds. Not for the first time in recent weeks she asked herself what Jack would have done. And not for the first time, the answer came faster than e.mail. Personal contact, girl, she could hear him say, with that amused, self-deprecating look of his when he dispensed good advice. Think. Who at NASA can help you short-circuit the system?

Alison leaned back in her chair and flexed her shoulders, pushing her reading glasses to the tip of her nose as she gazed at the computer screen, scanning through Zeralda's business research office's comprehensive list of who was who and who did what at NASA's Rockaway Project.

She could almost hear Jack Fitzrowan's chuckle as one name highlighted, and she blushed. George Davidson. Age forty-two. Married. Special Projects Executive. NASA's Washington Office. Ex-State Department. Educated Princeton and UCLA. Salary $168,000. Interests jazz, baseball, HD motor-cycles.

Christ. Was that only four years ago?

Alison had a vivid and embarrassing recollection of that night in the Willard Hotel when she had been representing Zeralda, her first month with the firm. Spread wanton on the king-size bed, room 703, naked from the waist down, climaxing with amazed gasps as George's tongue played her to perfection.

It had been the wine, or maybe the Jack Daniel's after dinner. Alison was not a great drinker. Whatever, it had happened. Neither she nor George had ever mentioned it again. But it had certainly been a very horny episode.

Face bright red, Zeralda's attorney prayed that the ubiquitous Sebastian Tree would not choose this moment to stroll in for another attempt at conciliation. But there was the name. Highlighted, just as she had stopped scrolling down. She smiled at Jack's ghostly amusement. You bastard, she muttered softly to herself. And felt a mixture of love for him, and desperate bereavement. And apprehension. For George Davidson, married, of NASA Washington, was precisely the person to short-circuit Rockaway's reticence to come clean about the cash-flow delay.

Alison Clancy reached for the phone. Nothing to be embarrassed about, she assured herself, we have met a dozen times since then. And there had always been a shared closeness about that one, unspoken night.

The NASA switchboard put her through. George's voice sounded reassuringly comfortable. 'Alison, hi, how you doing?'

She told him she was fine and he told her an uncomfortable story about his daughter's confirmation dress. Married men, thought Alison, there must be somebody else in the room. A secretary. He was probably doing it with her these days.

'George, I need a favour,' she said, ruthlessly exploiting her advantage.

'Sure. Name it.'

She told him about the delay in fund transference, and the sum involved.

George was all business. He noted everything, with reference numbers and due dates. 'Call you right back,' he said.

And twenty-one minutes later, he did. Six minutes after that, Alison was in Grace Hanrahan's inner office, with the door locked. She sat facing Grace as Zeralda's President stared at the memo she had prepared.

Eventually, Grace looked up, puzzled and angry. 'What the hell,' she said, 'do they mean, they don't pay for what they don't get?'

'It's all there,' replied Alison. 'Weekly deliveries from our Boston warehouse to Rockaway of platinum boards and ceramic microchips for the E-16 Project dried up three weeks ago.'

Grace made an exasperated noise, uncannily like the one Jack used to utter. 'Then they should have faxed us, got on the phone, for God's sake.'

Alison Clancy waited for a moment, then she said quietly, 'They did.'

In the silence, Grace gazed at Alison, waiting for bad tidings.

Alison went on, 'But their faxes and e.mail went into hyperspace. Grace, there is something you need to know. I wanted to wait till the time was right. Till I had more evidence. But this has . . . pre-empted me.'

And she told Grace about Sebastian Tree and the Katakura Corporation of Japan. She related Tree's telephone conversation with Tak Katakura that early morning about three weeks before and, being a prudent graduate of Harvard Law School, Alison merely said she had 'good reason to suspect' that Zeralda's CEO was engaged in insider dealing, with a view to damaging the firm's place in the market, to facilitate a second dawn raid by Katakura.

Grace sat quite still, hands clasped together as if in prayer, deep in thought.

Not a trace of panic, observed Alison. Just cold, calm deliberation. This was indeed Jack Fitzrowan's daughter.

Finally Grace Hanrahan spoke. 'Our overall cash flow is good. Question is, is it good enough to let us rob Peter to pay Paul in the short term? Maybe we can make other arrangements to service the banks.'

Alison smiled and handed over two slim portfolios with the finalized, unsigned Houston contracts, providing and updating electronic hardware to Shell, Mobil and Texaco.

'Gross turnover,' she said, 'for the next three years is guaranteed at eight hundred and eighty-nine million. With a cash flow of nearly twenty-five million dollars each month. More than enough to service First National, Chase and the Bank of Scotland, until we get the Rockaway Project back on line.'

Grace scanned the documents. 'This is flying on a wing and a prayer. By the time these are signed and the money comes in it could be too late. The moment we default by twenty-four hours word will get around. Our other credit will take a dive.'

Alison Clancy had thought about that. 'Zeralda's monthly repayments are made by electronic transfers on the twenty-eighth of the month. That's in four days' time. Immediately our Houston clients receive the signed contracts in front of you, their legal VPs will OK their accounts departments to wire, each, initial payments of just over eight point two million dollars.'

Grace's turn to smile, first time in a couple of days. 'Twenty-four point six million. How long will it take to reach T and C?' Zeralda banked off-shore in the Turks and Caicos Islands.

Alison had thought this through, 'I should fly with the documents personally.'

'Take the Lear Jet,' said Grace.

Alison nodded and went on, 'Deliver the documents and get them countersigned by noon tomorrow. I will impress on them I want the deal in place and fully paid up by the weekend. That's bog standard in such deals so they won't raise an eyebrow. With a fair wind and a following sea, there's no reason why we shouldn't be able to meet the monthly bank transfers as usual.'

Grace considered this. 'You are one hell of an attorney, Alison. I'm glad we poached you from criminal law.'

Alison shrugged. 'I got tired of dealing with sleazebags. Defending the indefensible is not my idea of a whole life.'

Grace studied her Legal Executive thoughtfully. 'Word is you were going places. There must have been one thing. One incident, a particular case . . . ?'

The lawyer met her gaze, slightly guarded, then nodded. 'Sure. Mafia boss. Murder, conspiracy, robbery, white-collar fraud. Should have gone inside for eternity. Good old Rawlince, Brooke & Maine, the firm I worked for, got him off everything but an IRS violation. Judge gave him the maximum. Four years. Guy went to Marion smiling. I guess I worked fourteen hours a day to help get that result.' She lifted her shoulders. 'I did not feel proud of myself. Shortly after that I heard Zeralda was looking for a legal eagle. And here I am.'

'Well,' smiled Grace, 'I'm glad you are.'

Alison got back to the business in hand. 'I strongly suggest you charter a freight plane and express Rockaway's microchips and hardware to reach them by the end of today, along with a team of technicians and programmers to install it free of charge. According to NASA's legal department, that would get us back on line. These hiccups happen, was the way they put it.' Alison put her reading glasses into her purse and clipped it shut, 'And it might be a good idea not to involve Tree until the thing is done . . .'

Grace stared at Alison Clancy and, slowly, that Fitzrowan smile of cool triumph appeared on her attractive young face. Without a word she reached down, slid open her drawer and drew out the bottle of Wild Turkey. She set it on the desk and produced two small, heavy tumblers.

Her eyes met Alison's. 'Booze is forbidden inside this facility,' she announced drily.

'Quite right,' replied Alison, and while Grace poured two stiff shots, she picked up the phone and told Transportation to get the Lear Jet ready for a flight to LA and an automobile and driver to take her to the airport.

When they had touched glasses and downed the fierce liquor, Grace remarked, 'LA? I thought you were going to Houston.'

'Sure thing,' said Alison, 'but that's between me, the pilot, and Air Traffic Control.'

After a moment, the two women rose and they embraced. It was the embrace of fellow conspirators. A friendship had been born.

5

Back at Hedge's Hall, near Oxford, Darcy had a fax, three phone lines and an Internet link installed in her study, a pleasant room, L-shaped, with windows on two sides, overlooking the apple- and cherry-tree orchard and part of the walled garden, where koi carp and huge goldfish swam in the ancient, stone-flagged pond. There she spent every morning furthering her researches into the secret birth and adoption of Oliver.

She had established that the adoption had been outside the law, for there was no official record of any Helen Costello giving birth in or around June 1954, in the whole of Ireland, either in the Republic or in the Six Counties of the North, which came under British law, records of which would have been kept at Oxford House in Belfast.

Darcy had flown to Belfast and had spent three days on her investigation, for she had inherited Big Jack's thoroughness. Next, she had trawled through official records faxed to her by the three private detectives she had engaged through the Quinn Investigation Agency in Dublin. They were a small outfit but Jack had used Quinn's many times in the past and they enjoyed a generous annual retainer from Zeralda Boston. And so, when Darcy had told them the firm wanted discreet researches into the antecedents of a possible rival, they had no reason for any quivering of antennae.

Thus, three weeks after the reading of the Will, Darcy Fitzrowan Bailey was searching through the Internet seeking details of Irish and US journalists' items about the illegal adoption lines which had flourished underground in Eire since poor, impressionable girls had believed the honeyed words of their seducers.

And those seducers had numbered married professional men, landed gentry, wealthy farmers and even the clergy. In a way, Darcy had become fascinated to learn that each group had its own secret circuit, to facilitate the quiet and smooth delivery and adoption of all those tiny 'embarrassments'.

The ecclesiastical hierarchy, she believed, as she scanned news-paper and journal articles going back to 1871, seemed to have taken the pragmatic view that, since abortion is a mortal sin, secret systems for the discreet reallocation of unwanted babies were not actively discouraged, illegal or not, provided they avoided any breath of scandal. And in rural areas, the most efficient keepers of secrets and arrangers of discreet events were beyond doubt the local priests and nuns and their staffs.

With such application and her not inconsiderable intelligence. Darcy was beginning to form a good idea of how the kitchen maid Helen Costello had been spirited off to some remote house, or even nunnery, where the boy-child she had so pathetically named Oliver in the short few hours he was at her breast was taken from her and handed over to some childless couple. American, it was rumoured.

But where? Which house? What nunnery?

Darcy had no idea which members of the clergy her late father's own parents had known well enough to entrust with such a con-spiracy. In any event, forty-three years after the birth, there was a good chance all the major players would be dead.

She pushed her seat back from the solid, Victorian partners' desk and gazed out at the orchard, where Edward was strolling with two of his students, pretty, attentive girls of about nineteen. Dear Edward, as if he would have noticed they were even female, but let them drop a bloody participle, she thought wryly.

Well, she decided, this is about as far as I can go without having an edge. That's what her daddy had dinned into them; never engage on any serious enterprise unless you had an edge. Time, therefore, for Darcy to draw a joker from the pack.

She opened her diary and found the number she wanted. She lifted the phone and tapped it out, then waited while the ringing tone sounded. After five rings it was answered, and a businesslike voice told her she had gotten directly through to her quarry.

'Why, Pronsias,' Jack Fitzrowan's elder and, some said, more desirable daughter purred. 'How would you feel about lecturing at Oxford? Dear Edward wondered if you would deliver a centenary lecture on the Irish legal system and, um, its application to torts . . .'

And Pronsias Stevenson's reaction? Suffice it to say that he munched his silent repast, in the company of his mad wife, in something approaching smugness.

Lieutenant Tom Hanrahan paced up and down his shabby office, while Marge watered the flowering cactus that never flowered, studying the Intel and Major Cases files on Peter Michelangelo Girolo, learning everything Boston PD, NYPD and the Feds knew about the guy. Which, while substantial, was not everything. Not nearly.

Indicted by a Grand Jury on charges of conspiracy, extortion and being involved in controlling organized crime, Girolo's lawyers had persuaded the trial jury to find him not guilty on all but involvement, on the testimony of two federal witnesses, Gianni Matta and Giusto Pizzuti, who subsequently had pitifully small funerals, attended only by a few relatives.

The judge had given Girolo three to eight and had specified a maximum-security federal prison.

'Marge, get me a report from Marion on Girolo, that thing is never going to flower.'

'They flower once every three years.'

'You're an optimist.' Tom glanced at Dan Tarantola coming into the peeling corridor from the stairs to the floor below. 'Danny, you got a minute?'

'Sure,' replied the detective. The two of them repaired to an interview room, with mugs of strong coffee and a pack of cigarettes.

Tarantola scanned the files on Girolo and sat back, watching Tom lighting up. 'You think there's a connection with the Flamingo homicides?'

'I think,' replied Hanrahan, 'we're talking out of town. That's what I think.'

'So where is Girolo? Where is he now?' asked Tarantola.

Hanrahan shrugged. 'Find out. Ask around.'

'Maybe I'll have a few mug shots run up. Ask around.'

'Maybe it's nothing.'

Tarantola considered. Hanrahan was nothing if not a good detective. 'The Feds will know,' he said. 'I'll get Jimmy Fitz on to it.'

Hanrahan shook his head. 'I don't want them in on this. Not yet.'

Tarantola stirred his coffee, thoughtful. 'Why Girolo?'

Tom took his time answering. 'Alberto Sanzo, first thing he did, when he heard the old man, Giuseppe, had been on the hit menu. He checks to see if Peter Girolo is still in the slammer.'

Tarantola took the spoon out of the coffee and laid it in the ashtray. 'Giuseppe was Peter G's driver, right? In Atlantic City.'

Not much, thought Tom, that Danny the Wop fails to hear, the guy keeps his ears nailed to the street.

'So,' he said, 'nice and easy with this, Danny. We could use a break. Let Major Cases and the Feds do their thing. We will quietly pursue the Girolo angle.'

Tarantola looked him in the eye. 'Is he a suspect?'

Hanrahan spread his hands. 'I just want to know where he is. What he's been up to. Start from there.'

Tarantola re-read the files in silence, sipping at his coffee. Without looking up, he said, 'About that other thing. One or two other things had maybe been . . . how can I say it? . . . maybe not as they should be.'

Hanrahan did not respond. He knew what Tarantola was up to. It was a standard thing for cops to change the subject. To confuse, wrong foot, the suspect.

The detective went on, 'The fo'c's'le pulpit, somebody had loosed off the screws. And the after decking on the starboard side, it had been greased with tallow.'

Tom waited.

Tarantola finished his coffee and glanced across at the Lieutenant.

'I read your wife is the new President of Jack Fitzrowan's Zeralda Corporation. Is that right?'

'That's right.'

'So between the two of you, you did not lose out.'

'I lost a friend. Grace lost her father. I would say we fuckin lost out.'

Tarantola nodded, slowly, then he met Tom's cold gaze. 'But not financially.'

'Fuck you.'

Houston, Texas. The William P. Hobby Airport is twenty minutes out of town. Jackson Earp, Legal Exec with Texaco, had, to Alison's pleasant surprise, telephoned the Lear Jet as it flew down from Boston and informed her a helicopter would be waiting to fly her directly into town and take her from rooftop to rooftop, so that she could visit the other signatory corporations, Shell and Mobil, without the hassle of city traffic.

'To tell you the truth, Mr Earp, I am impressed by your courtesy.'

Earp had chuckled. 'This is Texas, ma'am, that's the way we do things . . .'

The contract signings had gone off without a hitch, and while Alison was going about this business, back in Boston Grace Hanrahan had called in three senior managers and, impressing on them the absolute requirement for secrecy, explained enough to make them aware that, because of an administrative slip-up, the Rockaway Project was in danger of being scrapped.

Unless they could get a 747-load of essential micro-electronics and hardware to Miami International Airport by ten that evening, Zeralda would have to 'downsize'. By which they understood their jobs were on the line.

So by the time Alison Clancy had traded pleasantries, as if she had all the time in the world, with the legal eagles and business affairs secretaries in three of the USA's biggest oil and transport conglomerates, been helicoptered from rooftop to rooftop, and was sitting in the four-seat Texaco Bell helicopter, fluttering among the rooftops and derricks of the oil capital of America, with signed contracts in her attaché case and agreements to have the first payments in Zeralda's off-shore bank by close of play in two days' time, a Boeing transport 747 was winging its way south, chasing the sunset, on its way to Miami and Zeralda's Rockaway agents.

And in the Boeing, as Alison had recommended, sat a team of electronics engineers and programmers, courtesy of Grace Hanrahan, Zeralda's new President.

As the sleek, private jet sliced through the evening sky on its return journey to Boston, Alison went over and over in her mind the various events of the last twenty-four hours.

With the Houston money safely on board, which she would confirm on the Thursday night, she would effect a computer transfer of funds into the Rockaway Project account, so that the scheduled repayments of funds, $21.9 million, to First National, Chase and the Bank of Scotland would proceed without a murmur.

She would require Grace's authority to do that, for such dealings were not her responsibility. Sebastian Tree was CEO and Chief Accountant, but he could not be trusted to save Zeralda's reputation and it was more prudent to keep all of this piece of legerdemain absolutely under wraps till it was all over.

Boy was he going to be pissed.

Exhilarated, adrenalin coursing round her veins, Alison understood just what it was that had driven Jack, all those years. But Sebastian was nobody's fool. He would know that, somehow, Grace Hanrahan, Zeralda's President, no longer trusted him. What would he do next?

Any rational person, considered Alison, would resign. But was a man like that really rational? His schemings, as revealed in the computer files Alison Clancy had hacked into, bordered on the obsessive. What had driven him to that? Was it just greed, or had Jack Fitzrowan offended him in some way?

She decided, based on a hunch, call it a woman's intuition, to make some enquiries in depth into Sebastian Tree's background, before he came to Zeralda.

★

Dublin, when it rains, is a pretty miserable place. So is Boston, arguably Ireland's most westerly city, with nearly three thousand miles of Atlantic Ocean between them. And in neither place does a leading lawyer enjoy receiving written intimation that an attorney, at least his equal, is making carefully planned moves to pull the rug from under him.

Pronsias Stevenson stared at the letter from Medevik & Mac-Morrow on the desk in front of him.

MEDEVIK & MacMORROW

Attorneys At Law

118 Beacon Street Boston

Dr Pronsias P. Stevenson MA LLD
Stevenson, Stevenson & Malahide
32, Fitzwilliam Square
Dublin
Republic of Ireland

12 April 1997

Dear Dr Stevenson,

Zeralda Electronics Inc. of Boston, Mass.

v.

Estate of late Sir John Dunmill Fitzrowan Bt., MA MBA

We represent the above Corporation in its claim for the return of the sum of $207,000,000 (two hundred and seven million dollars) from the estate of the above deceased President of Zeralda Electronics Inc.

Papers have been filed in the Supreme Court of Massachusetts, stating cause and case.

Essentially, my client's case is that Sir John misappropriated the amount in contention, it being a finder's fee paid to Zeralda by the McDonnell Douglas Corporation (Avionics Division) Inc. and as such was Corporation money and not a personal payment to Sir John.

There is no record of the board of the Zeralda Electronics Corporation authorizing any payment of the contested sum and therefore we cite that the misappropriation is illegal and a felony.

This letter is to request your co-operation, as local executor of the late Sir John Fitzrowan Bt. estate, in arranging the return of said funds in the sum of $207,000,000 to the originating account.

Upon confirmation that the full amount claimed has been repaid, I am instructed by the Board of Zeralda Electronics Inc. to withdraw our class action in the Supreme Court of Massachusetts.

Yours sincerely,

Michael R. Medevik
Senior Partner

It says something for the hereditary principle of coronary heart disease that Pronsias Paudraic Stevenson did not expire precipitately. He certainly felt the thump of adrenalin and a familiar, fierce knotting of the muscles from his left shoulder to his neck, a precursor to one of his migraines.

Jack Fitzrowan's Will had made him the talk of the Dublin legal world. Word of the codicil had slipped out, and his colleagues and acquaintances, round the bar of the Shelbourne and on the golf course, were aware, he knew from their respectful demeanour, that he, Pronsias Stevenson, was the keeper of the codicil, master of the Fitzrowan estate.

He found it hard to swallow as he re-read Medevik's letter. Nobody, he swore to himself, was going to purloin his control over the Fitzrowan millions. Nobody, he determined, was ever going to relegate him to one of those nonentities who had to hang around the end of the horseshoe bar, fluttering a folded banknote in the hope of attracting the eye of one of the busy bartenders.

These days, a glass of stout was always handed to him as soon as he walked in the door. 'A drink, Pronsias,' they would say, a drink for the most powerful lawyer in the fair city. Why, Justice Shaughnessy himself had casually handed him a glass of Jameson only last Thursday.

Panic, for that is what it was, soon gave way to cold anger. The legal brain reasserted itself over the hidden but demanding ego. Stevenson pressed his intercom switch. 'Siobhan,' he said calmly, 'would you ever get hold of *Kidd and Delaney's US Corporates and Major Shareholders' Disbursements*.'

Siobhan asked him to repeat that, then reached for her index of US legal publications.

The Dublin lawyer relaxed in his chair, steepling his fingers and gazing over his half-moon glasses at a print of Robert Augustine Stevenson, his great-grandfather and founder of the firm. The noble head, regal almost in its confidence and patrician disdain, seemed to meet his eye.

By Christ, cursed Pronsias Stevenson, those two bitches Darcy and Grace are behind this, doubtless with that fey loon of a boy who has taken on such a mantle of gravitas, so ill-befitting his feckless reality.

By nine that night, eleven hours after his secretary had placed the Medevik letter on his desk, Pronsias Paudraic Stevenson had scanned a plethora of legal tomes and Harvard law papers, scribbling sheaves of notes in his tiny, neat, copperplate.

Now he sat lost in a world of torts and variances, counter-claims and rebuttals, his concentration quite tangible in the oak-panelled room, embers from his turf fire smouldering, his partners and staff gone, Fitzwilliam Square silent outside.

The telephone rang, a muted buzz. Stevenson lifted the receiver.

'Stevenson,' he intoned, as if he were President of the United States.

Silence.

Outside, he could hear the carefree voices of ordinary people.

'Hello?' he enquired tentatively.

Still, silence.

Over the silent line, he could almost hear the ormolu replica Princess Eugenie mantel-clock, from the *Antiquarian* catalogue, only two hundred in existence.

'I'm working late,' he said. 'It is something that has to be done.'

Silence.

'Sometimes,' the solicitor went on, 'senior partners have to do this.'

He could hear a faint squeak of car brakes, quite far down the street. Somewhere a car horn sounded.

'I see . . .' he said, to his mute caller. 'You have cooked the petit ragout en croute, riz vert and you have started without me.'

Not a word in response.

Stevenson smiled, the dead smile of a pierrot. 'Ahh, I can almost smell it from here. I'm the loser all right. Will you keep a little for me to warm up when I come home?'

Click. Dialling tone.

Pronsias Stevenson sighed, replaced the receiver and returned to *Weissman's Beauty Parlours* versus *Mildred Q. Weissman* (1971).

Peter Girolo sat quietly at a corner table in Ciao Bambino, a smart, chrome and glass eatery with Italian undertones, half-way along Boston's Newbury Street. He sipped a club soda with a slice of lime, on the rocks, and surreptitiously observed four men standing at the bar.

They were young – late twenties early thirties – with oiled-back hair, expensive, designer casuals, and enough Patek Phillipe and Breitling wristwatches and neck jewellery to buy a modest house in an OK neighbourhood.

Outside, two Harley Davidson motor-cycles, a cream Heritage and a scarlet and yellow customized Dyna Glide, sat parked on the sidewalk. And a silver Porsche and a brand new Mercedes SL600 were parked at the kerb.

The cars belonged to the guys. And the guys belonged to the mob. It was just, reflected Girolo, not without regret, that they had forgotten.

He had been to this place a few times, getting to know his territory, getting to take a good look at the players. And those four dumb, arrogant, and indeed violent, young men were all that stood between Peter Girolo and his intention to bring the Boston Syndicate under control, prior to expanding all over the eastern seaboard. Including New York City.

Girolo had been planning throughout his four years in Marion. He had his eyes and ears every place. And he felt as if he knew those four wop dummkopfs like family, so thorough had been his researches.

A bellow of laughter came from the bar counter. A pretty girl in a micro dress, waitressing behind the bar, was laughing too, clearly intent on getting real close to one of those four – probably any one – in order to get on the other side of the poor–rich divide. And who could blame her?

She was a nice, forward, independent girl. Good looking too. Girolo hoped earnestly that she would not be around at the time of the hit. For that time had come. Time to teach some rough and wildly arrogant guinea wops how to earn their money, and when to keep their heads down. Low profile, Girolo said to himself. That's what the survivors will have to learn.

The nice kid, the waitress, was flirting more with one guy than the others. Sal Spatola, wiry, good looking, like the Fonz in *Happy Days*, thousand dollar black leather zip-up, dark, wavy hair expensively cut by New York hairdresser Nicky Vine, flown up specially one day every three weeks to tend the locks.

Spatola's father had been *capo* of the Massachusetts Syndicate until the Feds put him away in 1993. That was the Johnny Spatola everybody had seen on CNN, refusing to testify before a Grand Jury, just before a bold attempt by his henchmen, including young Salvatore, to ambush the US Marshals' convoy taking him from Providence Superior Court back to East Massachusetts Correction Center.

The gunfight had run through two streets for eleven and a half minutes and had been likened by the press to the noisy, fast moving, terrifying street battles of various Al Pacino and Robert de Niro movies. At the end of it, Johnny Spatola had lain dead, his bloody corpse half in and half out of the bullet-riddled Marshals' Dodge van.

His son Sal had led the mourning at one of the eastern seaboard's biggest mob funerals. His face had streamed with tears, his shoulders had heaved. But Peter Girolo knew that the object of that wild display of intemperate force had been achieved; the death of steady, calm, pragmatic, unobtrusive Don John Spatola – and the rise to *capo* of his cold-eyed, high-profile, coke-snorting son, Salvatore.

Judging by Sal's attitude, the shock-waves and confusion caused by the Flamingo Club and Carmine Genovese killings had subsided. Sure, it was a mystery. But it ain't going to change our lives, it ain't going to change a thing. That seemed to be the attitude of those young Turks.

Wrong, thought Girolo. He sipped the last of his soda and indicated he wanted the check.

Alison Clancy arrived early on the morning of the twenty-eighth, the day that the Houston contracts money was due to be wired to Zeralda Electronics' off-shore fund in the Caribbean.

She had learned that there was no record of any telephone calls from Zeralda to the Katakura Corporation of Japan, except those made formally during the time of the abortive take-over bid. Therefore the telephone conversation she had overheard Sebastian Tree making must either have been an incoming call routed via a local number, or made on his own personal mobile phone.

That morning, however, there was no sign of Tree's silver Porsche coupé, because Grace had dispatched him overnight to Los Angeles to represent Zeralda at an electronics forum chaired by William Gates himself, on the subject of using DNA mathematics to cause microchip hardware boards, no bigger than the iris of an eye, to update themselves automatically in order to remain compatible with ever-improving systems.

This was a concept that would have thrilled Jack, she thought, and she could just picture his boyish excitement. And she reflected, not for the first time, that the reason Jack Fitzrowan had made millions out of his business was that he had truly loved the entire world of electronics. He felt, he sometimes said, like one of the early explorers, Christopher Columbus, or Vasco da Gama, half-way across some uncharted ocean, witnessing wonders every day, and being at the forefront of changing the perceptions of the world.

Anyway, Sebastian had gone to LA, warning Grace that unless the Rockaway Project paid out promptly, Zeralda's failure to meet her banking obligations would result in disaster.

As she sat in her office, balefully watching the printer and the screen for a fax or e.mail confirming that the desperately needed millions had arrived, the messenger boy arrived from the Dispatch Room with her morning's letter post.

Among the usual routine one envelope caught her eye, for the postmark was Vienna, Virginia. And there was only one business she had been dealing with in Vienna – Telford & Pollard, one of DC's most efficient and discreet private investigation agencies.

The object of their investigation was Sebastian Tree. Inside the sealed envelope was a treasure trove of documents, and an overview report which stated that this was the preliminary stage. There was much more work to be done, as sources opened up, and one lead led to another.

Alison smiled. Private eyes since the days of Raymond Chandler had always made their investigations seem time consuming, and therefore money consuming. She pencilled a note to herself to fax them saying time was of the essence.

As she scanned the reports, ranging from where Tree had attended high school to dietary fads and health record, Alison's printer chattered and spewed out the welcome information that the last of the three electronic transfers had been made. Just one hour later, the First National Boston, the Chase Manhattan and the Bank of Scotland, Boston, had each received their monthly tranche of around eight million dollars each.

Business went on. Zeralda had survived. And the entire nightmare had eluded the press. Alison relaxed for the first time in days. She reached inside her desk drawer for a couple of M&Ms, feeling she had earned them.

The telephone rang. It was Martin Dorman, financial editor of the *Wall Street Journal*. His wife had been at high school with Alison and was one of her three best friends. Martin and Debbie had been terrific when Alison's marriage to Mike Medevik came to an end.

'Hi, Marti.' Alison always liked to hear from the 6'7" bespectacled bear, soft-ball playing economics star of Yale '87.

'What's this about you guys defaulting on bank payments, Ali?' Embarrassing but true, they called each other Marti and Ali.

Alison frowned. 'What the hell are you talking about?'

There was an awkward pause.

'We received a press release,' said Dorman, 'purporting to come from Zeralda's Public Affairs office. Janice compared it with some of your other ones. It seems genuine.'

'Well it's bullshit and it did not emanate from here, Marti.'

'Good enough for me, Big Al.'

'Not so much of the big,' grumbled Alison, guiltily pushing shut the desk drawer with the M&M packet.

'But it sure looks like somebody is trying to shaft you, I mean, not you personally, hon, but Zeralda Electronics.'

Alison thought hard about how to respond. Martin was a good friend, but he was first and foremost a professional journalist.

'Still there?' enquired Martin.

'Yep.' She tapped her pencil on the desk. 'Listen, Martin, if I promise you an exclusive can you sit on this for a while?'

'How long?'

'Till we at this end have enough evidence to prosecute.'

Slight pause. It occurred to Alison her best friend's husband had just begun to tape the call. Or maybe he had been taping and in order to keep a good story to himself, had now switched it off. Paranoia, she realized, was becoming a facet of her thinking, ever since that morning she had overheard Sebastian's perfidious phone conversation with Tak Katakura.

'Can you give me a hint?' asked Martin.

'No.'

Another pause, then, 'OK. For an exclusive, I can probably do more than that.'

'Such as?'

'The *Journal* will not be the only rag to get this circular. I'll e.mail the people who matter and warn them the story is false and therefore libellous. So relax, no bad press for Zeralda today.'

Alison sighed with relief. 'Thanks, Marti.'

'But based on what you have said, Ali, you people have a problem. You'd better move fast, before the rat pack gets hold of that.'

'Yes. We're working on it.'

Alison hung up. For the first time, she was really worried, for she could glimpse a future in which Big Jack's thunderous success in building Zeralda into a world leader in its field could crumble, virtually overnight.

God, how she missed him. A tear ran down her cheek. The phone rang. It was Sebastian Tree, calling from LA.

'I can't get hold of Grace,' he said, 'and I'm concerned, as you can imagine.'

'Concerned?'

'Of course. The Rockaway money didn't come through, I take it?'

'I got to the bottom of that,' smiled Alison. 'Computer had wiped their delivery schedules off the production programme. They were talking to Mitsuko-Watanabe in Silicon about replacing us. And would you believe this . . . ? Katakura had offered to step in.'

The silence on the line was profound. Then Tree said, 'What are you talking about, Alison?'

'Sabotage, Sebastian. I'm talking about industrial sabotage. Some-body tried to fuck us.'

The outrage could have earned Zeralda's Chief Exec an Oscar. 'Nobody fucks with us!' he exclaimed. 'We owe that much at least to Big Jack.'

You are good, thought Alison, you are very good.

Tree went on, 'Give me the details.'

'It's not that easy,' said Alison. 'We managed to find somebody in NASA who would tell us what the problem was.'

'You did? Great!'

'And the problem was exactly what I just said. The computer had wiped the Rockaway Project from its schedule.'

'Oh, come on . . . the production managers would've come running to me. The Rockaway Project was what was going to pay for their pensions.'

'Is, Sebastian. Present tense.'

'Come again?'

'Rockaway is back on line. We flew the components down, along with a team of installers and programmers. On the house.'

'Nice . . . thank God.' He seemed quite emotional. 'Oh, thank God . . .'

'And the production managers were blissfully unaware, Sebastian, because nobody had cancelled the production line. Zeralda has been churning out the microchips. Our saboteur was more worthy an adversary. He, or she,' nice touch, thought Alison, reaching for the M&M drawer, 'merely cancelled the air freight bookings and left the stuff to pile up in a warehouse at Logan International.'

'Well we can easily find out who's behind this.' Tree was businesslike. 'You know, it could be Katakura . . .'

Wow! Is this guy good or is he something else? Alison asked herself, in reluctant admiration. She reflected she would hate to play poker with him before realizing that, in effect, was precisely what she was doing.

'Katakura? It hadn't occurred to me. Would they do that?'

'Tak Katakura, you know, I got to know the guy during the Indian arm wrestling match we had, the month before Jack's accident.'

Did you ever, mused Alison.

Tree continued, 'That man is capable of anything. And who else would have a motive?'

'You mean,' said Alison, 'with Zeralda in financial deep water, a second dawn raid would probably be welcomed with open arms?'

'I could see Katakura pursuing that scenario, Alison.'

Alison waited, not responding. Eventually, Sebastian Tree commented. 'Glad you sorted out NASA, between you and the President. I can understand why I was kept out of the loop.'

Alison Clancy held the phone away from her ear and stared at it. This was virtuoso stuff indeed. 'It was Grace's decision, Seb,' she said. 'I got the whisper from an old flame in NASA. Grace felt the vital thing was to get Rockaway back on track. It's not just you. None of the VPs is aware. You are actually the first, and maybe right now we should keep it like that.'

Sebastian agreed, almost too readily. The tension on the line was tighter than an E-string on a Cajun banjo. Alison Clancy's mind was racing. Does he really imagine we don't know? she wondered.

Or is he just pretending, like a good poker player, that he doesn't know that we know? She decided to play along with the charade. Maybe the guy was so arrogant, he thought he had fooled them all.

'Anyway,' she continued, 'that's the situation. Rockaway is back on line.'

Tree was magnanimous. 'Well that is fabulous. You two hardly need me at all.'

You can say that again, thought Alison.

'What a goddam shame . . .' said Sebastian. 'So goddam near, and yet, too late.'

'Too late for what?' enquired Alison innocently, beginning to enjoy herself.

'The bank repayments. It's the twenty-eighth of the month, Alison. First National, Chase and Scotland, three payments missed. Twenty-one, almost twenty-two, million dollars. When the trade finds out, and it will not take too long, well,' his voice dropped – he would have made a good professional mourner, considered Alison – 'that's going to be a body blow to the firm. To our firm, that Jack spent his whole life building . . .'

Alison could almost hear a New Orleans funeral dirge in the background. She grinned and announced, 'Oh, we made the monthly transfers, Sebastian. Bang on time.'

'Excellent!!' Tree shouted, as if we were at a ball game, 'Hallelujah! How come Rockaway paid up so damn fast?'

'Oh,' smiled Alison, 'we will not have the Rockaway twenty-one million for another three weeks. I managed to rustle it up from another quarter. I'm sure we have said enough over the phone. You coming back after the seminar?'

Now that was a mistake. That was bitchy, it was crowing, it was a challenge, and it revealed that Alison at least believed Sebastian Tree was behind the attempt to scupper Zeralda.

'Of course I am. Why, Alison?' the voice was silky, like Alison imagined an alligator's voice would be, if it could speak, as it slithered relentlessly out from its muddy lair, 'did you think I had some furlough coming?'

Alison Clancy laughed. 'I just wondered if you wanted to spend some more time in LA, with your old TV ad friends . . .'

Another dumb move. The line went chill.

'What do you mean by that?' asked Tree, his voice quiet and thoughtful.

'Didn't you mention,' said Alison, cursing herself, for she had just been reading that information on the Telford & Pollard investigative report on Sebastian Tree's background, 'that you once worked in Beverly Hills, making TV commercials?'

'No,' said Tree, in a voice she hardly recognized, 'I did not.'

'Well I'm obviously mistaken,' said Alison. 'See you next week.'

And they said their goodbyes, almost formally, false warmth, by mutual agreement, no longer necessary.

'Illegitimate adoptions?' The tall, skinny Little Sister of the Poor, Sister Mary Ignatius MacMurrough, gazed balefully through her pebble glasses. 'Do you mean illegal adoptions, or legitimate adoptions of infants born out of wedlock?'

Bloody hell, thought Paul Fitzrowan, his cranium still full of little men with chisels trying to carve their way out through his eyeballs, an inevitable result of his excesses of the night before – the night that Steve Doyle, manager of the up-and-coming Irish rock group Subterfuge had offered him a contract to play bass guitar on their first CD, *Head on the Wall* – bloody hell, a pedantic librarian, just what I don't need.

'I suppose,' he replied sweetly, 'I mean both of those . . .' and smiled his best John Belushi beam, the eyes wide and innocent behind his Ray-Bans.

'Hmm.' Sister Mary Ignatius pursed her lips and studied the face of this rather attractive young man in front of her. Same line of enquiry, she thought to herself, as the elegant, sophisticated woman in her early thirties who had been in with such a similar brief just the week before. And the same aquiline nose, reminiscent of those medieval stone faces on ancient gravestones.

'Is this a personal thing?' she asked, 'or are you by any chance carrying out research for some learned treatise on the subject?'

'Oh,' said Paul, either naïvely honest or a shrewd judge of character, 'completely personal. I'm trying to trace a possible sister.'

Not so stupid.

'Born about when?' asked the librarian.

'About nineteen fifty-four, fifty-five.'

'Do you have a date?'

Paul smiled helplessly, raising his shoulders. 'I'm not even sure, to tell you the truth, if the whole story is not a family myth. I just' – Sister Mary Ignatius almost reached out to the boy, he suddenly seemed on the brink of tears, and how was she to know that this was on account of his trepanning hangover? – 'I just need to know . . .' He took a gulp of air.

The librarian touched his arm. 'Sit yourself down. I'll see what I can do to help . . .'

And while Sir Paul Fitzrowan sat patiently at the same, small table where his step-sister Darcy had sat just five days before, the librarian put on the kettle to make the poor young fellow a restoring cup of tea.

She wondered if she should reveal to him certain items of information she had not felt obliged to pass on to the last person enquiring into the same subject. That elegant woman with her letters of introduction from Magdalen College, Oxford.

Which is how in the hunt for Oliver, Jack's bastard son, Paul, the seemingly least aggrieved of his children, came to lead the rest by a furlong. And which is how, just two days later, he found himself in a windswept Galway cove knocking on the door of a modest, stone-built Georgian house, its kitchen garden half-abandoned, the wooden cross on its stone setting half-eroded by Atlantic wind and rain.

A slack-skinned brown frog sat eyeing him from a discarded wheelbarrow wheel, the pneumatic tyre now a fossil. Paul knocked again. A zephyr of salt air breathed across the hillside, bringing with it intimations of rock-pools and seaweed, and salt water of profound depth. Two seagulls wheeled overhead, making desultory screeches, as if to say, you're wasting your time, there's nobody in . . .

He waited for a minute, then his feet scrunched on the remaining chips of pebble as he stepped on to the uncut grass and approached a window, where he peered in.

Paul blinked as he found another pair of eyes peering back. Old eyes, rheumy eyes. Eyes which showed neither apprehension nor interest. And a face to go with them. Almost mummified, clustered in sparse, dirty white hair like wisps of straw.

6

'This is the main halyard cleat,' said Danny the Wop Tarantola, with all the authority of a *cognoscente* of the nautical arts.

'Sure thing,' agreed Tom Hanrahan, resigned to a misinformed lecture on just how his colleague's Jack Fitzrowan murder theory was viable.

'And this is the lift stay cleat,' continued Tarantola.

'Yep. That's the one.' Tom could see where this was leading. He wondered if Grace would be late, he just had a feeling about it. And if it would all be O K. Boy or girl, he did not really mind. Well, a boy would be cool. But a little girl like her mom, that would be great.

'By which the height of the boom is regulated.'

'Yeah, yeah, sure. For Chrissake, Danny, it's me that sailed the fuckin thing.'

Tarantola stuck his hands in his pockets. 'Exactly.'

'Meaning what, exactly?'

'You must have made the same number of turns, to the nearest fraction, every time, every time you adjusted the stay.'

'I didn't always do it.'

'Who did? Who else?'

Tom shrugged, 'Jack . . . the crew.'

'But there was no crew on that particular day.'

'That's right.'

'And . . .' here Danny flipped open his thin notebook, with its grey cover and the Boston Police First in the Nation logo on the front, 'somebody called Sebastian Tree – you have to be kidding me – Sebastian Tree, was asleep downstairs.'

'Below.'

'Below what?'

'Down below. That's what we say. "Captain, are you sleeping down below?", like in the fuckin song.'

'Now you lost me.'

'You interviewed this Tree?'

'Not yet, he's been in LA.'

'That was last week, you been on this for a month and you ain't seen the guy yet?'

'We been investigating a multiple mob homicide, or is the Lieutenant suffering from amnesia?'

'So why are you suddenly back on the case, Danny?'

Tarantola glanced at Tom as if he were simple. 'It's gone quiet. First quiet day we've had.'

Tom Hanrahan flicked out the Winston from its pack, the Winston he had been trying not to smoke. 'You coulda played golf,' he said.

Paul stooped instinctively as he crossed the threshold, although there was more than enough room for his six feet two inches. The old woman had beckoned him in, from her seat at the window. The hallway smelled of damp. Strips of paper hung from its seeping walls. A grandfather clock faced the oak staircase, its carpet runner missing more than a few of the brass stair rods that kept it safe for unsteady, ageing feet.

It had once been a good clock. Paul loved clocks – at Crough Lake, he had gone round the entire house, as a boy, winding and oiling and polishing nineteen of them, ranging from Thomas Mudge escarp mechanisms to ormolu fantasies from the courts of the Czars. This had been a fine example, not outrageous quality but a decent timepiece, with its long case of mahogany, inlaid with yew and sycamore. M. Blassey of Cork, Paul did not doubt and sure enough, when he paused to examine the cracked, yellowing, Georgian face, there it was, the clockmaker's scrawled signature above the VII for seven o'clock. Enamel faded, inlay jaded, this was a clock that had long since ceased to tick or chime.

A raven croaked, from the parlour, or a crow, stranded perhaps, inside this time capsule. No, not so, for this raven had words: 'Are you ever coming in?' it croaked. 'Or are you here to rob me of me quiet?'

Paul breathed in the musty, dank air and stepped on through to the parlour. God help us, was his first reaction, I have been transported into *Great Expectations*. For there, at the window, like a dry, ancient, scrawny old bird, was the nearest thing to Miss Faversham anyone was ever likely to see in the flesh. If indeed it was flesh which kept this old biddy from transmogrifying into a pile of dust.

'I am not here to rob you of anything,' said Paul, gently. 'I am here to ask you for help.'

The old woman grinned, a terrible sight, and coughed, almost silently, its very soundlessness more awful than the wheezing rattle Paul was expecting.

'That's rare,' she croaked. 'Rare indeed. Me help, heh-heh. Me . . . ?'

'I believe you really can,' replied Paul evenly, addressing her as though she were both fully *compos mentis* and his equal.

For a while after that, there was silence. The salt breeze had never, it seemed, penetrated those crumbling, damp walls and Paul's senses were disturbed by mildew and decay, and the arid smell of withering decrepitude.

The old woman gazed at him, blinking from time to time, quite patient. He wondered if she was so far gone with dementia that this was a waste of time.

Then, the croak, 'I'll help you, then.'

Paul smiled, he had a nice smile, and cast around for some place to sit, but the dusty furniture looked as if it might collapse into molecules at the merest pressure.

'I was told this house belongs to the Church,' he said, in a comfortable, matter of fact sort of tone.

She nodded. 'Oh, yes. Holy ground . . .' and chuckled disconcertingly, her eyes twinkling in shared conspiracy. Behind her, beyond the unwashed windows, a pleasantly sloping hillside, and the faint screeching of seagulls.

'And it used to be a living, for the priest at Saint Sulspice?'

Paul's host nodded. 'Until nineteen,' she replied.

'Nineteen?'

Silence, then, 'Forty-seven.'

'And after nineteen forty-seven?'

The old woman nodded, her face framed in wispy white whiskers.

'What happened in nineteen forty-seven?' Paul enquired, patiently.

'Father Gerrard took a house by the church.'

'He moved out of here?'

She nodded, her eyes lost in memories, or the lack of them.

'We stayed, though, Sister Beatrice, Sister Agnes and me. We lived here. Taking care of the Lord's business . . .'

Paul's pulse quickened. Sister Agnes and Sister Beatrice had been two of the nuns whose names the church librarian in Dublin had given to him when she had passed on details of five parishes on the west coast where illegitimate pregnancies had been, in her words, 'catered for'.

Abortion being a mortal sin, the catering had taken the form of quietly arranged adoptions, mostly, but not all, legally effected. Some had been assigned by the local clergy to 'foster parents', a less-cumbersome piece of machinery, less paperwork than formal adoption, but legal all the same.

And on occasion, as the librarian had confided, a childless couple might be considered who, in the local priest's or mother superior's judgement, could give an unwanted child a good home, but who for one reason or another did not conform to the Church authorities' guidelines on adoptive parents.

What sort of couple would be both suitable and unacceptable at the same time? Paul had asked the librarian.

And the answer had been swift and frank. Americans.

And did money ever change hands?

Here the tall, bespectacled Little Sister of the Poor had given him the blankest of blank looks, and Paul had dropped the subject.

This Georgian rectory on the windswept Galway coast was the third such place Paul had visited since his return from Dublin. Of the other two, one had been demolished and the other was a thriving maternity home, run by nuns, just outside Cork city. The mother superior who ran it had been helpful on the recorded adoption side of things, but if his dad's father had been anything like Big Jack himself, there would have been no paperwork involved in pushing the baronet's heir's youthful indiscretion under the carpet.

'Now you would not,' said Paul, beginning to enjoy this piece of detective work, 'by any chance, be Sister Immaculata . . . ?'

The rheumy eyes glinted. The aged voice croaked, 'Not by any chance. By God's design.'

A survivor . . . Clinging to the wreckage.

'Sister, my name is Paul Fitzrowan. I believe an older brother of mine was born in this house, over forty years ago. And I wonder if you can help me find him.'

The old nun sat immovable, in stony silence.

Minutes passed. She reminded Paul of the leathery, motionless frog outside.

'I was the midwife, you know,' she said, and as she remembered, her voice seemed to mellow, the croak softening. 'I delivered the wee mites. God bless them every one.'

And the aged relic's face lit up, becoming almost angelic as a shaft of sunlight suddenly filtered into the room, motes of dust suspended in its beam, and shined upon her.

Darcy Fitzrowan Bailey sat in the conservatory of the manor house at Hedge's Hall, dipping a croissant into her black Colombian coffee and glancing through the minutes of the Aids and Elephants' Appeal Committee, of which she was chairperson.

'Do you have to wear Armani at breakfast time?' enquired her husband sweetly.

'My dear Edward, I have meetings all day. One committee after another.'

'Hmmph,' opined Edward Bailey, Professor Emeritus of Saxon and Post Medieval Linguistics.

'What's that supposed to mean?' Darcy asked.

Edward poured some honey over his muesli and solved another clue in the Telegraph crossword. Then he glanced up and brushed his mop of brown hair off his face. 'It means, Darcy, that I am not entirely sure if charities which combine the vogue but damp-squib disease of Auto Immune Deficiency Syndrome with the supposed threat to the African bull elephant are entirely a serious way for the lady of a Fellow of All Souls to comport herself.'

Darcy smiled that Fitzrowan smile which indicated cool displeasure. She was certainly her spouse's equal intellectually, and his growing reputation world-wide as an authority on Beowulf and the origins of the glottal stop left her perfectly unmoved.

'You want to get into my good books?' she asked, with just sufficient hint of promise to make him look up.

'Now how precisely would I do that?' he replied, with the tone of a husband who had exhausted all such avenues.

'I think Pronsias Stevenson is holding out on us.'

'On you, Darcy. I am not interested in all that money, we have more than enough, in my book.'

Yes and it all came from my goddam family, thought Darcy. She beamed at him. 'Darling, you are so full of probity I swear were you to burst, nothing would emerge but pietas, gravitas and dignity.'

'You hate me don't you?'

'No emotion quite so strong, I promise.' Darcy held his gaze, knowing he got off on such appalling treatment.

After a pause he said, 'So Pronsias is holding out. How would that get me in favour with you?'

Darcy dipped another end of croissant into her coffee and let it hang there for a moment. 'Invite him to Magdalen. Ask him to give a lecture.'

Edward Bailey almost did explode.

'You're mad,' he pronounced, and returned to five across – *The swimmer sings in D sharp, but not always*.

'The schoolroom . . .' breathed Darcy.

Edward stopped writing, his eyes fixed on the crossword.

'With contrition,' she murmured, almost inaudible, eyes lowered demurely to gaze at her plate.

It had been years since they had last indulged in contrition. Edward thought she had forgotten all about it. In fact, part of him rather hoped that she had. He felt undignified when he recalled how very excited and overheated he had become. For Professor Edward Bailey did like to maintain that dignity to which his elegant, beautiful wife had just alluded. But the sight of Darcy in her brief, grey, pleated Connecticut boarding-school skirt, with white shirt and navy blue knee-socks and her portrayal of innocent but available arousal had struck some chord in his psyche which had turned the dry academic into a raging satyr.

'With contrition . . . ?' His voice was hoarse. And when he met her gaze, he knew she would keep her promise.

After a moment, he asked, heart pounding, 'What in God's name could he lecture upon?'

'Oh,' replied Mrs Fitzrowan Bailey, 'I've thought of something.'

'He was a great man, your father,' pronounced Nicky Vine, as he snipped with expensive efficiency at Sal Spatola's long, thick, glistening black hair.

'Yeah, God rest his soul,' blasphemed the young *capo* who had arranged the murder of his own father.

'Going any place nice for the weekend?' enquired the hairdresser.

Spatola did not reply. He was in a black rage because his two-month-old Mercedes SL600, ice blue with cream leather, fully loaded, had been stolen from the drive of his heavily secure six-bedroomed house on the edge of the picturesque town of Concord.

Whoever did it was dead meat. His mind raced over possible perpetrators. Joyriding kids? He did not think so. Pro car thieves? Not unless they had a death wish. Somebody on the lam, who needed wheels? He could see that. And somebody who could by-pass the plethora of electronic security devices with which the $160,000 automobile had been fitted.

His rage was the greater because no Mercedes distributor in New England could get him an identical replacement model in less than ten days. And he had been looking forward to driving his new girl Amanda over to the exclusive Charles River Boat Club, where this college guy who owed for cocaine had arranged for them to have dinner in the Boathouse club bar and restaurant.

'. . . a shorter look?' the New York hairdresser was saying.

Sal shook out of his reverie, which had begun to involve chain-saws and Dexedrine. And H_2SO_4, otherwise known as sulphuric acid.

'Whadda *you* think?' After all, what the hell was he paying this fruit four hundred bucks for?

'I think just a tad off, shorter on the sides, kind of a brushy flat-toppish effect here, and long at the back.'

'Naw, there's a night-club owner in London has it like that, he looks like a scarecrow on acid.'

Nicky Vine put his hip to one side and eyed Spatola firmly in the mirror. 'That man is twice your age, Don Spatola, and that's being kind to him. Believe me, black and healthy, like your hair is, the effect will be like . . .' and here Nicky Vine proved himself versed in psychology, 'Al Pacino.'

'No kidding?'

'No kidding.'

'You know,' smiled Spatola coldly, 'if you fuck it up we send you home in the trunk of a cheap automobile.'

Nicky Vine giggled, and started on the left side of his mobster client's luxurious hair. At which point Dion Stomparelo comes in, without any knocking or hesitation. Dion is six feet four and two forty pounds of muscle, with a mini-Uzi under his left armpit and a .45 Colt auto in the small of his back.

'Boss,' he says, 'they just found your car.'

Salvatore Spatola hurried out from his offices above the pasta restaurant on the corner of Sheafe and Salem, in Boston's North End, a little piece of Italy, as anxious as a mother cat whose kitten has strayed. The car was unmarked, apart from a scrape on the front left fender and the left door sill.

'Kids, the cops figure,' said Dion. 'Abandoned at the Crystal Lake parking lot, on the Breakheart Reservation.'

'Goddam Indians,' said Spatola. 'They would steal the food from their mothers' hands.'

'High on moonshine, I figure,' agreed Stomparelo, getting into character.

Spatola gave an old-fashioned look.

'They wanted to keep it, so their stolen car unit could give it the once over,' continued D the Stomp, 'but I persuaded them to release it to me.'

Spatola nodded, he expected no less from his footsoldiers, his made men. 'Works OK?'

'Like a dream. Only thing, the fuckers started it with a fuckin screwdriver.'

Spatola shook his head as he crossed to the sleek convertible, its top down. 'Fuckin Indians. Check the trunk, I mean they ain't poured paint in it or nothin?'

'Clean. They left a quart of Sour Mash on the floor. Empty. Coupla joint stubs where the dash meets the windshield. And this . . .'

They had reached the car. A tiny Onieda-Menominee Indian stone charm, in the shape of a snake coiled round a bolt of lightning, attached to a worn, black leather neck thong, lay on the passenger seat.

Dion picked it up and handed it to the mafia boss, who weighed it in his hand, examining it. 'Nice,' he said. 'I'll give it to Amanda.' His eyes went to the ignition barrel, its delicate keyhole raped by a short-handled screwdriver which still protruded from it.

'Mercedes are sending a coupla guys over. It'll be right as rain for tonight,' said Stomparelo.

'Yeah . . . ? replied Spatola, thoughtful. 'Maybe we'll just take it for a spin.' He loved his coupé, it made him feel like somebody from one of those glossy ads in *Vogue* magazine. Amanda had been in *Vogue*, she was a model. She had also been in a porno video featuring three Mexicans and a German shepherd. This piece of art was, however, a rarity. For Sal Spatola had bought up all but two hundred and nine of the cassettes.

Frankly, Don Salvatore Spatola loved the Merc more than he loved Amanda, even though she was kind of cute and called him her favourite toad, which he accepted as a term of endearment. He opened the door and sat in the sculptured leather driver's seat, watched by the Stomp and Nicky Vine, still clutching his hairdresser's scissors and tongs.

'They musta been tall guys,' said Dion, 'they put the seats right back.'

Don Spatola was shorter than the average American male, a fact which had, in the past, proved close to fatal for those who had remarked on it. He turned the offending screwdriver to switch on the ignition, and smiled as the big six-litre motor purred into life.

Then he reached down with his left hand for the electronic memory switch, Number One position, which would raise and bring forward his seat, and lower and bring out the steering wheel to suit his particular diminutive build. Dion, his massive bodyguard, had the Number Two position pre-programmed, and Amanda, who was five ten, Number Three.

'I hope they ain't fucked around with the seat memory,' grumbled Sal Spatola and as his sound system started to play 'King of the Road', he firmly pressed the Number One memory button.

'Either,' observed the police pathologist attending the crime scene as he examined the dead man's undamaged head, which had landed, along with Sal Spatola's upper torso, unmarked, in Copp's Hill Cemetery, a block away from the site of the explosion, 'the blast sheared his hair real neatly on the right side, or the deceased was half-way through a haircut.'

'They found barber's scissors in the ceiling of an apartment across the street,' contributed Lieutenant Tom Hanrahan.

'Can you make a connection?'

'Sure,' said Danny Tarantola. 'There was a hand attached.'

Hanrahan's phone buzzed. He switched to talk. 'Yeah?'

'Tommy, it's me,' said Grace's voice. 'You want to eat in tonight? Or take a stroll down to the Farragut?'

The Farragut was a bar that served OK food.

'Not now, honey,' replied Hanrahan, 'I got a stiff.'

'Well, what can I say? Catch you later.'

The detective smiled. 'Any time.' And he switched the phone off.

'Lieutenant,' called Millicent Dunne, crime reporter on the *Boston Globe*, as she hurried across the graveyard, ignoring the attempts of uniformed patrolmen to keep her beyond the tape lines. 'Is this connected with the Flamingo and Carmine Genovese killings?'

She reached a gravestone, across from the canvas screens shielding Spatola's grisly remains. Tom scratched his neck, as if thinking about this, when he shrugged. 'What do you think, Milly?'

Millicent smoothed down her rumpled trenchcoat, adjusted the green chiffon scarf at her throat. Nothing, thought Tom Hanrahan, much as he loved the reporter's relentless pursuit of a story, could ever make her anything but homely and untidy. But he had a lot of time for her.

She frowned, meeting his gaze. 'Maybe,' she opined.

'Me, too,' smiled Tom, and nodded to big Joe Daly to escort her gently from the location. Milly glanced back and grinned as she was led away. Tom knew she would make at least two columns out of that. But you never knew when you might need the help of the press.

Danny Tarantola emerged from within the canvas screen, listening intently to his two-way radio. He glanced across to Tom, mouthing 'Jimmy Fitz . . .'

Tom gazed around the graveyard. Part of the windshield and front bulkhead had landed across the last resting place of one Ezekiel Grose, 1822–1887, haberdasher and, the detective recalled from his Boston University days studying forensics and jurisprudence, cross-dresser and suspected murderer of twin sisters who had last been seen giggling at him near the railroad station. Case had been thrown out by the DA's office owing to the fact that Grose's confession had been extracted by subterfuge and the suspect had not been alerted to his rights under the Fifth Amendment. *Plus ça change*, he thought. Miranda by any other name.

Danny the Wop shut down his radio and ambled over. 'Jimmy Fitz has been over to Intel,' he said. 'That Girolo guy. He has a share in a casino in Vegas. Rents a suite in the Caesar's Palace. Drives a BMW sedan with LA plates, registered to a girlfriend. Been seen around town. Two parking violations. Paid on time.'

Tom Hanrahan gazed at the pathologist backing out from the

canvas screens holding two small plastic evidence bags with God knew what inside them. 'What does that tell us?'

'Far be it from me to go for the fuckin obvious, Lieutenant. Maybe it means Girolo is living in LA.'

Tom fished for his pack of Winstons, digging them out from his coat pocket. 'And maybe it means, Danny, you should think like an Italian. Maybe you been around us Micks for too long.'

Tarantola hunched his shoulders. Stared at the nearest tombstone, then he nodded. 'You mean that's what he wants us to think.'

Hanrahan lit the cigarette and inhaled deeply. Aware that Danny Tarantola was watching him thoughtfully, his agile mind, as always, never far from that ketch, high and dry in the Coastguard dock, its hull seams suffering from lack of sea water. Hell, I didn't kill you, Jack, mused Tom. But this fuckin terrier here has got me wondering now, maybe somebody did.

He glanced at Tarantola, meeting his eye. 'I think I'm gonna keep this Peter Girolo's photo in my wallet,' he said.

Sergeant Danny Tarantola nodded slowly. Everyone in Homicide knew what that meant.

Tom's wife Grace, President of Zeralda Electronics, gazed at her Chief Executive and listened courteously to his calm, more in sorrow than in anger, litany of complaint against the Corporation's lawyer, Alison Clancy.

'I guess,' Tree was saying, 'what really offends is the suggestion I was not to be trusted . . .'

Perish the thought, Grace reflected.

'. . . and while I applaud the . . . finesse of your manoeuvre, using Texas oil money instead of NASA income to service our bank loans, my hair is falling out, Grace, when I think of the myriad things that could have gone wrong. Even now, were the media to get hold of this . . . I mean, it could still wreck Zeralda's reputation.'

'And how would they?' asked Grace, softly, her eyes firmly on his.

Tree smiled his open and frank, just-here-to-serve smile. 'You know how they do, Grace. You know the goddam press.'

'OK,' said Grace Hanrahan. 'Only three people know the particular and extraordinary circumstances of this one-time electronic transfer of funds. I have a fax from Tod Santez at NASA. Normal service has been resumed. He is particularly grateful for our complimentary provision of technicians to set up the new systems. Says it puts us back in the big-boys' league.'

'Nice words.' Tree raised his shoulders, pessimistic. 'But it doesn't pay the rent.'

Grace went on, 'He has today authorized resumption of monthly payments of twenty-one million dollars and change, including that which was due on the eighteenth of last month. And he has promised to phone me in person, or e.mail me wherever I am in the world, should there ever be another glitch.'

'Well that's just great.' Sebastian Tree looked so relaxed he could have been on Valium. Maybe he was, thought Grace, maybe he should have been. 'But it could have been a disaster.'

Get to the point, thought Big Jack's daughter. 'Sebastian, it was my decision. I moved alone, with legal advice. How was I to know there was not some . . .' she seemed to search for the word, '. . . conspiracy? Some attempt to ruin the Corporation? Mmm?'

Sebastian Tree did not even blink. 'Don't you think, if that had been the case, I would have been on to it?'

'So conspiracy is out?' enquired Grace gently.

Tree thought for a moment, then he nodded, emphatically. 'I have conducted a thorough investigation. Computer error is the cause of our failure to freight the regular NASA deliveries to Florida. If I had any faith in our dear lawyer, I would ask her to initiate a class action against MicroWare. But . . .' he shrugged eloquently.

Grace fought the urge to crown him with the nearest heavy artefact. 'Alison has my full confidence, Sebastian. She saved the day. You, on the other hand, failed to get to the root of a computer malfunction which almost ruined us.'

Sebastian Tree finally went quite pale. 'Meaning?' he said, charm draining from his voice.

Grace smoothed the documents on her desk, then looked him

square in the eye, 'Meaning, Sebastian, you had better watch your step. And sign this . . .' She slid a single sheet of close-typed corporation notepaper across the desk to him. 'It is a legally binding document, contracting you to total confidentiality on all Zeralda's banking and other sensitive matters. Break it, and we break you.'

She smiled coldly, as her Chief Executive's face went from white to glowing red, anger gripping him.

'I don't know, Grace,' he said, in a voice of controlled fury, 'if I can remain with Zeralda after this.'

'That is, of course, for you to decide.'

Grace rose, and as if on a signal her PA appeared in the doorway. 'Your brother on line two, Mrs Hanrahan.'

'Thanks, Diana.' Grace Hanrahan nodded to Sebastian Tree as he stalked from her office, then she lifted the receiver. 'Hi, Paul.'

Paul Fitzrowan sounded confident and excited. 'Grace, terrific news.'

'What's that, Paulie?'

'I've found him, Grace. I've found Oliver!'

Pronsias Stevenson stepped off the Aer Lingus shuttle at London's Heathrow Airport, looking for all the world like a lawyer on a few days off. The comfortably worn grey herring-bone jacket from Giorgio Armani in Boston's Newbury Street, purchased about four years before, when he had been over to brief Jack Fitzrowan on his various property acquisitions in Dublin and Cork city; the darker grey flannels from Brown Thomas in Dublin; shirt from Brown Thomas and shoes from Foster's in Jermyn Street, London, a present from Martina, who had sent away for them from an advertisement in the *Irish Gentleman*, a periodical which had foundered after three issues. Socks by Abercrombie and Ffitch, Boston.

A broad, middle-aged man in a slightly too tight raincoat and green pullover, battered brown pork-pie hat at a jaunty angle, appeared at the foot of the arrival hall stairs in Terminal One.

'Mr Stevenson?' he enquired, in slightly fractured quasi upper-class tones, with just a hint of something from middle Europe.

'That's me,' replied the lawyer.

'I am Mr Szabodo, Magdalen College bulldog,' the stout man announced, revealing as he smiled a missing front tooth. 'Do we have luggage?'

Stevenson looked the fellow up and down. He had heard of touts and cutpurses loitering at airports, ready to swipe your bags or dip your pockets. Then he remembered that some Oxford college stewards went by the quaint nomenclature of 'bulldog'.

'Just one brown valise,' he said, and they proceeded to the carousel where, without being prompted, Szabodo reached into the maelstrom of suitcases, golf bags and precariously tied cardboard boxes and hefted Stevenson's scuffed leather valise off the slowly revolving conveyer and made a polite gesture, ushering his charge towards the exit doors.

'This is very kind of you,' Stevenson remarked, as Szabodo drove the Baileys' Jeep Cherokee west on the M4 towards the M40 and Oxford.

It had started to rain, and although visibility was poor, Mr Szabodo seemed more than competent as he manoeuvred the Jeep past more cautious traffic.

'It is a pleasure to help out the professor,' he said. 'He is a gentleman of the old school.'

Around the time when this brief conversation was taking place, the aforesaid gentleman finally collapsed, perspiring, over the damp buttocks of one of the most beautiful women in Oxford, indeed, in Europe.

His wife.

And as he lay across her, heart pounding, his thick, brown hair lank with sweat, tumescence finally subsiding, he murmured in her ear, 'Are we contrite . . . are we now . . . ?'

And Darcy, who threw herself wholeheartedly into anything she embarked upon, even with her husband, lay quietly satisfied, reflecting that if such enthusiasm on his part occurred more frequently than once every other year, she might not be so tempted to stray.

'Oh, yes,' she whispered. Then the little devil in her made her continue. 'Almost . . .'

'Almost?' Edward whispered, licking her neck.

'My God,' his wife gasped, 'not again . . .'

And the Professor of Linguistics took a deep breath and grunted, 'Tally-ho!'

By the time Bulldog Szabodo drove the Baileys' Jeep into the circular gravel drive of Hedge's Hall, Darcy Fitzrowan Bailey and her erudite and pleasantly exhausted spouse – showered, changed, schoolroom toys put away – were standing on the Elizabethan steps to their manor house, sober and welcoming.

'My word, Pronsias, you do look well,' purred Darcy, while Edward thanked the bulldog and took the Dublin lawyer's leather valise.

'The Irish legal system is virtually the same, isn't it?' enquired Bailey as he led the way up to the guest bedroom, the ancient oak stairs creaking, their patina shining as spring sunshine suddenly broke through the grey rainy skies.

Behind them, Darcy smiled, it had never been Edward's way to indulge in small talk. No 'How was the flight?' for him.

'Except in certain areas, like our Constitution. And of course, jurisprudence,' replied the Dublin solicitor.

The spacious corner bedroom looked wonderful in the sunlight. Darcy had natural good taste and the room was furnished in big French and Italian eighteenth-century pieces, lighter wood than dark, English oak, with damask and southern Persian rugs. There were two French post-Impressionist oils of promenades, with faded, smoky, pastel blues and lightest of pale coffee colours, parasols, crinolines, straw hats and tiny splashes of poppy scarlet.

Stevenson was no parochial Irish lawyer. He had travelled the world on Big Jack Fitzrowan's business and, being an educated and inquisitive man, had learned along the way. He gazed around the room, thinking to himself how absolutely right each item was, and noting the degree of care which must have gone into it. Plus the price. He knew the two Boudins were genuine, for he had arranged the art insurance for Hedge's Hall. Over eight-hundred thousand pounds at the last valuation.

'Just perfect,' he breathed. 'Martina would be in seventh heaven.'

'You should have brought her, Pronsias,' said Darcy, meeting his eye as she stood behind her husband.

Stevenson smiled. 'Martina just will not fly, and the ferry takes too long.'

'I hate flying, too,' announced Edward, who seemed unusually jaunty, for Pronsias Stevenson had always thought the Englishman a mite too reserved.

'And elements of criminal law,' remarked Stevenson. 'We tend more to the European model.'

'Will you be incorporating that in your lecture?' asked Edward.

'I don't see how I could leave it out.'

'You will want a moment to freshen up, Pronsias,' said Darcy, interrupting this riveting interchange. 'Then why not come down and have tea with us? We'll be in the conservatory.'

'I'll just wash my face and be right there,' replied the lawyer.

'I have arranged,' said Edward, 'for you to meet the Centenary Committee in the Master's house. Glass of wine and a chance to become acquainted with some of the faculty.'

'Excellent.' Stevenson preened himself at the thought.

'Black tie, old boy. Throw on something casual for tea, we can change before we go.'

'Capital.'

'Do you have everything?' enquired Darcy, solicitous.

'We rise to tuxedos in Dublin, Darcy,' smiled Pronsias Stevenson. 'I even have a proper tie-it-yourself black tie.'

Edward grinned as he made his way across the galleried landing and back downstairs. Darcy touched Stevenson's sleeve and said, 'I'm glad you could come. Do you like Bach?'

Wary of such near effusion from someone who only weeks before had been close to going for his jugular, Stevenson looked back into her eyes. Coolly, he felt. 'Bach? Oh yes, Bach is very pleasant.'

'Then I'll play for you,' she whispered. 'On the harpsichord. Tomorrow, while Edward is in Oxford.'

And she was gone.

Pronsias Stevenson was surprised and even a bit annoyed, to find that his heart was beating just a little faster. Oh no, boyo, we are not going to fall for that one. He assured himself. And on the landing, a long-case Christopher Pinchbeck clock began to whirr, preparing itself to chime the hour.

Drive south on Highway 79 from Boston, through pleasant New England, and you reach the junction with Route 195, running west to east from Providence, Rhode Island. Drive on and soon you are out of Massachusetts and in the state of Connecticut. Off the highway, there is a road which runs along the shore of Mount Hope Bay, with a number of picnic sites and places for weekend sightseers to park up. During the week, of course, most of those places are deserted.

It was at one such remote vantage point that Peter Girolo climbed out of an Oldsmobile sedan and told his driver to wait in the car. He strolled over to the only other automobile there, a black Cadillac with coupe-de-ville coachwork. Its driver got out and held open the back door for whoever was inside.

Albert Genovese was inside, expensively dressed in a loose fitting silk suit, working on his teeth with a silver toothpick. Albert Genovese, you will recall, was *consigliere* to the *capo di tutti capi*, the Boss of Bosses, who presently languished inside Florence prison, Colorado, the last word in supermaxes, four floors underground and unlikely to see daylight before he reached his dotage.

Like Girolo himself, Albert Genovese was a lawyer, and as counsellor to the highest echelons of the *cosa nostra* he held the kind of power normally denied to all but ministers of state.

Beside him, dwarfed in the wide leather seat, were two children, a boy and a girl aged about six and eight respectively. Neatly dressed, more European than New York, it seemed to Girolo. Quiet kids, who gazed at him with a combination of curiosity and gravity he found disconcerting. He figured they were Genovese's grand-children and wondered what the hell they were doing there.

'Albert,' he said, by way of greeting. And his glance at the two kids meant, what's this?

Genovese turned to the children and smiled. It was the smile of a kind man, a man they seemed to trust. 'I'll be right back,' he said to them in Italian.

The children nodded gravely. Genovese climbed out and strolled towards the water's edge. 'With Salvatore Spatola out of the picture,' he said, when he and Girolo were out of earshot, 'these young hoodlums are running around like headless roosters. You figure on making a move?'

'Who are the kids?' asked Girolo.

'Just two kids, Pietro,' replied Genovese. 'Couple of orphan kids the *famiglia* is taking care of.'

'Whose kids?' Girolo enquired.

'Couple of kids whose father had to go.' Genovese put his silver toothpick back in its leather Cartier case. He meant the hapless father had been a senior *mafioso* who had transgressed the *cosa*'s code. 'His mamma,' Genovese went on, 'went crazy. Took her own life.' He crossed himself, without a blush. 'I'm taking them to the airport, the family will look after them, back in the old country.'

Girolo nodded. He knew such things went on, better than most, for there had been a time not long ago when he, the *cosa*'s top assassin, the *mana morte*, the hand of death, would probably have been the instrument of those two kids' misfortune.

'So, like I said,' Genovese was watching a sailboat on the far side of the bay, 'with Spatola out of the way, you figure on making a move?'

Girolo nodded. 'This is the time.'

'What do you need?'

Girolo shrugged. 'Just Joey and a couple of footsoldiers. Made men, clean, no punks.'

'We don't have punks,' said Genovese. 'We ain't the Cripps.'

'And nobody who has been involved in this earlier business,' said Girolo, referring to the multiple homicides at the Flamingo Club and the whacking of Carmine Genovese and his uncle Giuseppe, who had once been Peter Girolo's own driver and bodyguard. And when Girolo used the word business, it was no euphemism. He meant it. This was nothing personal, it was merely the way the mob went about restoring good order and discipline.

'You got it.'

Girolo stared out over the bay. It was one of those spring days when the first heat of the coming summer had made its presence felt. A pair of ducks winged their way above the gentle water, trailed by three busily flapping offspring.

And as he watched them, he thought to himself, if only life was that simple. It might not seem much, as portents go, but it was a moment the Sicilian was to remember. Like a waymarker in his personal odyssey.

'. . . the Vietnamese,' Genovese was saying. 'Violent and clever. They've been making moves into *cosa* territory, in the North Side and also Rhode Island, which is our hard-won turf, Pietro.'

Girolo nodded. Once he had reshaped the Italian crime syndicate, made it worthy of respect, it would not take long to make the expansionist Vietnamese dope gangs see reason. 'Tell me about the Russians,' he said.

In Marion, talk among his own people had been about the inexorable rise of the Russian mafia since 1993. They were ruthless and efficient, murdering opponents and assassinating rivals without compunction. Shooting, strangling and torturing their way into domination of organized crime in Europe and Asia. Even the Sicilians and the Neapolitan *comora* had been obliged to come to terms with the men from Moscow.

Genovese picked at his upper gum, reflective, then he said, 'The Russians are in Boston, sure. Since about two years. So far they have been putting their own house in order. A bit like yourself. Taking control of the Russian immigrant communities on the eastern seaboard.'

Girolo reflected the Russians were like a latter-day Mongol Horde, sweeping west through Europe and east and south into Kazakhstan and Azerbaijan. And now, across the ocean to establish a bridgehead in America. 'And once they have established a presence?' he asked.

Genovese removed the toothpick and met the Sicilian's eye. 'Watch out . . .' he replied.

The ducks seemed to squawk in alarm. And a cloud obscured the sunlight, casting a cold, grey gloom over the shore and the bay.

Paul has changed, thought Grace Hanrahan, sipping a cup of tea in the bar of the Ritz-Carlton Hotel, across the street from Boston Common, not far from Mike Medevik's office.

Her brother, his fair hair gleaming and swept back in a pony tail, had dispensed with the single gold earring, she noted. He was wearing a well-cut sports coat and faded jeans, with supple, comfortable boots, high in the ankle, which had been made years before, by John Lobb of St James's, London. A birthday present from his father.

Jeans were forbidden in the bar, where Boston's movers and shakers tended to gather for a drink or a lunchtime get-together. But the Vietnamese waiter had been so charmed by young Sir Paul's easy courtesy that he had either not noticed, or decided, since the place was almost deserted at ten after four in the afternoon, to let it go.

Paul sipped his Darjeeling tea and waited, quietly excited, while his sister read the couple of close-typed pages he had just given to her.

'How was your flight?' she asked.

'Grace. Please. Just read it,' he replied, unable to indulge in pleasantries at so momentous a time.

So Grace read on, and this is what she read:

Sister Immaculata, *née* Annie Frances Corkoran, of 144 Rafters Road, Drimnagh, Dublin, was one of two nuns of the Order of Saint Margaret the Meek appointed housekeeper and almoner respectively to the parish priest of Athgoe, in the County of Galway, in the year 1954.

Father Thomas Flynn, the parish priest since 1943, had a forthright view on the subject of illegitimacy. He believed that while fornication was a sin, and many hundreds of Hail Marys and Glory Be's were recited around Athgoe to give testimony to the fact, the ostracizing and social punishment of the unfortunate girls concerned was a greater sin.

Thus he established a residence, Inniscoor, bequeathed to the Church by a local landowner, where his housekeeper and almoner lived and where it became known, if unspoken, that women with child conceived out of wedlock could find a safe and discreet haven in which to live out their confinement.

Sister Immaculata was a trained nurse and it was she who performed the deliveries. In 1957, a third nun, Sister Beatrice, joined the household. She was a trained anaesthetist, so things were becoming fairly professional, and young women were by now arriving, with their suitcases packed, from all over the west coast of Ireland.

The identities of the pregnant women were kept from the nuns, and Father Flynn always found good foster homes for the babies.

It was only after Father Flynn passed away that among his papers was found a bank paying-in book, detailing deposits of sums ranging from £180 in 1947 to $4,000 in 1961. The paying-in book was in the name of Joseph O'Flynn, for an account with the Bank of Ireland in the city of Limerick. And at the time of Father Flynn's death, there was £53,743 in credit.

Grace glanced up at her brother. 'He was selling the babies . . .'

Paul nodded and said, 'The incriminating documents were taken away by a representative of the Bishop of Galway. Nothing was heard of the matter again.'

Grace shook her head and read on.

Sisters Agnes, Immaculata and Beatrice were warned by their Mother Superior never to discuss any of the events at Inniscoor. In 1971 Sister Agnes drowned while being rowed out to attend to a sick fisherman on board a Spanish trawler during a gale. In 1980 Sister Beatrice went to Cork, to a nursing home, where she ran the maternity ward until her death from natural causes in 1990, at the age of sixty-seven.

And the Order was perfectly happy to allow Sister Immaculata to live out her days in Inniscoor, content, more and more forgetful, looked after by the young novices, part of whose duties it was to care for the old and infirm, in the parish of Athgoe.

It might be yourselves some day, the Mother Superior had admonished, so do unto the good Sister as you would wish to be done by, in years to come should you, by God's good grace, reach such a ripe old age.

Grace looked up. 'Did you write this?' she asked.

Her brother nodded. The Vietnamese waiter appeared and asked if they would like some sandwiches.

'Egg and cress, if that would be possible, please,' said Paul and off the waiter went, so charmed by the young aristocrat that once again he seemed not to have noticed the banned jeans.

'How did you find this Inniscoor place? I take it that is where Oliver was born,' said Grace.

'Sister Immaculata would have delivered any baby born on or around June the fourteenth, nineteen fifity-four, at Inniscoor,' replied Paul. 'She remembers that when the baby was born an American couple arrived, to take the baby for "fostering".'

'Fostering?' Grace gave him a sceptical look.

Paul shrugged. 'Informal adoption would be more accurate.'

Grace snorted. 'Illegal adoption, it sounds to me.'

Her brother smiled. 'Illegal is about right.'

Grace, intrigued, returned her attention to the pages.

The infant was taken from his mother's breast, just four hours after the birth.

'Oh my God,' she breathed.

The mother, Helen Costello, was inconsolable. She sobbed for weeks, mourning the theft – her words – of the child she had called Oliver.

Grace glanced at her brother. He had a look of studied calm on his face, not unlike the expression on the oil painting of their own mother, Elizabeth, in the library at Crough Lake. It was close to serene.

She carried on reading:

> The American couple were called Webster. They arrived, according to Sister Immaculata, in an old Alvis shooting-brake with an Irish driver, who had a Kerry accent.
>
> A check of hotels in and around Limerick revealed that the Cashel Bay Hotel, not far from the airport, had in the late forties and early fifties, not one but two Alvis shooting-brakes.

'Paul, this is the business,' remarked Grace, thinking to herself that her brother might be able to make quite a contribution to Zeralda now that he was getting his act together. She returned to the report.

> And the present owners have, in their wine cellar, boxes containing old guest books going back to 1873.

Grace experienced a twinge of apprehension. Until now, the notion of ever actually tracing the Oliver child, a man now, forty-three years old if he were alive, had been just that. A notion, an abstract concept.

But as she read Paul's close-typed pages, the fact of a possible real, living, sweating, laughing (bad-tempered? sweetness-and-light? Who knew?) half-brother, fourteen years her senior, filled her with a variety of emotions.

Would he be successful? A down-and-out? Soldier? Salesman? Doctor? Janitor?

Grace ignored the waiter as he set down two plates of sandwiches and, aware of Paul's impatience, she read more.

> In the month of June 1954, a couple from the USA rented two adjoining rooms at the Cashel Bay Hotel, in the name of Pringle. They were accompanied by a young woman of South American appearance, with a baby just a few months old. She was in the adjoining room. They checked in on June the 3rd and left on June the 16th. The bill came to the princely sum of £92 16s 8d. which included the hire of one Alvis shooting-brake, with driver, on four occasions, including the 13th and 14th of June.

There the document ended.

Paul popped a sandwich into his mouth, triumphantly.

Grace gazed over it again, in its entirety, reading rapidly. Then she stopped Paul's hand as he raised another egg and cress sandwich to his mouth.

'You're still chewing the last one. You'll get indigestion,' she said.

'So what do you think?' asked Paul, pleased with himself.

'That South American woman with a baby in the next room, what was that all about?'

Paul grinned. 'If they were to acquire a brand-new baby, wouldn't they need a wet nurse, also someone who knew all about babies, having one of her own?'

Grace crossed her legs and gazed at him. 'I think you've done brilliantly. In fact the only thing lacking is an address for this Pringle/Webster couple.'

Paul seemed to be chewing his sandwich, preoccupied, then he met her gaze. '1548 Madison Avenue, Manhattan, New York City.' He dabbed a crumb from his mouth and beamed. 'Did I tell you I've got an album to do? We've recorded the first two tracks.'

'Paul, I'm glad for you but this is just a tad more serious. We have to contact Darcy.'

'Why? She's doing it her way. I could be wrong. Let Darcy worm some more out of Pronsias Stevenson, two angles of attack.'

Boy, thought Grace, a flash of his father, after all those years. But Darcy's playroom rages still haunted her half-sister. 'We can't track down Oliver without her being in on the act,' she argued. 'You know what she's like.'

Paul thought hard. To her surprise, Grace found herself waiting for his opinion. His new confidence was almost tangible. Maybe living in the shadow of Big Jack had inhibited the boy. Maybe – she felt guilty at the heresy – it had affected them all.

Finally Paul said, 'Not just yet. Of course we shall share with her anything of moment.'

'Like two hundred and eighteen million dollars . . .'

'Like one fourth of two hundred and eighteen million dollars,' replied Paul, gently.

Grace smiled. She touched her brother's hand. 'OK, go to New York, see what you can find,' she said.

7

Alison Clancy was working late. The contracts for the Houston project, all completed and signed at breakneck speed because of Zeralda's urgent requirement for the initial payments, were receiving her intense scrutiny.

The provision of a helicopter to facilitate her visit to the big three oil corporations, the rooftop welcomes, the board-room exchanges of signatures, all those things conspired to make Zeralda's attorney uneasy. If she had been advising the other side, she would have queried the sudden rush for deal completion.

However, as she painstakingly picked through the clauses and sub-clauses, nothing very daunting jumped off the pages. Maybe she was getting paranoid.

Earlier that day, while the now-deserted Zeralda complex had been humming with activity, her friend Martin Dorman, financial editor of the *Wall Street Journal*, had phoned to say that the whispering campaign against Zeralda seemed, for the present, to have dried up. And Tod Santez had e.mailed Grace from NASA to confirm that a payment had been dispatched that morning, to the Corporation's Boston office, of just over twenty-one million dollars.

All in all, it looked like Sebastian Tree's best efforts to weaken Zeralda in the market place had failed. For the moment.

Alison's telephone buzzed. She lifted the receiver. 'Alison Clancy . . .'

'Miss Clancy, it's Arthur Jamieson. Security. I have a Victor Jonson here. Something about a goldfish tank . . . ?'

Alison frowned. Jonson? Goldfish? Then she remembered. That was a code Telford & Pollard had suggested, to allow their investigator access to her at Zeralda without giving any cause for suspicion.

'Sure thing, Arthur,' she replied. 'Send him up.'

But Arthur, being a stickler for security procedures, sent a junior patrol guard up with Mr Jonson, a lean, affable man of medium height, wearing average suit and unremarkable necktie, with a visitor's pass clipped to his top pocket. He carried a briefcase with a sticker of a goldfish on the side.

Alison thanked the guard and invited Jonson in. After closing the door and offering him a soda, which the private eye declined, she sat down facing him and enquired, 'So, what do you have for us?'

Jonson scratched his chin, which looked as if it needed shaving every hour, on the hour. 'Did you know,' he enquired, 'that Sebastian Tree is an adopted child?'

Pronsias Stevenson's lecture went surprisingly well. The Master of Magdalen, Sir Geoffrey Thomas, graced it with his presence, along with several members of Oxford University's Hebdomadal Court, which met at that time each week. And the undergraduate turn-out was gratifyingly strong.

He dwelt, wisely, not on the similarities but on the differences between the Irish and English laws of tort and seized the opportunity to expand his brief to cover many aspects of Irish and English law, their mutual genesis and the political and religious reasons behind each divergence.

His learned and amusing anecdotes went down well, and by the time he invited questions at the end the atmosphere was one of relaxed respect for a speaker who had shed light on a hitherto grey area concerning the law in each country.

The Dublin lawyer wound up his lecture with grace and humour, ending with the words, 'So there we have it, ladies and gentlemen, two neighbouring nations, separated not just by a common language, but by the myth of two similar legal systems. About as similar, in fact, as a wedding in church, and a divorce in Reno.'

Polite if slightly mystified laughter accompanied the applause. The Master thanked Pronsias, and supper at the high table completed what for the attorney had been a quite perfect day.

Next morning, a maid entered his room at eight with a cup of tea and the *Daily Telegraph*. She bade him good morning and said that breakfast would be served in the conservatory at nine.

Stevenson shaved and bathed, read the paper, listened to the news on the radio and, relaxed and comfortable, daringly decided against a necktie and went down to the conservatory in his Giorgio Armani sports coat and a blue cotton shirt, open at the neck.

Darcy was there already, pouring herself a cup of coffee. She wore a chocolate Chanel miniskirt and *café au lait* cotton top. Chocolate and *café au lait* court shoes by Prada. All in all, the effect was stunning.

'I hear you went down rather well,' she said. 'Last night.'

Stevenson smiled as he took his seat, reaching for his snow white napkin in its Georgian silver ring. 'I did my best to keep it light enough,' he replied. 'After all, the laws of tort are fairly boring, even to a roomful of academics.'

'Well Edward is delighted. And, I dare say,' she dipped a toast soldier into her decapitated soft-boiled egg and placed one slender end of it in her mouth, her eyes still on the house-guest, 'surprised.'

She smiled as she munched delicately. Stevenson glanced around, there was no place set for a third person.

'He had to leave early,' explained Darcy. 'It's oral today.'

'Oral?' asked Stevenson, mildly confused.

'Matric. Oral examinations. Beowulf. You know, Grendel, the monster's mother.'

'Ah,' the lawyer nodded.

In the trees bordering the walled garden, a woodpecker had started to drill away, rat-a-tat-a-tat, and in the distance a rooster crowed. The sky was a lazy, faded blue, the sun warm. Intimations of summer. Darcy dipped another toast soldier into her egg. 'It's going to be quite hot, don't you think?'

Stevenson smiled. 'I'm sorry, I was miles away.'

'I said, I think it could get quite hot. This morning . . .' her eyes held his.

Pronsias Stevenson had not the slightest doubt why Darcy had inveigled him over to Oxford. Ever since he had received the letter from Medevik & MacMorrow, showing the heirs' intention to claw back Jack Fitzrowan's legacy and leave the bastard son Oliver, if he were ever found, high and dry, the Dublin lawyer had understood the gloves were off.

It had taken him four working days, days that he had charged the Fitzrowan estate twelve thousand dollars for, to find the flaw in Michael Medevik's claim that Big Jack had no right to use the McDonnell Douglas two-hundred and seven million dollars as his own. And having satisfied himself the estate would win in a US courtroom, he would merely reply briefly and courteously to the Boston attorney, thanking him for his letter and saying he did not believe there was a case to answer. In other words, 'See you in court'.

He wondered if the heirs would go that far. Either way, it would only benefit both his reputation and the bank balance of Stevenson, Stevenson & Malahide.

It had been clear from the moment he bumped into Darcy in the lounge of the Shelbourne that here was a woman, beautiful by any standards, just thirty-two years old, who would stop at nothing in her determination to find out all the secrets of her late father's codicil. And in so doing, trace Oliver. Thus it seemed that Darcy was embarked upon a stratagem of her own, just in case the lawsuit failed, as Stevenson firmly believed it must.

Well, thought the solicitor (the hen-pecked solicitor, he contemplated, with the mad woman of Shalott for a wife) God forgive me but if that's the way of it, who am I to turn down such an approach?

And so, to Darcy's mild surprise, he smiled back and said, 'You know, Darcy, I do believe the climate might be a little warmer than before . . . You were going to play me some Bach, were you not?'

Darcy studied him appraisingly. 'Indeed. If that's what you would like.'

Pronsias Stevenson inclined his head, his eyes not leaving hers. 'I could, um, turn the pages for you . . .'

Jesus and Mary, said Darcy to herself, he seems to be up for it. And despite herself, she felt a *frisson* of excitement.

★

As *frissons* go, it was perceptive. Darcy had barely completed twenty-four bars of Bach's Fugue in E minor, when it became clear that Pronsias Stevenson was finding it difficult to concentrate on turning the pages. She stopped playing and turned to gaze at him, sitting beside her on the long stool she and Edward used for playing duets.

'What is it, Pronsias?' she asked softly, in that husky voice of hers.

Pronsias Stevenson raised his shoulders. 'I'm sorry,' he said, and to her surprise, the buttoned-up walking lawbook seemed almost diffident. 'I lost concentration.'

He met her gaze in a way which left a very personal, even intimate, opening. Darcy straightened her back, one hand still on the keyboard. 'And what has stolen your concentration, Pronsias Stevenson, attorney at law?'

Stevenson shrugged. For all his pretence of worldliness, this was an uncharted sea he was adrift upon.

Darcy ran a fingernail along her long, tanned thigh. 'It couldn't possibly be a . . . physical thing? Mmmm?'

Stevenson swallowed, his heart pounding. He was a good lawyer, though, and he knew there were times when it was more prudent not to speak.

Darcy Fitzrowan Bailey smiled. She stood up and faced him. 'Perhaps this little bit of cloth is distracting you? Let's see . . .' and to the good lawyer's astonishment, she undid the zip and let her skirt drop to the floor.

There she stood, the object of years of desire, in a skimpy cotton top, the merest pair of white silk briefs and her Prada court shoes.

'The servants,' he heard himself choke.

'We are alone,' she whispered, and leaning forward, kissed him gently on the mouth.

For a second, Pronsias Stevenson had a horrible thought: the entire moment was a set-up, and the proceedings were being caught on video. Then, as he tasted her freshness and felt her soft lips upon his mouth, this pillar of the Dublin Bar thought to himself, 'What the hell!' and he kissed her with surprising passion and a skill which he had long forgotten.

In fact, the passion and the skill of those kisses were maybe a pleasantly remembered art as far as the solicitor was concerned, but Darcy was completely unprepared for the floodgates of sensual emotions they unlocked. His tongue was both gentle and tantalizing, his breath fresh and cool, and as he held her with one arm, he deftly removed her top and briefs, running his hands unerringly over her erogenous zones, including some even Darcy had been unaware of.

'Pronsias, for God's sake . . .' she gasped as, merely by stroking her bottom and pressing a thumb against her flank he brought her to near orgasm. 'You *are* a dark horse, ohhh, that's wonderful . . .'

Pronsias Stevenson smiled enigmatically and continued to play his seducer like a well-tuned violin. And how was she to know the closest he had ever been to putting those skills into practice had been in his mind, as he perused the pages of *Three Hundred and Eight Ways to Improve Your Love Life*, which Martina had sent away for from a tasteful advertisement in the *Irish Gentlewoman*.

Martina the Mad had been appalled by the frankness and explicit nature of its contents, and the tome had been banished to the bottom of the Wolfe Tone replica bookcase. Pronsias, however, had taken to sneaking it into the bathroom to read late at night. And being a lawyer who had passed his Bar exams by dint of a photographic memory, there was not an erogenous zone, a use of dick, tongue, finger or toe, nor any trick of an erotic nature, which that photographic brain had not stored away.

And here was Darcy Fitzrowan Bailey, temptress and seductress, having the best sex of her life with a man she could previously scarcely have borne to be in the same room, nay the same county, with.

After it was over, and her lover lay dozing gently beside her, she lit a cigarette and stared, slightly dazed, at the ceiling.

After two Marlboro Lites Darcy was herself again. She turned to Stevenson and kissed him gently on the shoulder and chest. He stirred and stroked her hair.

'Pronsias . . .' she murmured.

'Mm–hmm?'

'I wonder if you would come up to my study and take a look at my research notes. See if you think I'm on the right track.'

'What research is that, my dear?' enquired the lawyer.

'Oh,' her hand stroked his thigh, 'I'm trying to trace this Oliver character. See if I can win the finder's fee. I mean, twelve and a half per cent of two hundred and eighteen million is over twenty-seven million dollars.'

Pronsias Stevenson turned on his side and looked at her, naked and slick with perspiration.

'Put on your shoes,' he said. 'Just the shoes.'

Darcy reached for one of her Prada shoes, then paused and glanced back at him. 'Then will you help me?'

Again the enigmatic smile. 'As much as I can.'

It was another twenty minutes before they showered and dressed, and climbed to Darcy's private study on the top floor.

Sergeant Joe Reilly was Boston Police Department's explosives expert. There was nothing about things that went bang he did not know. An ex-marine, Purple Heart and Bronze Star from Vietnam, Joe Reilly was respected by the FBI and the State Department field offices in Boston and throughout Massachusetts and New England. The Department sent him on all kinds of courses and to law enforcement conventions to keep up to date on the latest methods, from terrorists and crazy survivalist militias to common or garden safe robbers and licensed demolition workers.

'It was RDX. I figure commercially obtained, in the first place, from the Milwaukee Ordnance Corporation. About two pounds. Under the driver's seat. That much, the way it was placed, acted like a jet fighter's ejector seat, but more indiscriminate to anyone standing around.'

Tom Hanrahan scribbled in his notebook, and asked, 'Placed like that deliberately? That means a demolition pro.'

Reilly shook his head. 'The configuration of a Merc SL600's transmission tunnel and seat-well would shape the charge to produce that effect. All anyone had to do was slide the device under the seat, towards the back.'

'So we are not necessarily looking for a serious mechanic?' ventured Tom. They were in his cluttered office at Homicide. Marge had brought in two big mugs of coffee and the brand of chocolate-chip cookies that Joe Reilly was partial to.

Reilly bit into one of those and shook his head. 'The device was primed and activated simultaneously, by prolonged, i.e. more than three seconds' pressure on one of the electronic memory seat adjustment switches. That takes skill. You are looking for a professional outfit. This guy was targeted and blown up by very serious people.'

'Modus?' enquired Hanrahan, searching his desk for a secret stash of sugar lumps he kept for his coffee.

'It's a method used by Mo Muldene, but he's in Attica, eight to life. Also Jerry Hobermeyer, but he works out of LA and right now he's doing special effects on the new *Die Hard* movie – I made an enquiry. Which leaves, among the mechanics I know of, one William Billy Giuliano, of Atlantic City.'

Tom Hanrahan nodded and retrieved just one sugar lump from a drawer that housed his spare pistol holster. He wiped it on his trouser leg and dropped it into his coffee. 'Mob?' he more or less stated. With a name like Giuliano it was hardly an inspired guess.

'Sure thing. He is free-lance, but mostly with the Gambino and Luchese families. Respected. Not even a parking violation against him. Took out Charlie Bagarella's two sons and two brothers, one running a casino in Italy, after Bagarella turned federal witness.'

'Where is he now?'

'Hey, I'm just the bangs man. Try Tim Murray. He'll get a handle on Giuliano. Best bet. Unless you want to go to the Feds.'

Tom smiled. He sipped his coffee. Lieutenant Tim Murray was one of three experienced Homicide detectives on the Cold Case squad. Their remit was to follow up and track down homicide suspects where the case had been shelved by operational Homicide squads owing to pressure of new business or just passage of time. The record of the Cold Case squad was solid, and they had a sixty-four per cent success rate, going back to a 1964 double murder where the killer had been arrested only a few months ago.

Tom called through to his secretary, 'Marge . . . ?'

'Yeah?'

'Is Tim Murray in? Along the corridor?'

'Hang on . . .'

The detective and Joe Reilly waited, relaxed, until Marge appeared in the doorway. 'Sure thing. He'll be there all morning.'

'OK, ask Jimmy to get me a printout on one William Billy Giuliano, from Atlantic City. Made man. Pro mechanic.'

'Right away.' Marge left. Tom Hanrahan thanked the bomb man and ambled along to the Cold Case office. He sat with Tim Murray for a few minutes, chewing the fat. Then Jimmy Fitz came in, with an NYPD printout, which Tom passed over to Murray.

It took Lieutenant Tim Murray two hours and four minutes to learn that Billy Giuliano was back in Atlantic City, after a four-day visit to 'Rhode Island and around there'. Rhode Island was less than an hour's drive from Boston.

By 3.07, Lieutenant Tom Hanrahan had been in touch with Number One Police Plaza, Manhattan South, and had arranged with his opposite number in NYPD to have Giuliano taken in for questioning.

'Thank God he's in New York,' he remarked to Danny the Wop, who had just come in. New York City had a different set of laws about arresting and holding suspects. In Boston, state law insisted that a suspect had to be charged before he could be held against his will. There were, of course, ways around that, but all in all, New York was good in this case.

'You wanna come?' Hanrahan asked Tarantola.

'Why not?' replied the sergeant. 'We can talk some more about the Fitzrowan thing on the way down.'

Tom Hanrahan shook his head. 'Never give up, do you?'

Dan Tarantola shrugged. 'Nope,' he replied.

The surviving mafia chieftains in and around Boston were alarmed. Just as they had begun to write off the Flamingo and Carmine Genovese killings as some aberration. Maybe an old score being settled, not their problem, they had figured. Then, dust settled, Sal Spatola and Dion Stomparelo are suddenly blown to smithereens right in the heart of their own turf, North Boston, Little Italy.

'Somebody is taking on the *cosa*,' growled Tomasso Riccobono, who it was rumoured sat for hours on end watching Al Pacino in *Carlito's Way*, and smoked forty a day, just so he could talk like him.

Riccobono was one of the four young hoodlum bosses who had been in the Ciao Bambino that time Peter Girolo had sipped his soda and observed them. Riccobono was one of the three survivors.

The other two were also present, in the darkened upstairs back room of the Cucina Napolitana spaghetti place on Salem Street, not far from Paul Revere's birthplace; Tony Bontate and Vito Greco.

Bontate, Greco, Spatola, Riccobono. These were all illustrious names in the mythology of the Sicilian mafia. Their fame had been won by the *uomi di rispettari*, the men of respect, who for three generations had dominated organized crime in the USA and in Italy, including the Vatican.

But this new generation, Tomasso Riccobono, Tony Bontate, Vito Greco and the late Salvatore Spatola had paid scant heed to the serious business of maintaining respect for their family names. Loose women, flashy, expensive European automobiles, bloody murder and needless violence for some imagined act of disrespect, or the merest whim, the personal drug abuse, the strutting around town like boxers or baseball stars, the indiscretion. All of that. All of that had turned the sprung steel of Boston's and the north-east's *cosa nostra* to shit.

They had thought nothing could touch them. Until recent professional hits on the three most able *capos*, and the impunity with which they had been carried out. And the absence of any obvious suspects. All of this had finally begun to touch them.

'No fuckin body is safe,' declared Tony Bontate, with his customary perception.

'And we do not,' said Vito Greco, 'have idea one about who is behind it. I mean, I talk to the Lucheses, they know shit. I get word to the *capo di tutti capi* inside Florence. Zilch. Nobody in Rhode Island –'

'Nobody in Vegas,' added Bontate, not willing to appear unconnected in the nationwide affairs of the mob. 'Nobody in Atlantic City . . .'

'And nobody in Miami,' growled Riccobono, who had actually taken to wearing a long leather coat, like Carlito Brigante in the movie.

In the street below, it would be no secret that a mafia council was in progress, for there were three carloads of soldiers parked outside, hoodlums on the doors front and back, personal bodyguards on the stairs from the pasta place below, and guys on street corners ready to radio a warning of any undercover cop presence. Only in the upstairs back room itself were there no footsoldiers. For this was a very private council of war.

Vito Greco poured himself a shot of grappa, from its flask on the check table cloth. 'So this is not, these fuckin murders, they are not sanctioned by the man, by the top don himself; they are not part of some fuckin *cosa* strategy . . . So we're talkin about some fuckin maverick. Some crazy person.'

'Wrong,' spoke a voice from a shadowy corner, and as the three hoodlum *capi* scrambled for their pieces, two men stepped forward from the darkness either side of a big old country dresser beside the doorway. One held a silenced .45 Uzi, the other a short-barrelled Remington pump gun. The voice went on, in Sicilian patois, 'Die if you want, gentlemen. Or listen first. Maybe you don't have to.'

The three sat motionless. Riccobono had got his two pistols out, held ready. The other two had their hands frozen on the butts, weapons only half-drawn.

'The decision,' went on Peter Girolo, as he too stepped into the gloom, 'is yours.'

Tomasso Riccobono, thirty-four years old, just sat and stared. The appearance of Peter Girolo in this room, at this time, was just about the worst news he could have imagined. For Girolo and his own father, Rosario Riccobono, presently languishing in Marion prison, eight to fourteen for conspiracy and racketeering, had been senior *capi* in the East Coast *cosa nostra*. And Girolo, as far as Tomasso had been aware, was still in Marion on the next landing to his father.

Fuck. Tommy Riccobono cursed himself for failing to visit his papa like a good Italian son. For here was Girolo with two men whose very presence, armed or unarmed, was even worse news than Don Peter Girolo.

The one with the Uzi was Rocco Trafficante, made man of the Luchese family and chief bodyguard to the wife and son of the *capo di tutti capi* himself, who continued to run Italian-American organized crime from deep inside Florence supermax, in the Colorado desert.

And the stocky man with the Remington pump was the stuff of nightmares. Joey Buscetta. Enforcer for the Five Families. His leathery face had seen it all. His battered ears had heard countless cries for mercy, the screams of the bereaved, the last coughing gasps of those who had the life beaten out of them.

In his fear, Riccobono was reminded of the cartoon character Deputy Dawg, Buscetta's face was like that. Fear does things like that. And, like Greco and Bontate, having recognized those three legends from the old mafia, Tomasso Riccobono had no illusions left about who was coming after the Boston Syndicate. It was the mob, and the Flamingo killings, the murders of Carmine Genovese and his uncle Giuseppe, the bomb that blew Sal Spatola over a street block into Copp's Hill Cemetery . . . all had been done with the knowledge and agreement of the mob. Of those at the very top.

'So,' Girolo took charge, 'guns on the table, please.'

The three apprehensive gangsters complied, laying their automatic pistols on the check table cloth.

Bontate glanced at the door to the stairs down to the main restaurant. 'You killed them all . . . ?' he enquired, unwilling to hear the answer.

Girolo smiled, without mirth. He pulled up a chair and sat facing them. Buscetta and Trafficante remained motionless, Uzi and shot-gun trained on them.

'What do you want, Girolo?' asked Riccobono.

'Everything,' replied Peter Girolo. 'Everything that belongs to the mob.'

The north end of Madison Avenue is not such a smart part of town as the street name implies. Life here can get a little rough, from time to time. Set between 91st and 92nd Street, it was probably more comfortable in the 1950s, thought Paul Fitzrowan to himself as he gazed up at the grey stone building, number 1548. There was a fruit shop, a shabby delicatessen, a shabbier convenience-food place, a laundromat and a cramped travel agency with dirty windows.

This was a part of town where people stopped and had conversations with each other. In other words, it was more of a neighbourhood than around the 60s and 80s, with their pricey Euro-trash restaurants and their Armanis and Versaces, their Ralph Laurens and their glittering jewellers.

Paul studied the building. Apartment 14 was the one that the Pringle/Websters had entered in the Cashel Bay Hotel guest book. His heart quickened, as he stepped up to the doorway and pressed the buzzer button marked 14.

After eight or nine seconds he pressed it again. A voice squawked out from the tarnished metal grille. 'Who's that?'

'I have something for the Pringles,' said Paul, cursing himself for failing to say something more calculated to obtain access. Then he glanced around the street and realized nobody was going to give access in this part of town, except to well-known and trusted voices.

'Ain't nobody here.'

Paul digested this. 'Are you Mrs Pringle?' he enquired.

'No.'

'Webster?'

'What's that?'

'Is your name Webster?'

'No.'

'Listen, I'm sorry to be a pest, can you remember, ma'am, did anybody called Webster or Pringle ever live in your apartment?'

'No.'

'Is that no they did not, or no you don't know?'

'Fuckin fruitcake,' said the aged voice, and that was that.

Paul turned away, more disappointed than he knew he had any right to feel. New York City was peopled by transients. It had been optimistic of him to imagine that the Websters/Pringles would have still been at that address, or that either of the names they had given might be genuine. Or even the address.

He sighed and, as he turned to go, noticed an old man in a battered fedora and shabby brown suit sitting outside the laundromat on a wooden kitchen chair, reading a two-week-old copy of *Corriera della Sera.*

'Excuse me,' said Paul.

The old man, a very old man, turned slowly and peered at him through tinted glasses.

'*Si?*' his voice was trembly with age. Paul was reminded of Sister Immaculata.

'Sir, have you lived here a long time?'

'Eighty-four . . .' The old guy was smart as a whip. 'I'm eighty-four years old.'

'Congratulations. When did you come to the land of the free?'

'Nineteen thirty-four. September.'

'And have you always lived here?'

'Why you ask? You from the government?'

Paul laughed. The old man's eyes glinted with something close to amusement.

'I'm from Ireland,' said Paul. 'I'm trying to trace some relations.'

The ancient Italian nodded, then volunteered, 'I been around here since forty-eight.' And with pride, 'This is my laundromat.'

'I see,' said Paul. 'Business good?'

The old man made a pained expression. 'It's a goddam laundromat, fella. I ain't takin no vacations in Aspen.'

'Couple called –' Paul stopped himself, changed tack. 'Couple who lived in that building over there. Apartment 14, in the early fifties, say nineteen fifty-four . . .' This is impossible, he thought, I'm going to return to Boston empty handed.

162

A voice behind him said, 'The Rosses.'

Paul turned round. A slightly crippled man, leaning on a walking stick, somewhere in his middle fifties, bad teeth, kind eyes, gazed at him earnestly. 'The Rosses. Mr and Mrs. Used to deliver the papers. I was thirteen then.' He glanced down at his crippled leg. 'Rode a bicycle. Racer.'

'You sure?'

'Oh yeah.'

Paul took a deep breath. Here we go, he thought. 'Did they have any kids?' he asked.

'Kids, you say?'

Paul nodded.

The man with the gimp frowned, deep in thought. Then he said, 'Sure. Nineteen fifty-four. The year of the truck. They had a baby. Never stopped bawling. But they doted on it. Quite old for having babies, I remember thinking. But then, I was thirteen . . .'

'Can you remember where they went, Mr and Mrs Ross and the baby? When they left here.'

'How's that?' said the man. 'My hearing ain't so good no more.'

'Where did they go,' asked Paul, louder, 'when they moved on?'

The man who had been hit by a truck in 1954 nodded. 'That's what I heard, they went home. Back to the old country.'

Paul smiled, at least now he had a name.

'Thanks.' He reached in his back pocket and produced a twenty-dollar bill.

'Please,' said the gimp, offended, and turned to limp away.

'I could always use it,' said the old Italian.

Paul grinned at such impertinence and strolled back towards the better part of town.

In the upstairs room at Cucina Napolitana, with Rocco Trafficante and Joey Buscetta's guns trained on them, the three surviving young *capi mafiosi* had no alternative but to listen while a relaxed Peter Girolo explained to them, in reasonable tones, exactly what was expected of them from now on:

No drugs to be pushed among family or friends.

No drugs to be pushed in immediate neighbourhood of home or semi-legitimate business (except night-clubs).

No violence except in the normal conduct of 'business'.

No killing unless cleared with the *capo di capi*, Don Peter Girolo.

No high-profile strutting. (*Mafiosi* were supposed to be low-profile men of respect.)

No secrets from the boss, Don Girolo.

Weekly accounts to be presented to Joey Buscetta, who would be staying on as Don Girolo's enforcer for the immediate future.

Any family disagreements to be judged by Don Girolo, whose decision was final.

No business to be conducted without the knowledge and approval of Don Girolo himself.

'And finally,' said Girolo, in that same quiet, reasonable tone, 'we do not use the product ourselves. We do not drink to excess. And we exercise restraint and . . . compassion, in resolving the problems of our countrymen in our territory. Our business, gentlemen, is in storing up debts of honour, so that we can call them in whenever. Our business is in restoring the respect which serious men, that is, men like ourselves, have to earn. So dress nice, but not fancy. Listen to what our countrymen have to say. Let them fear our wrath, but trust in our friendship.'

Girolo sat back and watched them, reading their faces, their body language. 'So that's the deal. Are you in or out? Tell me right now.'

Riccobono met Girolo's eye. He nodded.

Girolo said, 'Good,' and turned his gaze upon Vito Greco.

Greco was not happy.

Girolo glanced at Tony Bontate. Bontate inclined his head. 'It's OK with me, Don Pietro.'

Girolo said, 'Good.' And gazed back at Greco. A moment passed. Then Girolo asked, 'Vito?'

Greco was clearly very angry. He thought about it, then declared, 'Mr Girolo I can't fuckin sit still for this. My father and his father built up our territory. Nobody just moves in wid a bit of fuckin muscle and says hand it over. No deal.'

Peter Girolo stared into the man's eyes. Greco stared back. This guy knows what he is doing, thought Girolo. This guy knows what he has just said. He respected that.

'It's nothin personal,' said Greco, without a trace of fear in his voice.

'Sure. I know,' replied Girolo, and in an instant his Sig Sauer P220 .45 automatic was in his right hand, arm extended, the muzzle just a couple of feet from Greco's face, aimed right between the eyes.

Greco gazed back, unflinching, waiting for the end.

And something surprising happened.

As Peter Girolo's fist tightened on the pistol, taking first pressure on the trigger, his eyes focused on the target, he remembered those ducks, winging their way across the bay, drake and hen, with three offspring. He remembered thinking, if only life could be that simple.

What the fuck am I doing with my life? asked a still, small voice, deep inside his soul. The inanimate target's eyes came into focus, as they blinked, still unafraid, resigned to the inevitable.

Girolo eased the cocked hammer back to the safe position. 'You are a brave man, Don Vito,' he said. 'Will you leave my territory? Start up someplace else? Cause me no problems?'

A clock ticked in the corner of the room. Outside in the street below some people were walking past, laughing and talking in Italian.

All eyes were on Vito Greco.

Finally, he asked, 'What can I take?'

Girolo nodded and lowered his pistol. 'Joey Buscetta will help you. I will not send you away without respect. Joey?' His eyes did not leave Greco's.

'*Si, Padrino?*'

'See to it that Don Vito leaves my territory with enough to buy in someplace else. Tell the *capo di tutti capi* that is my decision.'

'*Si, Padrino.*'

And Girolo suddenly felt the cold breath of fate. This is a mistake, he thought to himself. I should have killed him. Rule One. You are losing your touch, Pietro.

Round about the time that Paul Fitzrowan was way uptown on Madison Avenue, his brother-in-law was also in New York City, in the 14th Precinct House, shaking hands with Lieutenant Sam Vargos of New York Police Department's Homicide Division.

'Tom, how's it goin?' enquired Vargos.

'OK so far,' replied Tom Hanrahan. 'You know Sergeant Danny Tarantola, you two guys have met?'

'Sure. Hi, Danny. I got Giuliano in here.' Vargos led them along a corridor and paused at a steel-clad door. 'His lawyer is with him, Jenny Puzzo. I already charged him with whacking Gino Lombardi, the guy who blew up when he pulled the chain in the Rockaways pool-hall john three years ago. You want to look at the file?'

Tom shook his head. 'No thanks.' He glanced to Danny Tarantola, who had spent the flight quizzing him about exactly who was where on the day Big Jack got hit with the boom.

Tarantola shook his head. Tom knew that his colleague had only one agenda on this brief visit to New York, and that was the Fitzrowan murder theory. Billy Giuliano, explosives expert and known mob contract killer, was a secondary consideration.

'Fine,' said Vargos. 'All they know is you have requested his help in a separate Homicide investigation. They do not know, or need to know, that you're from out of town . . .'

Billy Giuliano was surprisingly young for a pro hit-man. At six two, one ninety pounds, he could have been a football player. And a good enough looking guy, in a dark skinned, Mediterranean way.

Jenny Puzzo was petite and mildly overweight, still trying to squeeze into the dark business suit she had once felt more comfortable in.

'This is Lieutenant Hanrahan,' announced Sam Vargos, staying by the open door. 'Maybe you can help him.'

'My client has not been read his Miranda rights,' said Jenny Puzzo.

'I don't see it going that way,' replied Hanrahan. 'If it looks like it, I am sure you will point that out.'

The woman attorney met his eye as he smiled some Irish charm at her. She seemed unimpressed. 'Me, too.' She opened her briefcase and took out a small tape recorder.

'Leave you to it,' said Vargos, pulling the door shut with a gentle 'clunk' on his way out.

Tom Hanrahan and Dan Tarantola sat across the table from Giuliano and his lawyer. Tom took a long, slim notebook from his inside breast pocket.

Giuliano gazed at them unmoved, calm, and said in a toneless voice with shades of the Bronx, 'Who's he?'

Jenny Puzzo glanced up, and turned her gaze on Tarantola.

'Sergeant Tarantola. I'm with the Lieutenant,' said Danny, and patted his jacket for a stick of gum.

'OK, Billy, goes like this,' said Tom. 'An informer tells us you closed the deal on Salvatore Spatola in Boston North End. He says it was you.'

'My client now does require to be read his rights under the Miranda Act,' announced Puzzo, pushing her glasses back on to the bridge of her nose.

'Maybe not. Maybe not. Maybe he didn't do it,' said Tom, in a conversational, easy-going way.

'Whadda you mean maybe I didn't do it?' intoned Giuliano, which was not a statement his lawyer appeared to find helpful.

'Billy, let me do the talking,' she ordered.

'Billy does not need to say word one,' said Dan Tarantola. 'But the Lieutenant is giving him a chance to deny involvement. Quite frankly – may I, Lieutenant?'

'Be my guest,' answered Tom Hanrahan.

Tarantola went on, 'Frankly it could damage your client to remain tongue-tied at this early stage.'

'Meaning?' asked Giuliano, to Jenny Puzzo's annoyance.

'Meaning,' replied Tom, 'maybe you're in the clear. Meaning, maybe I just need to eliminate you from our investigation.'

'We've already excluded Mo Muldene. He's in Attica doing for ever,' contributed Danny.

'No comment,' responded Giuliano, aware of his lawyer's agitation.

'And Jerry Hobermeyer is working on the new *Die Hard* movie,' said Hanrahan.

Giuliano's face expressed interest. 'Jerry got that? Damn! I coulda done that.'

Tom Hanrahan nodded in sympathy. 'Didn't I say that?' he asided to Tarantola. 'So, Billy. Sal Spatola. Is my informant right? Did you rig that sweet little bang that sent the creep into orbit with half a haircut?'

'OK, that does it.' Jenny Puzzo was as fierce as a small, plump guard dog. 'Miranda. Now. Or my client walks outta here.'

Tom shrugged and explained to the killer his rights.

When he had finished, Puzzo said to Giuliano, 'You don't need to answer. If I step in, you stop in mid sentence, OK?'

Giuliano nodded.

'So,' went on Tom, 'did you do that?'

'Lieutenant, I swear I had nothing to do wid that. That was Rhode Island business.'

Giuliano meant that the Italian Syndicate in New England would look to the strong mafia base in Rhode Island for a Boston contract.

Hanrahan nodded. 'My problem, Billy, is this. I have two surveil-lance photographs of you in Rhode Island, with dates on the frames. Two days before Spatola takes a flying lesson, using his Mercedes ejector seat. I can place you in Rhode Island, sure enough.'

'My client has nothing to say,' Jenny Puzzo countered swiftly.

'Hey, listen,' said Tom, 'maybe I don't think he did this, OK? Maybe give him a chance to convince me, Miss Puzzo.'

In the comparative silence, Puzzo and Giuliano had a whispered conversation. Then the attorney said, 'My client was not involved in the Spatola murder.'

Tom shrugged. 'That's fine. I just have to clear one thing up.' He stared into Giuliano's dead eyes. 'Tell me why you met with the man I *know* you met with. Tell me why you had to go to Rhode Island to meet with him. And you know exactly who I'm talking about.'

'Oh no no no no no!' exploded Jenny Puzzo. 'What is this? Detective school? Come on, guys . . .'

Dan Tarantola was cool. He leaned forward and gazed at Giuliano. 'Calm down, Miss Puzzo. Billy knows why we are asking that question. It's the one question that will get us out of here and back to Boston.'

'Boston?' asked Puzzo, slightly thrown.

'Sure, ma'am. Boston Police Homicide Unit.' Tom Hanrahan kept his eyes on Giuliano. 'So why were you with such a serious *cosa* man? Was he maybe asking you to take out Salvatore and you declined?'

'That means you said no,' contributed Tarantola, helpfully.

'I know from declined, already,' responded Giuliano, who did not like to be treated as a dumb electrical engineer from the Bronx. This was why, prison psychiatrists were to theorize, he had become a professional assassin.

'Sure you do,' went on Tom. 'Was that it?'

Jenny Puzzo remained silent. She realized that Hanrahan was in effect offering a trade. The Boston Lieutenant had just indicated that, if Giuliano told him who had ordered the murder of Sal Spatola, he was not all that interested in charging him with the crime.

This she could understand. Cops like Hanrahan and criminals like Billy Giuliano lived in a world of deals and plea bargains. Hanrahan clearly figured, if Giuliano was going inside, anyway, and probably for ever, for the Rockaway Beach booby-trap killing of Gino Lombardi three years before, there was less mileage from the detective's point of view in getting the bomber another life sentence than in learning who was behind the Spatola contract.

In other words, it was the mob Hanrahan was after, not her pro-killer client.

The mob had chosen Jenny Puzzo's firm to represent Billy Giuliano because it had a long and respectable history of looking after the New York *cosa nostra*. But it was their misfortune that this particular counsel had no time for the mafia. They had killed her cousin and her cousin's husband during a labour dispute eleven years before, when Jenny was just nineteen. She had no love for the mob, and during law school she had become an FBI informer. It was the Bureau which had encouraged her to join one of the *cosa*'s favoured law firms.

Nobody in the 14th Precinct, or in any part of NYPD, would ever be aware of this. Tom Hanrahan and Dan Tarantola certainly were not. But when it became clear to Jenny Puzzo that Hanrahan was trying to get a handle on the men behind the Boston car bomb, she chose to remain silent. With the inevitable result that Giuliano talked too much.

Somewhat surprised that Puzzo had not jumped down his throat, Tom Hanrahan watched Giuliano wrestle with his conscience. For Giuliano too had guessed his reply might just get him off the hook. At least for now.

Finally he nodded. 'Sure,' he said. 'Joey told me it was sanctioned from the very top.'

Not daring to glance in Jenny Puzzo's direction, but sensing the dice were rolling for him, Tom pressed on. 'Which Joey?'

Silence. Tom Hanrahan waited for the guy's lawyer to explode. But she did not. Even when Giuliano glanced at her.

After a long moment, Giuliano said just the one word: 'Buscetta.'

'OK. Thank you,' Hanrahan said simply, and stood up.

'That's it?' enquired Jenny Puzzo.

'That's it, ma'am.' Danny pressed the door buzzer and somebody let them out.

Two weeks later, thirty-one-year-old Jenny Puzzo was killed, apparently by muggers, on her way home from the office.

Diana Prentice knocked on her boss's door and entered. 'Paul has just phoned, Grace. He's returning from New York on the five o'clock flight from La Guardia and would you like to have supper?'

Grace looked up from her video screen and smiled at her PA. 'Don't tell me. House of Blues.' The House of Blues is an eclectic, young people's haunt just off Harvard Square, across the River Charles in Cambridge. It was backed by the actor Dan Ackroyd, one of the original Blues Brothers, and every night there is a bluesy, jazzy gig, with gospel singers at Sunday brunch. It was one of Paul's favourite spots.

Diana grinned. 'He did mention it.'

Grace shook her head, 'Kid brothers! See if we can get a table.'

'For two?'

'For three. I haven't seen much of the detective recently.'

'No problem. And Alison would like a word.'

Grace stretched and rubbed a hand over her face. It was a gesture Big Jack used to make. She logged off from her computer and said, 'Send her right in.'

A few minutes later, Alison Clancy was sitting across the big antique desk which Jack had found at an auction in New Orleans. She noticed that the wooden desk board with JOHN FITZROWAN − PRESIDENT in gold letters had been replaced by one with plain white lettering: GRACE HANRAHAN − PRESIDENT.

'Is Sebastian showing any sign of leaving?' she enquired.

Grace frowned. 'Not officially. He did some work that day, after our confrontation.' She shrugged. 'He has taken an extended weekend. I guess he's working out his next move.'

'You have to get rid of him, Grace. After what he did.'

'It's not so easy. Say he wanted to cut up rough. Where is our proof? The bastard has covered his tracks really well. And he's clever. He even admits to having had informal contacts with Tak Katakura . . . although he says it was on our behalf.'

'I can't believe he's clinging on.' Alison separated two files on her lap. 'You as good as told him you knew he tried to ruin us.'

'He has a golden contract with us,' said Grace. 'What would it cost to fire him?'

'One point four million,' replied the attorney without hesitation.

'Are you kidding? I would not pay him dollar one. Either we obtain enough evidence to justify summary dismissal, citing breach of contract, or we tough it out and hope Sebastian is wise enough to leave before I decide to take him to court.'

'I take it he has not signed the confidentiality clause?' enquired Alison.

Grace shook her head. 'Not so far.'

'We can't force him. He's astute. He will have taken advice.' Alison produced her Telford & Pollard file, which was the real reason for this meeting. She had started with a general review of the Sebastian Tree business because she did not want to appear either fanciful or over-involved in the family affairs of the late Jack Fitzrowan, her dead lover.

As she thought that, Alison Clancy finally accepted the truth, and her heart missed a beat. Warm and lusty though her affair with Jack had been, and affectionate, it was only after he was so abruptly removed from her life that she realized she had been falling in love with him. And even with his passing, the emotion was growing every day. It was a healing thing. As if he were still around.

Alison took a deep breath and handed the file to Jack's daughter. 'T & P are doing a thorough job. Did you know, for instance, that Sebastian is an adopted child?'

Grace shook her head.

Alison Clancy read from her own file: 'Adoptive parents Emily Jean and Joseph St John Tree, of Elgin Hill, San Francisco. Father was a boat builder, mother listed as housewife. Only child, no brothers or sisters, either natural or adopted.'

In the silence which followed, Alison waited as Grace contemplated this information. Then Grace said, 'Date of adoption?'

'August twenty-one,' replied Alison, 'nineteen fifty-four.'

Grace scratched her chin, then asked, 'Are there details of an adoption agency?'

'Unclear. He was a foster child, mother unknown, a foundling. Taken into care by the Santa Maria Home for Orphans, San Francisco, in July of that year, formally adopted by the Trees a month later.' After a pause, Alison went on, 'I know. It occurred to me too.'

Grace gazed at her video screen, her mind miles away. Finally she said, 'He is the same age as Oliver.'

Alison shrugged. 'So are thousands of others. Probably hundreds of them were orphans.'

Grace digested this. 'Telford and whoever . . .'

'Pollard.'

'Are they going to trace the natural parents?'

Alison nodded. 'They're going to try.'

Grace was silent for a moment, then she remarked, 'Is that not something?'

'Bizarre coincidence. They happen.' Alison indicated Grace's copy of the Telford investigative report. 'I suggest you don't leave this lying around, Grace.'

'I'll take it home.' Grace slipped the file into her briefcase, still thoughtful.

Harvard Square is not really a square at all, it is more of an enclave around the main campus of Harvard University.

Grace and Paul had taken a taxi there from 85 Mount Vernon Street, the late Sir Jack Fitzrowan's Boston mansion. It had twenty rooms, with priceless furniture and works of art, a garage for six limousines, an apartment above the garage mews and a separate staff flat in the basement.

Grace had been putting off going back to the imposing house ever since her return from the funeral and the reading of the Will. The mansion, in addition to Crough Lake, belonged to Paul, to keep in trust for the rest of the family. The new baronet had felt he did not want to make any decisions about the place until some time had passed, and when Paul had arrived in Boston a few days earlier, he had politely refused Grace's invitation to stay with her and Tom at Farragut Road in South Boston.

Mount Vernon Street, he had observed, only half in fun, was the family seat in America. And he intended, as fifteenth baronet, to make use of it. The entire staff had been kept on and the big house had been spotlessly maintained. It still had the comfortable, welcoming atmosphere which had been so often remarked upon when Sir Jack was alive.

As they sat in the House of Blues, listening to a four-piece band flown up from New Orleans, Paul told his sister all about his visit to 1548 Madison Avenue, including the old man outside his laundromat and the cripple's information about the Ross family, who had indeed acquired a child just weeks after Oliver's birth and illegal adoption in Galway.

Grace laughed when Paul recounted meeting the ancient Italian. '"It's a goddam laundromat," he says, "I ain't taking no vacations in Aspen . . ." Hey, here comes Boston's finest.' Paul glanced towards the door, raising a hand in welcome.

Grace's expression softened as she watched her detective husband making his way past the line of waiting customers and moving towards her. She had half expected him to phone and say he was on some homicide or other.

'What'll it be?' asked the waitress as Tom reached the table. 'They ordered already.'

'Caesar salad,' said Tom, 'and blackened tuna, side order of fries.' He kissed Grace, said hello to her brother and took a seat.

'How's crime?' asked Paul.

'Crime is terrific. Don't knock it. It pays the rent,' replied Tom, aware he was deliberately ignoring the several million dollars of his wife, which might be considered to make a small contribution.

'Paul has found where Oliver was taken to,' said Grace.

'No kidding, which Oliver is that?' asked Tom, expressionless.

Paul grinned. He could not imagine anyone not liking his brother-in-law. 'This is really your territory. Bit of gumshoeing around, took me to New York City.'

Tom nodded. 'Sure, I heard.' He was too straightforward a guy to pretend his wife did not share such family business with him.

'And what did I find?'

'Surprise me. No Oliver, I bet.'

'How do you know?' asked Paul, deflated.

'It's all over your face, kid. Finding this long lost orphan of your daddy's, half-brother to you and Grace, which is as close as Darcy is, think about that.' Tom's voice became more serious. 'It's a drama, this codicil, kind of a bombshell for all of you.' Here he put an understanding hand on his wife's leg, gave it a squeeze. 'If you had found Oliver . . .' he thought about that, smiled, 'I would have known.'

'From my face,' Paul nodded.

'Sure. From your eyes.' He hijacked a passing waitress. 'Make mine a Michelob, two more of those – what's that? A white wine and Guinness? Roger that. Thank you.' Having taken care of the drinks, Tom went on, 'So, what *did* you find?'

'I found the house where a couple whom I believe were given the newborn baby lived.'

'Whom is impressive, Paul. My wife, your sister, she wants me to quit saying ain't and go for the whoms, am I right, Gracey?'

Grace shook her head. Paul, amused, continued. 'This couple, who called themselves Webster or Pringle in Ireland, in the week bracketing the birth of Oliver, gave an address on Madison Avenue, New York. I went there and as luck would have it, located the paper boy who delivered there in the year of Oliver's birth. He remembered the couple, he remembered a new baby suddenly on the scene. He remembered them leaving New York, a few years later, and he believes they went back to Ireland.'

Tom digested this. 'You get an address, back in the aul' sod?'

Paul shook his head. 'No, but I got their real name. It was Ross. Mr and Mrs Ross. The paper boy, he's in his fifties.'

The blues band had just finished 'Mustang Sally'. Tom joined in the applause, then he turned back. 'I need men with luck like you in Homicide. But you don't get promoted, Paul. Where are they now? Where is the baby? This forty-three-year-old baby? Back in Ireland? Or maybe he came back here. Maybe he joined the navy. What passport does he hold? Maybe he's dead. Maybe he's a missionary in fuckin China.'

'I wish you wouldn't swear like that,' said Grace.

'He's giving us professional advice, Grace. How can he be a

cop without swearing?' said Paul, and laughed at Tom's pained expression.

'Honey, I'm sorry.' Tom kissed her on the cheek. 'It won't happen again.'

She held his arm and kissed him back lightly. Paul smiled and hoped one day he would feel like that about someone. And that she would feel like that about him.

'There will be details of people called Ross,' he said, 'with the New York City authorities. Maybe Immigration if they were first generation – Irish to US citizen, or just residence permits. And in Dublin, I can trawl through Rosses buying property in the late fifties.'

Tom gazed at him. The kid has changed, he thought. This kid is more like a grown-up, these days.

The waitress brought the drinks and set them down as the band kicked into 'Polk Salad Annie', an old Tony Joe White number from the Mississippi white-trash swamps.

'Talking about orphans,' volunteered Grace, 'I learned today that Sebastian Tree is also adopted. Although legally, in his case.'

Paul knew all about Sebastian; his sister had told him during the last few days. 'Now there's a coincidence,' he said.

'It gets better,' Grace went on. 'Sebastian was born in the same year as Oliver.'

Tom and Paul exchanged knowing looks as if to say, poor woman, now she's going to imagine every adopted man aged forty-three might be this long lost love child and inheritor of over two hundred million dollars.

'But his adoptive parents are Americans from way back,' Grace pressed on. 'Tree is a New England name. They lived in San Francisco. His father was a boat builder.'

Tom Hanrahan stopped his beer half-way to his mouth. He set the glass down and stared thoughtfully at the table.

'*Polk Salad Annie . . .*' sang the singer with the band, '*Where do y'all come from?*'

After a moment Tom said, quietly, 'Whose father?'

'Sebastian's,' his wife replied.

'In San Francisco?'

'Right.'

'Any other stuff on the young Sebastian?' asked the detective casually.

Grace thought for a moment, 'Um, UCLA, Harvard Business . . . played football at college . . . Got some girl in the family way when he was seventeen . . . Daddy settled that with his cheque book . . . windsurf champion at Big Sur, nineteen seventy-four and -five . . .'

For Tom, the music had ceased to exist. He figured he knew what the answer to his next question was going to be. 'Windsurf, good for him. Any other nautical experience?'

Grace was enjoying holding her husband's undivided attention. 'Sure. He crewed the runner up in the Frisco–Vancouver–Frisco race. Three years in a row.'

Tom nodded, reaching for his pack of Winstons. 'So the guy is a sailor, then.'

'You bet.' Grace nodded. 'I guess it was inevitable, with his father being a boat builder. He built racing yachts. I am surprised Daddy never mentioned that.'

Hanrahan held his Homicide Zippo to the end of his cigarette, lit up and inhaled. 'I don't believe Jack ever knew that,' he murmured, and half closed his eyes as the smoke drifted from his mouth and nostrils.

He looked, thought Paul, like a contented dragon. But Lieutenant of Detectives Tom Hanrahan did not feel contented. He felt that tightness in his stomach which made his work, as the man said, not so much a vocation as a disease. And he owed Danny the Wop Tarantola an apology, for the Homicide Sergeant had been right all along.

Jack Fitzrowan's death at sea had probably been no accident. It had been murder.

As Tom Hanrahan sipped his beer, he resolved to bring the killer of his wife's father, and his own close friend, to justice.

It was just the kind of thing he was good at.

8

The slightly scratched tones of Dame Myra Hess playing 'Jesu, Joy of Man's Desiring' wavered around the big sitting room of Peter Girolo's Beaver Place apartment.

Girolo's collection of old 78 rpm records had been kept for him by the faithful Joey Buscetta while he had been in the slammer. He sat relaxed in a comfortable easy chair, eyes focused on nothing in particular, letting the music get to him.

In one hand was his usual tumbler of soda with a slice of lime. In the other, a cigar. It was one of the few indulgences he allowed himself. Partagas, they were his favourites. Partagas Number Threes.

Girolo was worried. He was worried about himself. For the first time in his life he had wavered in the fulfilment of his destiny, as taught to him by one of the mafia's most secret inner councils, the Scuola Dottrina Cosa Nostra, literally, the school of the doctrine of our thing.

The Scuola was at the heart of Sicily's ancient resistance movement, the original mafia – as much a spirit of antagonism towards authority and legal rule as a conspiracy of the lawless – which had made the island ungovernable since the Norman mercenary, Robert Guiscard, was made ruler of Sicily by the pope in the eleventh century. The English crusader king, Richard the Lionheart, had also attempted to rule Sicily and retired hurt, as had the German Papal Prince Manfred in 1266.

The island had been occupied by Romans, Normans, Germans, Moors and Turks. But native Sicilian resistance, deep rooted and cloaked in the secrecy of *omerta*, a conspiracy of silence, had always protected and asserted the natives' independence from outside rule. Which included metropolitan Italy.

Sicilian aristocrats had, from the beginning of Christianity, maintained close and secret relations with the Vatican, with the result that many grandiose schemes and manoeuvres to destroy the deep rooted and highly educated principal families of the resistance, the mafia, had been doomed before they started.

Times changed. Many Sicilians left to find work in Naples and Rome, Florence and Milan, far to the north. Later, there was mass emigration to America. The old mafia was taken over by criminal elements, who understood that its code of *omerta* and its essential Moorish ruthlessness and cruelty could be used to dominate organized crime in Italy and the USA.

However, the wiser of the new *mafiosi* also appreciated that ancient links with the Vatican were too advantageous to abandon. By dint of skilful diplomacy they reached an agreement with the original landowning Sicilian families from the hills and the mountain regions, and with those in control of Palermo's banking system, whereby the Scuola Dottrina Cosa Nostra was created. Each year, one or two bright children were handed over to the Scuola to be trained in the secret ways of the mafia, to be educated in the best universities, and to be sent wherever in the world the *cosa*'s affairs would benefit from their skills. Knights of the mafia. Samurai, if you like.

Pietro Michelangelo Girolo was one of those. The mafia was him, and he was the mafia. This was what he knew and it was his driving force. He had been educated never to question it, and he never had.

Until now. For as he sat in that room, without lights, while the sun went down, listening to the scratched but so moving tones of 'Jesu, Joy of Man's Desiring', Peter Girolo had only two images going through his mind: those ducks, winging their innocent way across the bay, and the grave, already calculating faces of the two kids in the back of Albert Genovese's Cadillac. *Couple of kids whose father had to go*, Genovese had said. *Their mamma went crazy. Took her own life . . .* And they had both shrugged and gone on planning to restore good order and discipline to Boston and the eastern seaboard, the territory the mob had assigned to their good and trusted *capo*, Peter Girolo.

As the scratched record played on, its pure strains of classical music filling the room, Girolo reflected that in order to bring Boston to heel, he had made more than a few orphans in the last couple of months. For all he knew, maybe a couple more girls, their husbands necessary victims in Girolo's business programme, were even now on the verge of madness or suicide.

He remembered the face of Vito Greco, composed in courage of a misplaced kind, expecting to be murdered within seconds by himself, Peter Michelangelo Girolo, the man who was a child of the Sicilian way. And he realized, with breathtaking clarity, why those two kids, dressed up for their flight to the old country, had struck such a chord that he could not get them out of his mind . . . They were destined for the same life as himself.

Those two orphaned children were the property of the mafia, and they were being handed over by Albert Genovese to the tender mercies of the Scuola. Why else would they be sent to Sicily?

In twenty years' time, that six-year-old boy might be the *cosa*'s top assassin. And the sixty-three-year-old Don Peter Girolo might well be his target. Girolo smiled wryly and took a puff on his cigar. It would, of course, be nothing personal. It would just be business. He shrugged and relaxed, trying to let the music soothe him. But something had changed. Looking into those doomed little faces, his emotion had been one of . . . pity. And he knew that pity had been not just for them, but for himself.

Before their tragedy, these had been two happy, boisterous kids. The signs had not yet been completely eradicated from their faces. Maybe one day he had been that innocent. That happy.

Girolo tried to shake himself out of such thoughts. What the hell was happening to him? One of the *cosa*'s most feared and respected chieftains. But four years in Marion had given him time to think, and deep in his mind, Peter Michelangelo Girolo knew that he was experiencing, for the first time in his life, very real doubts about his way of life.

Pronsias Stevenson sat in his Fitzwilliam Square office and read the draft of his letter to Michael Medevik.

21 April 1997

Dear Mr Medevik,

Zeralda Electronics Inc. and Estate of Sir John Fitzrowan Bt., MA MBA

Thank you for your letter of 12 April 1997.

I would draw your attention to US Federal Judge Koplowic's finding in the case of Lehman Toys Inc. of Worcester, Massachusetts v. Executors of Jacob Sydney Lehman, 14 October 1991.

Doubtless, upon consideration of Federal Judge Koplowic's ruling, you will advise your client that Zeralda Electronics Inc. has no claim upon the legal disbursements effected by the late Sir John Fitzrowan before his death.

I shall now be taking counsel's advice on whether or not your corporate client's President, Mrs Grace Fitzrowan Hanrahan, might have excluded herself from her late father's generous bequest of $2,684,000, by attempting to initiate a class action against the estate.

Yours faithfully

Pronsias P. Stevenson, MA LLD

The Dublin lawyer nodded to himself as he read and re-read the draft. He wanted there to be no mistaking the message he intended to convey between the polite if barbed lines. He imagined himself in Michael Medevik's position, for he needed to predict with accuracy the Boston attorney's reaction.

First, Medevik would send his legal assistants scurrying to obtain not only the Koplowic federal ruling but transcripts of the entire courtroom battle which preceded it. Next, he might make discreet contact, possibly on a social pretext, with Judge Ted Koplowic himself who, while based in Washington DC, was a fellow alumni of Medevik's from Harvard's Wadham House. Another generation to be sure, but those Wadham fraternity men did tend to stick together. And then? Stevenson felt that Medevik would come to the reluctant conclusion that his initial approach was flawed.

The Lehman Toys case had passed unremarked, it was only for a few thousand dollars, and the Koplowic ruling was hardly earth shattering, stating as it did that 'Where a corporation is wholly or not less than ninety-five per cent owned by its founder, who also holds the active office of corporation president, it is not necessary for that individual to obtain his nominal board's permission to expend or transfer funds, provided such action does not embarrass his corporation's fiscal liabilities or commitments.'

In other words, provided Zeralda had been left in a position to pay its debts, including wages, Jack Fitzrowan had been free to disburse any excess corporation funds as he chose.

'Always providing,' the judge had gone on, 'that such action is in all other respects legal and within Federal Revenue legislation.'

Pronsias Stevenson had discussed all of this with the head of his partnership's allied law firm in New York, and with his own senior partner, the sixty-seven-year-old Francis Malahide.

They had agreed there was only one course left open to Medevik which had a chance of success, and that would be to persuade the new board of Lehman Toys to appeal against the Koplowic ruling in the Supreme Court. But that would take years and would be prohibitively costly, Stevenson estimated several millions, for in order to use Lehman Toys as a vehicle, Zeralda would have to undertake both to recompense them and to bear the financial burden.

Maybe, with two-hundred and seven million dollars at stake, the Fitzrowan clan would think the gamble worth while. But a good attorney, and Medevik was the best, would be bound to advise that the odds against success were roughly four to one.

To follow up this right jab, Stevenson had chosen to deliver an uppercut in his warning that Grace Hanrahan risked being disqualified from inheriting anything at all by the very act of seeming to contest her late father's wishes, for it could be argued before that most unpredictable of animals, a jury, that she was merely using her position as President of Zeralda to obtain a personal financial advantage and was therefore, *de facto*, disputing Sir Jack Fitzrowan's codicil.

The wording stated plainly that any beneficiary who disputed the codicil was to be struck out of the Will. So if the jury found against her, Grace would have to return to the estate the $2,684,000 which Stevenson had only eleven days before paid into her personal account with a Bank of Boston offshoot in the Caribbean.

If Darcy and Paul had agreed, as members of the board of Zeralda, to sanction the class action against Jack Fitzrowan's estate, then they too could be construed as contesting the codicil and risk the same fate.

Stevenson felt something close to a warm glow at the symmetry of his approach. For if Darcy and Paul denied sanctioning Zeralda's action against the Fitzrowan estate, then the case, tentative enough, would collapse under its very own logic. For was the board of Zeralda not required to ratify any major decision concerning the Corporation, whether the transfer of funds, or the commencement of any potentially costly legal activity?

Stevenson smiled. There was now a strong possibility that Medevik would counsel his clients to drop Zeralda's class action, devised to claw back Oliver's lawful if hugely disproportionate share. And then? And then the hunt for Oliver would intensify. And that made Stevenson quietly content. For he would be back in control, and control was power and influence. And power and influence were reputation.

And reputation was very important to Pronsias Stevenson, MA LLD.

He pressed his intercom buzzer. 'Siobhan, that will be fine, let's Fedex this to Boston a.s.a.p.'

Siobhan came in for the draft and as she left, it seemed to her that the tight, buttoned-up old bastard was half-way to being human these days. Why, he had even smiled as he handed the document to her.

As the door closed behind his secretary, Pronsias Stevenson was still smiling. It was not huge, as smiles go, but there was most definitely an upturning at each side of the mouth, and a softening of the normally grave expression.

And behind the wistfully smiling Irish solicitor's eyes was not any thought of torts and variances, claims or counter-claims. Oh no, for Pronsias Stevenson was remembering. He was remembering that tanned and slender body, slick and bucking in unmitigated pleasure, as he took the object of seventeen years of unrequited lust for the third time in one morning.

He thought of the tiny white briefs, discarded, and Darcy Fitzrowan Bailey in nothing but a pair of expensive Italian shoes by somebody called Prada, shouting with abandon as he translated the words of page 191 ('Pleasure and the Ancient Persians') into deed.

And he smiled even more at the poor dear's anger when afterwards she had led him upstairs to her study, a kind of incredibly tasteful library-cum-sewing-room with computer terminal hooked into the Internet, and shown him the fruits of her researches into the origins and whereabouts of Oliver.

'Pronsias, darling . . . dearest Pronsias . . .' and she had licked at his ear, but by then even seventeen years of fantasy had been exhausted, and asked, softly, 'You know more, you randy old sausage, don't you?'

And when Stevenson had asked what she meant, Darcy had replied, 'You know where he went, I just know you do . . . You know who it was who took the baby from that poor kitchen maid.'

'Do I?' Stevenson asked, smiling coolly. 'I can assure you, my dear Darcy, I most certainly do not.'

A few more attempts at fawning and flattery were followed by blazing fury as that incredible woman, dubbed by *Vogue* 'one of the five most desirable women in Europe', came to understand that she had delivered up her perfect body, her most private tastes, *and had enjoyed it*, to this man who had no intentions of delivering up any vital, legal confidences concerning the key to over two hundred million dollars in return.

Pronsias Stevenson was still smiling when his secretary Siobhan came back in with the Medevik letter for signing. Mind you, he thought as he scribbled his indecipherable hieroglyphic, what a woman. And, despite himself, he found that the experience was something he could well do with again, at some time in the future.

But tell her about that night in 1954, as he had learned from others, as he had made it his business to learn, when the boy–child Oliver had been wrested from his child mother's bosom? Oh, no.

It would take more than a few hours of pleasure, however exquisite, to dislodge Pronsias Stevenson's best-kept secret. For secrecy was power. And power was as important to the Dublin lawyer as reputation.

He smiled as he pictured what those abandoned moments entwined with the delectable Darcy would do to his reputation. And he almost permitted himself a grin when he pictured the reaction of Martina the Mad, had she walked in on page 126, or even 58, which required a degree of agility he had never thought he possessed.

The strange thing was, at that very same moment, while shopping in the Chanel store in London's Sloane Street, Darcy Fitzrowan Bailey was thinking not dissimilar thoughts.

Back in Boston, it was just past two in the afternoon. Alison Clancy sat in the commissary, eating her Caesar salad and sipping a lacklustre diet soda, the consequence of a minor guilt trip after too many dippings into the M&M stash, when who should come striding over, big grin, large as life, but Sebastian Tree, tanned, relaxed and without a trace of either guilt or antagonism.

'Well, well, well,' he said, 'if it's not the saviour of the company. Mind if I join you? What's this, Alison, rabbit food? Hey you don't have to lose weight, look at you . . .'

Alarm bells.

Alison stared at him, less than welcoming, as he took a seat and set down his white plastic cup of coffee and a plate of macaroni, small portion.

'Surprised to see me?' he more stated than asked, and continued, 'Hell, I was mad at Grace for asking me to sign that goddam piece of paper. You know, the confidentiality contract.' He scooped up some pasta and went on, as he chewed, 'Then I figured, I bet everyone else has had to sign one. And I made some enquiries, I asked my secretary, I asked Security . . . you know Arthur . . . and sure enough,' he chuckled and waved his fork in the air, 'I guess I was getting paranoid.'

I don't believe this guy, Alison thought to herself.

'So,' said Tree, 'humble pie time. I came in a half-hour ago, apologized to Grace, handed in my signed thing, like everyone else . . .' He had paused, as if the thought had just struck him. 'Like you have, right?'

Alison looked him straight in the eye and replied of course, relieved she had taken the trouble to have every single employee sign an identical contract of secrecy, a vast item of administration, prudent enough but designed specifically to silence the firm's C E O, sitting across the table from her.

'And I owe you an apology, too. You did a terrific job, saved Zeralda's ass, Alison. I know Grace is talking to the family about a place on the board for you as a V P.' He nodded, asserting the veracity of this statement which was a pure lie, for if Grace had entertained any such idea she would first have discussed it with Alison, of that the Legal Exec had no doubt.

'Sebastian,' Alison responded, 'you are full of shit.'

Even this rolled off him, like water from a duck's back. Tree shrugged and dropped three sugars into his coffee. 'O K, I know you blame me for the . . . oversight.'

Oversight? The man had zero conscience.

'But,' smiled Tree, 'I am still here. And here I plan to remain.'

Alison gazed at him, looking him straight in the eye for a long moment. Then she said, very quietly, 'Sebastian, let's not fuck with each other. I know, and you know that I know, just what happened. Exactly. I know about the Katakura bid and I know about your attempt to ruin this Corporation.'

'Hey, hey, hey . . .' Sebastian Tree put his arms up, palms out, as if to ward off an attack. 'Harsh words. You can prove them?'

'If I could, you would be in front of a Grand Jury. But I have not finished yet. And when I have the evidence, this Corporation will come after you. So stay by all means. It will be easier to find you when the Feds come to arrest your sorry ass.'

Tree chewed thoughtfully, surprisingly unruffled. Finally he looked up. 'Well, Alison,' he replied, 'I have this contract. And I intend to see it through. Before I was in two minds, but you just convinced me.' He stared into her eyes, without blinking, for many seconds, then he smiled.

Except his eyes. As Alison sat in her office, an hour or so later, she remembered those eyes. They had been cold as Frog Pond in February. And that's cold.

Alison was perplexed. It was in her nature to go over conversations in her mind. Analysing them. Replaying them for nuance and inflection. Something about Sebastian Tree's controlled nonchalance had not been quite right. And she could not put her finger on it.

What the hell, she thought. Maybe she was getting too close to all this. It was Thursday, and she had planned to see Helen, an old law school friend, for supper. They were going to a small Italian place on Newbury that Helen was always going on about. It was called Ciao Bambino.

Ciao Bambino was a favourite haunt of the young mafia *capos* who had their pasta places, bars and delicatessens in Boston's North End, houses in the more expensive suburbs and kids at private schools. But all Helen knew was that they served great linguini.

Peter Girolo sat at a corner table, near the door. Two footsoldiers from Atlantic City, hand chosen by Joey Buscetta, sat at the next table covering the entrance and the back of the restaurant. Joey himself stood outside on the sidewalk, leaning against the navy blue Chrysler sedan which was Girolo's unobtrusive transport, and watching the street.

For now that the Sicilian don had taken a grip of the Boston mob, his profile had risen. Even *omerta* would not keep word of the new arrangement, and Vito Greco's banishment, from spreading within the closed ranks of the *cosa nostra*. So his personal security was to be taken more seriously, in case some ambitious young hoodlum, or an old vendetta, attempted to make a statement of a lethal nature.

Girolo had decided to visit the bar and restaurant from time to time, just to remind local mob bosses who was in charge, who was their boss, the *capo di capi*, in Boston and the north-east.

Tommy Riccobono was hard to spot at first, for the thousand-dollar leather jacket and Armani jeans had been replaced with a sober, grey-blue suit of European cut, slightly baggy, a white shirt and a bright blue and crimson necktie.

His two companions were similarly toned down and outside the silver Porsche was nowhere in sight. Instead, a Dodge two-door coupé in burgundy was parked across the street, with one of Riccobono's made men at the wheel, using mirrors and his eyes to watch out for problems.

But since the man who had ordered the killings of Boston's Italian organized crime syndicate chiefs had now taken charge of Boston's Italian organized crime syndicate, the chances of further trouble were minimal. Things were going to get quieter now. And more profitable.

Riccobono, instead of strutting his stuff at the bar, was sitting near the back, and the profound difference in his attitude and appearance pleased Don Peter Girolo. It was amazing what a look down the barrel of a .45 could do to make a guy see reason.

Girolo sipped his soda and contemplated his future, for he too had undergone a sea change. It had not been just the music in his apartment that evening, or the beauty of the sun going down, or the memory of those ducks making their innocent way across the bay. Something had happened, deep inside him, and nothing could ever be the same.

Being a highly intelligent man, the Sicilian understood that maybe he had reached an age in his life when the mafia was no longer his driving force. After all, what had he achieved? As he sat there in Ciao Bambino, Peter Girolo mentally did some reckoning; he was a wealthy enough man, with around $4.4 million tucked away in secret bank accounts, he had reached considerable heights in the *cosa*, with the entire eastern seaboard, including New York City, his for the taking, and his income from the Boston mob would be around two million every week, once he had reorganized things. Which would take about three months.

He commanded fear and respect, and to be frank with himself, he had enjoyed much of the life. The adrenalin involved was indeed a powerful drug, and his mentors in the old country had taught him how to harness it, to make him into a dangerous and calm adversary, which thus far had proved to be an undefeatable combination.

The Scuola had also taught Girolo the aesthetic satisfaction of being a top assassin. He was learned in the history of his profession, his art, and skilled in its myriad lethal ways. He could drop any man alive, regardless of height or weight or fighting ability, in just one second. And he had – more times than he could remember.

Which was a figure of speech, because Peter Girolo could in fact remember every act of violence, including murder, which he had ever committed. These were neither happy memories nor sad, certainly not exciting, and they were without remorse. They were just a part of his well-trained brain's accounting process.

He had mixed with legendary mafia figures, and some whom the world would be astonished to learn had the remotest link with organized crime. He had been blessed in a secret and probably blasphemous ceremony inside the vaults of the Vatican itself. A blessing which the rationalist in him had always thought had probably earned him eternal damnation.

And now, tonight, sitting in one of Boston's most chic Italian café-restaurants, Pietro Girolo knew he wanted out. And he knew this was something he could share with no one, certainly not the faithful Joey Buscetta, who was honour-bound to inform the *capo di tutti capi* of such an act of betrayal. For had not the child Pietro Girolo, at seven years old, sworn an oath on his blood and that of his local Scuola don, to remain in the *cosa nostra* for all time, until his last breath and his last drop of that same blood?

Sure he had, thought Girolo. And he felt a rare emotion; anger. For how could any organization visit such an obscenity on an innocent child?

Did he feel bound by that oath, in a dank room in the tiny chapel of an ancient Sicilian landowning family? Did he hell. But now that he had made the decision to get out, to whom could he turn?

Girolo was a loner. That was his strength. But he had always had the power of the mafia on call, the Joey Buscettas and Albert

189

Genoveses of this world. Could he survive entirely on his own? Really alone?

This was what the tall, good-looking gangster was reflecting upon when, across the restaurant, he saw someone he had not seen for four years. Girolo never forgot a face, and there was the young second counsel who had assisted in his defence throughout the trial in New York Supreme Court Number One, when the newspapers and the TV crime reporters were forecasting a minimum of three consecutive life sentences. But thanks to Girolo's superb defence team, the jury had found him not guilty on all but a minor revenue charge. And four years on, here he was, a free man.

He examined the woman, without appearing interested. She was eating with another young woman, who was almost as attractive, if more rounded.

What the hell was her name? Girolo cast his memory back to the time of his trial. First name . . . Alison. That was it, Alison Clancy. Second counsel with the firm of Rawlince, Brooke & Maine. He smiled to himself, she had been a bright star in those dark days of the trial. Whip smart, able, thunderous attention to detail, optimistic. He wondered if they had made her a partner. She certainly deserved it.

Girolo became aware that Tommy Riccobono was looking at him. He glanced across at the *capo* who gravely raised his wineglass in salute. Equally gravely, the man who had decided to get out raised his own glass in return. Both men inclined their heads, very slightly. Like steps in a sinister dance, they had just acknowledged each other's place in the mafia.

The uillean pipes produce an evocative, pre-medieval sound, a strange and moving discordant harmony which has graced and inspired the Celtic tribes since they were introduced to Ireland by Phoenician adventurer-traders before the dawn of Christianity.

'Uillean' is Gaelic for elbow, and sometimes the pipes are played slung over the shoulder and their bellows squeezed under the elbow like the more common bagpipes in Scottish and Irish pipe bands from Inverness through Cork to New York City. But the uillean pipes are smaller and more delicate, and they produce a reedier, more typically Irish sound.

When accompanied by the bodhrán, a deep-thunder drum, held in one hand and beaten with a double-headed stick, the effect on those with even a smidgen of Irish blood is to stir long-dormant tribal genes.

Thus Tom Hanrahan found himself at Joe Daly's wedding celébration in the back yard of the big patrolman's South Boston house, half-way through his third glass of Guinness stout and tapping feet with the best of them, as uillean (Detective Freeney), bodhrán (Sergeant Murphy) and fiddle (Motor-cycle Patrolman O'Connor) played jigs, reels and ancient Irish melodies.

Big Joe, at fifty-two, had astonished the PD by winning the heart of Nancy Gallagher, a civilian stenographer in Traffic, fourteen years his junior and as comely as Joe was large and battered. It was his second marriage, his first wife Mary having died three years before from gunshot wounds during a bungled drugstore hold-up by two thirteen-year-old kids from Mattapan.

Mary had stopped to buy some candles for their twenty-fourth wedding anniversary. It was a part of town she did not know well. Joe was devastated. He had hit a drink problem, roughed up one or two low-lifes, insulted his superiors, on occasion quite imaginatively. And even with all of the brotherhood understanding and supporting him, there had been one complaint too many and Sergeant Detective Joe Daly had found himself back in uniform as a plain and simple patrolman.

Larry Shauseau and the Commissioner had seen to it that Joe's pay remained commensurate with his years of service and his eleven commendations for valour.

Tom Hanrahan and Joe's former colleagues in Homicide had remained supportive but pessimistic about the big cop's future, even his survival in the force, when, it seemed overnight, he had pulled out of his nose-dive and slowly but surely became the same old Joe Daly they had all known and liked.

And the reason? Miss Nancy Gallagher, civilian stenographer and widow of Sergeant of Detectives Billy Kane, an NYPD

Narcotics cop who had been gunned down in Washington Square, South Manhattan, by two Afro-Caribbean pushers high on their own crack cocaine.

Nancy had come north to get away from New York. Her sister had found her a job among police officers, which had made her feel at home and given the young widow an insight into the life her late husband had lived, and what had motivated him to put it on the line just once too often.

She had watched Big Joe on his one-man auto-destruct mission and, for reasons known only to herself, had chosen to reach out a helping hand. She had gone to AA meetings with him, supported and encouraged him through the worst of the recovery programme, and restored his dignity and self-respect.

It had not been inevitable that they would fall for each other. But something magical had happened. Others in the Department quietly noticed, and held their breath for them. And now here they both were, just married and dancing a jig called 'Peter Byrne's Fancy', Joe as light on his feet as any Riverdancer, although sweating more than somewhat, his granite-hewn face sublime with happiness.

'Light on his feet,' observed Detective Tommy Boyle, sitting beside Hanrahan, as they watched the dancers, Grace among them, on the grass lawn hardened by lack of rain those last few weeks.

'He should save his energy,' remarked Larry Shauseau, Assistant to the Commissioner, leaning against the fence on Tom's other side.

'The boys ain't too bad . . .' announced Jimmy Fitz, as he came over with a jug of Guinness to top up their glasses.

'Considering five years ago they could not play note one,' agreed Shauseau.

Tom smiled. Everyone in the PD knew the story about Boston Police Department's pipe band.

About four years earlier one of their brethren, a bomb-squad sergeant named John Brady, had been killed trying to defuse a device planted by some extremist or other. The entire Police Department was moved by his death and messages of sympathy arrived from far and wide. The New York Police Department sent its fine pipe band to escort the cortège and to play at John Brady's graveside. It was a moving occasion and everyone commented on how fine the pipes and drums had sounded, how stirring and how fitting a send-off for a brave Irish-American to have had.

So much praise was heaped upon the NYPD pipe band, in fact, that during the wake a number of Boston's finest decided to form their own Celtic pipe band, and to that end a good number of officers put some dollars into the kitty to purchase musical equipment and to hire some bagpipe tutors.

The embryonic pipe band began to meet every Tuesday and Thursday evening, duty rosters permitting. And as the wheat was sorted from the chaff, those duty rosters were arranged so that the more promising bagpipe and side drum players, and Sergeant Dennis 'Molly' Malone on the big drum, the clanbeag, would be free to practise.

The band became the talk of Boston PD. After about six months it was generally agreed that, from the terrible caterwauling beginnings, there were occasional almost recognizable tunes emerging from the discordant bedlam.

Sadly, around this time, another Boston officer fell in the line of duty, shot dead in a liquor-store robbery. Public sympathy was again huge, and the funeral was attended by hundreds of police officers, many from forces as far away as Philadelphia and New York City. But this time, Boston Police Department's own pipe band insisted on performing the honours, playing the cortège on its route to the cemetery and again at the graveside.

Of course, there was no disrespect intended, and those men's hearts were for sure in the right place. But even the most sincere mourners soon found that among the tears of grief were tears of a different kind: tears of bottled-up laughter. For the Boston Police Pipe Band, God bless them, had not really been ready to be let loose on an unsuspecting public, and certainly not at an affair which demanded pomp and dignity.

Heads bowed, shoulders heaving, afraid to exchange glances lest the entire proceedings dissolved into unseemly mirth, there was not one among the assembled throng who would not carry to their own dying day the memory of that wonderful and absurd and sincere and so archetypically Irish Boston Police Pipe Band.

But just eight months later, stung perhaps by the stifled grins whenever they met their colleagues, that same pipe band went over to Cork, in the old country, and swept the board in the annual Irish pipe-band competition, winning first place and the Prize of Honour. Then, and only then, did the pipers and drummers concede that maybe they had first performed in public just a tad too soon.

Fitz moved on with his jug of beer. Larry Shauseau was hauled away by Joe's seventeen-year-old daughter Lesley, to partner her in the jig 'Madam Bonaparte'.

'So,' said Tom Hanrahan to Tommy Boyle, 'what did the Coast-guard find?'

Tommy sipped his beer, watching Danny Tarantola and his wife Stephanie dancing so neatly they might have been born and raised in Ireland. He knew that Hanrahan had no right to any information on the Fitzrowan suspected murder investigation, even though he outranked Tarantola. And he knew Danny Tarantola would not wish him to discuss the case with Tom, being as the Lieutenant had been the only witness to the electronics millionaire's violent end in a force five in the heaving waters of the Nantucket Sound.

Tommy Boyle had no problems with that. As he clapped to the music, he said, eyes still on the dancers on the grass, 'They found the boom stay had been let out eleven inches. There was a clear mark on the cable where it had been set before. You know, where it had usually been fixed.'

Tom nodded, smiling to Danny the Wop as the Sergeant reeled and jigged. 'Anything else?'

'Yeah . . . The step from the heads had been greased, then wiped clean. Forensics on the grease put it no more than ten hours before the incident.'

'I remember, Tommy, when Dick Freeney could not get a sound out of these things.'

'I remember wishing he couldn't . . .' The two men chuckled.

Tommy Boyle went on, 'Did the deceased tend to do his own mechanical work?'

'Sure.' Tom remembered Big Jack emerging from the engine compartment, grinning, face and hands black with oil and grease.

'So,' said Boyle, 'the diesel primer had been filled with kerosene.'

Tom was none the wiser. 'And?'

'Somebody switches on the reserve fuel lead. Blows his fuckin head apart.'

'It was like that? When the Coastguard checked it?'

Tommy Boyle shook his head. 'Traces, Lieutenant. Their forensics guy is O K.' O K in Boston Homicide parlance meant really good.

The music switched from jig to romantic. Wedding guests clapped as Joe Daly and his bride led the waltz.

'Anything else?' enquired Tom, who had not looked once at the detective during this brief exchange.

'That's it.' Boyle waved to young Lesley Daly and made a gesture indicating he approved of her dancing.

Tom Hanrahan was silent for a while, then he said, 'Tommy . . . ?'

'Yep?'

'So what makes you think I didn't do it?'

Tommy Boyle frowned, and shook his head. 'Aw, c'mon . . .' was his only reply.

Hanrahan smiled. Good to know somebody believed in his innocence.

The study at 85 Mount Vernon Street was on the top floor of the six-storey mansion house. Jack Fitzrowan had built an atrium to cover the central, sunken part of the original roof, with photosensitive glass which altered in shade, according to the strength of sunlight.

There were small trees and shrubs, flowering plants and two small, delicate fountains. The study area was spacious and furnished like a stateroom in an old trading schooner, the SS *Mark Twain* to be precise, built in Connecticut in 1847 and still plying the Azores and African coasts at the turn of the century.

The *Mark Twain* was designed and built by the same yard that built Jack Fitzrowan's beloved ketch *Zeralda of Erin* in 1923, and the keel and hull strakes had been taken from the original timbers of the old *Mark Twain*.

But the polished mahogany and teak, and the old schooner furniture, housed some state-of-the-art electronic communications and computer equipment, all neatly set into benches which Jack's carpenter had designed to resemble the interior of the old sailing ship's bridge.

It was at one of those benches where Paul Fitzrowan sat, examining the Irish Register of Voters, which had been put on to disk in 1989. The system the Irish Home Affairs Department used was considered inviolate and impossible to hack into. It was a system using security microchips supplied by the Zeralda Corporation's Security Division and the deal had been part of a much bigger contract Sir Jack Fitzrowan had negotiated with the Dublin government, covering its entire administration from education to defence.

The deal had been signed at a small but select occasion in the American Embassy in Dublin and had netted Big Jack a profit of thirty-eight million dollars over four-years. He did not feel bad about taking that much off the top, for the entire order had been subsidized by the European Community's Assistance to Minor States programme and it cost the Irish taxpayer nothing.

To describe any computer system as inviolate would, in fact, be extremely rash. When fourteen-year-old kids can hack from their untidy bedrooms into the Pentagon, what price the security of Dublin Castle's Voters' Register?

Not much, is the answer. And young Paul Fitzrowan had learned to hack into systems while sitting on his father's knee.

So here he sat, in the atrium-study-flying-bridge at the top of his Boston mansion, availing himself of list after list of surname Rosses, who had suddenly appeared round about 1956. Next he would purloin the immigration files, then the medical records.

Tom Hanrahan would have been truly shocked to learn just how easy such an intrusion was, to the son of the man who had installed the Dublin administration's computers in the first place.

Usually, Paul used his electronic skills in his music work, but there was nothing about hacking he did not know. Paul being Paul, hacking appealed to the anarchist in him, and it was a subject with which he kept right up to date.

But he was tired. The screen and the printouts had become blurred. It was not that there were too many Rosses. Just that they were all accounted for in a way which did not suggest they had come back from America, with a two- or three-year-old baby.

Paul sighed and pushed his chair back. This was going to take all night. Time to make a fuck-you jug of coffee.

And yet, even though his labours were proceeding exceeding slow, Paul Fitzrowan felt a certainty in his heart that he was on the right track. Somehow he just knew that his elder brother, half-brother, Oliver Fitzrowan, was alive and that he was going to trace him. It was probably the most single satisfying venture the young baronet/musician had ever attempted.

As he filled the base of the larger percolator, Martin Castillo, Big Jack's Spanish manservant, appeared at the top of the staircase, grave in his spotless white linen jacket.

'Is there something I can get for you, sir?'

Paul smiled. 'No thanks, Martin. I'm just making myself a pot of coffee. Much to do.' He shrugged, searching for the word for 'work'. '*Trabajo*.'

Martin nodded. 'Ah, *trabajo*. *Si* . . .'

Paul indicated the VDU screens. '*Mucho trabajo*.'

Martin almost smiled. A rare occurrence. 'Just like your father, sir. Always *trabajo*. Can I do that for you?'

'I'm OK. You want some?' This was Paul being mischievous. He had been around teams of servants all his life and understood perfectly about the protocol of such relationships.

Martin smiled a wan, Spanish, long-suffering smile, as if to say he knew that was a *gringo* joke. And the *gringo* was his employer, but he still had his pride.

'No thank you, sir.'

'OK . . .' Paul waited, polite, until Martin turned and headed back to the stairs. Then Paul Fitzrowan frowned. 'Martin . . .' he said.

The manservant paused, looked round. 'Señor Paul . . . ?'

'I'm sorry, what did you come all this way up for? There must have been something.'

Martin Castillo stood silent for a moment. He looked, half turned like that, with his slender figure, like a middle-aged bullfighter poised for a veronica. 'I wanted to say . . . your father was a fine man. And Mrs Castillo and I miss him.'

The dignified simplicity of that statement totally ambushed Paul, who really had believed he was getting over his father's sudden death. He swallowed, throat constricted and tried to say thank you, but as his eyes brimmed, all he could manage was a nod of the head.

Martin nodded back, courteously, and made his way down the stairs. When his manservant's serene head had finally bobbed out of sight, Paul Fitzrowan sank into the leather captain's armchair and let the tears flow.

Later, still slumped in the chair, comforted by the release of pent-up, suppressed emotion, the young baronet became aware that he felt closer to his father than he had ever felt while Big Jack had been alive. And with that came a mature understanding that his own behaviour must have been a great disappointment, not just the youthful pony tail and gold earrings, the rock groups and getting sent down from school for drugs, but his arrogance in turning his back on the family's wealth and reputation while at the same time taking advantage of both when it suited him. Living among dossers and rent-a-crowd protesters, snorting lines in unsavoury washrooms with bit-part players among the flotsam of rock 'n' roll's low tides.

Disappointment . . . he could just hear that little shit Pronsias Stevenson: 'Seeing as you were always such a disappointment to your late father . . .' And for once the little shit was right.

Disappointment . . . ?

Paul swallowed hard, forbidding himself the indulgence of further tears. Mere disappointment was more than he deserved. The fact that his father had not disowned him during the nadir of his conceits said much for Big Jack's big heart. Disappointment was too trite for the grief Sir Jack Fitzrowan must have endured as his only son, his only legitimate son, slipped away from all that the electronics millionaire had hoped and planned for them both.

Paul shook his head as he sat there, recollecting his deliberate rejection of so many attempts by Big Jack to forgive him and help him straighten himself out. Jesus Christ, he had even resented his father's generosity of spirit and chosen to repay it with something close to contempt, affecting to have been insulted by such 'interference'.

God, Dad, he thought, chest tight with regret and bereavement, I don't know how you put such a brave face on it.

He closed his eyes, as if in prayer, and said, almost silently, 'I am so sorry . . .' And a solitary tear ran down his cheek.

Get a hold of yourself, man. He could hear the gruff voice, never without charm. Get a fucking grip. That was the way Jack Fitzrowan talked to those closest to him. And the way he used to say it, it never really sounded like swearing. There was always too much love and fun in his heart.

So Paul Fitzrowan, Sir Paul Fitzrowan, took a couple of deep breaths and hauled himself out of the black dog he had slumped into.

To be fair, the last year or so had seen the beginnings of an improvement in his relationship with his father. The designer drugs were a thing of the past. He had understood that even in the rock music world, those who made a decent living out of it were the ones who kept a clear head and had some kind of a career plan. And since the accident, each passing day had seen his childhood slip away.

At the big house in Kerry, a couple of days after the funeral, Bridget the cook had put a plump hand on his shoulder and settled her bleary eyes on his. 'Young Paul,' she had said quietly, and he had listened, for of all the household, of all the family, only Bridget had never changed in her devotion to the wee fellow she had watched grow up from pushchair to 750cc motor-cycle. 'Young Paul, you know, don't you, you will never be a child again. It's gone for ever. And now, with God's good grace, has come your chance to be not just a man, but a fine one. Like your father.'

Paul had shaken his head ruefully and replied that he did not think he could ever be as fine as Sir Jack, but Bridget had grinned and said that Jack Fitzrowan had not always been an angel himself. And she believed in Paul. She had patted his arm and said God bless you, the way she had done since he was a baby, and waddled off back along the stone-flagged corridor to the kitchen.

That had been the start of the sea change. And sitting there now, feeling his father's presence all around, the new Paul Fitzrowan swore that he would bring added pride to the family name. He would find Oliver, if he could, for in so doing he was finding himself, and he would take control of the Fitzrowan family's fortunes, before those sisters of his turned the dynasty into a sideshow.

The whiter than white bow of the *Toshiro Maru* towered above the grey stone, dirty concrete and whitewashed corner-stones of the deep harbour wharf at Newport, Rhode Island.

The bleakness of the white steel was saved by scrolls and curlicues of gold leaf either side of the prow. From deep within the hull came the almost comforting, low, rhythmic throb of the ocean-going, 117-foot luxury upon luxury yacht's three 20,000-horsepower Mitsubishi diesel engines.

The luxury, while tasteful and understated like its owner, was remarkable even for a $27 million ocean-going motor yacht. Consider the existence of a 35-foot putting green, with real turf, a sand bunker and gyroscopic balancing for all but the roughest seas. Or the master stateroom with its polished sandalwood floors, tatami matting, live cherryblossom kept in bloom in a carefully controlled cool and mildly humid atmosphere, and lacquer-work baby dragons – a replica in miniature of the eighteenth-century Kyoto Prince Toshiro's quarters in his father the emperor's palace.

And the remarkable, understated owner of this powerful, ocean-going extravagance? None other than Takahashi Katakura, President of the Katakura Corporation of Japan. Tak to his acquaintants. Personal wealth estimated at around $36 billion.

'What does he look like?' asked Alison Clancy, when Grace had come into her office with a hand-delivered, hand-written note, brought to her from Newport by an Armani-suited Japanese aide, serious and polite, who had descended from the Boston sky to land by Bell helicopter in the Zeralda back lot. The note had read:

Dear Mrs Grace Hanrahan,

I have come to your country in order to purchase a golf club and an orchestra. After the sturdy rebuff which your late father delivered to my unworthy attempt to acquire your admirable company, Zeralda, undoubtedly a leader in the field of micro-electronics, I would very much like to show my admiration for such a worthy adversary and to enquire most humbly if you would consider, perhaps, to be my personal guest at a small and probably lacklustre banquet lunch which I shall be giving in the Ritz-Carlton Hotel, Boston, this coming Friday in honour of the Boston Symphony Orchestra.

I await your reply with bated breath, and hope that you will accept this possibly absurd attempt to smoke the pipe of peace.

I remain, your most obedient servant,

Tak Katakura

'There is no photo of him in any magazine or newspaper. He doesn't give interviews and by all accounts is a very private individual,' replied Grace. 'However, Jack got a few shots of him playing golf at a course he owns outside Tokyo . . .' She opened a slim leather folder and laid it on Alison's desk.

The man in the photo looked about forty, lean and fit. He had a strong face. Long and slightly fierce.

'He's quite good looking,' observed Alison, 'and tall, for a Japanese.' She handed back the hand-written note. 'What do you think he's up to?'

Grace raised her shoulders, shook her head. 'Who knows with these guys? Who knows with *this* guy? Our investigation showed up nothing but a family man, a golf fanatic, collector of Japanese art and artefacts. He has a first-class degree from Kyoto in Japanese history, he is considered an authority in calligraphy, he plays piano to concert standard, judo and aikido black belt, and is the third richest man in Japan. Don't you just hate him?'

Alison smiled. 'So you won't be going to his prom?'

Grace met her friend's gaze. 'Are you kidding? I wouldn't miss it.'

The silver Porsche convertible grumbled on to the quay and stopped behind the two navy blue Dodge 4 × 4 wagons and the understated, dark grey Cadillac coupé de ville.

Sebastian Tree switched off the engine and sat quietly, deep in thought, as he checked out the towering, fiercely white hull of the *Toshiro Maru*, with its elegant lines, and as much state-of-the-art electronic navigation and communications gear housed above and behind the bridge superstructure as any small warship.

Tree knew about such things, for the Zeralda Corporation supplied essential ceramic and platinum microchips to the US, Argentine, Australian and, of course, Irish navies.

A few crew members were quietly busy around the deck and in a small motor boat at the stern, where they were cleaning the immaculate transom with long-handled brushes. He could glimpse a couple of officers inside the bridge, doubtless going about the various items of administration required for docking in Newport harbour, or plotting the *Toshiro Maru*'s next course.

Tree glanced at his mobile phone, then back to the ocean-going yacht. And he reflected that he too was, sitting there, plotting his own next course. There was no future for him with the Zeralda Corporation, thanks to Alison Clancy and her relentless detective work. He knew that she had much more on him than she had revealed, and he had seen how close the Clancy bitch and dumb Grace Hanrahan, now President, if you please, had become.

And even if something awful (awfully fortunate, as far as he was concerned) were to happen to Ma'm'selle Clancy, Jack Fitzrowan's final whore in that endless line of strumpets, Sebastian Tree knew that Grace Hanrahan would never trust him again. He smiled. And why should she? Had he not so very nearly brought Fitzrowan's grand enterprise crashing to the dust? Had he not come within a hair's breadth of becoming President *and* Chief Executive of the reborn Zeralda Communications Group, a wholly owned subsidiary of the Katakura Corporation of Japan?

Had he not, in the meticulous manner in which Sebastian Tree planned everything, learned not only to speak Japanese fluently, but to read and write *Kanji*, the Nippon and Chinese form of written words? And golf? A game he found profoundly dull and boring, had he not achieved a nine handicap, just to find his way (was it only three years before) on to an exclusive course outside Tokyo in order to bump into Takahashi Katakura on equal ground?

And from those meticulously planned beginnings had he not become a secret confidant, on Tak and Seb terms, and Tak's deep-cover mole, right at the heart of Katakura's target for take-over – the Zeralda Corporation?

OK, maybe his two attempts to ease the Katakura offensive – the first by providing every most privileged and confidential detail of Fitzrowan's business, the second by pure sabotage – had not been entirely successful (failure was not a word in Sebastian Tree's vocabulary), but nobody could doubt that he had proved his loyalty and his worth to the Japanese electronics mogul. And now he was here to claim his reward.

Tree removed his Aviator Ray-Bans and checked his appearance in the rear-view mirror. Navy cotton polo shirt, soft leather zip-up windcheater, tan chinos and Timberland deck shoes. Tak was a military man at heart – Tree had always been impressed by the martial precision with which Katakura planned his work and his recreation. And Sebastian Tree had chosen his wardrobe carefully that morning, to give the right impression.

He looked at his mobile phone once more. To phone or not to phone? Or just breeze on board – just passing, Tak, good buddy, couldn't go by without paying my respects.

Yep. The casual approach. It always fazed the Japanese, whose ingrained courtesy forced them to welcome you.

He climbed out of the Porsche and strode past the parked cars to the covered gangplank, rising steeply to the deck of the *Toshiro Maru*, riding high on the tide.

★

Mike had not changed much, thought Alison Clancy as she sat across the desk from him in his office overlooking Boston Common. Still the same neat, dark hair, the same shy smile. It was a smile which masked a heart of railroad steel. And it was the essential coldness and lack of emotion in Mike Medevik's inner core which had led them to drift apart and, in the end, agree that divorce would be better for both of them.

It was strange, thought Alison, as she watched him stand at the bookshelf-lined wall, searching for his copy of *Kidd and Delaney's US Corporates and Major Shareholders' Disbursements*, to think they had once shared the shower together and wandered around naked or half-dressed getting ready for work in the morning – somehow far more intimate, in a way, than making love. Probably because they were both quite private individuals by instinct.

Sitting there, in a silence which was neither comfortable nor uncomfortable, Alison reflected this was exactly what had disquieted her when Grace Hanrahan had asked if she would mind taking this meeting with Medevik, as the Zeralda Corporation's representative, in the business of Zeralda versus Jack's estate.

Sure, Boston is a small place, and she and Michael had often seen each other around town. They had even been seated next to each other at a legal convention across the river in the law school, and had affected to be amused and sophisticated by the potential embarrassment of the situation, just a year after their divorce.

But this was different. For this roomy office, with its simple furnishings in such excellent taste, with those two high, Georgian windows overlooking the Common, was where Professor Mike Medevik had proposed to her, when she was just a junior counsel with Rawlince, Brooke & Maine. Eight years ago now. Before she had ever heard of the man she now knew, too late, that she was destined to fall in love with. Jack Fitzrowan.

'John Pearce Dunmill Fitzrowan,' intoned Mike Medevik, almost as if he had read her thoughts. 'A complex and complicated man . . .'

Alison shrugged. What was she to say? He sure was, and a wonderful lover into the bargain? She smiled enigmatically and nodded. 'Indeed he was.'

'How did you get on with him?' enquired her former husband as he grunted with satisfaction and prised out the volume he had been seeking.

Alison made a noncommittal gesture. 'He was OK. Always took care of his people.'

Medevik turned to gaze at her, letting his reading glasses drop to the end of his nose. 'He sure took care of you.'

Alison, who had been rated excellent by senior partner Dick Rawlince for her cross-examination technique, met Mike's eye without a trace of expression and smiled. 'It was my bonus. He wanted to make sure his successor wouldn't renege on the deal.'

'Three hundred grand . . . Quite a bonus,' remarked Medevik.

Alison held his gaze. 'Oh, I earned it.'

The top US attorney in the minefield of legacies and bequests seemed to consider this. Then he went back to his desk and flopped down on his leather swivelling and tilting seat. He opened the tome and thumbed through it.

A Georgian carriage clock on the mantelpiece ticked away gently. From outside, they could hear the sound of kids playing on the Common. Somewhere, a dog barked. Eventually, Alison Clancy's ex-husband sighed and leaned back in his chair, which tilted slightly, having been adjusted not to go too far. A bit like Mike himself, thought Alison, wryly.

'I'm afraid this guy Stevenson is correct,' he said. '*Lehman Toys* versus *Jacob Lehman* is a precedent which would . . . very probably, affect a judgment in Zeralda's case against the Fitzrowan estate.'

'Affect it how?' asked Alison, now very much the lawyer.

Medevik looked at her, noting the professional tone. 'Adversely,' he replied.

'Is that possibly, or probably?'

Mike raised his shoulders. 'Hmmm. Depends on the judge. Ted Koplowic, the judge who made the ruling, is considered an authority on wholly or almost wholly owned corporations. He was senior corporate law counsel with Reid, Palance & Palance before he made federal judge, a George Bush appointment. He is very influential in the careers of many top corporate lawyers. And of course now he's a pretty senior judge.'

'So no one would be keen to mess with him? Come on, Mike,' Alison shook her head, refusing Medevik's approach, 'that's bullshit and you know it. Half the young Turks at the Bar would welcome the chance to upset a Ted Koplowic ruling.'

Medevik appeared to be re-reading the judgment in his law book. Then he took a pack of Camel Lites from his desk, offering one to his ex-wife. 'Still smoke?'

'I gave up.'

'Good for you.' Michael Medevik, master of self-control, put the pack back in the desk and slid the drawer shut. 'There is one chance, if Zeralda feels like spending a fortune . . .'

'Persuade Lehman Toys to challenge the federal ruling,' said Alison, 'and bankroll them all the way.'

Medevik nodded, watching her with something approaching respect.

'Plus pay Lehman Toys something to make it worth their while. We could be talking millions.'

Medevik caressed the handle of the drawer with the Camels inside. 'We *are* talking millions.'

'And paying Lehman Toys for them fronting the appeal? Illegal I do believe, Michael.'

Medevik shook his head. 'There are ways round that.'

This was a powerful moment for a young lawyer. Alison Clancy knew that Grace, Zeralda's new President, relied on her and trusted her advice. Especially after the NASA–Seb Tree business. It was in her gift to make a decision which would cost millions of dollars, with no certainty of success, or to advise against. Which would leave the Fitzrowan heirs no option but to intensify their search for the missing Oliver.

The carriage clock delicately chimed the half hour. Alison ignored it. That clock had been her first wedding anniversary gift to the man with the neat, dark haircut sitting across the desk from her, leaning back in his chair, tilted. But not too far.

'I can't advise Zeralda to take such a course of action,' she replied.

Mike Medevik considered that. Then he let his seat tilt forward to the upright position.

'Which would be my advice too,' he announced, as if he were a judge himself, and Alison remembered with crystal precision just why she had divorced him.

'Fine,' she replied. 'I have no doubt the family will now be obliged to find the missing son. Their best hope is to go after the twelve and a half per cent of his two hundred and eighteen million dollars. For tracing Oliver.'

Mike Medevik crossed to the door, his expensive, dark grey London suit hanging in well-bred fashion around his spare, worked-out, sensible-diet frame. He opened the door and held out his hand, without a trace of irony. Alison actually wondered if he had maybe forgotten they used to be husband and wife.

'Unless he turns out to be dead,' he smiled, as they clasped hands. His was cool and firm. Hers was too, she hoped.

Their eyes met, and it was as if they had never once bucked and gasped in slick excitement, lost in sick-sweet pleasure.

'One way or the other,' said Alison, 'it looks like Oliver is the key, after all.'

And when she walked out of the room, she never did look back. Another of life's ghosts finally laid.

9

Tak Katakura stood in the sand bunker, on his gyroscopically balanced real grass putting green, below the stern deck of his luxury yacht, the *Toshiro Maru*. Sunlight strayed in from the large, oval portholes either side. He eyed the golfball at his feet and gripped the spoon-shaped niblik professionally.

'What's your handicap these days?' he asked Sebastian Tree, who sat on a stool at the small, palm-thatched beach bar, in the starboard after corner.

'Still nine,' replied Zeralda's Chief Executive.

'Hmmm . . .' said Katakura, deep in concentration.

After standing motionless for about two minutes, his breathing deep and relaxed, the Japanese billionaire allowed his club to rise then, without a pause, swung it abruptly, cupping the ball and lifting it up, out of the bunker to drop on to the cropped green and roll gently right up to the lip of the hole.

He exhaled slowly, then turned to face Tree. 'Is it not rash, Sebastian, to come here?'

Sebastian Tree grinned. 'Nice shot. They say practice is everything.'

Katakura was not in the mood for small talk. 'Is it not . . . inappropriate?' His gaze was cool.

Tree shrugged. 'I don't think it matters now.'

'Really? Why is that?'

'Grace Hanrahan and her attorney, the one Fitzrowan was humping before he died, they know.'

Tak Katakura climbed out of the sand bunker and walked over to the hole, his golfball poised on its lip. He touched it with his club and the ball dropped out of sight. Still looking down at it he enquired, 'What do they know?'

'Only how much of a help I have been to you, Tak,' said Tree. 'That's what they know.'

'Be more specific, please.'

'Specific? They know I shafted them.' Tree chuckled. 'Oh, they can't prove it or I would be up before a Grand Jury. But it's written all over their faces.'

Katakura still did not look round. 'That hardly explains why you are sitting here, Sebastian.' His voice was deceptively gentle.

Tree knew that tone. 'We have a deal,' he stated, courteous but firm, in the manner he knew was the only way to do business with Orientals.

The silence which followed was profound. Then Katakura turned and looked at Tree, thoughtful. 'Why,' he asked, 'did you hate Jack Fitzrowan so much?'

'I had my reasons,' replied Tree, thinking to himself, by God I did. From outside came the throb of powerful diesel engines as some harbour craft ploughed past.

'Will you tell me?' The question was so direct, for a Japanese, that it took Sebastian Tree unawares. And as he ducked his head slightly, he knew his discomfort showed.

'Oh . . . it goes a long way back.' He felt his neck stiffen, tension always did that.

'I take it you are here to make some form of accommodation.' Tak Katakura knelt down and retrieved his golfball. 'Under these circumstances, I really would like to know. It will go no further, you have my word.'

As the *Toshiro Maru* rocked gently in the wake of whatever had sailed past, Tree debated how to reply. Tak, as usual, had gotten directly to the heart of the matter. Sebastian Tree did indeed have his reasons for wishing eternal ill upon the Fitzrowan clan, but it was so deep in his psyche, such a very private and personal thing, he hardly permitted himself to think about it, far less discuss it with a comparative stranger. However, he was playing for high stakes. Katakura was a man to whom personal honour meant a lot.

Why not? thought the man who had betrayed Zeralda. He took a deep breath, and felt the old rage build up as he said, 'It was a long time ago, Tak. Jack Fitzrowan insulted my mother. And please. That is all I have to say.'

The Japanese tycoon straightened up, weighing the golfball in his hand. 'It must have been some insult.'

A vein in the side of Sebastian Tree's temple throbbed. 'Oh yes . . .' he replied. 'It really was.'

Katakura walked back to the bunker and threw the ball in, lightly, letting it drop at random into the sand.

'What deal?' he asked.

Tree did not enjoy talking to the man's back, but if that was the way Tak wanted to play it . . . 'I am here to take my place on the board of the Katakura Corporation,' he announced. 'That is the deal. That was what we agreed, if anything went wrong.'

Katakura turned to face Zeralda's Chief Executive, his face without expression of any kind. 'I am afraid that is out of the question.'

Sebastian Tree felt his blood pound in his chest, perspiration ran down his back. He forced himself not to show panic. 'Look, Tak, a deal is a deal. You are a man of honour. I have your word. Look what I have risked for you.'

Tak Katakura sighed. 'You risked nothing for me, Sebastian. You risked everything out of hatred, and a desire to betray.' He spread his hands. 'And if you can do it to Zeralda, you can do it to me. No thanks. No deal. You gambled and lost. There is nothing here for you. It would be better if you do not contact me again. Better for you, please believe me.'

And with that, the President of the Katakura Corporation of Japan returned to his sand bunker, breathing gently for his next swing, Sebastian Tree consigned to history.

His legs weak, the man who had hated Jack Fitzrowan so much, the man who had tried to ruin Zeralda, walked up on to the deck of the *Toshiro Maru* and down the steep incline to the rest of his life.

Like Jack Fitzrowan's other children, Darcy had inherited his lively intelligence and, when it suited her, the electronics millionaire's relentless determination.

Thus it was inevitable that, even without any help from her most recent sexual conquest, Pronsias Stevenson, or from Olive Oyl, the Church Records librarian in Dublin, she would eventually find herself on the edge of the village of Athgoe, in County Galway, the wind whispering through untidy, overgrown grass, stepping past an abandoned wheelbarrow wheel, towards the door of a crumbling, Georgian house called Inniscoor, its paint faded and peeling.

Darcy had used a family friend in the Civil Service to gain access to the untidy records of adoptions and foster parents in the vaults of the Government Records Office (Births, Deaths and Adoptions) at Dublin Castle. There she had, after four days of painstaking searching, discovered a brittle, close-lined, hard-covered, hand-written journal of yellowing pages, crammed with neat, copperplate entries in ink.

The journal had a stick-on label on the front, announcing: CHURCH LAY DOMESTIC AND AGRICULTURAL EMPLOYEES, CASUAL. ST MARGARET THE MEEK. 1946–1955. It would surprise only a foreigner to discover a record book more appropriate to Ireland's National Tax Office, or the Social Services Department, tucked away forgotten in the labyrinthine cellars below the small and dowdy offices of Births, Deaths and Adoptions.

Within those pages had been comprehensive lists of lay persons whom the Blessed Order of Saint Margaret the Meek had fed and housed, in return for 'domestic chores and general assistance', throughout the island of Ireland.

There were one thousand, six hundred and forty-three names of domestics. In the year of 1954 itself, one hundred and thirty-seven lay people had worked for the order, either for a pittance or for enough food to sustain them, according to the explanatory note on the first page.

The note also stated, somewhat cryptically, that on occasion, 'almoner and compassionate assistance was provided in lieu of subsistence pay'.

And after four days of searching, Darcy had found what she was looking for:

Costello, Miss H. – cleaner/cook. Athgoe. Almoner and Comp. Assistance. 22 Dec. 1953 to 21 June 1954. Total cost food and fuel; no cash.

So there it was, her father's 'one true love' had been sent off, on the eve of Christmas 1953, alone, pregnant and terrified, to this cold, stark house on Galway's barren coast, where, for a bed and a few crumbs, the child waited out her confinement, only to have the fruit of her labour taken from her and given, sold, to some childless couple from America.

Darcy assumed that 'Comp.' was a short version of 'compassionate'. A very bloody short version, she thought to herself as she banged on the huge brass door knocker. Behind her a frog, unnoticed, slid off the abandoned wheel and bounced away, multiple chins a-quiver.

As she stood there waiting the wind freshened and brought with it a tang of the sea. Three seagulls wheeled overhead, crying and steadying themselves against the breeze.

After a few moments she banged the knocker again. The house seemed to summon up a deeper silence, as if to say, there is nobody here, stop banging on my door, dammit. And in that still quiet, with just the flutter of wind rustling leaves and grass, Darcy felt she could hear the faintest voice, a rhythmic voice, male, rising and falling, almost inaudible, quite distant.

She left the porch and walked around the place, stepping carefully and peering through the several big, square Georgian windows. It was clear the place had been more or less derelict for years. Except, in the kitchen was a plate with a half-eaten lump of bread roll and a green and white striped coffee mug.

When Darcy got to the south-west gable, the faint, rhythmic male voice, which had come and gone as the breeze rose and fell, became more marked, although still indistinct. And there, about a quarter of a mile down the sloping hillside, towards the cove and the Atlantic Ocean, was a small cemetery and four people standing at a fresh grave. The voice came from a man in black, wearing a black hat. The local priest, Darcy had no doubt.

By the time she had climbed back into the car and found the tiny, old church of Athgoe and its cemetery, the funeral service was over. Two old women were being ushered into a car, a Ford which had seen better days, by a younger woman.

The priest had just said his goodbyes and was ambling back towards the church entrance, clutching his prayer book, with a slip of folded paper inside to keep his place and remind him who it was he was burying. Darcy hurried to intercept him and reached him on the shallow step of the arched porch, which had an aroma of fresh-mown grass and stale incense.

'Father, forgive me . . .' she started.

'This is hardly the place for a confession, my daughter,' replied the young priest, a twinkle in his eye. He could not have been more than thirty, and quite attractive in an unobtainable, patient sort of way.

'I really don't think there is enough daylight left for you to hear mine, Father,' she replied, grinning.

'Oh, dear me, I'm sure the Lord can do a bit of overtime,' he said. 'What can I do for you . . . ?'

'I was looking for a Sister Immaculata, I understood she was living at the old rectory, Inniscoor.'

The priest stopped smiling. He glanced back towards the cemetery, which was all he needed to do, really. That one glance said it all.

'Are you a relative?' he asked, in a more professional tone.

Darcy shook her head. 'No. It was to do with my research work. A thesis for my husband's work.' She too looked back at the cemetery, to make it easier for the priest.

'I'm afraid . . . I'm Father Murtagh, by the way . . .'

'How do you do?'

'I'm just fine. I am very sad to say, I have just buried the dear old woman, up there in our wee graveyard.'

'Oh, dear. I don't know what to say. I think I should just go.'

'Sister Immaculata was eighty-four. She had a good life, and a peaceful end. My housekeeper found her sitting dead at the window.

She used to love looking out over the bay. Have you come far? You don't look as if you are from hereabouts.'

'From Kerry,' said Darcy, unwilling to disclose her home these days was in England, for in west-coast Ireland, Kerry was a far better place to come from, 'originally. But I went to school in America and now my husband is a bit of an academic.'

'America?' Father Murtagh replied. 'Well we can't send you back without a cup of tea.'

So Darcy Fitzrowan Bailey went inside the small church which smelled of mown grass and stale incense, and old prayer books, and the sea, and took tea and cookies with young Father Murtagh.

And that was the beginning, the first real chink of light, in the hunt for Oliver, Jack Fitzrowan's long lost child, and heir to over two hundred million dollars, born to Helen Costello at Inniscoor at four in the morning of 14 June 1954.

For Father Murtagh, upon learning that Darcy was the sister of Paul Fitzrowan, entrusted into her safe keeping a sealed envelope which the deceased sister had been clutching in her dead hand when they found her, sitting at that window where Paul had first set eyes on her just four weeks before.

'To Sir Paul FitzRoan. Very Private', it had scrawled on the front, the word 'private' having been underlined several times. And the good Father Murtagh, because he was good, had not dreamed of opening it.

'I had no idea where to send it,' he had confessed to Darcy. 'And doesn't the Lord work in mysterious ways, to send the addressee's own sister here, on the very day we put the old lady to rest?'

Oh yes, Darcy had replied, he surely does. And after a second cup of Assam tea, real leaves, no teabags for Father Murtagh, she had returned to her rented BMW and driven a few miles before opening the envelope and reading its surprising contents.

Upon digesting them, she knew that it was now possible to track down her illegitimate sibling's adoptive parents, if they were still alive. And very probably, Oliver himself. If he was still alive.

Having memorized the dead Sister Immaculata's last letter, so obviously written with care and feeling, Darcy Fitzrowan Bailey had not the slightest guilt about her next action. She tore the letter into tiny pieces and scattered it along the winding road from Athgoe to Galway town.

A couple of big drops of rain appeared on the windshield, followed by others. Darcy switched on the wipers, content with her day's work. The clock on the dashboard read 12.43. Time to grab a light lunch in Galway's George Hotel and still be in Dublin by about four in the afternoon.

She smiled to herself, pleased that her painstaking detective work was paying off. It meant a flight to New York City, and more of the same, but at least now she knew what she was looking for. Whom she was looking for.

It was deeply satisfying to be one step ahead of her sister and brother, and closer now to identifying Oliver than she had ever expected to be. She had a feeling that Pronsias Stevenson also knew the truth about the couple who had paid $3,200 in cash to Father Thomas Flynn, in return for Helen Costello's newborn baby all those years ago. He knew something, that was certain. But he was never going to share it, being the control freak that he was.

Pronsias Stevenson. There had been no need to give herself to him, as it turned out. There had been absolutely no need for her to allow him to do the things he had done, during that morning of wantonness and pleasure.

Imaginative things, she conceded, as the road unfolded before her, wipers somehow soothing with their rhythmic swish-swishing. Decadent things. Exciting, let's admit it. Darcy became aware of her silk-clad thighs brushing together each time she touched the accelerator or brake pedal.

She glanced at the dashboard clock, and moistened her lips. To hell with a light lunch at the George. The electronics millionaire's daughter, a millionairess herself now, so beautiful she could have had any man she wanted even if she had been penniless, lifted her mobile phone and touched the buttons to recall the number of Stevenson, Stevenson & Malahide's Dublin office.

When the switchboard put her through, her heart quickened when that voice said, 'Pronsias Stevenson . . .'

'Pronsias, it's Darcy Fitzrowan here. I was, um, I wondered if you would be free for a cup of . . . tea? In Daddy's Dublin place.' Jack Fitzrowan had kept the two upper floors of one of his Georgian town houses in Fitzwilliam Street, just a block away from the Dublin lawyer's own office. It was now part of Paul's inheritance, but he had agreed to its use by the three of them.

There was silence on the line and Darcy reddened at the thought she had just made a prize fool of herself. The randy bastard probably screwed half his female clientele – how else could he have learned such things? – and her invitation was no doubt an intrusion.

Just as she was about to say forget it, Stevenson's voice replied, gently, 'I could not think of anything nicer. Do you have the keys? Or shall I bring a set?'

Her face hot with blushing, Darcy said, 'Oh, um, you bring a set . . .'

'OK. About four?'

She smiled, heart pounding in anticipation. 'Four is perfect.'

'Four it is then. I'm looking forward to it.'

'Me too,' answered Darcy, feeling as flustered as a schoolgirl. And she stepped on the gas.

'Rawlince, Brooke & Maine, how can I help you?' said a pert female voice.

Peter Girolo had placed a folded handkerchief over the mouthpiece of the payphone in the lobby of the Marriott Long Wharf Hotel. 'This is Heyman, Bartok for Miss Alison Clancy,' he replied.

'Are you sure you have the correct number? This is Rawlince, Brooke & Maine, attorneys at law.'

'Miss Clancy was with you four years ago. I have some family affairs which require her signature.'

'Please hold.'

Girolo let his gaze wander around the lobby. Nothing was happening, nobody was interested in him. After a few moments, a man's voice came on the line. 'This is Bill Brooke, to whom am I talking?'

'Hi, Mike Heyman here. Heyman, Bartok. I am winding up a family matter, old aunt of Miss Clancy's. There is a small inheritance, some furniture. I take it Miss Clancy has moved on?'

In the silence that followed, Girolo wondered if Bill Brooke was checking out Heyman, Bartok. That was cool. The firm did exist. Peter Girolo was a qualified lawyer with a degree from the same place as the man on the other end of the phone. Heyman, Bartok practised out of New York and Peter Girolo *was* Mike Heyman, whenever it suited him, for he had bankrolled the firm, back in 1983, and the real Mike Heyman would never be out of debt to the mob.

Finally Bill Brooke came back on the line. 'I believe Alison is with Zeralda Electronics, they're across the river in Cambridge, near the MIT. I can get you the number.'

'Don't worry, we'll find it. Thank you for your time, Bill.'

'No problem.'

Girolo hung up and walked out of the hotel. His two footsoldiers rose from the lobby couches, where they had been watching over him in case of trouble, and followed.

Girolo glanced at his wristwatch. Ten after twelve. As they reached the dark blue Chrysler, he turned to Sonny Favaro, one of his bodyguards from Atlantic City. 'Sonny, I got a coupla things to do. Take a powder and I'll catch up with you.'

Sonny, who chewed gum even when he was eating, frowned. 'Joey says never to let you outta my sight, Mr Girolo.'

Girolo clapped the hoodlum on the shoulder of his loose grey worsted coat. 'Be a good boy. I'll bleep you when I need you. Some things a man needs some privacy with, OK?'

As Sonny met his gaze, Girolo reflected that Joey Buscetta had chosen well. This was a protection man who used his head. Then Sonny grinned. It had to be a woman, or at least about sex. That much he could figure.

Sonny Favaro nodded. 'You take care, Mr Girolo.'

Girolo smiled. 'You bet.' And as his bodyguards climbed into the Chrysler he stepped into a waiting taxi and gave directions.

Forty minutes later, wearing a beat-up old leather windcheater and a tweed cap, like Robert Redford in *The Sting*, he was at the wheel of that same taxi, parked near the Zeralda Corporation complex. The driver, a black guy from Summerville, was enjoying a day off with his girl and their two kids, one thousand dollars richer.

And three hours and eighteen minutes after that, a green BMW coupé, with the number plate 502 PLAINS, emerged from the Zeralda parking lot and headed for Longfellow Bridge.

At the wheel was the woman Peter Girolo had last seen a couple of nights before in Ciao Bambino, whom he had recognized as Alison Clancy. He slipped the taxi into gear and followed at a discreet distance, for he had things to say to the young attorney. If he felt he could trust her.

And if, after making his initial approach, he decided he could not?

Girolo earnestly hoped it would not come to that.

Sebastian Tree glanced through the letters and spreadsheets Amy Schofield, his secretary, had brought for him to sign, while Amy stood patiently at his desk.

'Two young men are washing and valeting the company Bentley for Mrs Hanrahan,' she announced. 'Young black fellows, very nice. It's nice to see young people prepared to work for their money these days.'

'How much are they charging?' Tree asked, not really interested. Except his Porsche was kind of dusty and he was going to a barbecue that evening with one of the younger Kennedys and her controversial Irish husband, a former prisoner of the British, who was running for Congress. It would look better if the car was clean.

'Fifty dollars.'

'Tell them they can do the Porsche for thirty. There's less to clean.'

Amy smiled, thinking to herself she could always make up the difference from her own pocket. Amy was a practising Christian and she liked to encourage honest toil. 'I'll have a word with them.'

'How's your mom?' asked Tree absent-mindedly as he scribbled here and there in margins, or signed letters with his usual hiero-glyphic.

'She's just fine.'

'Pasta salad tonight?' went on Tree, who practised easy charm the way a pickpocket might steal matches from coats, just to keep in shape.

Amy beamed. At thirty-eight, she was no longer sure that the Prince Charming her mother and she so often used to dream about was just around the corner. In fact, she wondered these days if he was even on the next block. But if she could have chosen her own prince, it would have been the tall, tanned, Chief Exec whose every administrative need she had serviced those last five years.

'Pasta salad is on Tuesdays, Mr Tree,' she said primly in mock reprimand, and immediately wondered, Oh God, I hope he doesn't think I'm being impertinent. Impertinent was a favourite word of her mother's, whom one day, she fantasized, she would probably murder. It was just her little joke, of course.

'Tuesdays. Right. Excellent . . .' murmured Tree, who seemed more than usually preoccupied. The poor man had so much on his mind. He worked so hard, often into the wee hours. Amy wondered if the Management, as she referred to Mrs Hanrahan and Alison Clancy, in her meticulous diary, were aware just how much dear Mr Tree did on their behalf.

Finally Sebastian Tree handed back the files and thanked her. Amy Schofield beamed and muttered that tonight was in fact mozzarella and tomatoes, with olive oil. She could never bring herself to use the term extra virgin; he might think she was being coarse.

When he had given his PA his car keys and thirty bucks, for the valet cleaners, and she had gone, closing the door behind her, Tree took his mobile phone from his briefcase and made one call. He waited as the ringing tone continued for a few moments, then a voice answered.

'Yeah?'

'Mr Apple, please.'

Slight pause, then, 'OK, this is he, who is this?'

'Mr Lemon. What time is it where you are?' Tree had been rehearsed in this simple code. He found it idiotic but it was a small price to pay for professionalism and discretion.

'Yeah, let me see . . .' said Mr Apple. 'You mean what time is it in Pennsylvania, or Seattle?'

'Eastern standard time.' That completed the recognition ritual. Now they had established who each other was.

'So, Mr Lemon, what can I do for you?'

Sebastian Tree waited for a second. Did he really mean this? Had things really come to this? Once committed, there was no going back.

But logically, there was only one course left to him. He checked that his door was shut, then he spoke quietly into the receiver. 'I would like you to proceed.'

Silence, for a couple of seconds. 'Are you sure . . . ?'

'Quite sure.'

More silence. Then, 'Fine. This number will be history, the second you hang up.'

'OK.'

'So there is no going back.'

'I understand.'

Silence. It took Sebastian Tree a few moments to realize that Mr Apple was no longer on the other end of the line. And with that irrevocable moment spent, much of his tension evaporated.

Tree slumped into his leather chair and exhaled. He could see a glimmer of light now. He could see the future, and it worked.

Down in Zeralda's yard, back of the complex, as most of the staff were leaving after work, two young coloured men worked on the Chief Exec's Porsche, one working wax into the metalwork, the other inside, vacuuming the carpets and emptying ashtrays. A radio on the ground played James Brown, 'All aboard the night train . . .' with lots of bass, but not too loud.

Their names were Big Time and Jebediah. They did a good job and Amy Schofield gave them the full fifty and an extra five for a tip.

Arthur the chief security guard nodded to them as they left two hundred and five dollars richer, having cleaned the Bentley, the Porsche, Alison Clancy's BMW and Grace's own car.

'Hey,' said Tom Hanrahan, as Detective Willie Big Time Caldwell and Sergeant Detective Jeb Kingdom strolled into his Homicide Department office and deposited three developed contact sheets of Sebastian Tree's fingerprints on his desk. 'If I had known you guys could do a job like that you coulda washed my own car.'

'Well now, would that be politically correct, Lieutenant?' Kingdom asked and although he was grinning, Tom knew that he meant it. The days of black cops washing Irish lieutenants' cars were long gone. At least this far north.

'So, we got all ten, nice and clear?'

'Left three has not come out well,' said Big Time. 'I dunno. It was good on the steering wheel. And on the gear lever,' he shrugged. 'Maybe the guy has a gimpy left three.'

Tom Hanrahan nodded, studying the contacts. He looked up and offered the detectives from a pack of chewing gum. Big Time took it. Jeb Kingdom ignored the offering.

'Thanks,' said Tom. 'Anything else? Anything interesting?'

Jeb Kingdom stuck his hands in his dungarees pockets and studied the various rosters and shift sheets on the walls of Tom's office.

Big Time frowned. 'Diesel oil. Heavy duty. The kinda stuff you find on docks, or harbours.'

'Yeah,' contributed Jeb. 'Like tar. A dockside kind of smell. Oily.'

'On what? The tyres?' enquired Hanrahan.

Both men nodded.

'Lieutenant?' asked Jeb Kingdom, examining the next month's roster.

'Yeah?'

'That Thursday the nineteenth. I'll maybe switch with Jimmy Fitz, if that's OK with you. My brother's fighting that night.'

Jeb Kingdom's youngest brother had been a patrolman in the Department, and an amateur welterweight with a drop-dead combination of double-southpaw hooks followed by a straight right,

221

and even though his opponents knew that was his ace in the hole, they never could get out of the way of it.

Luke Kingdom had gone pro just after Christmas and now he was fighting his way up through the card, and would soon be among the contenders.

Tom nodded. 'Sure thing. Maybe some of the guys would like to go along. If you can square the roster it's fine by me.'

Kingdom smiled, a real one this time. 'Thanks, boss. Oh, one other thing.'

'Uh-huh?'

'In the tool-bag were a couple of items you could never use on a Porsche, on any car, come to that.'

This was why Tom liked being a detective. This was why he liked his detectives. Homicide had the pick of the crop, and of the six squads, the one with Jeb, Big Time, Jimmy Fitz and Tommy Boyle was probably just ahead on points.

'What kind of items, Jeb?'

'Well, a marlin spike, like they use on yachts for ropes and cables. And a long-spouted oil can, for getting deep into places, um . . .'

'Places,' contributed Big Time, 'where short-spouted ones can't reach.'

They laughed, and as Jeb finally helped himself to some chewing gum, Tom nodded, satisfied.

'Do you think,' he asked, 'you could break into the car sometime real soon, and get a hold of that can?'

'Without a warrant . . . ?' protested Big Time, affecting to be appalled.

'Sure,' said Kingdom. 'For forensics?'

Tom nodded, opening his drawer for a fresh pack of Winstons.

'Then we put it back?' asked Big Time, who actually did not like the idea of stealing somebody else's property, even a suspect's.

'Then we could put back a replica. They sell them in the Long Wharf chandler's,' suggested Jeb Kingdom, popping a strip of spearmint gum into his mouth.

'Sure. And we keep the original for evidence,' replied Hanrahan, who was never surprised by Jeb's devious initiatives.

222

'We allowed to know what this guy has done?' asked Kingdom.

Lieutenant Tom Hanrahan lit his cigarette and waved the match about till it expired. 'One of these days,' he said. 'But in the meantime, keep separate notebooks and we do not discuss it.'

Both men said sure thing and moseyed on out.

Tom Hanrahan gazed at the sheets of fingerprints and felt grimly satisfied. If the long-spouted can had traces of the kerosene which somebody had put in the diesel ignition chamber, plus traces of diesel oil around its spout, plus Sebastian Tree's fingerprints, that could well be the start of the evidence which would prove Tree had murdered Jack Fitzrowan.

Alison Clancy, meanwhile, stopped off at De Luca's on Charles Street and bought four lamb cutlets for her supper and, from the wine and cheese shop next door, some frozen spinach, fresh-baked granary bread, Greek honey, yoghurt and Panama coffee. She did not notice the yellow taxi stopped a half-block down the street, as she got back into the BMW and turned left into Mount Vernon Street.

By the time Alison had found a place to park and was walking along the mews, choosing the right door keys from her Americas Cup key ring – a present from Jack – the yellow taxi had cruised past, turned round and had stopped across Mount Vernon Street, from where its driver, Peter Girolo, could see into the mews.

Alison unlocked the three locks on her front door and let herself in. Inside the small hall, she closed the door behind her and put the brown paper bags with her supper in them on to a pine surface in her kitchen. She pressed the message playback on her answer machine and listened to Marta, her cleaner, saying she had a cold and could not come in, her mother in Seattle saying why had she not phoned since a week last Sunday and her dentist's receptionist reminding her she had an appointment with the dental hygienist the next day.

Suddenly she felt tired. It had been kind of hectic recently. Things had not stopped since Jack's funeral. It had been strange sitting in Mike's law office, talking business as if they had never been married. It had been quite unsettling walking in and out of Big Jack's office with fewer signs each day that he, so vital and full of life, had ever existed.

And it had been weird, how that creep, Sebastian Tree, had just come back to work as if nothing had happened.

Alison climbed wearily upstairs and stepped out of her skirt. She turned on the shower and peered at her face in the mirrored wall above her washbasin. God, she looked weary. Maybe a mud pack and some new make-up. Not that she used more than pale lipstick and a little eye-liner. But shopping for make-up and lovely, aromatic oils and skin lotions was a wonderfully therapeutic indulgence.

As she stripped off her day's clothes and put her hair up, Alison resolved she would spend all Saturday morning on Newbury Street, buying goodies to pamper herself.

And, she promised, as she turned sideways and studied her lithe tummy in the glass – lithe but maybe not so slender as it had been before Jack died – no more M&Ms. Not until she had lost about four pounds.

And look at her skin. Yes. Definitely a mud pack. She would put it on before cooking the lamb cutlets. Before defrosting the spinach? Sure. Wouldn't take more than a few minutes.

While this domestic activity was going on inside the little mews house, Peter Girolo sat in the taxi deep in thought. Having studied the girl over the last half-hour, he had made certain that this was indeed the Alison Clancy who had been second counsel at his trial.

The four years since then had certainly improved her. He remembered a slightly earnest young woman with a sensible walk and dull, law-firm outfits. But now she had a confidence in her step, and quietly expensive clothes. Still very much the reliable professional executive, but dressed these days by Ralph Lauren and Max Mara, rather than some chain store recommended by the head of the typing pool.

And the kid had lost some weight, he thought to himself. Amused that, so busy had he been since coming out of Marion, this was the first time he had found himself really noticing a woman, the way nature had intended.

He sat there, wondering how he should make the approach. And assessing her at the same time. Until he could be sure of his hunch that this was not only a person who would listen to his proposal, and would be able to further it in the right quarters, but one who could be relied on to keep her mouth shut and remain discreet.

Then there was the question of where? Going to her home was out of the question. He had already established that she drove to and from work, and occasionally ate out in the evenings. She did not wear a wedding or betrothal ring, so she probably was not married. Did she have a boyfriend? A lover?

Did she share the house in Willow Mews with anyone else? A paying tenant? A sister? Someone who was close enough for Alison Clancy to impart Girolo's secret business to?

All of those questions were going through Peter Girolo's mind when he noticed a pattern of events in and around Willow Mews which very few others would have understood. But he, a product of the Scuola, recognized it very well.

It was not just the builder's van parked near by, in a pricey residential street, at an hour when every builder on planet earth would long since have clocked off for the day. Who ever heard of a builder working after six o'clock? Who ever heard of them working after four thirty? It was not just the two men in their thirties who had arrived in the van together, and were now strolling around the area as if they did not know each other. And it was not the action each took to avoid being noticed by other people who occasionally passed by.

Nor was it the fact that each had the unmistakable gait and other mannerisms of the prison yard and landing, mannerisms which Girolo himself had worked hard not to acquire during his four years in the slammer. It was not even the interest they took in several houses in Willow Mews, including the one Alison Clancy had gone into.

It was none of these things individually. But together they added up to one of two things: a break-in robbery, or a hit.

This was not idle conjecture on the *capo mafioso*'s part, any more than a diagnosis of pregnancy or heart disease would be on a physician's. This was his work, his profession. And he was never wrong, because even once might be fatal.

At first, as he watched the business going down, he was merely an interested observer. After all, did he give a damn if somebody got burglarized or rubbed out? Only if such an act smacked of competition on his territory. That could not be tolerated. Which was the sole motive for the mafia *capo*'s continuing interest. Sure, maybe he wanted to alter the course his life had taken. But he was a prudent man and he was still the *cosa* chieftain in and around Boston.

His next question was, how professional are these guys? After a half-hour, during which time it had become dusk, his opinion was, professional enough. Not top of the league, but they knew what they were doing.

Those two were making a thorough reconnaissance of the locale. Walking and timing a number of alternative approaches and escape routes. Measuring, by pacing, the varying widths in Willow Mews, maybe to check if two cars could pass in opposite directions, or if it might be necessary to place a false road sign at the junction with Mount Vernon Street.

Was this the robbery team? Or were they the advance men? And was it a break-in or a hit? The more he observed them, Peter Girolo's instinct told him it was probably a hit. Their attitude, the seriousness of their demeanour, everything in his experience suggested these were two scouts, preparing the way for a pro-cleaner. He also guessed the star of the show would be around later, either that night or within the next twenty-four hours. Longer than that, the recon would be out of date.

Girolo decided it was time to move, and eased the taxi away from the kerb, driving up Mount Vernon Street towards the State House, right into Joy Street where he parked near the Beacon Hill intersection. He got out, opened the trunk, dropped his tweed cap inside and changed his leather jacket for a long raincoat.

He wished he had brought his Sig Sauer .45 pistol, but he did not believe it was fitting for a man of respect, a serious don, to carry except on very serious occasions.

He put on a pair of clear glass, gold–rimmed spectacles and strolled down Beacon Street, returning to Mount Vernon via a side street with more old, terraced houses.

When he walked past Willow Mews, looking as if he knew where he was going, the two recon men were making their separate ways back to the builder's van.

A few minutes later, the van moved away, lights on, with both men sitting in the front, which Girolo considered was kind of unprofessional after all the trouble they had gone to in the street. This was clearly not the A-team, in the business of client termination.

He checked his wristwatch. Ten after seven. Well, he had no other plans for the evening.

About four hours later, in the living room of her mews house, Alison Clancy switched off the TV and put her two plates and knife and fork into the dishwasher. It had been a typical evening, since Jack's accident. Flicking through the channels, contemplating watching a video and not getting round to it, sipping some apple juice.

She had not realized how much time having an affair with Jack Fitzrowan had taken up. The suppers in town, nights in his mansion, flights at least once every week to New York, Washington, New Orleans or San Francisco. And about every three weeks they would be off to Dublin, London, Paris, Rome, Singapore or Tokyo, often in the Lear Jet, which Jack liked to fly himself – just take-offs and landings, he would leave the boring parts to Johnny Hernandez and Mick Rogers, Zeralda's pilots.

It was interesting that Grace seemed to be able to run the firm without such peripatetic forays into the territories of clients and rivals. Alison smiled as it occurred to her that maybe Big Jack had just enjoyed travelling. The man was a legend, and as he himself had said, half the legend was achievement, the other half, life-style.

'And that, kid, is a damn sight better than most assholes in the pages of *Fortune* . . .'

You bastard, she thought to herself. How could you have gone and got yourself killed like that? I miss you so much . . . And she brushed the moistness from her cheek, as she switched out the light and climbed up to bed, realizing she had completely forgotten about the facial mud pack. Once again.

It was just after eleven o'clock.

A half-hour later, the man walking up Mount Vernon Street went past Willow Mews, stopped, glanced at his wristwatch, checked out the area, then turned and strolled back into the mews, made dark by its narrowness and the angle of the pallid moonlight. He wore a loose overcoat and seemed confident, the way he carried himself. His name was Joseph Cranmer. His ancestors had come over just eight years after the *Mayflower* and his great grandmother had been the New York beauty Henrietta Cranmer, who was the toast of Manhattan in the 1930s just before the Wall Street crash.

Henrietta's husband, the banker J. D. Parker, had lost everything and he had been one of the two ruined millionaires who really did step out of a window (26th floor) of the Chrysler Building to spread himself over the sidewalk below.

The beautiful Henrietta, after a succession of unwise and scandalous affairs, had turned to drink and had died penniless on a derelict wharf, within sight of Riker's Island. Her two sons had gotten involved in loan sharking and the movie business. But only Albert, the loan shark, had prospered, albeit briefly, before NYPD had bust his operation and he had spent seven years in Attica prison.

Joseph Cranmer was Albert's son. He was as far away from the ethos of the *Mayflower* as Ho Chi Minh City. He had graduated from night-club bouncer to brothel owner to small-time coke pusher to bartender to gym and health club manager.

Joseph had unwisely fallen into serious debt with the mob, round about 1986. They had asked him to do a small favour, in return for time to pay. The favour was to have a word with a tailor who had fallen behind in his payments.

Joseph's 'having a word' had resulted in the tailor's premature departure from planet earth. But the manner in which he had contrived to make the death look like an accident, and his total lack of remorse or conscience, had drawn him to certain people's attention and ever since then, Joseph Cranmer had found gainful employment as a professional killer – a mechanic, a cleaner, a hit-man. Joseph Cranmer was not major league, top-drawer, *numero uno* like, say, Peter Girolo. But neither was he a third-rate punk. Joseph was somewhere in between.

He passed Alison Clancy's house without a glance and moved on until he came to number 31, which was set back, behind a wall, covered in wistaria and clematis, just beginning to flower.

Number 31 was unoccupied. The owners had moved to Wisconsin and the place was advertised in the window of Hunneman & Company's realty office near the corner of Mount Vernon and Charles Street. Cranmer let himself in, unlocking the wooden gate and closing it behind him. He had no need to go into the house. Instead, he found the wistaria and outside water pipes his scouts had described to him, and like a figure from some Gothic horror story, coat flapping, he swarmed up the sheer side of the mews house and crouched on the angled rooftop, getting his breath back. After a moment, Joseph Cranmer moved stealthily over the clutter of different rooftops, until he was directly above number 25, where Alison Clancy lay in bed, drowsily poised on that brief precipice between wakefulness and sleep.

His scouts had said the skylight was easy, and they had already ascertained that the primitive alarm system would not be active while the occupant, the target, was inside.

Cranmer produced a couple of simple tools and before one minute had elapsed was easing the heavy skylight open. Beneath the skylight was a shallow loft and Cranmer smiled to himself as he drew the honed Bowie knife from its sheath across his chest. The client had asked for this one to look like a random prowler, a sex pervert, and the killer felt a cold thrill of anticipation. He could professionally allow himself some fun, in the termination of what would be victim number nineteen.

At first, for the merest fraction of time, he thought his neck had touched a piece of guttering, a water pipe maybe. But when a thump of adrenalin in his chest and the sudden pounding of his heart coincided with the hairs on the back of his neck actually rising – he could feel them move – Joseph Cranmer knew something very bad was occurring. For this was no water pipe, this was the cold, unfriendly snout of a pistol.

The voice was gentle, it seemed . . . reasonable, and it breathed the words, 'Live or die, choose fast, lay the knife down quietly, and shut the skylight.'

Joseph contemplated rolling left and thrusting the hunting knife up and into the gentle and reasonable whisperer. But his legs had started to tremble uncontrollably. This was no night patrolman, no Boston Irish cop – which had been his immediate thought. This man would kill him. It took one killer to recognize another. And the predator in him instinctively recognized his nemesis, as if he had always known when this moment would come.

Joseph Cranmer slid the Bowie knife back into its sheath and very quietly, very carefully, closed the skylight.

When he came to, he was so overwhelmed by the smell of gasoline that it took a moment to realize he was trussed like a chicken, and another moment to realize he was in the trunk of a yellow taxi. The man who had so easily taken him stood gazing down, the wreck of a big Dodge truck looming large behind him. They seemed to be in some kind of cemetery for wrecked trucks.

The tall guy was holding a Zippo lighter in one hand. In the other, held loosely at his side, was a plastic gasoline can. The kind you keep in the trunk for emergencies.

'I have made some enquiries,' he said, relaxed and conversational. 'It seems to me you are Joseph Cranmer, a.k.a. Jackson Heights.'

Cranmer swallowed. This was something. To identify him *and* know his mob nickname . . . this guy surely was something.

'So, Joseph,' went on his captor, 'you want to die?'

Joseph Cranmer shook his head, he guessed there was fear in his eyes.

'Kind of strange, isn't it, Joe?' went on the guy with the gently terrifying voice. 'Here we are, you and me. We take life, in the course of our business. And yet, when it's our own that's on the line . . . suddenly it's very precious.'

Spare me, thought Cranmer, a fuckin philosopher. But his frightened eyes kept looking into his captor's, searching for a glimmer
of weakness. There was none. How was he to know this was the
chief of the Boston mafia?

'Who wants Alison Clancy dead?' asked Girolo.

Cranmer shook his head. 'I don't know. It's not how I work.'

Girolo appeared to turn this over in his mind. And he seemed
to see the sense of it.

'Sure,' he said. 'Well, that's that.' And he flicked on the Zippo,
its tiny flame ready to ignite the gas fumes so heavy in the air.

Christ, shouted Cranmer's survival instinct, he's gonna do it!!

'Desmond Dekker . . .' croaked his voice, failing him in his time
of need, so parched had it become as fear in his mouth dried up
the saliva.

Girolo held the flame cupped in his left hand. 'A seventies pop
singer has taken a contract on a businesswoman?' He shook his
head and readied the flame, holding the lighter nearer. 'I don't
think so . . .'

'No, no!!' croaked the contract killer. 'This Desmond Dekker
is a fixer.' A fixer was someone who brought information, hired
robbery teams, found fences, laundered money and, on occasion,
acted as a middleman, a cut-out, between people who wanted other
people dead and those who had a good track record for such
services.

Girolo shook his head, amused, closed the Zippo, killing its
flame. 'OK, where does he live?'

Joseph Cranmer squirmed. 'Come on, I can't tell you that . . .'

Peter Girolo flicked the lighter back on, shrugged and stepped
back.

'Sudbury. Near the Boathouse,' breathed Cranmer.

Girolo shut the Zippo and took some car keys from his pocket.
'Exactly where?'

Joseph Cranmer felt that, as long as he could stay alive, he
had a chance. 'I'll guide you. It's kinda hard to find, without
directions . . .'

Girolo said OK and slammed the trunk shut. In his dark,

gasoline-fumed coffin, Cranmer tried to figure out how to get the drop on this arrogant son of a bitch.

Twenty-seven minutes later the taxi stopped and the trunk was opened. The *capo* hauled Cranmer out and stood him, propped him, against the side of the car.

'Joe, this is Sudbury now, near the Boathouse. So, where, exactly?' he enquired softly, without a hint of malice. And the man who had been looking forward to killing Alison Clancy, even though he did not know her, began to tremble and weep.

Twelve before one in the morning.

Alison slept soundly, in her mews house, unaware of her brush with the Grim Reaper. She dreamed about a new store which had opened on Newbury. Her ex-husband was there, serving at the counter, oblivious of her presence.

She knew Jack Fitzrowan was there someplace, and it was frustrating being unable to lay her eyes on him. And someone was watching her, someone who made her feel uneasy. Then she was walking by a stream, in the countryside. A man was walking beside her who gave her great peace and security. At first she assumed it was Jack, but when she turned to look up at him it was someone else, a much younger man. A man she had never seen before.

And across the stream, on the other side of the stream, which had become wider, deeper, stood the unmistakable figure of her beloved, Jack Fitzrowan.

He smiled to her and raised a hand in greeting. He seemed very real and very happy. In her sleep, Alison Clancy smiled and fell into a dreamless slumber, secure and content.

Twelve before one in the morning.

In the Fitzrowan mansion, not far away, at 85 Mount Vernon, young Sir Paul was not asleep. The light in his attic study glowed as he worked at the bank of computers.

One thing was clear to him. Nobody called Ross had applied for education, medical care or insurance for a child who had not been registered legally and correctly at birth, on 14 June, or four weeks either side, in either the Republic of Ireland, Britain or the USA, in the year of the birth of Helen Costello and Jack Fitzrowan's love child, Oliver.

There were no adoptions registered to anyone called Ross and in the Dublin police, the Garda Síochána, records of investigations into illegal adoption and fostering, there was not a word about the trade in babies at Inniscoor, although four legal adoptions of infants born out of wedlock were recorded in the Irish Civil Service's national register at Dublin Castle.

Paul felt tired and spent. He had been so thrilled by his piece of luck in New York, when the man with the limp had told him about the Rosses and the sudden arrival of a noisy boy-child. For the Rosses had occupied the very apartment old Sister Immaculata had revealed to him was the Manhattan address of the couple who had taken charge of the baby Oliver, that awful morning of 14 June 1954, an event that had almost deranged poor sixteen-year-old Helen, love of his father's life.

And the limping man had seemed quite certain, when he had said that a few years later they had returned to the old country. Paul shoved a hand through his hair. This was a dead-end. Either the name Ross had been false all along, which would be strange when they had employed two aliases in their visit to Ireland to adopt the baby, or the man with the limp had been mistaken.

Or making it up. Lying.

Paul Fitzrowan felt himself blushing. It had begun to look as if he had wasted all this time on the mendacious whim of an eccentric New Yorker. What a klutz.

Twelve before one in the morning.

Tom Hanrahan eased himself out of bed, trying not to disturb Grace, who was sleeping peacefully, a pillow clutched over her head to drown his alleged snoring, which he always denied.

He had got to the phone on the third ring, and on the other end, Luther had said, 'They just fished one of your snitches out of the Mystic River at the Wellington Bridge. You want the case?'

'Who is it?' he had asked. Tom never jumped to conclusions. But when Luther had told him he had sighed and said sure, he would take it. It was the least he could do, after all.

Twelve before one in the morning.

The doorbell was ringing loudly in the Dekker residence, in Sudbury, in the vicinity of Boston, not far from the Boathouse bar and restaurant. The white and grey house was detached, clapperboard and stone, and stood in its own acre, shielded from the road by trees and a small landscaped mound.

It took Desmond Dekker all of four minutes to come to the door. You could hear him on the other side, staring through the spyhole, then unlocking locks and slipping off security chains. Desmond Dekker took no chances.

Finally the door swung open. He was angry. An angry man in purple shorts, holding a MAC-10 machine-pistol loosely at his side. 'What the hell are you doing here?' he demanded, staring at the gasoline-damp Joseph Cranmer. 'You should know better than to come here. You do the job? You get your money, but I don't keep money here, everybody knows that. You'll get your fuckin pay-off tomorrow. Canvas grip, usual place, twenty big ones in hundreds. Used notes. What the fuck is that smell? You spilled gas? Is it kerosene?'

'It's gas,' said a voice from beside the door.

'Aw, great, who the fuck –' Dekker stepped forward in his purple shorts and peered to his left. His expression vaulted from pissed off to curiosity. There was no fear because he was the guy with the gun.

'My name is Girolo,' said the *capo*, softly. 'You maybe have heard of me.'

Dekker stared at him, a tall man in a raincoat, dark hair and an unforgiving gaze, and the look of curiosity changed to one of unease. 'You're the mafia guy . . .'

'There is no mafia, Mr Dekker,' replied Girolo. 'Just a business network. Sometimes we have to remind people who runs things, you know how it is.'

234

Joseph Cranmer watched the two men, alert, figuring if now would be a good time to jump Girolo. But he knew the man's reputation, and one spark would turn him into a torch.

Dekker too was figuring things out. A simple contract on a dame. Forty thousand dollars for nothing. Twenty to Joe Cranmer, twenty to himself. Money for nothing. What the hell did that have to do with the mob? Unless, of course, the victim had been somebody's girlfriend.

Fuck.

'Was the lady under your, uh, protection, Mr G?'

'Let's just say nobody does that kind of business in my town. Unless I say so.'

Dekker digested this. Thoughtful. Absurd in his purple undershorts. And highly dangerous, finger still on the MAC-10 trigger. He knew about how Peter Girolo had brought good order and discipline to the Boston *cosa*. By a ruthless and surgical programme of murder.

He wondered if Girolo would make him pay over the contract fee in compensation for the woman he mistakenly believed Joseph Cranmer had butchered. If so, fine. Forty thousand was a cheap price to pay to avoid incurring this serious mobster's displeasure. Everybody knew Girolo was on his way to taking over New York City. It was rumoured Boston was just the hors-d'œuvre.

'Joe,' he said, still looking at Girolo, 'what the hell have you gone and done?' And without turning his head, he abruptly raised his gun arm to the side and squeezed off a burst which knocked the professional killer off his feet and dropped him on his back, on the gravel.

Girolo watched Dekker, ready to make his move if the guy even looked like pointing that thing at him. Cranmer twitched and trembled for about half a minute, then he was dead.

Dekker set the MAC-10 to safe and propped it against his doorway. He stepped over to Cranmer's corpse and stooped to grasp the ankles before dragging it into the shadows beside the front porch. He went inside and came back wearing a towelling bathrobe and with a couple of rugs which he threw over the body. Then, like a housewife who has completed a chore, he turned back to Girolo.

'You can't get the help these days. I really, really, did not know the Clancy woman was under your wing . . . What can I do, Don Girolo?' He remembered his manners. 'You wanna step inside?'

'This is fine,' replied Girolo. 'You can tell me who wanted her dead.'

'Say what?'

Girolo's eyes glinted. 'Who is the client?'

'Ah, Mr Girolo, please . . .' Dekker essayed a worldly chuckle, which came out as a snigger. Probably not a great idea, in the circumstances. 'We are professional men you and me.'

'You want to live, don't you?' Girolo's voice sounded almost kind, sort of remorseful, as if he meant I don't want to kill you, have you killed, but I surely will.

Desmond Dekker knew when it was time to quit playing a losing hand. 'It's a guy called Tree,' he said. 'Sebastian Tree. He's senior VP or some such with an electronics company. In Cambridge, near the MIT building.'

'Tree,' said Girolo.

Dekker nodded. 'Sebastian. Sebastian Tree. He calls me Mr Apple, I call him Lemon.'

'Mr Lemon . . .'

'Sure. Mr Lemon.'

'How much?'

'Thirty grand,' lied Dekker, who just could not help himself. 'You can have it.'

'I don't want your money.'

Dekker nodded, big nods this time. 'Of course, Mr Girolo. No offence intended. No disrespect.'

Peter Girolo produced a mobile phone from his left raincoat pocket. He threw it to Dekker who caught it. 'Call him,' he said.

'Ah, that's not the arrangement.'

'Call him.'

'Sure thing.' And his hands shaking slightly, Dekker tapped out Sebastian Tree's home number.

236

Sebastian Tree was sitting in his oak-panelled study, listening to Beethoven on his state-of-the-art Bang & Olufsen eight-speaker pro-logic system. His eyes were closed and he nursed a balloon glass of 1928 Exshaw Cognac.

It would soon be all over. One of these nights the Clancy bitch would be butchered, a victim, the police would conclude, of some crazed sex killer. The papers would be full of it for a day or two. The *Globe* would run a piece on serial killers, digging up references to the dormitory slayings, Geoffrey Dahmer, Son of Sam and so on. He would attend the funeral – he had decided on the black Ceruti two piece, European three-button jacket, white shirt and navy necktie.

Tree smiled as he imagined days ahead, free of Alison Clancy, where he could run rings around Jack Fitzrowan's daughter Grace and gently manoeuvre Zeralda Electronics back to the precipice. Was he going too far? He grinned, as the overture swelled towards a crescendo. Nothing but total destruction of the myth that Jack Fitzrowan had built up around himself would do.

My God, when Sebastian Tree thought about his mother, not the cloying, adoptive one, Emily Tree, who still imagined that money and the occasional phone call equalled parenthood, but his real mother. When he thought about the fear and loneliness she must have felt, carrying that bastard's unwanted child. And the pain when, over forty years before, he had been taken from her arms and handed over to the Trees, via some third party who had made that long journey to collect him, when he thought of all that, of his inauspicious entry into the world, his blood quite simply went cold.

Whunk!

He would never forget the sound that boom had made when it had smashed Big Jack's head and swept him into the heaving seas off Nantucket Sound. Vengeance is mine, sayeth the Lord? Not this time, baby, thought Tree to himself, as the overture climaxed, volume high.

It was only in the silence which followed that he realized the phone was ringing.

Sebastian Tree muted his sound system, using the remote switch, and lifted his phone receiver.

'Tree residence,' he announced.

'Mr Lemon . . . ?'

His heart thumped as he recognized the voice of Desmond Dekker, Mr Apple. 'Why are you calling me here?'

'Tonight was the night.'

Hallelujah! Tree could not keep the grin from his face. Annoyed though he was that Mr Apple had traced his unlisted number, Sebastian Tree's relief and joy were too great for him to carp. 'Excellent. I trust . . .' he paused, 'I trust it was not without pain?'

Silence.

'Hello . . . Mr Apple?'

'It wasn't possible.'

'What do you mean?'

'I'm returning your money.'

'I don't want the goddam money, I want the bitch dead.' Maybe it was the brandy which had loosened his tongue. Maybe it was the enormous disappointment.

'Your money is on its way back to you.' Time stopped, for this was not the voice of Mr Apple who, in spite of his lethal connections, Sebastian Tree felt he could manipulate. This was a calm, quiet voice, somehow familiar in a vague, unsettling sort of way, like an aroma you could not quite pin-point.

'Who is this?'

'You will not contact Mr Apple again.'

'No kidding? Says who?'

'You will not harm the woman. Since you did not have the balls to do it yourself that is probably not a problem. Now, Sebastian, listen to me . . .'

Fuck. Sebastian. After all the trouble he had gone to to disguise his identity.

'If you try to contact Mr Apple again, you die. Harm the woman, you die. The woman slips on the soap, pray she does not, for again, you die. Clear?'

Tree's heart was racing so fast he thought he might pass out. 'Is this a hoax? I have no idea what you are talking about . . . !'

Silence. Then the line went dead.

The first thing Sebastian Tree contemplated was leaving town. The next was to keep the Beretta pistol he had acquired years before in LA close to him at all times. And by the time an hour had elapsed, at three in the morning, with a jug of strong black Panama coffee inside him, Sebastian Tree had convinced himself he had the balls to see this one out.

He guessed that the low-life Dekker probably never had the connections he pretended to. And because he had suddenly gotten scared at taking Tree's money, twenty grand in cash (the rest on proof the bitch was dead), he had probably decided on this little drama just to get off the hook. That was it. But nobody could fool Sebastian Tree so easily.

Tree double locked all his doors and went to bed, sleeping the sound sleep of one who enjoys a consummate ability to delude himself.

'Body had been in the water maybe three hours, no more.' Barry Maguire the police pathologist greeted Lieutenant Tom Hanrahan with those words as the detective climbed out from his dusty Aston Martin, probably unique with its blue strobe light along the dash and back window, and held out a mug of coffee, which Tom accepted with a nod.

Together they walked along the grassy bank, ducking under the plastic POLICE – STOP – CRIME SCENE tapes towards a lonely cluster of battery powered Forensic Department lamps on precarious slender aluminium stalks, casting their pale glow over a haphazard arrangement of canvas screens that protected the victim from curious gaze.

Actually, at one thirty-seven in the morning, on the bank of the Mystic River below Wellington Bridge, there were not many curious souls abroad.

Except, of course, the tenacious Milly Dunne, still pursuing her mafia turf-war story. She had, as usual, ignored the taped cordon and was standing at the open aperture to the screened-off area, taking photos of the corpse of the dead man.

'Cause was not drowning, though,' the pathologist was saying, as Tom's eyes glinted upon seeing the *Globe* reporter. 'Two bullets, nine millimetre copper jacket, fired from a Colt, I would guess.' Tom knew this was because the rifling inside the barrel of Colt pistols was anti-clockwise, unlike most other handguns. A slug which had not been too mutilated would show rifling marks under any kid's drugstore magnifying glass. He carried one in his coat pocket, next to a piece of plastic for helping reluctant locks to open.

'Milly, get yourself outta here,' said Hanrahan, meeting her welcoming grin with a glare. 'If you have no respect for the Department at least have some respect for the fuckin dead.'

'I love you too, Lieutenant,' replied Millicent Dunne. 'So. The victim. Regular low-life from what I can gather. Also rumoured he was a snitch. Not a good insurance risk, mmm?'

Tom Hanrahan pushed her aside and stared down at the sodden, broken, once-living thing, looking for all the world as if it had been dropped from an aeroplane. Crumpled, limbs askew, the right half of the head gone, most of the brain too. On the blue-grey face an expression of . . . peace. At last.

'Alberto Sanzo was OK,' he said quietly. 'Alberto Sanzo had a big heart, and I suppose . . .' he sipped his coffee, 'he was kind of a friend of mine.'

'Me too,' said Sergeant Danny Tarantola as he joined Hanrahan, blocking Milly Dunne with his broad, Italian back.

'So was this another mob killing? Are the citizens of Boston supposed to brace themselves for a return to the Prohibition era?' the reporter asked, completely unmoved by the humanity just displayed.

Tom was silent for a moment, as if he were praying, which is just what he was doing, a prayer for the soul of Alberto Sanzo, small-time criminal, pimp and stoolpigeon. When he had finished, he turned to Milly Dunne. 'Millicent Agnes Dunne, I am arresting you for wilful obstruction of a police officer in the execution of his duty, one, and two, for refusing to leave a crime scene after repeated instructions from a police officer so to do.'

As Millicent Dunne grinned a 'you cannot be serious' grin, and opened her mouth to say some wisecrack, Tom nodded to the big uniformed cop who had just arrived and was standing behind her, 'Joe, read Miss Dunne her Miranda rights, then take her into custody and call for transport to move her downtown. Charge her and lock her up.'

Milly Dunne's normally cheerful, been-there-seen-it-done-it expression had become frozen with consuming outrage. 'Oh boy,' she hissed, 'you are really arresting a member of the press? Harassing an accredited crime reporter with two Pulitzer runner-ups? Thanks for a great story, Tom.'

Tom Hanrahan gazed at her, as he might look at a lab specimen. 'You have no respect for the dead. While you're sitting in the paddy wagon, while you are in your cell, for the few minutes till your attorney springs you, just think about this man's sister, two hundred pounds, forty years old, with the brain of a five-year-old child. This quote-unquote low-life in here looked after her, fed her, clothed her and gave her love and hope. Dignity even. What is going to become of her now? Kids laugh at her and throw things at her in the street. She goes with men for a bar of candy. You maybe think you're a hard-assed crime reporter. You're playing at it. Get a fucking life.' He turned to Joe Daly. 'Get her outta my sight.'

Joe took Millicent Dunne by the arm and led her away. As they receded, she turned her head and called back, 'I wonder if you would have been so goddam righteous before you married money . . . the millionaire cop gets emotional? You can afford it, pal. Playing at it? You would know . . .'

Danny the Wop watched her go, shrugged and turned to study the corpse of Alberto Sanzo. After a moment he said, 'Oh, well.'

'Alberto knew the score,' replied Tom Hanrahan. 'It had to happen . . . now that the grown up mob is back in town.'

'Intel confirm,' said Tarantola, 'that one Peter Girolo is reliably reported to have taken over Italian organized crime from north of

New York and is based in Boston. You read that in their weekly digest?'

'Sure thing,' replied Hanrahan.

'They say he's something.'

'Sure looks that way.' Tom Hanrahan tugged a stick of gum from its pack and, as he unwrapped it, resolved to pull this Peter Girolo in and have an eyeball to eyeball. For this was not the mafia's town, it was Boston PD's.

Time to remind everybody.

10

Darcy was preoccupied, scarcely noticing the run-down grey and brown stone buildings of Queens, or the surreal graffiti, in its fluorescent pinks, mint greens, lilacs and yellows which adorned or defaced, whichever your point of view, every surface accessible to a spray can.

She was preoccupied by two separate matters. One was her feeling that soon she would know the identity of the family who in 1954 had gone from New York to Limerick in the Irish Republic, and thence to Inniscoor, to pay Father Thomas Flynn cash in return for the illegal adoption of Helen Costello's newly born male child, whom Helen had called Oliver.

Darcy's other preoccupation was more disconcerting.

She had left Dublin just over eight hours earlier, taking the TWA flight direct to JFK. Normally she would have slept soundly until the big 747's wheels touched down Stateside, but this time she had remained awake, dozing only fitfully, for events of the previous evening – late afternoon and early evening – had once again given her more pleasure than she had imagined possible.

Pronsias Stevenson had been there when she had arrived at the Fitzwilliam Street house, in Dublin. He had opened the door to her, the same old, boring old Pronsias she remembered from her teens. This is a mistake, Darcy had told herself. What the hell am I doing here when I could be hot on the trail of Oliver and all that money? And if it was a little diversion she had wanted, there was always her athletic and enthusiastic Americas Cup skipper, who could be relied on to perform and keep his mouth shut.

Then the Dublin lawyer had smiled and, as he closed the door, he had touched her hand and brushed his mouth gently against her hair . . .

And here was Darcy Fitzrowan Bailey, one of the most desirable women in Europe, according to *Vogue*, one of the most desirable *around*, according to *Vanity Fair*, sitting in an air-conditioned Lincoln, oblivious of the graffiti of Queens and the looming Queens Bridge and Manhattan skyline that had never before failed to stir her soul, weak with memories of five hours and eleven minutes in the company of the only man who had ever brought her complete – complete? – unbelievable, sexual fulfilment.

And not just once.

Darcy smiled dreamily as memories of those five quite incredible hours occupied her thoughts, to the exclusion, she could hardly believe it herself, of the imminent identification of her Daddy's mystery bastard and twelve and a half per cent of $218 million.

Pronsias Stevenson, you dark horse, she mused, why could I not have met you years ago? She imagined what might have happened if she had accepted his invitation that hot afternoon of the Kentucky Derby, at Churchill Downs, when Pronsias had asked her to dinner. And her legs went weak.

Pronsias. She smiled, like a schoolgirl. It was a lovely name . . .

There were television and press cameras outside Boston's luxury Ritz-Carlton Hotel, capturing the glittering guests of the Katakura Foundation's Boston Symphony Banquet.

Senator Olympia Snowe was there, along with the Japanese ambassador, who had flown up from Washington DC. So too was Van Morrison, along with André Previn and Kiyo Miyagi, the nineteen-year-old violin virtuoso from Kyoto. Robert de Niro, Al Pacino and Nicolas Cage were there, and so was Tom Clancy, ex-President George Bush with Mrs Bush, and Miriam Rockefeller, all dressed to the nines, relaxed and comfortable to be guests at an event so unambiguously in good taste and non-political.

Cameras popped as Grace Hanrahan stepped out from the Zeralda Corporation's midnight blue Bentley, the door held open by Edwin the chauffeur, as resplendent as any senator in the grey morning coat, brocade silk waistcoat and black bow tie, an ensemble he had insisted on wearing. All he needed, Grace had thought, was a black top hat and he could have led any New Orleans Dixieland funeral with pride. But of course she had told him he looked great which, on reflection, he really did.

'Mrs Grace Hanrahan, you are so incredibly kind to have graced us with your presence. I just can't believe my good fortune.'

Grace turned and there he was, tall, thick black hair, greying, slightly unkempt, glowing with fitness, eyes twinkling with good humour.

Tak Katakura.

She extended her hand, smiling coolly and saying it was good of him to invite her and she did so enjoy an evening out, in such a good cause, when all the time, inside, her stomach had tightened. Not because this was the man who had tried to ruin her firm. Grace was too tough a businesswoman for that. Oh no, her stomach had been gripped by surprise, for upon setting eyes on this six foot three inch stranger, from the other side of the world, there was no getting away from the absurd and improbable fact that they had each taken one look at the other and found they really liked what they saw.

Absurd. So absurd that Grace knew she must look quite angry, a reaction she had always had when she met someone she found attractive, ever since her first school dance.

The President of the Katakura Corporation of Japan politely offered his arm and escorted his guest into the Ritz-Carlton, under a red and gold canopy. And anyone watching would have assumed she did not like him one bit.

'I hope you are not still mad at me for the take-over bid?' Katakura asked solicitously.

'Not a bit,' replied Grace, with a coolness that bordered on hostility. 'Business is business, after all.'

When wooden sailing boats are neglected, it shows. The stays and rigging lines become slack. Teak decks lose their spruceness and take on a dirty, grey dullness. Aluminium gets frosty with sea salt and brass turns dull and jaded, with verdigris in the joins and corners.

The sails become hard and dry in their sailbags. Wood map tables and shelves accumulate that heavy calibre dust which docks and harbours produce all over the world. Portholes get smeared and greasy, stained with rain polluted from the city and halyards rattle and screech, orphaned and uncomfortably exposed in dry-dock.

Thus it was with *Zeralda of Erin*, once Jack Fitzrowan's pride and joy. Sailing with Jack aboard *Zeralda* was like being in the last century. He loved to get her beam over, sailing hard into a stiff breeze, the noise of bow hitting choppy seas almost an aphrodisiac, he used to say, as spume and spray hit his tough, granite, Kerry features, dripping off his eyebrows and running down his sinewy, muscled neck.

Just look at her now. All that's missing are the cobwebs, thought Tom Hanrahan, as he stood by the main saloon coachroof, gazing over the abandoned ketch.

Edward Bailey, to whom Jack had left *Zeralda of Erin*, had written to Pronsias Stevenson saying that happy memories of sailing with Sir Jack really made it too painful to enjoy being on board the craft without him. And he would like Pronsias to handle the sale of the ketch. Edward had also asked the Dublin lawyer not to mention this to his wife Darcy since, as he understood it, the craft had been willed to him personally and was his to dispose of in any way he wished.

Pronsias Stevenson was used to odd goings on in the business of legacies and bequests, and he had passed the letter on to Grace, saying that since she was based in Boston, she might like to discuss with her sister and 'young Sir Paul' if they would like to keep *Zeralda* in the family.

This was a calculated insult to Paul, who as head of the Fitzrowan family had authority in such a matter. But Pronsias Stevenson's contempt for him had become apparent in several ways since the reading of the Will.

Stevenson had also advised Grace that he would prefer not to be the first to discuss the matter with Darcy, since he considered Edward had *de facto* retained the good offices of Stevenson, Stevenson & Malahide in the matter.

So Pronsias Stevenson could keep a secret. Tom Hanrahan was wondering what other secrets the Dublin lawyer had kept close to his chest when Tommy Boyle emerged from the after cabin hatch, which gave access to the engines, and called, 'Hey, Lieutenant, we got a match.'

Sitting in the main saloon, sipping strong coffee and smoking Winstons, Tom Hanrahan and Tommy Boyle compared a fresh set of prints with those obtained by deception when Jeb and Big Time had washed some automobiles out at the Zeralda plant in Cambridge.

'No question,' opined Detective Boyle. 'There is the scarred left three, just like all over his Porsche.'

Hanrahan nodded, studying the two sets of prints carefully. Tommy Boyle had found them on a bulkhead above the diesel primer valve, in which Coastguard forensics officers had found traces of kerosene which would have blown the face off anyone trying to prime the port engine, for a quick start from cold.

'And the long-spouted can . . . ?' asked the Lieutenant.

'Sebastian Tree's prints, thumb and l's three and four, where he held it while unscrewing the cap on top.'

'What did they find in the can?' enquired Hanrahan.

'Traces of kerosene, commercial code matches the stuff found in the diesel primer in there . . .' Tommy Boyle jerked his head aft, in the direction of the engine compartment, 'which would link Tree to that particular act. Show probable cause and we have intent, maybe conspiracy. Prove he tampered with the boom . . .' he hit the side of his head with the flat of his right hand, 'we have enough circumstantial to go to the DA.'

The Lieutenant nodded. Tommy was doing a good job co-ordinating all this, but he was kind of racing ahead. The long-spouted can would look good in a trial if produced at the right psychological moment . . . *Mister Tree, this can contained the same rare brand of kerosene, traces of which were found in the diesel primer chamber of the murdered man's ketch. If activated, the chamber would have exploded in Jack Fitzrowan's face. Can you explain what this exhibit was doing in the trunk of your expensive sports car, hidden in a bundle of rags . . . ?*

But how often would a DA counsel have the wit to use police evidence in such a damning way? Sadly, in Tom Hanrahan's experience, not always.

'So,' asked Tommy Boyle, 'do we pick him up?'

Hanrahan shook his head, part of his mind still thinking about the previous night's murder. The detective felt instinctively that Peter Girolo must be behind Alberto Sanzo's killing. But how had Girolo figured out that Sanzo was a squealer, when the snitch had been so careful?

He turned to Boyle. 'Not yet. We need to prove motive. OK we have method, we have opportunity. But motive? Murder is a big step. Bigger than something in the heat of the moment. To plan and go into such detailed preparations, and go through with it, that takes resolve. Let's face it, it takes guts. A perverse determination. What reason would Sebastian Tree have to kill Jack Fitzrowan in cold blood?'

As he asked the question, Hanrahan remembered that Grace had told him about Tree's insider dealing with Tak Katakura, and the CEO's attempt to sabotage Zeralda's NASA contract, worth over twenty-one million dollars each month. But did all that add up to a motive for murdering Zeralda's President?

If so, was Tak Katakura behind that? And if he was, was Big Jack's daughter, Tom's wife, safe, attending at that very moment a banquet at the Ritz-Carlton with the same Tak Katakura who might be implicated in her father's death? A death which, with each new forensic revelation, was looking less and less like a simple accident at sea.

Tom's bleeper sounded. He checked the tiny display screen.

2 X H SUDBURY. 231 HAWTHORN. GSW VI+V2 1144 BOTH. YOU WANT?

Which meant a double homicide in Hawthorn Drive, one of Sudbury's more expensive roads, both victims known criminals, died of gunshot wounds. Did Lieutenant Hanrahan want the case?

That address, 231 Hawthorn, rang a bell. Why should he know it? He lifted his radio handset from the saloon table and called in. Luther's gravelly voice responded, 'Tom, yo.'

'Who is it this time?' asked Hanrahan.

'Desmond Dekker, it's his place. Plus a New York button man name of Joseph Cranmer, a.k.a. Jackson Heights. Local crime scene supervisor says it looks like a gunfight and both got fatal.'

Damn. Tom frowned. Organized crime homicides in the Boston area were getting to be an epidemic. He had wanted to be in the Bentley when it collected Grace from the Katakura affair at the Ritz-Carlton. But if this was also the work of Peter Girolo, he would have to attend, for he had made Girolo his top priority, which was pissing off the Superintendent in charge of Major Cases, not to mention the FBI.

He sighed and turned to Tommy Boyle. 'Could you do me a favour?'

Tommy Boyle was way ahead of him. 'Go with the limo to pick up Grace?'

'If that's OK with you.'

'You got it.'

'I owe you one. And uh, get hold of Danny Tarantola,' said Hanrahan, thoughtful. 'Tell him to meet me at the crime scene. I got a couple of things to discuss with him.'

A string quartet from the Boston Symphony Orchestra played some light Mozart, while the invited guests enjoyed a banquet of petit filet de sole, sauce d'homard followed by melon sorbet, then chicken consommé, with a main course of delicious rack of lamb, then the finest cheeses, exquisitely kept, and a delicate pudding of crushed meringue and tiramisu.

Wines were California's best, a diplomatic touch of the Japanese host's, and by the time they had reached the pudding, Grace and Tak Katakura had quite gotten over the initial surprise that they had hit it off on sight, and were discussing all manner of things as if they had never been, corporately, at each other's throats. All manner of things that is, except anything remotely important.

Until Katakura glanced at his wristwatch and murmured, 'Speech time pretty soon . . .'

'Good luck,' smiled Grace, thinking to herself, watch this charmer, he still means to put you in the poorhouse.

The Japanese tycoon grinned and launched into a humorous and detailed description of how his eight-year-old daughter had just failed to get elected to the Tokyo music conservatoire, only a year, as Katakura put it, after he had made a 'fairly generous' donation.

Grace was amused. She knew from her own comprehensive file on him that 'fairly generous' meant two point eight million dollars.

'Which just goes to show,' Katakura was saying, 'that my country's most élite music school is incorruptible.' He smiled ruefully. 'Dammit.'

Grace found herself laughing. He was quite a guy, this Tak Katakura. Urbane, able to laugh at himself, good fun; it was hard to remember he was as ambitious and ruthless as her own father. And even more successful.

Some flunkey banged a gavel and the buzz of conversation died away. The director of the Boston Symphony Orchestra stood up and made a speech welcoming the assembled, glittering company, ending with a warm tribute to Mr Takahashi Katakura, whose generous patronage had funded an entire season of BSO concerts.

As the guests applauded, Katakura rose and replied. His speech was relaxed and sincere, amusing and to the point. Then, to Grace's surprise, the electronics billionaire went on to say, '. . . About four months ago, the success of an American electronics company caused my business advisors to warn me that, if it went on growing the way it looked like, Zeralda Electronics, with its headquarters here in Boston, was headed to grab a vital share of Katakura's world microchip markets.

'The success of Zeralda was attributed to just one man, the legendary Jack Fitzrowan, US citizen and son of Ireland, who single-handedly built up his multinational corporation from an attic workshop in Los Angeles.

'Now I took a long, hard look at this man and his company, and was impressed, and worried, by what I found. For there was nothing Jack Fitzrowan set his mind to that he did not conquer. His hugely successful business, concentrating so cleverly on the design and manufacture of just a few electronic components, a few vital components which were, and are, so reliable, so constantly ahead of their time that even Japanese companies like Sanyo and Sony were ordering them in vast quantities, in preference to my own.

'His Americas Cup contender, *Criterion*, which won the Mackinac Race, with Big Jack himself, not too proud to crew under the skippership of that inspired master sailor, Rich Calhoun, and which looks set to win again, unless someone does something to stop him . . . his string of race-horse winners, the Derby, Longchamps, Churchill Downs, Hong Kong, Ireland . . . where did the man get his energy?

'And I made a mistake . . .'

Katakura paused and sipped from his glass of water. He glanced down at Grace and she thought she could detect a hint of a smile, a friendly one. Then he went on, 'I tried to buy him out.'

In the silence, every eye was on him. Bill Gates, Bob de Niro, Ted Turner, Kay Koplowitz, they all gave him their undivided attention.

'I see the owner of the *Wall Street Journal* is here. Well, his paper gave the inside story of how I failed. I should have known better than to take on Jack Fitzrowan. And not only did he beat me in a . . . fair? No, a very dirty, fight. He snatched a multibillion dollar deal with McDonnell Douglas from under my nose. This was street fighting and the cleverest and the harder man won.

'My old *sensei* who led me through the ways of the martial art, aikido, had dinned it in to me; never, ever fight unless you absolutely *know* you will win. Never, ever fight unless you know you are the master of the moment.' Tak Katakura grinned, shrugged his shoulders. 'I should have listened.'

The guests chuckled. Here was a multinational business tycoon sharing his life with them, taking them into his confidence. Katakura continued, 'Shortly after destroying my dawn raid, Jack Fitzrowan, whom I had come to admire greatly, died, as you will all know, in a tragic accident sailing his beloved ketch in the Nantucket Sound. Well, today I am honoured to have as my personal guest, Jack's daughter Grace . . .'

Grace blushed as the glittering guests applauded politely, and bobbed her head in recognition, wondering all the while what the hell this guy was up to.

'Grace Fitzrowan has taken over Zeralda, and as I would expect from the daughter of Jack Fitzrowan, is just as able and just as tough, and this time I will listen to my *sensei* . . .'

Laughter.

'From now on, and Ted Turner you heard it here first, it is peaceful co-existence between the Katakura Corporation and Zeralda . . .' He turned and raised his glass to Grace, who smiled what she trusted was a cool smile and raised her own in reply.

Later, when the string quartet was playing more Mozart and the limos outside were getting ready to receive the lunch guests, she turned to the Japanese and said, 'What was that all about?'

Tak Katakura met her gaze. 'Pipe of peace. Listen, Grace, this is not the place. Can we meet again, during the next few days?'

'Why?' asked Grace so bluntly there could be no question whose daughter she was.

'I have a proposition,' he replied.

'And how can I trust you, after all that has gone down between our firms?'

Katakura considered this. Then he leaned closer and murmured in her ear, a sensation she was perturbed to discover she did not mind. 'Do not trust Sebastian Tree . . .'

Alison Clancy stepped out of Mike Medevik's offices on to a sunlit Beacon Hill. It was nearly the end of May, and June looked like it might bring a real summer. She strolled up towards the traffic lights on the Charles Street intersection, planning to walk down through the Common, back to her car, which she had parked on Marlborough, near where Tak Katakura was holding his banquet.

Alison had returned to her ex-husband with Grace's instructions that, if he really believed an attempt to claw back the McDonnell Douglas millions from Big Jack's estate was too risky a venture, he should drop it and come up with some other way of keeping what was in fact Zeralda's hard earned money out of the clutches of some adventurer. For if Oliver was still alive and could be traced, who knew what he would be like?

The guy might be a success in his own right, like Jack, or a no-hoper, like young Paul. Although, meeting him in Grace's office the other day, Alison had been struck by a new gravitas about Big Jack's only legitimate son.

Saint or hobo, it stuck in Grace's craw, Alison had reported, and in Darcy's, that the Zeralda fortune should be thrown away, which had never been Big Jack's intention. Even Pronsias Stevenson had conceded that Jack Fitzrowan could not have foreseen his untimely death, just days before he had planned to fly over to Dublin and alter that damned Will.

Mike Medevik had commented he was quite surprised no word of Jack's remarkable codicil had leaked to the media. Just imagine the circus that would bring.

As she shuddered at the thought, the attorney became aware of a tall, fit looking man standing beside her. Now no city dweller shows the remotest interest in their fellow inhabitants, as if somehow that is a talisman against mugging or, God forbid, conversation, but even without looking at him directly, she noticed he wore a well-cut dark suit and carried himself with quiet confidence. Alison smiled to herself. I must be returning to the human race, she thought, if I am beginning to notice good looking men, waiting to cross the street.

She crossed on the light and headed for the gate to Boston Common South. As she started to walk down towards the small bridge over the lake, which had recently been nearly drained for some reason of maintenance and was beginning to smell in the late spring heat, the tall man in the good suit overtook her, walking easily with big loping strides.

Once he was a few yards ahead of her, Alison thought he looked kind of familiar, even from the back, and she was casting her mind over where she might have seen him before – maybe the guy was a lawyer – when he glanced back and paused, a shy grin on his face.

'Miss Clancy, is it not?' he enquired.

Alison relaxed, at least he was not some odd-ball. 'Yes. Alison Clancy, have we met?'

He looked awkward, almost shy. 'Uh, I don't know if this is the right thing. You were on my defence team, nearly five years ago.'

Of course. Peter Michelangelo Girolo. The mob boss who had been predicted around a nine hundred year sentence, before Dan Maine, the senior counsel, had demolished a lazy case by the DA, who had subsequently lost his job, and the only indictment which had stuck was a fairly minor IRS misdemeanour.

The judge had thrown the maximum four years at him. Alison remembered the case with complete recall, for this was the man who had made her sick of defending the indefensible.

'I remember too well, Mr Girolo. You were, um . . .'

'Fatter,' he smiled.

'Prison was obviously a good chance to get in shape,' she heard herself saying, and just stopped from asking him how the food was. Maybe a couple of months in Sing Sing was just what she needed to get back into those suits she had worn at the trial. Two months with no cookies. And definitely no M&Ms.

He had fallen into step beside her. Alison would always remember how he had so easily led her into walking with him, rather than stopping to talk.

'I should have gone down for life, Miss Clancy. Thanks to you guys I didn't.'

Well that was frank. The man was a trained assassin with a law degree and heart of tungsten. The only possible thing in his favour was that he had run his various organized crime ventures with strict rules about not harming 'civilians'. Unless they got in the way.

'You deserved to,' she replied, glad this conversation was taking place in the open air, with plenty of folks around.

'I sure did,' Girolo agreed. 'I sure did . . .'

Alison was not impressed by the note of remorse. She had spent enough time in criminal law, before switching to business, to learn all the weasel ways of hardened career hoodlums and gangland Napoleons. They could be better actors than actors. So Girolo's tone made zero impression.

As they walked on, reaching the bridge, he paused and gazed over the parapet at the few ducks still trying to pretend nothing had happened to their almost empty lake.

'You made a big impression on me, Miss Clancy,' he said.

Oh great, I have a major crime boss here who has a crush on me, thought Alison. Gimme a break.

'Yes,' she said, 'you were fatter. And you had more hair.'

He glanced at her and chuckled. 'Anyway. I would like to retain you. It's delicate. But I was impressed. You have integrity. You have ability. You are smart as a card-sharp. And this is a very, extremely, confidential matter . . .'

OK, so he was not hitting on you, thought Alison. That's a relief. She turned to face him. 'I don't do crime any more. I'm sorry. And if you need someone to act for you in a confidential matter, I suggest you can do better than ask the first person you meet in a park.'

In the silence which followed two of the ducks rose, squawking importantly, from the sparse pool of water and winged their way up towards Frog Pond, flying low over the heads of kids and dogs and ambling parents who had never heard of the mafia except in the movies.

Peter Girolo seemed deep in thought. Alison was deciding to say bye-bye and walk away from him, when he spoke, in that quiet voice she was to come to know so well.

'Last night, a man called Cranmer tried to kill you.'

'I'm sorry?' Prison had obviously got to this guy. Alison was glad one of Boston's Mounted Police was sitting astride his horse just fifty yards away, keeping an eye on things. Then her world turned upside down.

'He was hired,' said Girolo, 'by Sebastian Tree.'

Webster had of course been their real name. That much Darcy had deduced. For they must have entered the Irish Republic with genuine passports. No adoption, illegal or otherwise, was worth going to the risk of forged passports, and anyway, where would ordinary people get such things?

Oh yes, her daddy, Sir Jack Fitzrowan, he would probably have known a man who knew a man. Daddy's millions had bought many things the family preferred not to know about – political favours, commercial advantages, union leverage – but a couple of moderately comfortable New Yorkers? She didn't think so.

So here she stood outside 1548 Madison, on the frontier of North Manhattan, feeling just a tad out of place with her pale linen Chanel suit and Dior shoulder bag.

Stanley Ralph, Zeralda New York's driver, sat in the office's silver Buick, at the kerb, keeping an eye on things.

Darcy walked past number 1548, avoiding a rather scruffy old man sitting on a wooden kitchen chair on the sidewalk, reading the sports pages of *Il Tempo di Milano*. He was in his eighties if not older, in a brown suit that looked straight out of *Guys and Dolls*. He even wore a fedora, pushed back on his head, its beat-up brim crinkled this way and that and he watched as she went into the Dime Busters laundromat.

Inside the dark and humid hell-hole, with air dank and suds-foul from the moisture of fifteen coin-operated washing machines and eight tumble driers, she became aware of a dozen pairs of eyes on her, eyes in faces of every hue known to God or man. A large woman of indeterminate age loomed out of the rain-forest gloom.

'Yeah, lady, what's up?' This gorgon pushed her face close to Darcy's, who wished she had trained in some form of unarmed combat, for assault seemed an imminent probability.

'Webster,' squeaked Darcy, alarmed and for once not in control of the situation.

'Sure, that's me,' the dragon woman grunted, hauling a plastic sack filled with unspeakable undergarments, pulling them out like some hellish conjuror and shovelling them with her enormous paw into an open machine.

'You?' Darcy was still squeaking as she struggled to regain composure.

'Sure.' The woman, reminiscent of some medieval torturer in the bowels of Notre Dame (Darcy had never been much of a historian, but confusing Quasimodo with Giles de Rey was forgivable, in the circumstances). 'Henrietta Webster. You got a whole trunkload in the Buick? Forget it. I close at four.'

'Let me get this straight,' said Darcy Fitzrowan Bailey. '*You* are called Webster? How?'

The washerwoman, right out of Degas, decided Darcy – with a touch of Bram Stoker – peered at her as if she were real stupid. 'Well that's my name, lady. On account of, I am his daughter . . .' She jerked her head at the ancient man on the sidewalk.

Darcy took all this in. 'How old are you?' she demanded, eyeing the monster up and down, the way she would a horse.

'Mind your own goddam business,' came the reply, and Darcy beat a dignified but hurried retreat from this bowel of Hades.

Back on the sidewalk, she waved discreetly to Stanley Ralph to let him know she was O K, unscathed, and moved over to the old man.

'Howdy,' she smiled sweetly. 'Am I addressing Mr Webster?' (I don't think so, her brain replied.)

'*Che?*' replied old walnut-face, revealing a missing couple of teeth.

'Webster. Web-ster.' A wasted journey, thought Darcy. So much for the late Sister Immaculata's personal and private letter to her brother Paul.

'*Si.* That's me. I'm eighty-four you know.'

'No kidding. And have you always lived here?' Darcy felt like a game-show host.

'No. Does it sound like I always lived here? I'm from Genova. That's Italy.'

'I know Genova. We used to take a yacht there, stopping for a couple of nights at Portofino.' Hotel Splendido but no point in mentioning that, the man could be a communist.

'I come over in thirty-four. Wid my family. We rose from the slums of Genova to this . . .' He inclined his head at the laundromat. 'It's a rags to rags story.'

Darcy's mind reeled, this was not happening to her. 'Listen,' she said, revealing two hundred-dollar bills, in the palm of her hand, 'is there someplace we can talk?'

Giovanni Webster, as he turned out to be, raised his hands expressively. 'You wanna go back in there?' He shook his head as he said it, meaning, you *don't* wanna go back in there. Then he gestured at another kitchen chair by the laundromat door. 'This is fine, hardly nobody speaks English, what's so important?'

Darcy went over to the chair and looked at it, perplexed, until Stanley Ralph hurried over from the Buick and placed it so she could talk with the old man.

It was a conversation which proved Darcy to be a better sleuth than young Paul, who had walked away when Giovanni had offered to take his twenty-dollar bill.

In the next twenty minutes, sitting there on that North Manhattan sidewalk, she learned that this was the man who, with his late wife, had flown to Ireland, complete with Mexican wet-nurse, and paid $3,200 for a baby which was not theirs.

'Of course we were doing OK then,' said old Giovanni. 'We had three laundries and the Milano Café in Queens. Plus Betty had inherited some dollars. Few thousand. And Betty was going crazy to have a baby. I think she mighta left me if we hadn't gone over and bought that *bambino*.' His rheumy old eyes softened. 'Great little guy, just so big, brand new. That's why we needed the suckling nurse, she had her own kid. We flew them both over with us. Nice baby, no mistake. One of the nuns said his natural mother called him . . . Gilbert?'

Darcy's mouth was dry as a strip of jerky. 'Oliver,' she prompted.

The ancient Italian nodded. 'Oliver. How could I forget such a thing?'

'Why did you change your name?' asked Darcy. 'When?'

The old man smiled, lost in his memories. 'Thirty-four we came over. The whole family. My three brothers. Marina my sister. Uncles, you name it, we coulda started a tribe. Moved to this neighbourhood in forty-eight.'

'Webster. Why Webster?'

Giovanni glanced at her, old eyes suddenly bright. 'Betty was from Ireland. Her papa had a bar way downtown, west Broadway. Jackie Flynn. Johnny, he says to me, you are a good Catholic boy, and I am glad you two wanna get married. But I can't have my Betty running around callin herself Betty Biondino, you will never get anywhere in this land of the free without some all-American name. So I changed it. On account of I wanted to marry his daughter.'

'Why Webster?' Darcy persisted.

'That was the name on my dictionary.' Giovanni explained. 'Webster's Dictionary. Italian to American, American to Italian. Nine dollars.'

At which juncture, the monstrous Henrietta came out with two cracked tumblers of iced tea.

Darcy thanked her, and as she stirred at it with a thick straw she said, as casual as you like, 'So, uh, what name did you give him? Hmmm?' And she smiled her most alluring smile. 'You did not call him Oliver, I'm quite sure.'

'I bet you break a few hearts, with that,' said the old man, and before Darcy could figure out a reply, he went on, 'Rodney.'

'You called him what?' exclaimed Darcy, the Irish in her outraged at even a bastard brother having such an up-your-ass English name.

'Rodney,' replied the ancient. 'What's wrong with Rodney? We called him after Rod Steiger, the actor. I mean, how American can you get? We used to go see all the western movies.'

It could be worse, thought Darcy, they could have called him Trigger. But this was it. Here was Oliver's adoptive father, Giovanni Webster, an Italian immigrant who had married an Irish girl.

Sitting there outside his laundromat, to Darcy he was a signpost which declared '$218,000,000 THIS WAY'. Like unwrapping a special Christmas present, for she could scarcely contain her excitement, Darcy said, 'So, Mr Webster . . .'

'*Si?*' The way he slurped his iced tea, it occurred to her he had probably worn one of those huge Italian moustaches, most of his life.

'Is, um, Rodney here? In New York?'

The old man let his rheumy eyes rest on hers. He blinked, as if trying to cope with a question on advanced quasar physics, asked in a foreign tongue.

Eventually, having worked out his reply, old Signor Webster spoke. 'These things happen . . .'

She nodded, keeping silent.

'It's common,' but he was definitely embarrassed, 'like . . . these things happen.'

He seemed to relax, content with that response and appeared to imagine it would be enough for his designer-clothed visitor. He nodded, to convince himself. 'They happen all the time.'

'What things?' asked Darcy, the two hundred-dollar bills in her hand suddenly becoming three.

Webster drank some more iced tea, wiped his upper lip, and responded, bright as a light, 'Betty got pregnant. Well . . .' he spread his arms, 'once Henrietta arrived and Rodney was eating us outta house and home, we gave him away.'

Darcy's world stopped right there.

'I'm sorry?' she said.

'We gave the kid away. Don't give me no looks. C'mon, money was tight. They paid cash. Wealthy folk. Good family.'

'I see,' replied Darcy, with saintlike equanimity. 'And where is this family to be found?'

Old Giovanni Webster thought about this for a long moment.

Darcy thought he had maybe decided he had said too much.

Then he slipped his dry old palm over hers and when he had the three hundred dollars safely in his pocket . . . he told her.

It was the last thing she had expected.

There is a seedy Dunkin' Donuts place on the north end of Boston Common, on Tremont Street. It was not the sort of place Alison Clancy had ever imagined she would be inside for more than a moment, ordering a coffee to go. But here she sat, near the back, with the man she had helped to defend, more than four years before. A man whom she had fully expected to get more than a hundred years in prison, had it not been for the combined skills of her senior partner and, she supposed, herself.

The Girolo case had been a Damascus Road experience for her, with its revelations of organized crime in the United States, and the realization there was a big future for her if she chose to specialize in such cases.

Bernie Schechter, the federal trial judge, had praised her work as second counsel at a law school dinner a few weeks after the trial, and assured her she was on the way to partnership and a lifetime's very lucrative work defending mob bosses and serial killers.

You have a certain skill in saving such low-life, was the way Schechter had put it, with his usual knack of damning with barbed praise.

Alison had thought about that for several weeks, before she had heard that this guy Sir Jack Fitzrowan was looking for a legal exec who had not come up the usual corporate route. The rest, as they say, was history.

Except, after this *mafioso*'s revelation, which had not really sunk in, that Sebastian Tree had taken a contract out on her, here she was, sitting at a cramped table in the back of the Tremont Street Dunkin' Donuts listening to one of the most bizarre pitches she had ever heard in her life.

It seemed, if he could be believed, that this major hoodlum, boss of all Italian organized crime north of New York City on the eastern seaboard, had become sick of his life and wanted to go straight. Even *mafiosi*, she had decided, can get flaky.

And yet, as she examined his handsome face, and let her lawyer's mind look behind those deep, grey-green eyes, there seemed to be, bizarrely enough, a fundamental integrity there. The man was intelligent, very damned intelligent. He had a self-deprecating sense of humour and he was clearly trying hard to convey the sincerity of his intent.

'We both know I should have gone down for life,' he said candidly, 'but even those four years were tough. Marion is no picnic. But if it wiped the slate clean, I would do another six, that would make me about fifty when I came out. And after that?' He turned his palms upwards. 'Maybe I'll go to Santa Lucia and start a boat charter business. You ever been scuba diving?'

Scuba diving? Alison had other things crowding her shocked

mind. 'Sebastian Tree really has put a contract out on me? To kill me? Tell me you are not serious . . .'

Girolo checked in the mirror beside them, but the place was deserted, even the waitress had disappeared. He nodded. 'I could not be more serious. The man wants you out of the way. You both work at Zeralda. I figure it's either you are a threat to him, money, career . . . liberty. Or it's an emotional thing. Like love, you know . . .' The way he said the last bit, he could have been talking about life on Mars. Emotion was clearly a stranger to this Peter Girolo.

Alison Clancy shook her head in disbelief. 'The bastard.' Then it hit her, and she found herself trembling, and it would not stop.

Peter Girolo smiled and placed a cool, dry hand on hers, not a come-on, just a friendly gesture. It was strangely comforting. 'You'll be all right now. It's taken care of,' he said, and from the look in his eye, he meant it.

Alison tried to sip some coffee, but it spilled. 'All right? With this asshole trying to kill me?'

'I need your help,' replied Girolo. 'You are under my protection. He will not find anyone to do the work.'

Alison shivered. By work, this gangster meant murder. And why would Girolo need her?

'What exactly can I do,' she asked, 'that your teams of shit-hot mob lawyers can't?'

Peter Girolo pushed the ice around his glass of soda. Then he met her gaze. 'You are honest, you are straight. And you are a good negotiator. They will listen to you. I want you to approach, discreetly, the Justice Department. Do your best to cut me a deal. That's all I ask, your level best. Say, six more years, then I can wipe the slate clean. And why not my own people?' He laughed, ruefully. 'Miss Clancy, if they knew what was on my mind, they would kill me.'

Alison Clancy's heart went cold. Her world had spun from Zeralda and its suddenly frivolous problems to the concept of imminent death, in the space of a walk through the park. Death not just for the man sitting opposite, but for her, herself.

'OK,' she said, and could not believe how easy it had been to decide, but there was something about this new Girolo. He had changed, and she sensed his remorse was genuine enough. 'I need to know, in detail, precisely what it is you propose . . . and what it is you have done since you came out of jail, for I figure, if you had gone straight then, we would not be sitting here right now.'

And Peter Girolo smiled, ruefully. 'Miss Clancy,' he said, 'I knew I had come to the right place.'

Sonny Favaro had been waiting when Peter Girolo got back to his apartment in Beaver Place. Tony di Angelo was outside, near the Chrysler, keeping an eye on things, which was sensible, in the circumstances.

Girolo had noticed four other footsoldiers, all Atlantic City men and loyal to Joey Buscetta, in two cars parked in the street, facing in different directions for quick getaway or pursuit.

When he had let himself in, Favaro had been like a fussing mother. 'Boss, where you been? We been worried sick,' he said, in that monotone of his, and had poured a mug of strong coffee for his charge.

Girolo had replied that everything was fine, and he complimented Favaro on the increased protection. And on the coffee. By the time he had let the big goon make him some hash browns and scrambled egg, and nodded that they too were OK, the peeved tension had evaporated.

The fact that Sonny had made him breakfast at one forty in the afternoon was not unusual in the world they lived in. Clubs had to be seen to, money had to be counted, the minor bosses had to be kept in line. One forty was average for breakfast.

'So, you know, Joe is kind of worried too.' Favaro had meant Joey Buscetta.

'Sure.'

And after Girolo had eaten on, in silence, Sonny Favaro, whose job and probably his life depended on Peter Girolo's continued welfare, had enquired, 'Yeah, and, uh, so everything's OK?'

'Sure. Tell Joey I'll see him at five,' Girolo said, indicating that was enough with the questions.

And now he was in the back of the tan Chrysler New Yorker he had decided to use instead of the navy one. He had begun to get used to the blue automobile and that meant it was time for a change, for others would get used to seeing him in it.

It was two twenty in the afternoon, round about the time that Grace Hanrahan and Tak Katakura had been dancing around each other, metaphorically, as they sat at that banqueting table, beginning to discover maybe there was another way for them to do business, apart from insider dealing, industrial espionage and general corporate delinquent behaviour.

Joey Buscetta sat in the back beside the *capo*. Sonny Favaro was up front, riding shot-gun, with one of the Atlantic City fellows driving. There was a grey Dodge 4 × 4 right behind and some more guys in a green Chevvy sedan a few cars back, but ready for trouble.

The reason for all this was not, as Peter Girolo had supposed, a result of the deaths of Desmond Dekker and Joseph Cranmer, out at Sudbury in that house on Hawthorn Drive.

It was, potentially, a more serious problem. And it was a problem that was not going to go away, a problem which had brought Albert Genovese, *consigliere* to the Man, the Boss of Bosses, way out there in the Florence supermax, beneath the desert and still running the *cosa*, back up from New York City for an urgent consultation.

Life was getting no simpler.

Life was getting no simpler for Girolo. For reasons he would never have dreamed of just a few weeks before.

It had started with the goddam ducks. Peter Girolo was nobody's idea of a romantic. And ducks were for shooting, as far as most Italian men were concerned. But there had been something about that family of ducks, winging their way over the water, the last time he had met with Genovese, on the shores of Mount Hope Bay, Connecticut, which had moved his soul.

If only, he had thought, life could be that simple.

Then he had spared the life of Vito Greco. Big mistake. Greco had left town and was building a new territory in Seattle. The usual way. With a ruthlessness Girolo should have demonstrated to him, instead of letting the hoodlum go with enough to get started all over again.

And Desmond Dekker. Girolo knew he would have let Dekker live too, if the guy, just after he had made that phone call to Sebastian Tree, had not made the mistake of going for a Colt .45 pistol he had kept under a plaid scatter rug for such an occasion.

Girolo had shot him once in the head, using a .22 reduced charge shell, while still on the phone to Sebastian Tree, and not looking round from the mirror where he had been watching Dekker make his fatal mistake.

It was not the eighty minutes it had taken to re-arrange the scenario so it would look like Dekker and Cranmer had killed each other in an exchange of fire that was annoying, disquieting, Peter Girolo.

It was that he had not wanted to kill Dekker in the first place.

Now that was not something the professional assassin, the graduate *cum laude* of the Scuola had ever experienced before. And even though he had decided he wanted out of the mafia life, even though he had even then resolved to meet with Alison Clancy to enlist her help, it pissed him off.

And he blamed the goddam ducks.

'Joey,' he said.

'*Si, Padrino*,' responded the faithful Buscetta.

'This woman . . .' he scribbled the names of Alison Clancy and Sebastian Tree on a scrap of paper and passed it to the enforcer, 'is not to be harmed.'

'Sure thing.' Joey Buscetta studied the names, then flicked his gold Davidov lighter and lit the scrap of paper. 'And the other name?'

Girolo thought about that. In normal times he would have simply had Tree negotiated, which in *cosa* parlance was a terminal state. 'He does not wish her well.'

Buscetta nodded, as the burning scrap of paper crumbled into ashes, and replied in Sicilian patois, 'No problem. I'll have a word with him.'

'We're here,' announced the driver, turning into an alley behind the Aquarium.

'Pietro,' Albert Genovese advanced across the roof of the Marriott Long Wharf Hotel, 'we got problems. The fuckin Russians have decided to start their East Coast operation in Boston. You are gonna need soldiers. You are gonna have to be ruthless. Explain to these commie shitheads we got an all-American syndicate here and there ain't no place for Boris the fuckin Terrible Stateside. This is from on high. You gotta go to war. We give you everything you need. Kick their asses all the way back to Khazak-fuckin-stan, all right?'

Beautiful, thought Girolo. Thank you, God. Just when I was coming over to your side . . .

After the Katakura lunch, Tak had escorted Grace Hanrahan to the lobby of the Ritz-Carlton where Tommy Boyle, in check shirt worn loose over his dark pants, was waiting to escort her to the Bentley double-parked outside.

Grace had thanked her host and once again had experienced a feeling of annoyance at her mixture of emotions when he had gripped her hand and looked straight into her eyes, smiling that inscrutable smile of his.

'I hope you will consider meeting,' Katakura had said, 'when I can put my proposition before you. Bring Miss Clancy, she seems to have a good head for business.'

Grace had thanked him, without making any promises, and the Bentley had taken her back to Zeralda, where she had changed into a black skirt, cream shirt and loose, navy jacket, all by Donna Karan, Prada shoes and the Snoopy wristwatch Tom had given her three birthdays ago.

She had noticed Sebastian Tree's silver Porsche in the car lot, and as she ran a comb through her hair she wondered how in hell he had the nerve to continue working on as if nothing had happened.

When Grace came out of her executive washroom, there was her brother Paul, with Diana, her PA, reading and discussing a pile of spreadsheets, laid out on a side table.

'Hi, Paul,' said Grace, slightly annoyed at his intrusion. As if the boy knew anything about business. It was embarrassing that he should pretend.

'Hi, Sis,' replied Paul. 'I must have got the dates wrong . . . but Diana is just giving me a crash course in Zeralda spreadsheet data.'

'Dates? Dates for what?'

'Board meetings. Last Friday of every month. I felt being in town I should make the effort. But apparently Darcy is in New York, and you were at lunch so . . . when do we have them, these days?'

Grace was thrown. Certainly, when her daddy had been alive, she and Big Jack would retire to the board room and go over the previous month's business and future plans, usually with Sebastian Tree and Alison Clancy in attendance, with Diana to keep minutes.

But in the four months since the funeral, with just herself in the driving seat, and the Sebastian Tree situation, it had come down to Grace and Alison sitting in the President's inner office, with a couple of glasses of bourbon, at the end of each week. That was as close to board meetings as they had gotten.

And after the first slight flush of guilt, Grace found she was uncharacteristically angry. How dare Paul, who until recently had been more concerned with his goddam rock 'n' roll music, his recording sessions which got nowhere, and his generally hippy life-style, suddenly breeze in and pretend he had the remotest interest in Zeralda?

'Well, as a matter of fact,' she announced, 'since you and Darcy have shown zero inclination to get involved, I have been coping here, with Alison's help. You know about our problem with . . .' she lowered her voice, 'Sebastian.'

Paul nodded and straightened up from bending his tall, slender body over the side table. While Diana affected to be deeply busy in some detail in the files, he crossed to his sister and just stood there, gazing down at her, a tender smile on his face.

There was something about his eyes that reminded Grace, for the very first time in their lives, of their late father. It was that mixture of tenderness and steel.

'I'm sorry . . .' he said, gently, and reaching out, touched her shoulder. 'I am truly sorry. I should have been here a whole lot sooner.' And he held Grace to him, patting her shoulder, as she found the tears coming.

Diana glanced at the two of them and diplomatically left the room, thinking it was about time somebody helped Grace with her burden, which Diana had noticed was becoming hard for the new President to bear on her own. In fact, as Diana had mentioned to her own husband, an intern at Mass General, it was Zeralda's great good fortune that Alison Clancy did not seem inclined to use her position of trust and influence to her own advantage, for Grace Hanrahan had come to lean on the young attorney for reassurance and advice.

Alone together, Grace's shoulders heaved as she wept. And Paul patted her shoulder and stroked her hair, just like their daddy would have done.

Soon she was O K and, sniffing a bit and laughing at her embarrassment, Grace took a white hanky from her desk drawer and blew her nose a couple of times.

'I'm sorry, Paulie,' she said. 'I should have arranged board meetings, it was just, it seems like no time since Daddy died . . .'

'I know. I still shed a few tears when I least expect to,' Paul replied gently, and he sat on the edge of her desk. 'Listen, I have no plans to go back for a while. And Dad taught me more about software and modem surfing than I had realized, until I started hunting for Oliver.'

Grace reached out and gripped his hand.

'I am not a complete klutz,' Paul went on, 'when it comes to business concepts. It's just my natural laziness that put me off before. But you're my big sister, and it's maybe time I pulled my weight around here.'

Grace blew her nose again and shook off her blues. 'What about that band you have a recording contract with? Sabotage, is it?'

'Subterfuge.' Paul shrugged. 'The recording session's in August. I could hang around in Dublin and London, enjoying the life of rock 'n' roll millionaire groupie, and believe me that can be a fun life. Or I can grow up and try to behave like one of the family . . .'

He took a pack of Panther cigarillos from his jacket and lifted one out. 'Unless, of course, I would be in the way.'

Grace leaned back in her chair and studied her brother. Tom had been saying there was more to the kid these days, and her detective husband was a good judge of horse flesh.

'If you're serious, I really could use some help,' she said.

'Oh I'm serious, Splodge,' he replied, with a grin. He had not called his sister that since he was about twelve.

Grace laughed. 'OK, welcome to Zeralda. But first, let's get up to speed on that damn legacy codicil and the search for Oliver. You go first. After all, over two hundred million is sitting doing nothing until we find Daddy's long lost illegitimate son . . . How old would he be now?'

'Forty-three,' replied Paul, without hesitation.

In the outer room, where Diana had slipped out to get a decent cup of coffee from the ground-floor commissary, forty-three-year-old Sebastian Tree stood beside the intercom, which he had switched on at low volume.

It was the first he had heard about the codicil. Or Oliver.

And he felt a great peace come upon him. It was as if the hand of fate had touch him.

Two hundred million . . . He smiled quietly.

Maybe Jack Fitzrowan had not been such a bad bastard after all.

11

The house on Hawthorn Drive was festooned in blue and white
POLICE – CRIME SCENE plastic tapes. There were two mortuary
vans, local Sudbury police vehicles, a Homicide forensics team
Dodge van, the pathologist's Mazda sports car, Lieutenant Tom
Hanrahan's unmarked Homicide Department Ford and Sergeant
Detective Danny Tarantola's unmarked Toyota coupé.

Blue and red strobe lights on the police vehicles flickered relentlessly, there were chalk marks and tapes in white, pink, yellow and
mint green, denoting where the bodies had lain, bullets had ended
up and shell cases fallen. Homicide forensics men and women
moved around slowly in green or white coveralls and the overall
effect was like the aftermath of some macabre *bal masque*.

'Here is Desmond. Right?' Dan Tarantola stood in the front
porch, very much like Desmond Dekker had done when he opened
the door to Cranmer. 'He opens the door to find Joseph Cranmer,
a.k.a. Jackson Heights, facing him. Cranmer has two weapons, one
in each hand. The guy is a cleaner, known to the deceased who is
an underworld denizen –'

'Say what?' asked Lieutenant Tom Hanrahan.

'A denizen. Low-life. I read it. It's a word.'

Tom shrugged. 'OK.'

Tarantola pressed on. 'He sees the guy has a piece in each
hand.'

'Who has? Dekker?'

'No.' Tarantola shook his head.

'The denizen.'

'Correct.' Danny Tarantola was getting into this theory.
'Desmond clocks the denizen is holding two pieces, held out,'

Tarantola demonstrated, arms outstretched, 'the twenty-two, for neatness. The forty-five, should things get unforeseen.'

'And what?' asked Tom. 'A pro-cleaner shoulda blown him away, bap-bap-bap.'

'Who knows? Maybe they talk.'

'They talk?' Tom gave the detective a long look. 'The denizen engages in conversation? With the patsy?'

'And now he's dead,' said Tarantola. 'He made a mistake.'

Tom shrugged. 'Nobody's perfect.'

Tarantola nodded. 'My point entirely. Desmond Dekker uses this opportunity to fire eighteen from his MAC-10, and Joseph Cranmer blasts off the three from his twenty-two, one of which is a bull's-eye, and four from the forty-five, two of which connect in the left shoulder and upper arm.'

Tom opened his pack of Winstons, glanced at the two remaining cigarettes, then shut the pack and put it back in his pocket.

Tarantola smiled. Since he had stopped smoking he had become something of an evangelist. 'Feel better?'

'No,' replied Tom, 'the angles are wrong.' At which moment Barry Maguire, the police pathologist, emerged from inside the Dekker residence carrying four plastic evidence bags. Tom glanced at him. 'Doc, what do you reckon? One on one? Or is that what we're supposed to think?'

Maguire stopped, considering his reply. He was a businesslike pathologist who did the job and preferred simple results. He was not the type to look for complex angles, but he was not lazy. There had been, for instance, this Jewish guy in Mattapan, the year before, murdered his eighty-year-old mother after raping her. Alleged he had enjoyed carnal knowledge with her for years and the old woman's death had been an accident. It was Doc Maguire who had proved otherwise, against both Homicide's and the DA's own opinions. Maguire had made himself unpopular when he could just as easily have signed a death certificate for natural causes.

'The purely pathological evidence points to this . . .' said Maguire. 'This one opens the door, this one fires and misses . . .' He pointed to the four chalk circles above and to the left of centre, in the wood and wall behind the porch entrance. 'This one, in his undershorts and towelling bathrobe, fires his MAC-10 maybe even when mortally hit.'

'Dead man's grip,' volunteered Danny Tarantola.

'Maybe. Anyways, Tom, that's what all the forensic and pathology evidence tells me and that is what will be in my report.'

Tom watched Maguire as the Doc moved past. He smiled to himself and, for some reason he could never figure out, he decided to wait till he had the doctor on his own before asking him what was not right about all this.

It was probably a wise decision.

Later, as he and Danny the Wop shrugged out of their crime scene overalls and tugged off the Latex gloves, standing at the trunk of Hanrahan's Department Ford, Tom Hanrahan said casually, 'So Danny, you still think I killed Jack Fitzrowan?'

Tarantola paused, thinking about it, then he raised his shoulders. 'I ain't seen anything to prove otherwise . . .'

Tom reached into the trunk and produced a manila envelope. Inside were evidence photographs and formal statements from Tommy Boyle, Big Time and Jeb which pointed the finger at Sebastian Tree, along with sworn affidavit evidence from California that Tree was a licensed off-shore yacht master, a fact he had hidden from the Fitzrowan family and indeed everyone in Boston, where he seemed to have started a new life, re-inventing part of his past when it suited him.

'What's this?' asked Sergeant Tarantola.

'Read it.'

Danny opened the envelope and skimmed through the contents, pausing to study a detail, glancing at the Lieutenant from time to time.

Finally he looked up. 'You figure this lets you off the hook, Lieutenant?'

Hanrahan met Tarantola's gaze. 'No apology will be necessary, Danny. You were doing the job.'

Without a blush, Tarantola re-sealed the package and remarked, 'I ain't convinced. All this proves is the victim was probably murdered. Which is where I am coming from in the first place.'

'Wake up, Danny, smell the coffee. Everything points to Sebastian Tree.'

Tarantola wrinkled his Italian hooter. 'Yeah, I dunno. Maybe . . .' he stared pointedly at the Lieutenant, '. . . maybe the man is being framed.'

Alison walked along the corridor towards Grace's office, passing the Chief Executive's open door. Inside, Amy Schofield sat with micro-weight headphones on, typing out dictation from her boss, Sebastian Tree.

Alison shuddered and walked on, going over in her mind Peter Girolo's promise to ensure her personal safety, and the tall hood's almost naïve belief that, after a lifetime of crime and homicide, he could somehow do a deal with the authorities, to plea-bargain around five or six more years inside, then wipe the slate clean.

She could, she supposed, make a few discreet enquiries; she still knew a few people at Justice.

Girolo was a typical criminal. If only he had taken the decision to go straight when he walked out of Marion, having served his sentence, he could have gone off to pursue his dream of a boat charter business in the Caribbean. Instead, what had he done?

Girolo's brief, laconic information that he had in a few weeks carved his way to control of organized crime on the eastern seaboard, north of New York, on his own admission added up to a thousand years from a lenient judge.

If it were not for the fact that Girolo was in a unique position to protect her from Sebastian Tree, Alison had no doubt in her mind she would have told the mobster to take a hike.

Still, lucky for me, she reflected, that he finds me useful. Otherwise Sebastian Tree would have been able to have me rubbed out and nobody could have saved me.

At which juncture Sebastian Tree emerged from the office which had been newly provided for Paul Fitzrowan, the prodigal Fitzrowan brother, who had come on board. Alison struggled to keep from flinching as Tree paused, all grins as usual, to pass the time of day.

'Hi, Alison. How's it going?'

'I'm absolutely fine, Sebastian. In the pink.'

He nodded, cheerily. 'In the pink, eh? That's wonderful. Could you let me have last week's draft agreement with Hughes S and C? I need to plan a production schedule.'

Alison said sure she would, and they parted. It was a strange, almost dreamlike situation, knowing that only the night before he had sent somebody to kill her.

Could she really trust Girolo? Or should she do the sensible thing and speak to Grace's detective husband, Homicide Lieutenant Tom Hanrahan? For some reason which did not seem hugely rational, Alison felt instinctively that she could trust the gangster. At this stage.

'Alison . . .' it was young Paul, stepping into the corridor from the office Zeralda had provided for him, kind of a waste of space, thought Alison privately, 'do you have a moment?'

Alison smiled and went back. She was surprised to see how spartan the room was, with three computer terminals, four VDU monitors and an independent main box console, set up in a corner and running independently of the main power system off solar battery panels. The cardboard cartons this equipment had come from were still scattered around the room.

'Grab a chair, forgive the mess.' Paul pushed a hand through his hair, using his fingers as comb. It was a mannerism Jack used to have and Alison immediately felt a warmth towards him.

Paul sat down and with surprising skill pulled down all kinds of information: flow charts, complex equations and financial spreadsheets which became scattered around the four monitor screens.

'You did the Houston contracts didn't you?' he enquired.

Alison nodded. 'Yes . . .'

'Terrific job.'

The cheek of him, thought Alison. Talk about strolling in and throwing your weight around, as if this kid could even read the clause numbers on a contract.

'There is one clause . . . let's see . . .' said Paul, his fingers racing over the keyboard. 'Yep. Forty-four D two. How did you get them to agree that?'

With her brain still dwelling on Sebastian Tree's contract to kill her and the sudden entrance into her life of a major gangland figure, it took Alison some seconds to force herself to concentrate on the legal document Paul had brought on to his main screen.

It was the Houston Oil Contract and 44(D)ii gave Zeralda the exclusive future option to re-supply computer microchips as and when the current orders were superseded by technical advances.

'Well, they were impressed by Jack's, your father's, pitch in the first place. They knew Zeralda is top of its field. It was not too difficult, really.'

Paul sat back in his chair, amused. 'It's not a clause many lawyers could have pushed through without a fight. Words like endeavour to, or give favourable consideration to, no problem. But this puts Zeralda in a very strong position just to go on making money. I mean, who's to define superseded?' And before Alison could reply he gave the correct answer to his own question. 'It means they trust us. And that means Zeralda's reputation is untarnished by the NASA fiasco that was going on at the time the big three oil companies signed this.'

Paul wiped the clause off the screen. 'Alison, Zeralda owes you a great deal,' he said softly. 'I can see why Dad voted you a huge bonus. We need you here, I hope you don't get itchy feet . . .'

Three surprises in one day. Alison wondered what more was around the corner. What had happened to the feckless youth, as Jack had referred to his only son? His only legitimate one.

'You're quite a wiz with those things,' she said, indicating the computers.

When Paul looked up at her, she, like Grace, saw his father's eyes. He smiled. 'It's my birthright . . .'

Dublin. Seven ten in the evening. Pronsias Stevenson was working late. Martina had enrolled in an art appreciation course, two nights each week, and he used the opportunity to catch up on the huge backlog of work Stevenson, Stevenson & Malahide had acquired since word of the Fitzrowan legacy got around.

He and his partners had been the souls of discretion, but you only had to read the papers to know that there was about $230 million at stake, the bulk of which was the subject of some dispute. And he had not denied, among his professional and equally discreet colleagues, advocates and judges to a man, that he, Pronsias Stevenson, was holding the ring, and was final arbiter.

So with a pot of tea, in a knitted blue and yellow woolly tea-cosy – which Martina would not allow in their house (she thought he had done as he was told and thrown it out) – and an illicit pipe of Dunhill's Standard Mixture, he sat at his desk, wearing a threadbare old grey cardigan Martina had also banished from the marital home, and pored over documents concerning a limited liability dispute between a farmer in Dundalk and the proprietors of a petrol-station chain who alleged his cattle had strayed on to their property and contaminated 30,000 gallons of fuel, both leaded and unleaded.

Stevenson was just formulating, in his academic way, some schoolboy joke about how many cows does it take to contaminate a gallon of unleaded petrol when the phone rang. It was his private line and when he lifted the receiver, he expected to hear Martina's dulcet tones, berating him about some transgression or other. Maybe he had not folded his bathtowel in the correct shape. Being married to Martina was like being hitched to a gunnery sergeant in the US Marine Corps.

'Stevenson,' he announced.

'Are you alone?'

His heart skipped at the sound of Darcy Fitzrowan Bailey's voice. 'Yes . . . Where are you?'

'Dublin Airport. Can I come over?'

'You've only just gone. Jesus Mary and Joseph, you must be swooning with jet lag.'

A quiet chuckle at the other end of the line made him weak at the knees. 'I'm fine, Pronsias. Can't wait though . . .'

To the Dublin lawyer's surprise, he realized the prospect excited him. 'Will I come to the house round the corner?'

Slight pause, then, 'I would like to come to your office.'

'*What?!*' Pronsias Stevenson found his face flushing, 'Out of the question. For goodness' sake . . .'

'OK, I'll take the next flight to London. Edward has a dinner with the Master of Magdalen. I'll be in time for the port and coffee. Dear Edward, he always misses me so . . .'

Lust and jealousy were two emotions utterly foreign to Stevenson. Well, certainly jealousy. He glanced around his room this way and that, already guilty at what had been proposed. And at what he was probably going to do.

'I suppose,' he said, 'you could always come into the office for a quiet drink.'

'I'll bring some caviare, got it at JFK. Are you feeling horny?'

At which moment Stevenson's secretary poked her head round the door and smiled goodnight.

Stevenson wiggled his fingers at her in farewell and muttered into the phone, 'Absolutely . . .'

'Excellent,' said Darcy. 'And I have a surprise for you. I am almost ready to claim the finder's fee.'

Stevenson knew she meant in the hunt for Oliver. Well, New York was always the place to look. He could have told her that. But he doubted if the delectable Darcy would have achieved much more than to find herself in another blind alley.

'I'll see you soon,' she whispered, and hung up.

He smiled to himself. No need to disillusion the girl until afterwards. He knew by now that greed aroused her more than any man.

Sebastian Tree said goodbye to Amy Schofield and took the elevator to the ground floor. He was a worried man, for on the neatly compact, international multi-frequency Sony radio he kept on his desk, he had just heard the local news station give a breathless account of the discovery of two mobsters found dead at the million-dollar Sudbury home of Desmond Dekker, one of the victims, the other being one Joseph Cranmer, a hoodlum and known professional button man from Little Italy, in South Manhattan.

'Police are considering the theory of a double homicide, resulting from a quick-draw shoot-out. A source at Boston Police Headquarters said that no third party is being sought in connection with the slayings, at the present time . . .' announced the newscaster jauntily, before going on to give details of an imminent visit to Boston by the leading yachts in the international Whitbread Round the World Race.

The double homicide would have occurred not long after Dekker had made that call to him, at ten to one in the morning, just fourteen hours ago.

Jesus. Tree's blood froze. What if the police traced one of the dead man's phone calls back to him? What if it had been recorded? It was more than likely a little scumbag like Dekker would have done just that, with a view to putting the arm on Tree later, to blackmail him over his attempt to have Alison Clancy murdered.

Perspiration began to trickle down Sebastian Tree's back as he fought a sudden feeling of panic. Tree needed to be in control of every aspect of his life. Part of his legacy from his bastard father leaving him and his poor frightened mother abandoned to their fate.

'Leaving early today, Mr Tree?' said Arthur the security guard cheerfully. It was one of those remarks that meant nothing very much, a mere pleasantry, but in his current mood Sebastian Tree scowled and replied that he worked hard enough to be able to leave before six every now and then. Arthur shrugged and returned to reading his *National Enquirer* which alleged that the government was hushing up the fact that several small half-fish half-human females had been found alive in the Bermudan Triangle. Jeez, thought Arthur, these could be mermaids.

Oblivious of such profound reflections, Sebastian Tree crossed the yard to his silver Porsche 911 Carrera 4 Turbo convertible and as he opened the door, a sleek, if dusty, Aston Martin DB7 coupé growled its way into a parking space and Tom Hanrahan climbed out.

Tree raised a hand in casual greeting and stooped to get into his car, but Hanrahan kept looking at him in a way that meant he wanted to talk. Fuck. They did not waste much time, those Homicide guys. He decided he would say yes, some weirdos did phone him in the middle of the night, but he had hung up on them. And pray the cops did not have a tape of that last, insane, conversation with Dekker.

Tree straightened up and waited till Grace's husband got closer.

'Hi, Tom,' said Sebastian Tree. 'Great wheels.'

Tom had known that Tree would be impressed by the DB7. 'We should take them out on Route 90 one of these days,' smiled Hanrahan, 'see what they can do.'

'That would be fun. You wouldn't book me for driving too fast?'

'I might,' replied Hanrahan, still smiling, but maybe not so much.

Typical cop, thought Tree, they love to make you sweat.

'So,' he said, 'taking some time off today?' Just making small talk.

Hanrahan seemed to think about that. 'Sebastian, you remember that day on *Zeralda*, the day Jack was killed?'

Tree frowned. 'How could I forget it?'

Tom Hanrahan nodded, sympathetic. 'That's good. I want you to do something for me.'

'Name it,' said Tree, almost swooning with relief this was not about the Dekker phone call. Hanrahan was OK. Tree had a lot of time for him – after all, the guy was not a Fitzrowan. And as a matter of fact Sebastian Tree often felt he too would have made a good detective. The deduction, the observation, the intuition and the power, all of those things appealed to him. But the money was shit. OK though if you had a rich wife and a nice inheritance to back up the sixty or seventy grand a year.

'Write down for me,' said Hanrahan, 'everything you can remember about that day, from parking your Porsche at the wharf to mooring the ketch with the ambulance crew and police waiting.'

Tree tried to read the Lieutenant's expressionless face. 'Sure. They lose the first one I wrote?'

Hanrahan shrugged apologetically. 'Different departments. I would appreciate it.'

A tiny alarm rang in Tree's mind. Tom Hanrahan was with Homicide, everybody knew that. What the hell did Homicide want with an accidental death report? But instead of asking that simple, natural question, Tree just nodded, as if Hanrahan's request was the simplest thing in the world and replied, 'Fine. I'll do it over the weekend.'

'Appreciate that,' said Hanrahan and nodded, walking back to his car.

As Sebastian Tree nosed the Porsche out of the Zeralda lot, he noticed Hanrahan get back into the Aston Martin and back out from its parking bay, clearly not intending to go into the building to see his wife, which would have been normal.

Zeralda's Chief Exec frowned, and drove out of the complex, heading for Memorial Drive and Longfellow Bridge. Don't get paranoid, he decided. The death of such a big noise as Jack Fitzrowan was bound to get investigated in depth. Nothing to worry about. Mere routine.

But he wished he had kept a copy of his original accidental death statement, written on board *Zeralda* on the same day they had brought back Fitzrowan's waterlogged corpse. Christ, how heavy it had been. He would never forget the effort of hauling it back on board. And he shuddered as he remembered the eyes, still open, the expression somehow . . . angry. And as the dead man's head had lolled in his arms, the eyes had seemed to stare directly into his, accusingly.

Back in the Boston Homicide office, Tom Hanrahan walked past the front desk and let himself into the staircase leading up to the first floor. Marge was in her room, slightly stooped, peering at the Easter cactus, a tissue in her hand, which she had been using to wipe the many prickly leaves.

'It'll never flower,' said Tom.

'Look, here's something.' Marge was determined the plant would one day do the business.

'It's a lost cause, any calls?' He hung his jacket on a peg behind his door, glancing around the walls with their crime scene photos, suspect surveillance photos, charts and sketch maps.

'Doc Maguire is with Jimmy Fitz, he said to tell you if you came in.'

The pathologist was in the squad room drinking coffee and going over his notes on a recent murder, a domestic row that had ended with not one but three kitchen knives embedded in a bullying wife.

'It's a hell of a lot of knives,' remarked Maguire to Jimmy Fitz.

'The guy was a chef,' explained Fitz. 'He killed her in the kitchen.'

'I know the feeling,' replied Maguire, who was known in the Department to be something of a cook himself.

'Barry,' said Tom Hanrahan, coming in, 'still the chicken à la King king?'

'That Sudbury crime scene,' announced Maguire, who did not believe in small talk, 'just too perfect.'

Tom patted his pack with the two Winstons, maybe he would have one with his coffee, because, soon as this pack was finished, that was it. No more cigarettes.

'How's that?' he asked.

Maguire handed back the kitchen knives file to Fitz and moved over to the Lieutenant. 'Normally at a homicide, there are one or two . . . surprises, conundrums, unanswered questions. The random element. You come to expect it, in forensic terms.'

'And . . . ?'

Maguire scratched his rump, thoughtful. 'Everything out there was just too perfect. No unanswered questions. No surprises, in terms of the pathology of the event. Nothing I could say in court, nothing I could write in my report.'

'So what are we talking about here?' enquired Hanrahan.

Maguire shrugged. 'It's as if . . . oh, I dunno.'

'As if,' volunteered Jimmy Fitz, 'somebody had set the scene. Re-arranged the cadavers? I've come across that before.' He glanced to Hanrahan. 'Remember the Passover murders? That was like that.'

Tom Hanrahan nodded. 'As if,' he said to the pathologist, 'maybe a third party had done the killing, pumped another few slugs into them, and laid the bodies so that we would write it off as a mutual exchange of lead that produced what we saw . . . is that a possibility?'

Maguire sipped his coffee and nodded. 'That would certainly explain things. But there's nothing I can write, or testify, that would support such a theory.'

The three of them thought about that.

'Work of a real pro . . .' said Jimmy Fitz, and his eyes met Hanrahan's. They both knew he meant Girolo.

'Time to catch up with this guy,' announced Tom Hanrahan. As he turned to leave he said, 'Jimmy, get a car, and a couple of guys for back-up.'

'Big Time and Jeb. On their way back from Brookline,' said Fitz, grabbing his jacket and radio, 'I'll give them a call.'

And as they went down the stairs, Tom Hanrahan found himself thinking about Dan Tarantola, and asking himself questions one cop should never have to ask about another.

Driving back to his immaculately restored colonial pepper-box house in Charlestown, on Boston harbour between the Mystic and Charles rivers, Sebastian Tree took stock of events.

The Dekker/Cranmer double shooting. Well that figured. Cranmer must have been the other voice on the line, the voice that had chilled his soul, no mistake. So they fell out about something, each pulled a gun, fired virtually simultaneously. Both dead. Neat result, for there was nobody left to testify that he, Sebastian Tree, had commissioned the killing of Alison Clancy.

Except for the man in LA he had gotten Dekker's name from. And since that individual was a mafia made man, who understood the culture of *omerta*, the conspiracy of silence, Tree felt no threat from that quarter.

Tom Hanrahan's request for a second account of the day of Jack Fitzrowan's death at sea did not really worry him. Police routine was famous for its slowness. Probably somebody in the Accidental Death Unit had lost the original and he had asked Tom to get another statement, knowing he and the Chief Exec were friends, well, acquaintances.

He had gotten rid, just days before, of the incriminating long-spouted oil can and other items from the trunk of the Porsche.

Tree smiled as he drove, listening to the overture from Rossini's *Thieving Magpie*, with the volume turned up loud.

Which brought him back to the problem of Alison Clancy. The bitch was determined to have him prosecuted, just as soon as she could amass enough evidence, for insider dealing. Breach of contract. Industrial espionage. Tree had read a recent case where a Wall Street VP had been sent to jail for seven years for the same kind of thing.

Well, Alison Clancy had to go. So, as the orchestra of the Tokyo Philharmonic took *The Thieving Magpie* to a crescendo, Sebastian Tree resolved to fly back to LA and make contact once again with the mob boss he had met while working as a twenty-seven-year-old business affairs manager with the Oasis Hotel, Beverly Hills, Los Angeles.

In those days, Tree had uncovered a scam on the part of the hotel's casino cashiers, and when he had shown Bobby Scipio, the owner on paper of the Oasis, how the scam was being worked, Scipio had given him a ten grand bonus and told him if ever he needed anything and etcetera and like that.

So naturally it had been to Bobby Scipio that Sebastian Tree had turned when he had decided to have Alison Clancy removed from his life.

The music reached a crescendo, Sebastian Tree felt back in control of his destiny. And able to concentrate on the biggest and best news he had ever had. Jack Fitzrowan had bequeathed a legacy of over $200 million to his long lost and illegitimate son, called Oliver, by his poor mother, before being taken from her breast.

Ever since Tree had learned the truth of his illegitimate birth, and had met up with his natural mother just before her tragic end, he had known he was somebody special. His vow to destroy Jack Fitzrowan had sprung from that poignant encounter and his only desire had been revenge. For his own cold upbringing by the Trees, his adoptive parents, devoid of affection, and for the casual way in which Fitzrowan had discarded his real mom.

There had been no element of greed in his secret vendetta. But $200 million . . . it almost gave him a belief in benign providence.

It had not been too difficult, since that first overheard conversation between Grace and the bitch Alison Clancy, to obtain more information. A study in his accounts spreadsheets of telephone calls from Zeralda's President's office, to that of Medevik & MacMorrow, a perusal of Grace Hanrahan's personal/legal file, stored on computer, easily accessible to Tree who, like Fitzrowan's legal heir Paul, had been coached by the big fellow himself in the art of hacking, and after three hours' work, at his desk on the fourth floor, the entire last will and testament, including the bombshell codicil, had become available for his perusal.

And in his attaché case, on the seat beside him, was a printout of those documents. Documents which were his passport to untold wealth. And all perfectly legal, for the legacy was his to claim, and any test would prove it.

Tears poured down Sebastian Tree's face, tears of sadness, tears of happiness, tears of rage, tears of relief that his bastard father had loved him after all, and he gunned the gas pedal, swooping the Porsche round the last bend before his beautiful house, and up the sweeping incline, through the scattered trees, when the massive rear of a huge truck backed out on to the road ahead of him.

Tree stepped hard on the brake and slammed the gear into second. Tyres screamed and singed rubber assailed his nostrils as the car's immaculate German brakes brought it smoothly, if fiercely, from 78 mph down to a stop.

Boy . . . Sebastian Tree relaxed.

Wham!!

The Porsche rocketed forward, not of its own volition, as a big 4 × 4 rammed it from behind, slamming its neat, sloping nose, metal shrieking, under the side of the backed-out truck.

Tree's head jerked back, then forward, and his head hit the steering wheel just as the air bag exploded around his face, smothering him momentarily.

He did not hear the door being forced open and the big cutters slicing through his seat-belt straps, and even as he was hauled out on to the road, it still in his confusion seemed to be some ongoing concomitant of the accident.

It was only when he was forced to stand on his feet, the noise of the crash giving way to profound silence, that Sebastian Tree focused on the leathery face in front of him. His arms were pinioned to his sides by two other men.

He was never to know that these men were Joey Buscetta, Sonny Favaro and one of Buscetta's soldiers from Atlantic City.

'This woman . . .' Buscetta thrust a photograph of Alison Clancy up to Tree's face. Tree recognized it as one of those he had provided Dekker with, for the killer's information. 'You got two options. She stays well.'

In the long silence which followed, Sebastian Tree was about to ask what the other option was, when Joey Buscetta told him, 'Or get hold of a blunt saw and kill yourself.' His leathery face just an inch from Tree's, he went on, 'For that will be nothin compared to what I will do to you . . .'

Buscetta stepped back, his flint eyes on Sebastian Tree's. For a long moment he stayed like that. Then he said, quietly, 'Tell me, Sebastian.'

Tree's mouth was suddenly dry. He swallowed and nodded. 'I leave Alison Clancy alone.'

'If you don't, we will find you, Sebastian. And I will skin you alive. I like to start with the ankles.' Suddenly there was a long, surgical knife in his hand, like an elongated scalpel, and Buscetta held its tip against Sebastian Tree's face. Just beside the right eye. He smiled, almost sadly. 'But I always get to here in the end. Then . . . ? I cut out the heart. Some of them are still alive, and they can see it, in my hand.'

The enforcer snapped his fingers, the two footsoldiers released Tree, who almost collapsed on to his knees, head swooning.

The three men climbed into the Dodge 4 × 4. It reversed, executed a smooth J-turn and as abruptly as the entire nightmare had started, it was gone.

A bird chirruped in the high trees.

Somewhere, a woodpecker was drilling away.

Sebastian Tree stared at his Porsche. It was wrecked.

★

'This guy is like the Scarlet goddam Pimpernel,' said Jimmy Fitz, leaning out of the driver's window of his undercover Mazda coupé, stopped alongside Lieutenant Tom Hanrahan's blue Ford sedan with the Lieutenant in the passenger seat and a smugly satisfied Joe Daly at the wheel. Big Joe had finally been reinstated from patrolman to detective, it had been the Commissioner's wedding present to him, and here he was, assigned to Tom Hanrahan's squad.

'He sometimes hangs out at the Ciao Bambino,' said Hanrahan. 'Somebody should check it out.'

Joe Daly lifted the car radio handset and tasked Jeb and Big Time to take a look at the Italian bar and restaurant on Newbury.

'What about his apartment?' asked Tommy Boyle, Jimmy Fitz's partner in the Mazda.

'Place is crawling with Joey Buscetta's boys from Atlantic City,' replied Hanrahan. 'For my opening shot, I want a nice quiet face-to-face with Girolo, on neutral ground.'

'I saw him on Boston Common the other day,' announced Tommy Boyle, known in the Department as 'the quiet man'.

'Terrific,' said Fitz. 'We should stake out the Common on the off-chance that he walks across it again some day. Maybe even this year . . .'

Hanrahan grinned as the pair of detectives bickered over this good natured put-down.

'He was with some woman,' said Boyle. 'Good-looking, seen her around. You know who it was . . . ?'

Still amused, Tom Hanrahan replied, 'No, who was it?'

'I don't know what she does, boss, but she works at your wife's place. What's it called? Zeralda.'

'What does she do there?' asked Hanrahan, assuming it must be some assembly-line girl, or maybe a typist, or a secretary.

'She's something legal. I met her at your barbecue, last September. Great legs, small boobs. Dark hair, straight, good cut. We talked somewhat. She has a place in Willow Mews. Father was a vet.'

'Vietnam, huh?' nodded Joe Daly, who had been a combat marine, wounded at Khe San.

'Horses. He was a veterinarian, Joe.' Tommy Boyle shook his

286

head. Marines, especially Vietnam veterans, it seemed to be the high point of their lives, even his brother, a big noise in Boston's finest, running a Major Cases unit, saw himself as a combat marine first and cop a close second.

Tom Hanrahan filed this information about Alison Clancy in his prodigious memory. He knew, having read every scrap of intelligence information, plus all the old newspaper cuttings, that Zeralda's Legal Exec had been second counsel on the Peter Girolo trial, the trial when Girolo had beaten all counts against him, except for that four-year sentence, which the guy had done in Marion, ruling the place from his cell.

Hanrahan had read the FBI report on the prison killing of a Jamaican drug king who had ordered the gang rape of Girolo, soon after the mafia boss had arrived, presumably to let him know who was boss. A fatal error on the Jamaican's part.

But why would Alison have anything to do with Girolo now? Unless they had merely bumped into each other in the park. Best thing was to ask her. Grace and Zeralda owed a lot to Alison Clancy, and she had proved many times over to be trustworthy and loyal.

Sure, best thing was to ask her.

The radio crackled. 'Yeah, boss, this is Big Time. We got that guy in the North Side, Mario's restaurant on Clark.'

Hanrahan took the handset. 'Just arrived, or leaving? You figure he might be there for a while?'

Jeb's voice came on the radio. 'Jeb, boss. The guy is looking at a menu.'

'Who's with him?' asked Joe Daly, leaning over to borrow the car microphone.

'Three or four, maybe more. Three cars.' Jeb again.

Then Big Time. 'I think he's just having supper.'

Hanrahan considered this. 'OK,' he said, 'easy does it, this is a low-profile thing. I just want a quiet sitdown. Nothing heavy.'

'You got it,' replied the laconic radio voice of Sergeant Detective Jeb Kingdom.

★

'Where on earth,' enquired Darcy Fitzrowan Bailey, almost coyly, as she fastened a stocking top to her garter belt, 'did you learn to do *that* . . . ?'

Pronsias Stevenson, naked but for his shirt, sprawled relaxed and damp on the old leather chesterfield where his secretary usually sat to take dictation, or rehearse his engagements for the next few days. He smiled as he puffed on a slender Cuban cigar from the humidor on his desk.

'Well now, that is for you to ask. And for me to keep my own counsel,' he replied, as he watched this magnificent specimen of female beauty step into her crimson leather high heels.

To her surprise, Darcy found herself quite shy in the gaze of her latest lover. Her legs were still trembling slightly, following an entire hour of imaginative, unalloyed sexual fulfilment.

'You must have had some wonderful lovers, Pronsias.' And as she said his name, she felt her stomach flutter. What in hell was happening to her, Darcy Fitzrowan, whose life had been filled with wonderful men, from young Greek gods to exciting middle-aged political leaders and international tycoons? Not to mention two Hollywood stars who were household names. And both in the same night.

None of them had taken her to the heights of pleasure this neat, unadventurous, unremarkable Dublin lawyer had achieved with such calm confidence and magical skill.

Stevenson puffed away at the Havana, not saying a word. He waited until she had slipped her black and burgundy Donna Karan silk dress over her head and shrugged it down, smoothing it over her hips and thighs. She turned her back to him and said, 'Zip me up, please.'

Stevenson laid his cigar down and without getting off the leather couch, zipped the dress up, then relaxed again while Darcy deftly clipped her three-strand pearl necklace around her elegant throat.

Wait for it, he thought. Not long now.

'Pronsias . . . ?' said Darcy sweetly.

Here we go, Pronsias Stevenson smiled. 'What is it, Darcy, my dear?'

'You have not even asked about Oliver.'

'I was sure you would tell me,' he met her eye, 'once we had gotten more important things attended to.'

She glanced at him, giving that sideways look which had driven him crazy with desire since he had first set eyes upon her, aged fifteen and riding Big Jack's champion Arab Kismet, at the Connecticut Junior Horse Show.

'Pronsias . . . ?'

'Yes, Darcy?'

'Was it really more important to fuck me than to learn what I've discovered about Oliver?'

Pronsias Stevenson winced at that word. Was that what he had been doing? Fucking Jack Fitzrowan's elder daughter? Good God, when he had been transported into some erotic, almost unreal dream world. Bringing the pleasures of that tome in Martina the Mad's Wolfe Tone replica bookcase to life, pleasuring the object of a lifetime's desire.

He had not really been able to believe it was happening. And now she had said it. Plain speaking. Just like her father.

Fucking her?

A slow grin took the place of that controlled little smile. Fucking her? You bet. That was precisely what he had been doing. Hell's teeth. Himself. Pronsias Paudraic Stevenson, pillar of the Bar. Fucking a client.

He chuckled. It was probably the first time in his life that Pronsias Stevenson had ever chuckled.

'What's so funny?' asked Darcy, suddenly ready, the way women were, to perceive some insult.

'Oh yes, of course it was. Of course that was more important. It's you I'm mad for, not bloody Oliver and his millions.'

Darcy's heart skipped a beat. She searched his eyes. 'You really mean that, don't you?'

'I can prove it,' Stevenson replied, with a look bolder and with more promise than she would have imagined possible just a few weeks before.

'How . . . ?' Darcy realized her voice was hoarse, with . . . lust?

She hoped it was merely that. And as he sprawled there, half naked, it became extremely evident just what he had in mind.

'Pronsias . . .' she exclaimed, 'you are a clever boy.'

'Lift your dress up around your waist,' he commanded, very quietly.

Darcy did as she was told. She had not gotten round to putting on her underwear.

'Now turn round and grip the desk . . .' he said.

Heart pounding, legs weak, Darcy turned and bent down to grip the desk, aware that her lover was rising from the chesterfield and was approaching. She spread her legs and stuck out her excellent bottom.

After a second's unbearable pause, she gasped as her father's lawyer entered her.

'Oh, Jesus, Pronsias, you bastard. You dirty, randy, randy, dirty bastard. Fuck me senseless, you fucking . . . stud.'

The shriek was that of a banshee, chilling the blood.

Pronsias Stevenson jerked out of his overheated lover as if electrocuted.

Darcy Fitzrowan Bailey's knees gave way and she dropped to the floor.

Two more shrieks and then an awful, solid kerrump, and their two faces, wide-eyed at the worst nightmare having happened, turned in unison to examine, appalled, the prone form of Mrs Martina Stevenson, lying sparko on the Ottoman rug, a present from Justice Malahide upon Pronsias receiving his partnership, eighteen years before.

'Holy mother of God,' breathed Pronsias Paudraic Stevenson, MA, LLD. 'Now we are well and truly fucked . . .'

Peter Girolo hated spaghetti. Maybe because he had been fed a diet of pasta as a child in Sicily. He liked Mario's on Clark Street, in the Italian enclave of North Boston, because they did the best osso buco he had tasted anywhere outside Louise Junior's on East 62nd Street, in Manhattan Central. The cook used red wine and paprika, with just the right amount of olive oil and garlic, and the meat simply fell from the bone. Delicious.

He nodded his approval to the *padrone* and politely waved away the complimentary bottle of Chianti the owner had produced.

'I'm sure,' he said in Sicilian patois, 'it is an excellent bottle, Signor Barresi. But fizzy water is OK for this evening.'

Mario Barresi smiled and withdrew. He knew that the Boston *capo* did not touch alcohol, but he too was a Sicilian and he understood the etiquette of honouring a senior don who had graced his humble establishment.

Girolo ate in silence, deep in thought. He had met with the woman Alison Clancy two more times now, in secret, having sent his bodyguards away and stolen a couple of hours to be alone. Alison had made contact, informally, with John Foley, a Federal Attorney who had been a fellow student at Harvard Law School.

But the word was less than encouraging. Foley had said that Girolo's actions since coming out of jail were quite simply, in his words, 'beyond the pale'. The entire United States were aware of the bloody taming of the young hoodlum bosses of the Boston mob. And a recent piece which originated in the *Boston Globe*, then was syndicated nation-wide, by some crime reporter called Milly Dunne, had named Peter Girolo as the new *capo mafioso* of Boston and the north-eastern seaboard.

And in Dan Rather's *60 Minutes* television show, the same Millicent Dunne had sat there and itemized the Flamingo Club slayings, the Carmine Genovese killing, Sal Spatola and his exploding Mercedes, and she had voiced suspicion that the Boston mob, and therefore Peter Girolo, was somehow behind the double homicide at Sudbury of Desmond Dekker and Joseph 'Jackson Heights' Cranmer.

Where did this Milly Dunne get her information, Albert Genovese had wanted to know, presumably on behalf of the Man himself, locked up four floors underground in the Florence supermax jail, out in the Colorado Desert.

Girolo shook his head at the naïvety of those people. In the days of CNN and in fact since 'Deep Throat' and the fall of Nixon, nobody was safe from investigative, all-intrusive journalism, be it presidents or *capi mafiosi*.

Genovese had asked if he wanted Milly Dunne taken care of but Peter Girolo had replied you could not cure acne by removing one zit. The trick was merely to obey the eleventh commandment: 'Thou shalt not get caught.'

Then Genovese had returned to his theme, in reality the Boss of Bosses' theme, that Girolo had been chosen by the *cosa* to take the war to the Russian Syndicates, which had spent the last five years putting the arm on their own immigrant communities which had taken root in every major American city.

Girolo, an educated man, felt like some Roman general, Hadrian or Marcus Aurelius, maybe even Caesar himself, stuck way out on the frontier, fighting a successful campaign to secure the territory, when a messenger arrives from Rome with a fresh command from the emperor. To open an offensive on another front. Promising the earth, reinforcements, equipment, gold, when all the time the general was really on his own. And the Senate in Rome, with the remote, unworldly emperor at its head, was hoping his growing power and military might would be curtailed by the enormity of their increasing demands.

Well, Peter Girolo knew that Russian organized crime was a monster still unhatched, but the functionaries who had arrived piecemeal, undetected by the US Immigration Service, from Moscow, Kiev and Chechnya, had just about completed their work.

Soon, the major crime bosses, czars as opposed to *capos*, would be arriving to take command. They had enough soldiers, they had identified their rivals in the Italian mafia and the Colombian, Jewish and Vietnamese crime syndicates, and Girolo had it from one of the best criminal intelligence systems in the USA, the major league prisoners inside Marion, that it was just a matter of months before the Russian mafia made its move.

It would be bloody, it would be costly, and there was every chance an accommodation would eventually have to be made to share the *cosa nostra*'s business with them, coast to coast.

But sitting out there under the desert, John Gotti would have read the papers, watched the CNN reports, and a *Time* magazine profile on the inexorable rise of Peter Michelangelo Girolo, the mystery don from Sicily via Harvard and the Sorbonne, rumoured to have worked his way up from white-collar assassin.

He would have read Millicent Dunne, he would have listened to the Larry Kings and the Dan Rathers on TV, he would have nodded when Milly Dunne had theorized that Peter Girolo was not going to stop at Boston and all points north of New York City.

Nothing, she had written, will satisfy this Attila of hoodlums, until he is sitting with his feet under the table of Giovanni Luchese's spaghetti house in Tribeca, downtown Manhattan, having usurped the mantle of John Gotti himself. Even, she had written, if it means wiping out the heads of the Five Families to get there.

Well, Albert Genovese and Joey Buscetta had laughed along with Peter Girolo whenever they had read or heard such nonsense. But Girolo did not believe the man four floors underground in that Colorado supermax would have laughed quite so heartily. For in truth, until his Damascus Road experience with those damned ducks, until he had become sickened by his bloody career, control of New York was precisely what Peter Girolo had been aiming for.

That had indeed been his secret agenda. And after New York and the entire East Coast down to Miami? Why, Las Vegas and California beckoned. For Peter Michelangelo Girolo was not only a clever and a ruthless and a careful operator. He had also inherited a profound breadth of vision and ambition. He had the gift to see ahead and, unlike most of us, the ability to understand precisely how to obtain his ambitions.

Plus, he had never been afraid of either hard work or responsibility.

Girolo smiled to himself as he ate his supper. Such musings would appear conceited, almost megalomaniac, to some eavesdropper into his mind. But he was a practical man, not a dreamer. A realist. He had merely been following his destiny, as taught to him by the Scuola Mafiosi from the age of seven.

And the *capo di tutti capi* and his counsellors would have understood this. And they would have become cautious, maybe regretting the ruthless ease with which Peter Girolo had subdued the crazy Boston banditos who were pissing their *cosa* inheritance up against the wall.

Maybe, he reflected, Boston had been allocated to him as an impossible task. Maybe, Boston had been supposed to be his Alamo.

Well, he sipped at some mineral water, too bad. And now he had changed his mind.

Outside, Jeb and Big Time's unmarked Chevrolet turned into Clark off Hanover Street. It was, noted Joey Buscetta, sitting in the tan Chrysler outside Mario's, the third time that cop car had appeared in fifteen minutes.

Detectives Jimmy Fitz and Tommy Boyle in their Mazda coupé entered from the Commercial Street end, opposite Sargent Wharf at Boston harbour.

When both automobiles had taken up position, covering the street around Mario's restaurant, Fitz spoke into the concealed microphone above the windshield. 'OK, we're here. We got three vehicles on the other team. Tan Chrysler, Dodge four by four, colour grey, and a, uh, burgundy Oldsmobile.'

'Burgundy?' came Lieutenant Tom Hanrahan's voice. 'Good year is it, Fitz?'

Jimmy Fitz grinned, 'Ninety-two, wrong side of the valley. Two inside the Chrysler, two on the sidewalk beside the four by four. Two inside the Olds . . .'

Jeb Kingdom came on the air. 'Plus he has two soldiers inside the joint.'

Tom Hanrahan thought hard, the last thing he wanted was a dramatic confrontation. He was investigating seventeen homicides in which he believed Peter Girolo was involved: maybe the guy did not pull the triggers, but he sure as hell gave the orders.

And he did not have enough evidence to haul Girolo in for questioning, let alone make an arrest. So a low-key face-to-face was his chosen approach. He had hoped Girolo would be eating with just a couple of wing men. But eight men taking care of him . . . 'The guy,' remarked Hanrahan to Joe Daly, 'must think he has need of protection.'

'The guy,' replied Daly, laconically, 'has made a whole lot of people very angry.'

It probably happened because of the way Jeb and Big Time got out from the Chevrolet sedan. Sometimes it just takes the wrong body language to set these people off. But as the two black detectives strolled across to cover the entrance to Mario's restaurant on Clark Street, Sonny Favaro and Tony di Angelo climbed out from the Oldsmobile and blocked the doorway. Tino Sciascia and Michael Angel Eyes Binelli moved over fast from the Dodge 4 × 4, unbuttoning their coats and sweeping the jackets aside as they reached for their pieces.

Tom Hanrahan, sitting in the Ford, now stopped in the street, closed his eyes as Jimmy Fitz and Tommy Boyle slewed their Mazda in a handbrake stop, diagonally across the road in front of Sciascia and Angel Eyes.

So there it was, guns out, waving around in the goddam street. Everybody yelling and shouting, 'Police officers, freeze!' 'Drop the fuckin gun! Drop the fuckin gun!' 'You don't go in there!' 'Face down in the fuckin street!' 'No way, asshole!' stuff like that.

Everybody excited. Everybody overheated. Soon, thought Hanrahan, as he hauled himself out of the car, somebody is going to get shot, and sure enough right on the button – *Bang!* And straight away two more shots and more yelling and everybody is seconds away from a war zone and there is nothing more disconcerting at such times than being on that bleak and barren expanse of asphalt between sidewalk and the safety of some nice store doorway, with the imminent prospect of gunshots from several directions and the crack of lead zipping past your ears.

'For fuck's sake!' muttered Hanrahan to Joe Daly who, good man that he was, had materialized by his side, his massive bulk trying to shield the boss from bullets marked 'to whom it may concern'. 'All I wanted was a quiet talk.' Detective Daly took in this information, digested it, nodded then strode off, walking among the shooters, both hoodlums and his cop colleagues, batting them over the heads and shoulders, cuffing their ears and yelling, 'Cool it! Cease firing! Cut it out! He only wants a quiet talk! Put that fuckin piece away or I'll take you round the back and jackets off, boyo! Cool it!! Calm down . . . Come on now. Put it away . . .'

And to Tom Hanrahan's awe and astonishment, this big, ex-marine, former quarterback, as he moved among the detectives and Atlantic City soldiers, was joined by none other than Joey Buscetta, legendary New York enforcer, still leathery and heavy muscled in middle age, who got out from the Chrysler and joined Daly in calming things down until, as swiftly as it had started, the gunfire was over and that whole bunch of hard-faced detectives and hoodlums had backed off, somewhat shamefacedly, and retreated to sullen mutual suspicion.

And being that particular quarter of North Boston, there was not a passer-by to be seen, no civilians on the street, not a face at any window.

Buscetta approached Hanrahan. 'Lieutenant, I seen you on TV. Wid your beautiful wife at the Princess Diana ball in the Boston Marriott. Mr Girolo's inside. Please, by all means . . . have the quiet word. He shoulda be at the coffee by this time.'

And Buscetta opened the door to Mario's restaurant and almost bowed, like a medieval courtier, as he ushered the detective inside.

It was not hard to spot Girolo; he was the only man in the restaurant, apart from the two bodyguards and a nervous waiter who was mopping up the coffee he had spilled over the wooden floor when the shooting had erupted.

'I had been hoping for a quiet word,' said Hanrahan as he sat down opposite the *capo*.

A flicker of a grin passed over Girolo's face. He signalled to the waiter. '*Due caffè.*'

The waiter scurried away.

Girolo gazed at Tom Hanrahan. 'Everybody is kind of jumpy,' he remarked. Hanrahan presumed he was referring to the kerfuffle outside.

'Why would that be?' he asked.

Girolo shrugged. 'The Russians. You must have the same problem. Anatoly Groszhnin flew in from Petersburg Friday.'

Hanrahan nodded gravely. Not being in the Major Cases squad, run by Tommy Boyle's big brother, Russian organized crime was not high on his agenda.

'Groszhnin, is that a fact?' he replied.

'He would not have come here,' said Girolo, 'unless they were ready to make some moves.'

Whoever this Groszhnin was, he must be a piece of work to make an impression on Girolo. Hanrahan filed the information away, to pass on to Intel and Major Cases.

They sat in silence while the nervous waiter laid down two large espresso coffees. Hanrahan showed his Police ID. 'I'm Detective Lieutenant Hanrahan, Homicide . . .'

Girolo nodded. 'I know, I saw you in the society columns with your wife. A beautiful woman.'

'You know,' sighed Hanrahan, 'it really pisses me that nobody recognizes me from the arrests I make.'

Girolo smiled. 'The public are fickle. They're more likely to remember you standing beside Donald Trump and Daryl Hannah.'

'But you ain't the public, Peter,' remarked Hanrahan softly. 'You kill people.'

Girolo dropped one sugar cube into his espresso and remained silent. But he did not look away.

Hanrahan went on, 'In fact, you are killing so many people, Peter, the law is beginning to look stupid. And I am the law, in this particular instance. Believe me, I do not like to look stupid.'

Girolo shook his head. 'These are serious allegations. Are you arresting me?'

Hanrahan's eyes narrowed. 'Listen to me. You came out of Marion and the *famiglia* offered you Boston, if you could take it. The place was a battleground with young idiots running around making like Al Capone.' He lifted his cup with a rock-steady hand and gazed over the rim into Girolo's eyes. 'You will not be surprised to hear there are some in the DA's office who think you have done Boston a favour.'

Girolo's face remained devoid of expression.

'But I just do the job.' Tom Hanrahan sipped his espresso. 'I am investigating twenty-one homicides in and around the city. OK, the chef who killed his wife, the guy in Mattapan who strangled his sister, the kids who robbed a liquor store near the Marriott Long Wharf, where you have a suite, and killed the old woman behind the counter, the Vietnamese hoodlum who was chopped up by his own folk . . . none of these do I look at you for. None of those four murders.'

Tom Hanrahan drained his coffee and set the cup down. He tugged his pack with the two Winstons in it and shook one out.

'That leaves seventeen.' He glanced sharply at Girolo, as he lit the cigarette. 'Seventeen murders, Mr Girolo.' After he had exhaled, savouring the nicotine, the Lieutenant said, softly, 'Seventeen for which I am looking at you. How many years is that in Marion, or Florence? Hmm?'

Girolo was not impolite. He did not look as if he had other things to do. It was almost as if he felt . . . sympathy, for this Homicide cop who just happened to have gotten caught up in his career.

This made Hanrahan mad. But he did not let it show.

'OK,' he said conversationally, 'it's time for a line in the sand. One more mob killing and I arrest your ass, and I arrest all those penny-ante scumbags you have hanging around you. Sure, your lawyers will get you out. So I arrest you all over again. I will have every one of your enterprises searched, regularly, closed for breach of fire regulations, investigated by IRS, busted for dope, pandering, money laundering . . . you will never have a day without Boston PD crawling all over you. *Capisce?*'

In the silence which followed, Hanrahan affected to be more interested in his surroundings and his cigarette, but all the time he was observing his opponent. And it was strange; in fact, two things were strange. The first was that Girolo seemed to be deep in thought, not a process the cop associated with organized crime bosses, as if reflecting on what Hanrahan had just said. The second thing was that it was almost as if he knew this guy. Maybe fatigue was playing tricks on him. He had hardly been home at a decent hour for days, maybe weeks, with all this homicide work courtesy of our friend sitting across the table.

Grace was not letting it show but she was very pissed with him. Ever since they had talked about making babies he had hardly been awake enough to go to sleep, let alone make love to his wife with the tenderness and excitement he felt she deserved.

'. . . laws of harassment and infringement of my civil rights,' Girolo was saying.

Hanrahan nodded at the waiter for more coffee. 'Run that past me again?' he said. 'Rights? I could have a SWAT team here in minutes to disarm your made men the fuckin hard way. You want a body count? Boston PD can help some.'

'My associates,' said Girolo, 'are licensed to carry concealed handguns. They are employees of a private security firm I run. When you people arrived in plain clothes, so aggressively, they thought it was a Russian hit. It's something we were expecting.'

Hanrahan grinned, bleakly. 'There was a kid, John di Falco, a young man who worked as a cook in the Flamingo Club, out there in Mattapan. You ordered his death, when all he wanted to do was save enough for his own bar and restaurant. For that one killing, I will not rest till I see you in fuckin leg-irons.'

He stubbed his cigarette out in the newly arrived espresso and stood up.

Girolo met his fierce stare. 'I read about that. My condolences. He was a relation?'

Hanrahan shook his head, more sad than angry. 'You people never get it, do you? He was a human being, Mr Girolo. No relation. But I did hold his mother while she cried her heart out. You should take care,' he patted his inside pocket, 'I mean to get you.'

The Lieutenant walked out, not looking back. His detectives faced off Girolo's men as he got into the Ford, and Homicide cars moved away, turning right into Atlantic Avenue.

Joey Buscetta went inside and sat at Girolo's table. 'What was that all about?' he asked.

Peter Girolo looked thoughtful, then he said, 'Nobody gets whacked for a couple of weeks. It would be bad for business.'

'Sure thing, boss.' And in his Sicilian sign language Buscetta moved hands and wrists, succinctly. They asked the question, 'What about the Russians?'

Girolo slowly turned to look into Buscetta's soul. 'Are you here to keep an eye on me, Joey?'

The enforcer looked shocked. *'Absolutamente non, Padrino,'* he replied.

And Peter Girolo noted that was the first time his strong right hand had not been able to look him in the face.

Six a.m. Darcy had not slept well. After the nightmare of Pronsias's wife collapsing in a dead faint on his office floor, Stevenson had thrust her purse and underwear into her hand and let her out, first looking this way and that, furtively, to ensure nobody was around.

'Go back to your father's house,' he had said. The Fitzwilliam Street town house was just round the corner. 'I'll call you.'

And Darcy Fitzrowan Bailey, millionairess and international society beauty, had walked briskly away, knickers in her handbag, slightly flushed. The way, she contemplated, with the beginnings of a return of her sense of humour, she had done a few times before.

By the time she had reached 8 Fitzwilliam Street, she was relaxed and close to being amused. After all, shock though it must have been for Pronsias's tight-mouthed squeaky clean spouse to have breezed into her boring husband's office and found him *in flagrante* with a stunning (yes, thought Darcy, let's not be modest) woman, the high drama of collapsing in an unconscious heap was maybe just a tad over the top.

Then at two fifty in the morning, the phone had rung and it was Pronsias. He had dressed, revived Martina and, bizarrely, had tried to convince her she had been hallucinating, unkindly reminding her of her sojourn in Saint Theresa's, under medication. But Martina knew what she had seen and when she had searched the office and found, as Darcy had surely meant her to, one of Darcy's sapphire and diamond earrings, between two cushions on the leather couch, she had become, according to Pronsias, disconcertingly serene.

'She wants a divorce,' said the Dublin lawyer.

'Oh, dear,' Darcy had replied.

There had been a long silence on the other end of the phone.

'"Oh dear" . . . ?' Pronsias Stevenson had sounded confused. 'Is that all you can say?'

Darcy had shrugged, lying there in bed, gazing through the tall Georgian windows at the night sky and the rooftops of one of Dublin's better neighbourhoods. Pronsias had never discussed his marriage in their brief and torrid relationship, nor had she talked about Edward.

Frankly, my dear, she felt, to quote Rhett Butler, I don't give a damn. But poor Pronsias was clearly shattered by this turn of events.

'Pronsias, I'm sorry. But it was always a chance you had to take.'

'Are you really that heartless?' Stevenson had said.

'I'm just a realist. It gives me no pleasure to be involved. Pleasure without cost is a rare commodity,' she replied, thinking perhaps for the first time in her life, what a hard-hearted bitch you can be, Darcy Fitzrowan.

Stevenson had sounded drained. He had made some mundane remark about sure, she was right. He must have been mad. What a fool he had been, etcetera.

And he had said of course he would never allow her name to be dragged through the courts. And just as he had been about to say goodbye, the lawyer had chuckled sadly and remarked that he had still not learned her dramatic news about the hunt for Oliver.

Then he had said goodbye. And the way Pronsias Stevenson had said it, Darcy knew he did not mean *au revoir*. Well, too bad, she had thought, and pulled the bedclothes over her head and tried to get back to sleep.

But sleep was elusive.

At first Darcy put it down to fatigue from jetting across the Atlantic from New York, exhilarating sex with her new and now former lover, and the drama of Martina bursting in on them like that. But as dawn came, and still she lay half-awake, Darcy knew that her restlessness came from a new and unwelcome emotion. For the first time in her life, she had begun to like someone for themselves. Liked? Stronger than that. Cared about. As much, well, nearly as much, as she cared about herself.

And now he was gone. And the clouds of scandal loomed.

Darcy had no doubt that Martina Stevenson would lose no time in making the most of her husband's infidelity with a Fitzrowan heiress.

Poor Edward. The saddest thing about him was that she had not the least doubt he would forgive her. Again. Well, if the dull professor believed such generosity might earn him another perverse ceremony of contrition, he had another goddam think coming.

On the other hand, divorce settlements in England these days were becoming almost as costly as those in the USA, and Darcy was damned if the boring Edward Bailey would enjoy any of her few millions. So maybe she might just put up with another of his rare moments of lust. It was simple economics when you came to think about it.

These were Darcy Fitzrowan Bailey's thoughts when, at 6.04 in the Dublin morning, the doorbell sounded. One long ring. It was an old-fashioned doorbell and it always reminded her of fresh breakfast cooking and home-made marmalade and scones, and the laughter of her sister and brother, when their daddy had juggled hot boiled eggs and pieces of toast as they popped up from the toaster on the white linen table cloth.

Ringgg . . .

There it was again.

Looking like shit, she felt, but not caring, Darcy pulled on her father's big dressing-gown and padded down to the front hall.

She opened the door expecting to find a postman or some such and there was Pronsias Stevenson, neatly dressed and crisply shaved, but with part of his shirt sticking out over his belt, and a scrap of tissue where he had cut his chin shaving. His eyes were red with fatigue.

'Pronsias,' she said. 'What is it . . . ?'

The lawyer looked so tired, yet somehow years younger.

'Darcy, I want to marry you,' he declared.

302

12

Sebastian Tree, maybe because of his background, needed to be in control, not just of himself, but of his life, its surroundings and anyone who related to those in any way.

Tree's single-minded campaign to destroy Jack Fitzrowan and his globally successful electronics corporation stemmed from the simple, but all-powerful, psychological need to remove the cause of so much random instability in his life so far.

Jack Fitzrowan had spawned him on a whim of casual pleasure, and discarded him, casting him to the wolves of Fate. Therefore, by destroying Fitzrowan and all that he stood for, the Zeralda Corporation, then Fitzrowan's Americas Cup hopes, then the Kentucky and Kerry stud farms, and of course the bastard Jack himself, Sebastian Tree had intended to free his troubled psyche from the control that Fitzrowan's rejection had put over his life.

It would have been more satisfying to have brought Zeralda crashing down before Big Jack's death, but the opportunity that weekend on his ketch *Zeralda of Erin* had been too good to miss. And, reflected Tree, he had not even realized that with Fitzrowan's death, he, Sebastian, would become one of the wealthiest men in the USA, which was to say, in the world, merely by submitting himself and the history of his birth to some Irish lawyer, and by changing his name to Oliver Fitzrowan, to conform with the terms of the codicil.

That ought to give him some degree of control . . .

He smiled grimly, sitting in his den, a little light jazz coming from his Bang & Olufsen state-of-the-art sound system.

The wreck company had offered him $25,000 for the remains of the Porsche, and he had just ordered a new Jaguar XK-8 on the strength of his coming legacy.

$218,000,000. He scribbled it for the umpteenth time on his desk pad. At eight point seven per cent per annum, which he could easily realize, that would provide him with around twenty-six million dollars every year. Since he did not anticipate spending more than around six million, his capital base would roll over and increase, as would his income, year after year after year.

What bliss.

For the first time in years, maybe even in his life, Sebastian Tree relaxed.

And the hoodlum who had sent his gorillas to lean on him?

Tree smiled grimly. Nobody messed around with the son of Jack Fitzrowan. There were certain powerful, ruthless genes at work. Plus he had friends in the mob.

He lifted the phone and dialled a number in Los Angeles.

A woman's voice announced, 'Thank you for calling the Oasis Hotel, Los Angeles.'

'Get me,' he commanded, 'Bobby Scipio. Tell him it's an old friend . . .'

The house on Farragut Road was in darkness, except for one soft light on the top floor, in a small room off the third-floor balcony. The door to the balcony, with its white, wood railed balustrade, was half open, letting cool air into the room, which Grace used as her study and den combined.

It was her private bolt-hole and at two in the morning she sat in the old rocking chair that her daddy had given her not long after she and Tom had married, saying, with that grin of his, it might be more comfortable than a wooden kitchen chair, when it came to nursing a 'little fellow'.

But the only thing she was nursing that night was a mug of hot chocolate, as she gazed out over the bay towards Castle Point, her heart heavy as she contemplated her situation.

Here she was, nearly thirty years old, married four years to a good man, a kind and loving man. But was he the right man for her?

Grace had all kinds of plans when she got married. Tom to run for Senate. With her daddy's backing, there would have been few problems in getting him at least well into the nomination stakes. Her husband had a good mind and just the strength of character and honesty of purpose that had been so lacking in another famous Massachusetts dynasty, now tarnished and largely reviled by its indulgences, misdemeanours and its arrogant hubris.

But dear Tom was wedded to the Police Department. And worse, he was a Homicide detective with few ambitions to become Chief of Police. With his law degree from Boston University, there would have been nothing to stop him from switching from the Department to the DA's office.

Her father had told Tom several times, on the golf course and sailing on board *Zeralda*, that he could be Boston's District Attorney within three years of quitting the police. But Tom had just grinned and said he felt he had something to contribute in Homicide, and the height of his immediate ambition was maybe to transfer to Major Cases and head up the fight against organized crime, and continue to build on Boston PD's unusually good working relationship with the Feds, Customs, the DEA, the US Secret Service and other agencies.

Grace reflected on all this, and while she admired Tom for his integrity, her heart was heavy. For with her daddy gone, and with Zeralda Electronics taking so much of her time, here she was, living a life she had not planned, anticipated, or even contemplated.

Tom Hanrahan was dreaming about *Zeralda*, in heavy seas, in the Nantucket Sound. There was a fog, the spray was blinding him as he fought with the big steering wheel. And Jack Fitzrowan, in of all things his pyjamas, but wearing a black bow tie, was slithering down the hatch cover, his arm outstretched for Tom to grasp it. But it was impossible to hold the wheel and touch Jack's reaching hand and both men knew that to let go the wheel would result in *Zeralda* capsizing.

Crying out, 'Hold on, hold on . . .' Tom woke up, his left arm stretched out, knocking over a glass of water on the bedside table. Heart pounding, he took a couple of seconds to realize where he was. At home in his own bed.

Calming down, he sighed and rolled on to his back, moving to feel the warm comfort of his sleeping wife. But she was not there.

Tom Hanrahan opened his eyes and felt the empty space. He sat up half-way and saw the bedroom door open and a faint glow of light from under the study door, across the hall.

He looked at his watch: 2.07 a.m.

Sitting in her rocking chair, Grace was aware of the door behind her opening and Tom standing there.

'Baby, do you know what time it is?' asked Tom, concerned.

Grace did not turn round. She nodded.

'Hey . . .' said Tom, and moved over to her, so that he could see her face. It was wet with tears.

'Aww . . . Grace, honey . . .' He put a comforting hand on her shoulder. She almost flinched.

'Is it Pop . . . ?' he said, a statement more than a question.

Grace gently pushed his hand away, shaking her head.

'What is it then? More problems at work?' He wished he could tell her about Sebastian Tree, but the time was not right. Pretty soon he planned to go to the DA with a case against Zeralda's Chief Exec and arrest his ass.

But again, Grace shook her head.

'Come on . . . everything seems so much worse in the middle of the night, hon.' He thought of his own recent nightmare.

But Grace just sighed and said, 'You could not even come to the Katakura thing, to pick me up.'

'Gracey, I was on a double murder . . .'

'There's always a double goddam murder, Tom. And just where does that leave us?'

Tom Hanrahan stared at his wife. Every couple has rows, and he and Grace were like anyone else, but he knew this was different. And that disquieting feeling of losing somebody so close, that had wakened him calling out, heart thumping, just minutes before, suddenly returned. That feeling of inevitability and helplessness as in his dream he had watched Jack slip away, over the side of his ketch, into the heaving sea, was now real For there was a sad resolve in Grace's attitude which gave him a sense of emptiness.

'I love you, darling,' he said softly.

'I know you do,' his wife replied, and more tears began to run down her face. She wiped them away and glanced at him. 'I know you do. And I love you. But I think I've had it. If I didn't think it was so corny, I would say I just can't take any more . . .'

Silence.

'Jesus,' said Tom and he pulled a chair over and sat beside her, gazing at her, almost afraid to hear any more.

After a while, he spoke. 'Gimme the full nine yards.'

Grace sighed, and sniffed. Tom produced a tissue from her neat bureau, overlooking the trees and the water beyond.

'Thanks,' said Grace and blew her nose, less delicately than they had taught her at that exclusive Connecticut boarding school. She took a couple of deep breaths and turned to look at him. 'Tom, you are a dedicated cop. It's your life. You live and breathe it. Look at me. Thrust into running Zeralda at the age of thirty. A corporate psychopath intent on ruining the firm, and nobody, apart from Alison, to lean on for advice and . . . comfort.'

OK, decided Tom, enough is enough. 'You have to get rid of Sebastian Tree,' he said. 'The man maybe murdered Jack.'

Grace stared at him, trying to get a handle on that. 'But Daddy was killed in a yachting accident.'

Tom raised his shoulders. 'There is evidence the boom was tampered with. And the two suspects are Sebastian and me.'

Grace frowned, and suddenly she was her father's daughter once more, with that core of steel. 'When did this come to light?' she asked.

Tom shrugged. 'A few weeks ago.'

'Weeks?' Grace looked shocked. 'Weeks, and you haven't told me?'

'I couldn't,' said Tom. 'I didn't want to worry you, you had all that NASA stuff going on, and at first it was only me under suspicion. And then only from one direction.'

'What direction?' Grace was actually looking at him as if she too believed he might be guilty.

'Sergeant Tarantola.'

'Danny? On what evidence?'

'Oh . . . he had a hunch. I followed it up, unofficially, with the help of Tommy Boyle, who is working with Danny on the investigation. Danny has something. He's wrong about me, but there is accumulating circumstantial against Tree. Pretty soon I will have enough to charge him with.'

Suddenly much of his wife's hostility went. She reached out a hand to him and said, with sympathy, 'Poor Tom. You kept all that to yourself . . .'

'Well . . .' Tom replied, seizing the chance to turn Grace's feeling of being left to her own devices back at her, 'you were so busy with Zeralda.'

And her eyes flashed, at first recognizing the cheek of that riposte, then amused, as Tom held her gaze and made what she called, in happier times, his John Belushi eyes.

Then the glimmer of a smile, and she said, 'That was real cheap.'

'I know,' he admitted, without a blush.

The worst moment, when Grace had taken their marriage towards the abyss, slipped past. But it would be a while, Tom knew, before he could describe it as rock steady, the words he would have used before walking into the room just minutes before.

'OK, let's get back to sleep.' She stood up and laid her cup down, avoiding his eyes.

Tom rose and put his arms round her. She did not resist. 'You want to make babies . . . ?' he murmured, as he nuzzled her hair.

Grace shook her head. 'Maybe not just yet, honey,' she replied and gently pulled out of his embrace and padded back out of her study towards their bedroom.

Music was important to Peter Girolo. He had a piano in the Beaver Place apartment, and whenever he had the chance, he would practise. He had, in fact, been practising ever since he was eleven, when the Scuola had decided musical ability, a facility to play jazz and classical, might well be an asset to their little assassin in the future.

But whereas the boy had excelled at languages and mathematics, history and physics, gymnastics and weapons handling, the truth was he had never really mastered the keyboard, even though he loved listening to music, and had a natural sense of rhythm.

Thus piano practice, even thirty-three years on, was conducted in conditions of as much secrecy and privacy as any confidences of the *cosa nostra*. It would be unfair to say it was awful. But it would be less than honest to say that it was awfully good.

Peter Girolo knew this, yet still he persevered.

Marion prison had musical facilities, a piano, saxophones, guitars, electronic keyboards and a couple of drum kits. It also had an opera society, with about seven talented prisoners who would put on everything from *La Bohème* to *Porgy and Bess*.

But it lacked privacy, and so Girolo had four years of missed piano practice to catch up on.

That Sunday afternoon, apart from four of the Atlantic City boys down in the street, keeping an eye on things, he had the place to himself, and the Boston *capo* sat at the keyboard of a Bechstein upright piano, playing passages from Leoncavallo's opera *Pagliacci*.

To an untutored ear, it probably sounded quite talented and the word among his hoodlum footsoldiers was that the boss was gifted. But Peter Girolo felt anything but gifted as his fingers roved, less than effortlessly, among the keys.

His mind, however, was not on the music score, but on the opera's tragic story of a clown caught in a doomed love. Clown was right, he thought, as his mind went over his life's path. It was as if he had been in some kind of trance for the last thirty-five years.

He had been conditioned to serve the *cosa* without question and he had been taught that his almost unique way of life was both honourable and at the same time a great honour. The business of unemotional killing, in the service of the mafia, the complex hierarchy and the conspiracy of silence, the culture of *rispeto*, respect, and unquestioning loyalty had been inculcated by his tireless teachers, and mentors, and had until very recently been his motor, his driving force.

It had never occurred to Girolo, in all other respects an intelligent and educated man, that his career, although criminal, with its reliance on fear and brutality, conspiracy and murder, was fundamentally and profoundly evil.

In fact he would have shrugged at the notion and pointed to the history of many respectable nations, tribes, clans and dynasties, in Europe in the Middle Ages, in Asia for thousands of years and in the Americas until quite recently. He would have argued convincingly that his particular profession was an honourable one and if he had put his skills at the disposal of a European king, or the USA during two world wars and one cold war, he would have become a respected servant of the nation instead of a national bogeyman.

Well, those two doomed kids had changed all that. The kids and the goddam ducks. And other things, like the fundamental decency of Alison Clancy, who was very wary of him and who still doubted, he knew, the seriousness of his intentions. Even so, she had made informal contact with a federal attorney in the US Justice Department, and had been doing her best to get some kind of deal for Girolo, no doubt in return for his saving her life.

Before his re-awakening, Girolo would have been satisfied that Alison owed him a favour, the biggest, for he had saved her life. It was the family's way of doing business. But now, as he played the *Pagliacci* overture, the *capo* felt regret that he had not been able to approach her without any leverage, of any kind, and persuade her to represent him on his own merits.

Merits? he thought wryly. What merits?

His digital, relatively secure, mobile phone buzzed. Only Joey Buscetta and a handful of trusted others had the number. He picked it up. 'Hello.'

'Hello, Mr G. This is Alison.'

Alison Clancy was naturally discreet. Peter Girolo was surprised to discover he was pleased to hear her voice, she really was a nice woman.

'Alison, what can I do for you?'

'I've managed to persuade the man I have been talking to, off the record, to take a meeting.'

Girolo frowned. 'A meeting? What kind of meeting?'

'He would like to hear your side of the story. I would be present. And there would be no funny business.'

By funny business, Peter Girolo assumed Alison meant nobody would try to throw him in handcuffs and leg-irons and return him to prison, charged with all kinds of stuff.

After the surprise appearance of the cop Hanrahan, in Mario's restaurant, in the heart of Girolo's fiefdom, Girolo guessed it would not be long before the law put together a case for indictment before a Grand Jury.

Hanrahan had impressed him, the man was a pro to his fingertips. That visit had been a cold warning. We are going to get you, it went, so be cool, and don't add any more crimes to the list, if you ever want to see daylight in your old age.

Hanrahan had not scared Girolo, but his warning had been timely. Caught between police heat and the mob's insistence that he take the war to the Russians all along the eastern seaboard, Peter Girolo could not think of a better time to get out for good.

There was an island in the Caribbean, as yet untouched by the drugs traffickers or the mob's casinos. It lay to the east of Saint Kitts and Nevis. It had beach bars and a couple of small hotels, and was five hours from the Venezuelan coast.

Years before, Peter Girolo had purchased a small bar there, with its own bay and wooden dock. He paid a local fisherman and his wife to run the place, and he visited it about once a year.

Nobody in the *cosa* knew of its existence, and Dean Arthur, his bar manager and deep-sea fishing wizard, believed that his senior partner and benefactor was one David Grant Morgan, a contracts lawyer from Washington DC.

Girolo had also made discreet financial provision for a new life, unknown to anyone else, not even his confessor in the Vatican, whom he still visited every other year or so.

There were safe deposit boxes in Switzerland, Monaco and the Cayman Islands, with cash totalling $4.4 million, along with several new identities, handguns and the other paraphernalia of his profession.

Well, he would not be needing the assassin's tools, ever again, but the cash and new identity would allow him to disappear into a new life as beach-bar and fast-cruiser owner, renting out his and Dean's services for deep-sea fishing, scuba diving and general lazing about in the turquoise waters of the southern Caribbean.

'Mr G . . . ?' Alison Clancy's voice.

Girolo shook himself out of his reverie. 'What in your professional opinion would such a meeting achieve?'

Alison replied, 'If he can be persuaded of the genuineness of your decision, *vis-à-vis* the rest of your life . . . I would try to sell him on the idea of using your example, and an imaginative approach from his side, to convince others like you to . . . reform.'

Girolo smiled. The kid had a good brain, this was an interesting angle.

'What happens if they jump on me and arrest me on the spot?'

'They would if they could, but so would Tom Hanrahan and he does not have enough to persuade the DA, and neither, I understand, do the Feds.'

But time, reflected Girolo, is running out.

'Say I say yes. When and where?'

'Today. Come to the Aquarium, leave by the staff entrance. There are painters working there and the door is left open. I'll be in my car, waiting.'

Big risk, thought Girolo, this could be a perfect set-up. But what the hell, they could more easily come and knock on my front door.

'I'll be there in forty minutes,' he said and switched off the phone.

Round about the time that Peter Girolo was on his way to the Aquarium, Paul Fitzrowan could be found in his father's office in Zeralda Electronics. He did not really think of it as his sister Grace's office, even though it was her name, nowadays, on the wooden plaque on the President's desk.

He liked working on a Sunday, because the building was deserted apart from three security men and some Mexican cleaners. It gave him time to think and space to mooch around and get a feel for what had been going wrong since his father's fatal accident, for something had been going wrong, of that he had no doubt.

Sure, the Sebastian Tree episode with NASA had rattled the corporate cage more than slightly. And certainly Alison Clancy's quick wits had saved the day. But that did not explain the lack of new business.

It seemed, from reading through the firm's sales records and existing business, that repeat sales to clients were on target, but new clients were either not biting, or they were not being tackled hard enough.

Paul had signed out the sales manager's office keys and now he sat at his late father's desk reading through the sets of computer floppy disks detailing Zeralda's sales effort over the last five months.

One common denominator eventually trickled through. The more important customers' technical services advisors had become aware that several computer parts companies were neck and neck in research and development of the as yet mythical self-improving microchip, which would update itself to come into line with advances in main-frame micro-engineering.

This rang a bell with Paul, for he remembered in one of his brief conversations with Alison Clancy that she had mentioned how interested his dad would have been in such exciting and imaginative research.

So for the past three hours, Paul Fitzrowan had been trawling through the R&D files of any and every company in the same line of business, whose defences he could penetrate, downloading only in the few instances where he felt that company was seriously on to something.

Was this piracy? Was this against international copyright law? Was it theft? Industrial espionage?

Paul smiled.

It was the electronics business at the end of the twentieth century. Dog byte dog.

His father had been punctilious in his business relations, with a reputation for straight dealing and reliability. But he was a ruthless player in the big boys' game of computer research. How did anyone think Big Jack had gotten where he was? Why, one US government agency had done a deal with him (the deal was he would avoid prosecution) to sit down and teach their own technical spooks his state-of-the-art techniques of hacking into the most closely protected computer files, downloading, and by using a computer security code, instructing the dumb machines that this was part of a routine service and they were to erase any record of having been raped and pillaged.

Computers being essentially obliging, when treated right, they would do just that, and thus there was no trace of Jack Fitzrowan's acts of piracy.

By four twenty, Paul had enough material to take home and work on, in his own computer den, with a view to designing a DNA-type string which would programme certain micro-micro-chips into re-forming themselves in order to stay in line with main-frame equipment as each fresh improvement occurred.

Paul knew there would be a finite time for the life of such micro-microchips but he figured his task was to make that life at least four years longer than anyone else could.

He also made a list of those members of Zeralda's sales team who seemed to have relaxed their effort since his father's death, and he took home the files Alison Clancy had received from Telford & Pollard, the Washington-based private investigation agency who had produced considerable background on Sebastian Tree.

As he left the Zeralda complex, two carrier bags groaning with floppy disks and documents, the senior security guard on duty, not Arthur but his deputy, Jon Szbegneci, waved him a smiling 'take it easy' kind of wave and pressed the remote control to open the heavy duty wire mesh security gate.

Paul steered his Pontiac through the gateway with its impressive 'Zeralda' logo and smiled back, returning the guard's cheery wave and making a mental note to remind Security to institute a system of spot searches of staff leaving the premises.

The New England Aquarium is built on the landward side of Central Wharf, on Boston's Waterfront. The plaza which fronts it was busy with Sunday afternoon strollers, milling around a huge, scarlet sculpture, 'Echo of the Waves', which reaches high into the air and rotates slowly.

What with the 'Echo of the Waves' and, on the left of the Aquarium entrance, an exhibitionist flotilla of seals diving and rolling in the harbour, there was more than enough to divert the casual observer from Peter Michelangelo Girolo as he went inside.

He paid for his ticket and strolled past the penguin pool, where a girl in blue wetsuit bottoms was feeding a gaggle of small, bustling, tuxedoed lodgers.

Soon Girolo had found the stairs to the staff exit and he made his way down, past a couple of men painting the walls, and out into the yard beneath the supports of Atlantic Avenue, the main highway by-passing the Waterfront.

He saw Alison Clancy's BMW 320 and, as if he had not a care in the world, paused, hands in pockets, to check out the environment. She was alone.

'Hi,' said Alison as Peter Girolo opened the passenger door and got in.

'Hi yourself,' smiled Girolo. 'Where are we going?'

'Not far,' replied the lawyer and as she started the car and drove out of the yard, the mafia don found himself appreciating the faintest aroma of her scent.

'That's nice, what is it?'

'What's what?' she replied, with a sideways glance, as she turned right on to the John Fitzgerald Expressway.

'You smell great,' he said, suddenly feeling both shy and annoyed with himself. He hoped she did not feel he was coming on to her, for this was strictly business.

But Alison merely replied, 'L'eau Hadrien.'

'Ah yes,' nodded Girolo, 'Annik Goutal.'

Alison was genuinely surprised. 'How did you know that?'

Girolo smiled. 'When I was in prison, I used to get *Vogue* and *Vanity Fair*. It was the closest I ever got to the ladies . . .'

Alison thought about that, and wondered about the obvious. And as she wondered that, she found herself blushing.

Peter Girolo just smiled again, and pointedly gazed out of the window as Custom House and Quincy Market flashed past beneath them.

'John, this is the man I have been talking to you about,' Alison Clancy said to a mildly overweight, sandy haired man, about 5'10", with a droopy moustache and rimless glasses, wearing blue jeans and a grey Ralph Lauren Polo shirt with USA in big letters on the front. And Gucci moccasins.

Girolo offered his hand, which John Foley, Federal Attorney with the United States Department of Justice, ignored.

'OK,' he said, businesslike, 'I do not want to know your name.' He did, of course, but he was not going to speak off the record and then have it replayed in court from a wire. 'Miss Clancy has posed a hypothetical question, and since I assume you are probably a legal colleague of hers, I can discuss the matter on that basis.'

His podgy face had not shown any emotion and despite being so obviously unfit, the man had good eyes. Honest eyes. Tough, in their own way, and intelligent.

They were in an underground car park, not far from the Charles Hotel, in Cambridge, Boston's twin town, across the Charles River.

Girolo had told Alison to let him out on the ramp descending to the lowest level, and he had checked out the entire area before joining Alison and Foley standing beside Foley's Lincoln sedan.

'That suits me,' replied Girolo. He had been around prosecutors and jailers enough to know just how to temper his attitude. Not too servile, not aggressive.

Foley glanced around, nodded and said, 'Fine. Step into my office.' He got into the back seat and moved over to the far corner, a nice gesture, meaning he was not intending to drive off with Girolo inside.

Wise man, thought Girolo, and he slid in after Foley, as Alison got into the front passenger seat.

'OK,' Alison said, 'the hypothesis is this. An organized crime boss comes out of a high security penitentiary after serving four years for tax evasion. The federal system is well aware that the man has been up to his eyes in conspiracy, extortion, murder and the controlling of major crimes for years.'

'But you got him off with only four years,' remarked Foley, peering balefully over his spectacles at Alison.

'My firm did its work to the best of its ability, John. That's what the law requires.'

Foley raised his hands. 'Sure thing. Go on.'

Alison continued, 'He comes out, every bit as much a *capo mafioso* as when he went in. The mob tells him he can have Boston and everything north of New York City, if he can take it back from the banditos who have reduced Italian-American organized crime in the territory to the level of inter-gang delinquency. Quite lethal delinquency, with guns and drugs and fast cars and acting out the stuff they watch in the movies.'

'So this hypothetical guy, this ex-con . . .' Foley let his gaze fall on Girolo, 'takes on the job.'

Alison nodded. 'Sure. He restores good order and discipline to the *cosa nostra* in and around Boston, and in the process, a number of banditos die not of natural causes.'

Foley glanced at her. 'There is a school of thought that for these people to die like that *is* natural causes.'

Maybe this fellow is going to be a help, thought Girolo, and had a momentary picture of coming out of jail in five or six years' time, the slate clean, and able to take his place in society. He had a notion he might be able to square it with the Man himself, so that the family would let him go. After all, they owed him enough. And he would have those few years inside to negotiate a new life on his release.

'Then,' Alison went on, 'our hypothetical person has a change of heart. It's genuine, it is true remorse, and he becomes sickened with his way of life.'

'He wants out?' asked Foley.

Alison Clancy nodded. 'He wants out.' She turned to Girolo, 'Right?'

Peter Girolo inclined his head. 'He wants out,' he agreed, and met Foley's searching gaze.

'But,' said Alison, 'will he be able to cut a deal with Justice? He knows what he has done. He is an educated and, oddly enough, a sensitive man. The guy has finally, after all those years, discovered a conscience.'

'Kind of late in the day,' observed Foley, drily.

'But too late?' asked Alison. 'I wonder. Our man knows in order to wipe the slate clean and start afresh, he will need to do time.'

Foley agreed. 'That's for sure.'

'So the hypothetical question is this,' Alison went on. 'If the Justice Department believed, by showing clemency to a genuine repenter, that this would encourage others like our . . . subject, to renounce their lives of crime for ever, would it not be a bold move to cut the person a deal? Say five or six years in a penitentiary? Which would still allow him the rest of his life to be a useful citizen.'

In the silence which followed, Alison wondered if her advocacy would have any effect on John Foley, whom she had known as a student. He had been good fun in those days, a football player who liked his Budweiser. But that was ten years ago.

And Peter Girolo was asking himself was that true what Alison Clancy had said? Did he really, genuinely repent, regret, his life at the top of the major crime league?

To his relief, he knew the answer was yes.

Eventually, Foley, who had seemed to be in an almost zen-like trance, grunted. He turned to Alison. 'Alison, level with me. Do you trust this guy? This hypothetical guy?'

Without hesitating, Alison replied yes, she did. And avoided Girolo's grateful if surprised glance.

'And,' went on the Federal Attorney, 'would you be prepared to vouch for him, if released earlier than the thousand years he has undoubtedly earned for himself?'

Alison frowned. She looked at Girolo, thoughtful, then she said, 'You know, John, I believe I would, but as his attorney, I am precluded by law from such action.'

Foley thought about that. Then he said, 'I hear what you are saying.' He turned to Girolo. 'How serious are you?'

'Serious. I'm serious,' the *capo* replied.

'You know we have a witness protection programme . . . ?'

'I am not informing. I am not giving word one on anyone or anything. That is not on the table.'

Foley sighed. 'Hypothetically, of course.'

'I am no rat. I do not squeal.'

Silence.

'Last word? It could make things so much simpler.' Foley watched Girolo carefully.

'Positively. I give myself up, but nobody else. Apart from any . . . misplaced you maybe think . . . sense of honour, witness protection or no witness protection the *cosa* would get to me. This I know how?' He smiled and it chilled Foley's blood. 'You know how. Hypothetically . . .'

He meant because he had done it. Peter Girolo had personally taken care of three top *mafiosi* who had been under the federal witness protection programme. And he had managed to do that without harming one innocent bystander, or even a Fed.

John Foley thought hard for a few minutes, then he opened the car door and turned to Girolo. 'Thank you.' He got out and opened Alison Clancy's door, and as she climbed out from the Lincoln he said, 'I'll be in touch.'

Alison thanked him, they both shook hands and Foley drove off, without a backwards glance.

'I'll make my own way back,' said Girolo, who had located a service elevator in the shadows, behind some concrete pillars.

'Whatever,' replied Alison Clancy, and there followed one of those awkward silences.

'So, uh, thanks,' said Girolo. 'Thanks for trying.'

'You don't sound too hopeful,' said Alison.

Girolo shrugged. Suddenly she felt sympathy for him. She had never known a man so alone. Self sufficient? Not even that, for he had needed her. Her advice, her legal contacts.

'Maybe,' she said, 'we'll get a pleasant surprise.'

'You were very good.' Girolo looked her in the eye. 'Thanks for saying that. That you would vouch for me.'

Alison moved a foot, gazing at her shoe. 'You could have done so much, Mr Girolo. In the real world. I get the impression you would have gone really far.' She met his gaze. 'I knew a man like you. And funnily enough I often thought to myself, if he had not made it in the legitimate way, he would have made one hell of a gangster.' She chuckled. 'He had that same ruthless quality.'

'In what way?' asked Girolo.

She thought about that, then said, 'He made his own rules.'

Girolo smiled, and it was only when his face relaxed that Alison realized how much strain the man was under. 'That,' he said, 'I can understand.'

In the silence they could hear a car's tyres squeal as it manoeuvred on another level.

'I'd better be off.' Alison held out a hand.

Peter Girolo clasped it, and said, 'It's none of my business. But he was a lucky man. Whoever he was . . .'

Alison suddenly felt a tear spring in her eye. She nodded. 'Thanks.' And she turned and walked back to her car.

Girolo watched her go before heading for the service stairs, to the left of the elevator. As he climbed towards street level, he had much to think about.

The Beverly Wilshire Hotel, on Wilshire Boulevard, Rodeo Avenue intersection, in California's Beverly Hills district of Los Angeles, is grand, tasteful, expensive and spacious.

Sebastian Tree sat at a low corner table in the bar, sipping a margarita. He wore a pale linen suit, just the tan side of white, which had been made for him by the London tailor, Doug Hayward, a navy blue cotton-silk shirt, top button undone, and a turquoise and lemon silk necktie, worn loose, by Hermès.

His calf-length supple leather boots were by John Lobb & Sons of St James's and his Rolex was plain silver and stainless steel. All in all, the effect was terrific, he felt, and he was comfortable about himself as he listened intently to his companion, a tanned, wiry, well-muscled man in his fifties, deep-set brown eyes that missed nothing, lime green sports coat, Italian out of Miami, Tree suspected, dark, well-cut pants, and intricately tooled cowboy boots.

Tree noted that Bobby Scipio wore a solid gold Petak Phillipe wristwatch and round his neck a ton of bullion clearly visible under a patterned silk shirt, open to the chest.

This man, his apparel stated, is probably not a Baptist minister.

Sebastian Tree was listening intently because Scipio, owner on paper of the Los Angeles Oasis Hotel, where Tree had once worked and saved Bobby, and therefore the mob, several hundred thousand dollars, was patiently explaining to him why the 'organization' was not prepared to harm a hair of Alison Clancy's head.

'. . . To cut a long story short, Seb my friend, let's just say the lady is now a protected species, like the Bengal tiger. Did you ever see that programme? Only fifteen left in the world. Who cares if they eat a few villagers from time to time? Villagers the world has plenty of . . .'

Sebastian Tree nodded, gravely. He had a feeling his acquaintance was being serious. 'Protected how?' he asked casually.

Scipio glanced at him. 'Well they got laws, they send patrols and stuff into the jungle regions. They ambush poachers and shoot their asses, and like that.' He sighed and lifted his tumbler of Wild Turkey, contemplating the amber liquid. 'And still they lose a few every year. Pretty damn soon they could be extinct.'

'I hope not,' sympathized Tree, and taking a deep breath went on, 'Miss Clancy. What makes her, uh, protected? Like the tigers.'

Bobby Scipio sipped his drink and put the glass down. He glanced around. Nobody was listening, nobody was near, the place was not too busy, but not too quiet either.

'I spoke to friends in New York. I spoke to a man who looks after the new boss in Boston, Mass. She is under his personal protection.'

'She is under the *capo*'s protection?'

'We don't use such words. We speak American, *capisce*?'

'Sure. I'm sorry.'

'Forget it. You ain't made; you don't know these things.'

They both drank some more. Sebastian Tree had read the Millicent Dunne piece in the *Boston Globe* about this mobster called Girolo. What Scipio was saying was that the same Girolo had taken Alison Clancy under his wing. Perplexed, Tree asked, 'But why . . . ?'

Scipio shrugged. 'Who knows? Maybe he's fucking her. Maybe they're related. Maybe he owes her a big favour. Whatever, he's the Big Boss in your town. That's it. You don't argue with the Man. That's it.' His deep, alert eyes glanced at Tree. 'I would not advise taking any private action against her. By rights I should not be telling you this.'

Sebastian Tree waited, suddenly uncomfortable, for he could guess what was coming. And Bobby Scipio's eyes examined his face as if maybe remembering it for the last time.

'Your name came up,' he said.

'My name?' Sweat began to run down the hollow of Sebastian's back.

'Your name came up, when I asked about finding somebody to do the business. The man I was speaking to, in Boston, says, "You ain't doing this for that asshole Sebastian Tree?" Pardon me, Sebastian, but those were his exact words.' Scipio raised his hands, 'I said no. I said I never heard of you.'

'Thanks,' said Tree, wryly.

'But pal, you should maybe think about leaving Boston. The man of whom we speak, he don't mess around.'

They sat there in silence. Sebastian Tree putting his considerable memory to work. For something was nagging at the back of his mind. Girolo, Girolo, Girolo . . .

Then he had it, Peter Michelangelo Girolo. When Big Jack had recruited Alison Clancy for Zeralda, he had told his Chief Exec her background. Tree could remember it as if it were yesterday; Jack Fitzrowan had been striding through the workshops, encouraging the women on the assembly benches, joking, asking after their families, and saying, 'The girl has quite a brain, Sebastian. You know that mafia guy who we all thought was going to jail for ever and a day? She was second counsel on the defence team. Peter Michelangelo Girolo. That was the guy. Big-time hoodlum. Law degree. Professional killer. It turned her sick to her stomach. Getting such a man off with just four years. So she now wants corporate,

322

she has a good degree. And thinks on her feet. We need a brain like that. You two should work well together.' And Big Jack had grinned. 'She's quite a looker, who knows? Maybe you'll end up married.'

And they had chuckled.

And of course Alison and Sebastian Tree had disliked each other from day one.

Then she had become Jack's (Sebastian Tree's own father's) whore. Yet another strumpet to add to the list of all those with whom the bastard Jack Fitzrowan had dishonoured Tree's real mother's precious memory. Sebastian smiled, it was all going to be all right, he could feel it in his bones. He had 218 million reasons for living. It was time to move against the only possible fly in his multi-million dollar ointment.

'Bobby . . . what do you know about the woman?'

Scipio shrugged. 'Clancy? Nothing. I know more about the Borneo orang-utan. Only one thirty-four left in their natural habitat.'

'Well, let me help you.' Sebastian Tree leaned forward, lowering his voice even more. 'Alison Clancy was second counsel on Peter Girolo's defence team. When he got off with a four stretch.'

Bobby Scipio relaxed and grinned. 'Ah . . . so he owes her a favour. There it is then, *esta simplice cosi*.'

'Except . . .' said Tree, 'she hates the mob. It makes her, I quote, sick to her stomach.'

'Sometimes people say that to distance themselves. It's a very Italian thing to do. It's prudent, particularly if she works in the legal field.'

'No, I've worked with her. She hates you people.'

The made man started to shrug that off, assuming Sebastian was merely groping around for some angle, some edge. But Scipio had rare antennae, necessary to survive in his business. 'Tell me about her,' he said.

Scipio was interested, not on behalf of the man sitting beside him, but because, unknown to Sebastian Tree, and he would never hear it from Bobby Scipio, the word from New York had been that the *famiglia* was becoming less than comfortable about Peter Girolo.

Certain of his recent actions had been considered by the mob's hierarchy to smack of . . . weakness? Or worse – independence. Whatever, there were intimations of the beginnings of a degree of unease about the Boston *capo*.

Sebastian Tree's own intuition picked up those unspoken vibes, and he proceeded to tell Scipio about Alison Clancy, her hatred for the mob, and the fact that he had noticed, while checking Zeralda's phone company accounts, record of a couple of phone calls made from her mobile to the Boston field office of the FBI, telephone number 617-223-6100, and the US Department of Justice in Washington.

It was a conversation that was to seal Girolo's fate.

'I am so very glad you agreed to this meeting,' smiled Tak Katakura, after the helicopter which had lifted Grace Hanrahan from the Zeralda Corporation's yard down to Newport, Rhode Island, and had clattered away from the after-deck of his ocean-going yacht *Toshiro Maru* in a roar of engine noise and a minor hurricane from its rotor blades.

As comparative silence returned, Grace shook the hand of her Japanese rival and gazed around the luxury craft. 'This is a tad larger than the ketch my father used to have,' she remarked, and nodded approvingly. 'Very nice.'

'I find I can work better at sea,' said Katakura. 'Even back home, I tend to live on board. There is a bay near my home at Shimizu, not far from Mount Fuji. *Toshiru Maru* regularly anchors there.'

'Did you sail all the way here?' asked Grace, and Katakura smiled.

'I flew to Miami and picked her up after she came across the Pacific and through the Panama Canal,' he admitted.

Grace laughed. 'That's cheating . . .'

The electronics billionaire smiled and ducked his head, slightly embarrassed. It was endearing, thought Grace, in a man who had everything.

'Would you like to see the ship?' he asked, and Grace said yes she would.

Later, lunching on delicious, freshly prepared Maine lobster, with a delicate lime dressing, and sliced mango with mineral water, Grace gazed around the stateroom, fans revolving overhead, and said how marvellous an atmosphere had been created, blending the nautical with the very best of traditional Japanese interior design.

Katakura thanked her, then said, 'Well, Grace, I mentioned I had a proposition to put to you.'

Grace nodded. 'Fire away . . .'

He laid down his fork and dabbed at his mouth with the snow white linen napkin, thinking. Then he said, 'I wanted Zeralda badly. Not because Katakura has some megalomaniac desire to swallow up the competition, but rather that Zeralda has a parallel and very successful business operation in place, covering outlets and markets that we, the Katakura Corporation, have not yet fully conquered.'

Grace thought about that. 'You mean, why spend a fortune in research and development, and on production lines, if you could have simply acquired a rival company which was already in there and thriving?'

'Just so.'

'And you failed,' she said, meeting his gaze.

Katakura agreed readily. 'I failed and it cost me a contract worth several hundred millions with McDonnell Douglas. That made your late and excellent father over two hundred million in personal fees.'

'Well,' said Grace, 'it made the Zeralda Corporation over two hundred million.'

Katakura did not miss the point of her remark. 'But the money had been moved out of Zeralda by Sir Jack. And presumably redistributed among your family.'

Grace studied her plate and replied, 'Something like that.'

'Something like that?' Tak Katakura shook his head. 'I hear that there was a codicil, a somewhat – forgive me this is absolutely none of my business, Grace – a somewhat unequal legacy in favour of a . . . how shall I put it?'

Grace had gone quite pale. She felt her heart beat stronger. She laid her knife and fork down and stared hard at her host. 'You're quite right, Tak. It *is* absolutely none of your goddam business.'

'Oh, dear. I have offended you. My dear lady . . .'

'I'm surprised at you,' replied Grace. 'You can't avoid fighting dirty, can you?'

In the silence, white-tunicked waiters came and took away the plates. Tak Katakura waited, then he said, softly, 'On the contrary, I asked you here not to fight at all, but to hear my probably ridiculous proposition. Which is for you, Zeralda Electronics Incorporated, to enter into a partnership with Katakura. We would fund your marvellous R&D programme, and share with you our international electronics order book. Katakura–Zeralda would dominate the industry. No other company could compete. You would be joint President, along with me. I have spreadsheets and projected analyses for your management team to study.'

Katakura sat back, clearly excited by the prospect. 'We are looking at profits of billions each year. I have a slim, most confidential, proposal document prepared.' He clicked his fingers and a slightly built young woman in a black business suit by Prada appeared as if from nowhere and quietly laid a russet coloured leather-bound case, like a jewel case, on the table in front of Grace.

The girl bowed and withdrew, walking backwards with grace and deference.

Intrigued, but still angry, Grace glanced at the case, then at Katakura. And when their eyes met, she was startled to feel that animal attraction she had last felt many years before, when she had met a certain young detective investigating a robbery at 87 Mount Vernon Street, the mansion next door to her father's Boston town house.

'I know you are mad at me,' said Katakura, who would not have needed to be a mind reader, for Grace Hanrahan's Irish eyes were glinting with anger, 'but please, I promise you will soon have reason to believe I brought up the subject of the legacy for a very good reason.'

He let his gaze fall on the russet leather case.

Grace, more to take her eyes off his handsome face than anything, reached out and took the case in both hands. She opened it and inside was one 3.5-inch computer disk. High density.

'That is Katakura's proposal,' said Tak Katakura. 'I would be honoured if you would take it with you and consider. Together, I can offer you, and you, Grace, can offer me, the world. In terms of our business. And we can make history. There are new developments, which we can share with you, and Grace, they are quite . . . breathtaking to the imagination.'

Grace studied the disk, then she closed the box and inclined her head. 'We'll take a look at it,' she replied.

Katakura put both hands on the table and again, that shy movement of the head. Damn, thought Grace, how on earth can I feel attracted to this man? He tried to wreck Zeralda. And anyway, I am a happily married woman.

And a still, small voice inside her asked, 'Happy? Are you really, Grace Fitzrowan . . . ?'

'Thank you,' said Katakura, then he poured some rose-petal tea, which a servant had brought, entering and retreating as quietly as a ghost. 'Well. Please permit me to tell you why I had the appalling rudeness to mention your late and excellent father's legacy, and above all, the codicil.'

'I'm surprised you found out about it,' replied Grace, determined not to be drawn. The man probably had only heard a rumour or two, and she had no intention of unwittingly increasing the sum of his knowledge.

'You employed a first-class firm to investigate me,' Katakura smiled, raising a hand as if to say, we're all grown up here, 'and as you would expect, I did the same. The Katakura Corporation has its own Intelligence Department, although I call it something else.' He waved his arm, self deprecatingly. 'Occasionally, they earn their keep.'

Grace stared at him – this was indeed a bizarre occasion. She tried to think what Big Jack would have done, in similar circumstances. But she could not imagine her father having agreed to come here in the first place.

'And so, I can bring a . . . dowry, to accompany my proposal for our two firms. A personal gift to you, dear Mrs Grace Hanrahan, from me, Takahashi Katakura.'

What a charmer, thought Grace to herself. Well, boyo, you will not be getting round me, whatever baubles you offer.

'I'm agog,' she said, flippantly, wondering when the helicopter would arrive to whisk her back to the real world. 'What is this . . . dowry?'

Katakura paused, aware of the drama of the moment, then he spoke. 'I know who Oliver is,' he said, and while his guest stared at him, her face going pale, he continued, 'And I know *where* he is . . .'

13

'You don't know me, Pronsias darling.' Darcy Fitzrowan Bailey lay curled against her lover on the big leather chesterfield in the family's Fitzwilliam Street town house. She wore her late daddy's oversize, beige coloured cashmere sweater with holes in the elbows, her long legs clad in silk stockings. 'You know nothing about me at all . . .'

Pronsias Stevenson, clothes in a heap on the floor, stroked her hair and said, '*Au contraire*, I know all about you, Darcy Fitzrowan. I have been in love with you since you were fifteen years old.'

'But you can't marry me.' Darcy toyed with the black hairs on his chest. 'You are married already.'

Pronsias grunted.

'What's that supposed to mean?' she enquired softly.

'I told you. Martina wants a divorce.'

Darcy smiled. 'She's in shock. It's not every day, I presume, Pronsias, that she has been confronted with such a sight as her husband making out with a female client over his desk and shouting "*Madre mia*".'

'And I will oblige her,' said Stevenson. 'I don't wish to sound disloyal, but life with Martina has been no kind of life at all.'

Darcy thought about that. Martina did not know what she had been missing.

'But you know, Pronsias,' she leaned round to gaze into his eyes, 'it will not always be like this.'

'And why not?' the lawyer asked.

'You will grow tired of me. The thrill will wear off.' Darcy thought about Edward, who had become so dull once he was sure of her, and about all the others. 'It's a fact of life.'

Stevenson frowned, then, when he smiled, her heart melted.

'The thrill of you will never wear off,' he answered. 'I have spent too many years waiting for you.'

'Anyway,' said Darcy, 'I already have a husband.'

Pronsias Stevenson stroked her back. 'Do you love him?'

Darcy shook her head. 'I don't want to talk about it.'

'That answers my question, I think,' replied Pronsias Stevenson.

They lay like that, in each other's arms. Darcy felt confused. The idea of actually marrying this man, the only one who had ever satisfied her so completely, simply was not on the cards. After all, she was actively scheming to get hold of the Oliver codicil millions, precisely to get out of one marriage. Why get into another when soon, if she succeeded, she would have the financial and personal freedom she had always wanted?

'Now then,' said the lawyer, 'you can reveal all.'

'I thought I already had, darling,' Darcy murmured.

'I meant,' continued Stevenson, 'the fruits of your research in New York City. Do you really,' he enquired sceptically, 'believe you have identified Oliver?'

'I know who he is, and I think I can find him, at least if he is still alive.'

They kissed, a lingering, lovers' kiss.

'And who, pray, is he then? I must confess I am excited at the prospect,' said Pronsias Stevenson, and Darcy leaned close to his ear and whispered.

His eyes widened. 'Given away? How very Dickensian. To whom was he given? And where is he now?'

Darcy gazed down at him, teasing him, the revelation beginning to take the form of a sexual game.

'He was given to a family called . . .' she paused, mischievously. They kissed again, her lover becoming aroused.

'Tell me, you strumpet . . .' he murmured, stroking the hollow of her back.

'Oliver was given by the Websters in New York to a family who were not Irish-Americans but . . .' she paused as he breathed gently on her neck, and licked her earlobe. 'Oh, God . . . the things you do to me . . .'

At which moment, Pronsias Stevenson's mobile phone rang.

'Leave it, it'll be her . . .' gasped Darcy.

'I'd better get it, we have *MacDowell* versus *Blaney* in court tomorrow.' Stevenson reached down and lifted the phone, putting it to his ear.

'Hello . . . ?' he said.

'May I speak to Mr Pronsias Stevenson?' replied an American voice.

'This is he,' said Stevenson.

'Mr Stevenson, I am coming to Dublin later today, and I need to see you on a very confidential and important matter.'

'Really? And what would that be?' asked the lawyer.

'You will want to conduct a few essential tests. DNA, that kind of thing.'

'DNA? What are you talking about, Mr . . . ?'

'It will soon be Fitzrowan, Mr Stevenson. I am Oliver, and I can prove it . . . I trust you have taken good care of my two hundred and eighteen million dollars.'

Joey Buscetta had changed in his unswerving loyalty to Peter Girolo. It was nothing tangible. No one particular moment. No definable glance or mannerism. Nothing he had said. Nothing he had done.

There was no disrespect, no hesitation in carrying out Girolo's orders. But Peter Michelangelo Girolo was a survivor. Before assassin, before organized crime boss, before mafia politician, he was a consummate survivor. And he perceived, in his bones, that the New York enforcer's attitude towards him had altered.

They were in that upstairs room, over the Cucina Napolitana restaurant, where Girolo, Buscetta and Rocco Trafficante had laid down the law to the surviving under-bosses, Tomasso Riccobono, Tony Bontate and Vito Greco.

Riccobono and Bontate had fallen into line. They had mended their ways and Joey Buscetta kept an eye on them. The mob had returned to low-profile, financially profitable organized crime. Things were going well.

Vito Greco had moved to Seattle, with some money from the Boston operation's coffers to get started all over again. Word was, Greco was doing well. The *capo di tutti capi*, in his luxury prison cell, suite of cells, four floors under the Colorado desert, was real pleased with him, so the word went.

In fact it looked like Greco could be a contender to take over the New York family syndicate.

Girolo wondered, as he did several times a week, if his act of mercy, sparing Greco's life when the entire mafia ethic dictated he should personally have killed him, would one day return to destroy him.

No doubt about it. It had been a mistake.

For neither Greco nor anybody else was aware that he wanted out, and was actively in discussion with the Justice Department about a deal. So to Vito Greco, Girolo would still be the number one obstacle in his way to complete control of the family.

'Boss,' said Joey Buscetta, who had just come off the plane from Atlantic City, 'the Man wants to know about the goddam Russians. He asks me to tell him what you're doin up here, when he gives you already a direct command.'

Girolo wondered who had brought up the subject first, Gotti or the faithful Buscetta.

'What did you tell him?' he asked.

'I tell him you got soldiers out there, in the commie territory.' Buscetta was not one to regard the fall of the Berlin Wall and the collapse of the Soviet Union as any intimation that all Russians were not still commie bastards, 'eyeballing the opposition and making a timetable of their movements, wiretapping their phones, identifying their vulnerable shit, and like that.'

'Good. That's exactly right. We move when we are strong. Unless they want me, the men at the top, to move too soon and get our asses wasted.'

He held Buscetta's gaze and he could tell it was hard, even for a pro like Buscetta, not to look away.

So there it was.

Somebody up there did not like him any more.

★

Paul had been working at home, in the atrium study at 85 Mount Vernon, when Grace had phoned from the office and asked him to come in. She had urgent things to discuss. He retrieved all his work files from the computer and transferred the originals to a virtually irretrievable path, hidden deep inside the printer program and disguised as a simple series of commands in computer grammar.

Eighteen minutes later, the Pontiac Firebird swept through the security gates and by ten before five, Paul Fitzrowan was walking into his sister's office.

'You rang . . . ?' he said, with a grin.

'You look very pleased with yourself,' said Grace.

'I took some Research and Development disks home on Sunday. I think I might be able to beat all our rivals. Give us an edge for years to come.'

'That's nice,' Grace replied, as if he had just told her he had been playing with his train set.

'You're all dressed up. Going someplace special?' he asked.

'I've just come back,' Grace responded. 'Close the door and I'll switch on the anti-bug.'

Paul closed the door, while his sister flicked switches to render the room relatively safe from all but the most sophisticated eavesdropping.

'Number one, Paul, Tak Katakura has made a proposition that Zeralda and Katakura combine. Together, he says, we could dominate the market.'

'No kidding? And you trust him, after he tried to destroy us? Placing that bastard Tree inside our board room? Please. You told him to stuff it, I trust.' Paul shoved a hand, exasperated, through his mop of hair. Grace smiled, reminded again of their father. She had never seen Paul so forceful. Or confident.

'I told him we would get back to him.' She came round from her desk and sat down facing him. 'We, Paul. You and me. And we should consult with Alison. I know you are cool towards her, because of Daddy, but she has a good brain. And she is right on side.'

Paul spread his hands. 'Sis, I don't want to pre-judge the issue.

But all my instincts say tell Takahashi Katakura to go take a jump in Tokyo Bay.'

'He's given us this proposal, Paul.' Grace handed her brother the 3.5-inch disk Katakura had given to her. 'You're the wiz in that department. Check it out and see what we think.'

Paul examined the disk. It looked innocent enough. 'You have not put this into any of our own equipment,' he asked, turning it over in his hands.

Grace shook her head. 'I do know about viruses, Paul. Tec Section have set up a brand new IBM, sanitized and separate from our own hardware.'

Paul nodded, approving. 'OK, let's take a look.'

But as he rose, Grace laid a hand on his arm. 'There is more, it's dynamite. Sit down.'

Intrigued, Paul sat down.

His sister seemed almost on the verge of tears. 'You said, when you came in, and I quote, that bastard, Sebastian Tree . . .'

'I did,' agreed Paul, unrepentant.

Grace took a deep breath. 'Prepare yourself for this. That is exactly what he is. A bastard.'

'A trifle pedantic, Grace. We know he was adopted. It figures if the man is illegitimate.'

His sister shook her head. 'No, Paulie. He is *the* bastard.' She shrugged and sighed. 'Tak Katakura has given me proof, he called it his dowry. And I believe him. Sebastian Tree is our half-brother . . . Oliver Fitzrowan.'

'What the hell is he doing here?' whispered Darcy to Pronsias Stevenson, as they stood in the Arrivals Hall at Dublin Airport watching the passengers come off the Aer Lingus Flight from JFK, New York. It was ten past seven in the morning.

'Who?' asked Stevenson, scanning the travellers, some tired, some elated and glancing around for friends or family, and others glowing from the excesses of complimentary in-flight alcohol.

He had tried to quiz the mystery caller further but the man claiming to be Oliver Fitzrowan had merely asked to be met at

Dublin Airport by Stevenson 'with a limo', and had said he would respond to a uniformed chauffeur wearing a peaked cap and holding a placard with the name 'Oliver' written on it.

'Sebastian Tree . . .' Darcy and Stevenson were standing to the side, away from the chauffeur, so that they could take a look at the claimant for $218 million of Sir Jack Fitzrowan's money. 'What's he doing in Dublin?'

Pronsias Stevenson knew all about Sebastian Tree from Darcy and her sister, Grace, who had sent him a letter outlining why Zeralda no longer trusted their Chief Exec and warning Stevenson to have nothing to do with him and to treat him with extreme caution, should he ever try to contact the Fitzrowan family lawyer in Dublin.

As they watched, Tree strolled up to the chauffeur and introduced himself, smiling. The chauffeur took Tree's travelling bag and led the way out to the car park.

Darcy, furious, was almost spitting blood.

'The goddam cheek of the guy,' she exclaimed. 'Fancy trying that! Well,' She turned to Stevenson, 'if he proceeds with this charade, Pronsias, I am instructing you, as a Fitzrowan and beneficiary of my daddy's legacy, to have him arrested and charged with conspiracy to defraud. With such an amount involved, the asshole will get three or four years and serve him right!'

Stevenson gazed after Sebastian Tree as he followed the chauffeur out of the Arrivals Hall.

'Don't worry, Darcy. You leave it to me.' He gently released her hand's fierce grip on his sleeve. 'It would be better if I handle this alone. Why don't you drive on back to Fitzwilliam Street?'

Seething, fighting to control her famous temper, Darcy said she had a good mind to go and drag the impostor out of the hire car by his throat.

'Well now,' smiled the lawyer, who had always found such outbursts engaging, 'I am not at all sure if that would help the course of events, my love.' He kissed her lightly on the forehead. 'I am quite capable of dealing with rogues like him.' He looked into her eyes, so full of rage and passion. 'I'll call as soon as I have sent him packing.'

So Pronsias Stevenson took a taxi back to his office (he had instructed the chauffeur to take his time so that he himself got there first) and Darcy drove her rented BMW back to the Dublin town house.

Alison Clancy looked thoughtful.

'Penny for them,' said Grace, as they strolled through Production Floor E, where a score of skilled workers sat quietly at benches, assembling porcelain and platinum micro-circuit boards.

'Have you seen or heard anything about our Chief Executive recently?' asked Alison.

Grace considered how to reply. Tak Katakura's bombshell that Sebastian Tree was in fact Oliver, fruit of her father's loins, her half-brother and heir to the enormous legacy was something, she felt instinctively, to be kept within the family. She had phoned her sister Darcy at her Tudor manor house near Oxford, but neither the servants nor her husband had any idea where precisely she was. Edward thought New York, but he was vague about how to get in touch with his wife.

Grace glanced at Alison and shook her head. 'I think, after all that's happened, and word of my lunch with Tak Katakura will have reached him, I'm pretty damn sure . . . I suppose even Sebastian will not have the sass to show his face as if nothing has happened.'

She would bring Alison into the loop as soon as she had told Darcy, but not before, that would not be right.

'We'll need to replace him,' advised Alison, who was husbanding her own secrets, although it was tough keeping from Grace Hanrahan, her boss and friend, the distressing news that Zeralda's Chief Executive Officer, Sebastian Tree, was reliably reputed to have taken out a contract on her own life. Thwarted only by the coincidence that a major league mafia boss had happened to have taken an interest in her, because he wanted to do a deal with the Justice Department and reform.

Just precisely how, reflected Alison, appreciating the dark

humour of her predicament, would I explain that to Grace here, without sounding as if I were out to lunch?

'What's so funny?' enquired Grace.

Alison shrugged. 'I can't believe Sebastian. In all my days I have never known anyone to be so . . . well the guy is practically deranged.'

'How is the private investigation doing?' asked Grace, thinking if Tak Katakura's people are right, sooner or later Telford & Pollard will unearth the same evidence, identifying Sebastian as Oliver Fitzrowan.

'We know which nursing home the Trees got him from. But the identity and origin of the mother is still a mystery. Ed Telford's theory is that the baby was abandoned on the steps of a nearby orphanage.'

'Abandoned?' Grace grinned. 'Maybe the real mother had a premonition how he would turn out.'

'Grace . . .' Alison and Zeralda's President laughed quietly at their shared dislike.

Suddenly Grace became serious. 'Alison,' she said, 'how would you feel about coming on to the board, as Chief Exec?'

Alison Clancy was close to being amazed. It was something she had not even contemplated.

And with that thought, she realized why she had not seen such an obvious, and personally rewarding, career move on the horizon. It was because of everything that had been going on in her private life. If you could call a failed murder attempt against one's person and a confidential professional liaison with a major gangster part of her 'private' life.

'It's a man, isn't it?' asked Grace.

Alison shook out of her reverie. 'I'm sorry?'

Grace touched her arm gently. 'When somebody offers you a vice-presidency of a global electronics company, and a hundred thousand a year raise, with bonuses, and you are not listening . . . I figure it has to be a man.'

Alison said absolutely not, no way, and went on, 'I'm . . . what can I say? Flattered and surprised, pleasantly.' Both of these were true, she had not contemplated being offered such a tempting career move. 'Can I think about it?'

Zeralda's President smiled and said, 'Of course. And don't protest too much, Alison, it's OK. I have been thinking it's high time you met somebody. It's none of my business I know, but I can see how you and Mike Medevik fell out of love.'

Alison blinked. This was a question she had asked herself, felt so terribly guilty about, for the two years since the divorce.

'How?' she asked.

Grace looked her straight in the eye. 'You need a man with nine balls, Alison. You need a strong man with no regard for bourgeois safe life-styles and conventional safety nets.'

'I do . . . ?' replied Alison, vague alarm bells beginning to tinkle.

'You sure do. My daddy knew what he was doing when he fell for you . . . and you know why you fell for him. Why you were still falling in love with him, with his memory, until very, very recently.'

'Grace . . . !' exclaimed Alison, surprised and somehow thrown by the accuracy of her employer's perception.

'And now, you have met somebody in the land of the living. Am I right? I have the gift you know, being Irish and all that.'

Alison stared at her. It was as if a curtain had been thrown aside, letting the light in, and she was both embarrassed and annoyed with herself.

'Absolutely not,' she said, haughtily. 'Good grief.'

And Grace Hanrahan just smiled and said of course, how silly of her, and she apologized. But her eyes were still smiling, knowingly. Which Alison found disconcerting.

I mean, she thought to herself, the only man in my life right now is Peter Michelangelo Girolo. And, excuse me, I really don't think he is exactly my type.

But Alison spent the rest of her morning thinking about that.

It always came back to this damn boat. It was like visiting Jack's grave, for there was an atmosphere of decay these days around the ketch that had once resounded with the big man's laughter.

Tom Hanrahan gazed at the rusting steel mast stays, shackles and windlass gear. The brass was green with verdigris and the teak and iroko on decks and cockpit surround was peeling grey and settled with a layer of dockside grime.

Nothing that could not be cleaned up. Tom reckoned it would take about two weeks to restore *Zeralda of Erin* to her former pristine condition. Maybe he and Grace should buy it from Edward, for his detective's instinct told him the Englishman would not resist a good offer. The guy had not even enquired about *Zeralda* since the day he had inherited her.

It seemed a hundred years since that morning he had stood there, just back from Big Jack's funeral and the reading of that Will. Jack sure knew how to make his mark, even in death.

It seemed a hundred years since Danny Tarantola had stood there, right there, and quietly, without fuss, accused him of murdering a good friend.

Tom leaned on the small wooden jump seat, beside the steering wheel, where he had been standing that dreadful day. He checked the height of the boom, and tried to remember exactly where Grace's father had been sitting, grinning, exuberant, when 1,134 pounds of solid teak had lifted him overboard, smashing his head and killing him outright.

The Coroner had established the boom had killed Jack, because there had been no water in the dead man's lungs.

As he sat there, Tom Hanrahan felt a terrible, hollow sadness. For, try as he might, he could not remember, precisely, at that moment, just what Jack Fitzrowan had looked like. He felt that was an act of betrayal.

A soft footstep sounded as somebody stepped on board, behind him. 'So, Lieutenant,' he heard Tarantola's voice. 'Why did you bring me out here?'

Hanrahan turned round and looked at Sergeant Detective Danny Tarantola for a long moment.

'What was that sister of his called?'

Tarantola frowned. 'Sister? Whose sister?'

Hanrahan shook a piece of chewing gum from its rectangular pack, offered it to Tarantola, who declined.

'Alberto's sister,' he said.

'Alberto who, chief?' asked Tarantola, with a look that said, are you wasting my time here?

'Sanzo,' said Tom Hanrahan, 'Alberto Sanzo.'

'Aw, who knows? Who the fuck knows? Eh, Janis, Jezebel, something like that. She's a fuckin mongoloid, two hundred pounds of putrid fat. Takes guys three at a time, for a bar of candy.' Tarantola shook his head. 'Not even three bars, boss. She humps whole teams just for the one bar.'

Tom Hanrahan did not laugh. Nor did he smile. He popped a strip of wintergreen flavoured gum into his mouth and chewed it for a minute before saying, 'She's in Mass General. Tubes in every orifice. BP eighty-five over forty. Two shots of adrenalin and a stomach pump kept her alive. For the present.'

Tarantola seemed less than appalled. 'So she overeats. It'll get her in the end.'

'She tried to kill herself,' said Hanrahan quietly.

Danny Tarantola shrugged. He took a Chesterfield from its pack and stepped across the deck to the port side, holding his Homicide Zippo close as he puffed against a mild breeze which was gathering strength.

Hanrahan moved to join him. They gazed across the harbour to watch the police boat *Saint Michael* make its way towards Constitution Wharf. Its skipper was a Sergeant Tommy Boyle, who was no relation to the Detective Tommy Boyle who was in Hanrahan's Homicide squad.

'She wanted, still will when she gets discharged I guess, to end it, Danny, because her brother used to protect her from herself. Alberto used to feed her, you know. She spills stuff. He would wash her, take her clothes to the laundromat. Keep her from dropping off the last rungs into the pits of human society, and tumbling, confused like she is, into a half-life of vagrancy and prostitution. Filthy and bewildered, trusting everybody, Danny. The way mongoloids do, God bless them . . .'

Tarantola glanced at the Lieutenant, who looked pale with anger. This Sanzo's goddam sister had surely touched a nerve.

'Maybe,' said Hanrahan, 'maybe – give me a goddam cigarette – maybe I am a fucking mongoloid too.'

'You, chief?' enquired Tarantola as he handed over a Chesterfield.

'Sure.' Hanrahan leaned to take a light from the Sergeant. 'I mean,' he inhaled, deep, 'I trust everybody.' The smoke tumbled from his mouth as he said that. 'In the Department that is . . .'

'We gotta do that,' Tarantola nodded sagely. 'We all gotta do that.'

'Sure.' Hanrahan took another, briefer, drag on his Chesterfield. 'When did you start again?'

Tarantola spread his hands. 'A few days.'

'After how long?' Hanrahan had been using Danny the Wop's self discipline as a model to follow.

'More than a year. About a year and a bit.'

Hanrahan nodded. It was a year and a day more than himself. 'You don't really think I killed Jack Fitzrowan, do you?'

Tarantola made a very Italian face. 'I don't want to. Just doing the job. You would do the same, sure you would. You know it. Without fear or favour, right?'

Hanrahan seemed to think about that. 'Alberto Sanzo trusted us.'

Tarantola nodded. 'The guy got careless. It's kinda inevitable when you play stoolie wid the mob.'

Tom Hanrahan nodded and flicked the cigarette over the tarnished rail, turned on his heel and moved across the deck to the gangplank with its tattered and grimy POLICE – CRIME SCENE plastic tapes.

'Hey, Lieutenant . . .' called Sergeant Detective Dan Tarantola.

Hanrahan stopped, turned slowly and stared at him. 'Yeah?'

Tarantola raised his shoulders, puzzled, and pissed at having been brought all this way. 'Is that it?'

Hanrahan nodded. 'For the present.' And he turned and walked on to the dock and towards the waiting Ford, where Jimmy Fitz sat at the wheel.

Tarantola sucked on his Chesterfield and watched as the

unmarked Homicide sedan drove away, bumping over all those things cars bump over on docks.

'Well, fuck you,' he said, as Hanrahan's car disappeared from sight.

Going straight was going to be tougher than he had ever imagined. Those at the top of the *cosa* had not taken long to get a sixth sense that Peter Girolo was no longer *their* Peter Girolo. Joey Buscetta was a good man, a loyal enforcer and a good friend. Until just a few days ago, Girolo would have trusted him, had trusted him, with his life.

But things were changing. Imperceptibly to most, but not to Girolo. The temperature had definitely dropped.

Well, here he was, kneeling in a place he felt awkward to be. The House of God. He had gone for a walk, telling the two footsoldiers assigned to look after him, Sonny Favaro and Michael Binelli, to take the afternoon off. Sonny was a good man and he had decided the boss was seeing a woman, on the quiet. This was always what he told Joey Buscetta when the older man enquired about the *capo*'s movements, which was more regularly than before.

This particular walk had no ulterior motive. It had been so that Girolo could be alone. Then, strolling down Washington Street, with an unquiet feeling he was being watched, he had seen the church, the Holy Cross Cathedral, its doors open and the faint but comforting sound of some choirboys practising coming from way inside.

Partly to shake any tail, but also because he felt a certain inevitability to it, Peter Michelangelo Girolo had gone up the steps and into the cathedral.

And there he knelt, the faint sound of choir practice coming from some room near the vestry. And as he reflected on his life and his crimes, and his sins, he found himself, for the first time in his life . . . diffident. In the presence of something far greater than the *cosa nostra*.

Even in the cellars and catacombs of the Vatican in Rome, he had not experienced any particular religious awe. But this was different.

Here was God.

And His presence was so profound, that Girolo felt, to his mild surprise, tears begin to run down his face.

Of course you can pray, he felt Someone say, believe it or not, my son, I've heard worse.

So he prayed. And he prayed in Italian, for that was his native language. And he told God that even if nobody on earth believed him, he knew that his maker, who was all seeing, and who understood everything, would know that he was genuine.

Well, Pietro, he could hear this voice say, you seem to doubt it yourself.

Girolo sighed. There it was.

Was he really and sincerely repentant? Did he really and truly want to disappear to that small West Indian island to run a bar and take dumb tourists deep-sea fishing and diving?

Sure you do, he felt God say. It's your age, Pietro. But here is how to test the level of your sincerity. That is, if you really want to know . . .

God, come on. Gimme a break, Girolo had lapsed into American. I do. I really do.

He imagined God frowning at this less than formal approach, but his priest and confessor in Paris, where he had attended the Sorbonne, had always said that the Almighty could be spoken to just like a friend, a *compagno*, a pal.

Cool it, Pietro, he felt God say. We got a long ways to go before you and Almighty I get on friendly terms. You want to know the test?

Yes, please, prayed Girolo meekly.

So here it is. Imagine your entire attempt, your plan to do a deal with Justice, your nest egg stashed away, your brand new identity, turns to shit. And the *capo di tutti capi*, in your pygmy *cosa vostra* finds out and sends somebody to waste your ass.

Say all that happens . . . Will you still repent? Will you still, in your very heart, live the life of a reformed man?

Will you still love me tomorrow? Hmmm?

And Peter Girolo knelt there and laughed, quietly.

He crossed himself, stood up, faced the cross, genuflected, crossed himself again, and turned to leave.

And there, facing him, just a couple of feet away, was Vito Greco. Seattle *capo*. The man he had humiliated and kicked out of Boston.

The man the Man in Florence supermax regarded so highly.

'Hello, Don Peter,' said Greco, his eyes boring into Girolo's. 'They gave me the contract. You know, the contract on *you* . . .'

And somewhere, Peter Girolo could hear a heavenly chuckle.

In Dublin, round about the same time, Pronsias Stevenson sat playing and replaying a tape recording of the Sebastian Tree interview, which had taken place within an hour of Tree stepping off the New York aeroplane.

It went like this:

s: 'I will be taping this, Mr Tree, for reference and accuracy, unless you have any strong objection.'

t: 'No that's fine by me, Mr Stevenson.'

s: 'What is your name?'

t: 'Sebastian John Tree.'

s: 'Date of birth?'

t: 'Uncertain. I was a foundling, so they always told me.'

s: 'Do we have a year?'

t: 'Nineteen fifty-four.'

s: 'Uh-huh. Place of birth?'

t: 'Again, uncertain. I was adopted aged around eighteen months by Joseph St John Tree and his wife, Emily Jean, of San Francisco, California. At that time I was in the care of the Santa Maria Roman Catholic Orphanage, in Boston, Massachusetts. Enquiries there, when I was in my mid twenties, elicited the information, by means which I would prefer to keep confidential, that my natural mother had been identified, and that her confinement had been in a house owned by the Church, location unknown, where a parish priest's housekeeper lived.'

s: 'And what is the basis of your claim to be the son of John Pearce Dunmill Fitzrowan, of Crough Lake, County Kerry in the Republic of Ireland and of Helen Costello, kitchen maid, of the same address?'

t: 'I obtained access to the records of the Santa Maria Orphanage, which was difficult because it had moved, lock stock and barrel, to Louisiana in the late nineteen fifties.

'Those records show that the costs of keeping me at the orphanage, from 1955 through to the spring of 1956, were paid by one John Fitzrowan, a student at Massachusetts Institute of Technology. And subsequent to my adoption, the same John Fitzrowan continued to take an interest in the affairs of the orphanage. He helped facilitate the move to Louisiana, and from time to time made financial donations, including, it is recorded, a bequest of twenty-five thousand dollars in his Will.

'I graduated at UCLA with a degree in accounting and for the last six years I have been employed by Zeralda Electronics Inc. of Boston. During that time, I was able to obtain samples of hair and saliva from Zeralda's President and major shareholder, Jack Fitzrowan, without his knowledge.

'I have the results here, from DNA tests carried out by the Zeigler Laboratory of 185 Hudson Street, New York City, and I present them in evidence at this point.

'They establish beyond doubt that Sir John Pearce Dunmill Fitzrowan was my natural father. Thus I claim to be the son of the aforesaid John Fitzrowan and of Helen Costello, God rest her soul.'

God rest her poor soul, indeed, mused Pronsias Stevenson. Well, the results of his own DNA comparison would be there within the hour. Then they would see.

Sebastian Tree had been co-operative about providing samples of hair and saliva. Big Jack had left a lock of his Helen's hair, along with other samples, upon his return from Zurich and his beloved's cremation. He had also provided samples of his own hair and blood.

There was a small knock on his office door, and in came Mr Justice Malahide, Stevenson's partner.

'Pronsias, do you have a minute?' enquired Malahide, his voice lower than usual, which is how it generally went when he had something to discuss in confidence.

'Of course, Francis. Please come in.'

Malahide entered, closing the door firmly and quietly behind him, and sat himself down on the leather couch which Stevenson and Darcy Fitzrowan had just a day or two before made slick with pleasure.

'I've just had Martina on the phone,' said the Judge.

'Ah, well,' replied Pronsias Stevenson, 'I am afraid that was inevitable.'

Malahide raised one eyebrow, something he was famous for in court. 'Inevitable, Pronsias? How?'

'Well . . .' Stevenson raised his shoulders, 'she no doubt gave you chapter and verse *vis-à-vis* my . . . shenanigans. With a lady client. And she told you she wants a divorce.'

Malahide removed his half-moon spectacles and polished them thoughtfully on his tie. He replaced them, blinked, peered at the lawyer, and nodded. 'Oh, yes. I must say, Pronsias, one does take rather a dim view of these premises being used as a, um, a sort of knocking-shop.'

Stevenson found himself blushing. 'It was an error of judgement, Francis.'

Malahide thought about that. He fixed his courtroom stare on his partner. 'Heat of the moment and all that. I am sure it will not happen again.'

Pronsias Stevenson was surprised. 'You mean you don't want me to resign?'

Malahide made an almost eighteenth-century gesture of dismissal. 'Stuff and poppycock. I would have left that dreadful woman years ago. God alone knows how you stood it. I suggested Myer & Reilly to represent her in the divorce. All right by you?'

For the second time in his recent life, Pronsias Paudraic Stevenson felt a warm glow of pleasant surprise. 'Oh, yes,' he said, 'Myer & Reilly. They will be fine.'

Justice Malahide slapped his knees and stood up. 'Well done,' he announced simply, and walked out of the room, crossing with Siobhan, Pronsias Stevenson's secretary, who was carrying a sealed buff envelope.

'This is from the lab, Mr Stevenson,' she said, and dropped the results of the Sebastian Tree DNA comparisons on his desk, giving her employer a glance which might be described as appraising.

The room empty once more, Pronsias Stevenson studied the fateful envelope, reflecting on his senior partner's reaction to what must have been a most unpleasant phone call from Martina the Mad, soon to be the ex-Mrs Pronsias Stevenson.

As he slit the envelope open with a replica Javanese sacrifice knife, scaled down, the phone rang. He lifted the receiver.

'Stevenson . . .'

'Darling, how is everything?'

He smiled, it was nice having someone who cared about him. 'Fine. Just fine. The divorce is going through. Francis Malahide, my partner, has been quite, um . . . wonderful about it.'

'No, you banana, Sebastian Tree. The DNA tests. Do you have the results?'

'Oh, yes,' replied Pronsias Stevenson, letting his reading glasses slip to the end of his nose. 'I am looking at them even as we speak . . .'

Peter Girolo sat in a pew half-way towards the altar, half-way from the doors to the front porch and the street. Beside him sat Vito Greco, head bowed as if in prayer.

The blasphemy of the *mafioso* reminded Girolo of the hypocrisy of so-called guerrilla groups, of whatever religion, who murdered and prayed and found priests to bless both acts. The mafia too had its priests, even at the fountainhead of the Church in Rome, as Girolo knew only too well.

But on this day, when maybe he had, or maybe he had not, had a private talk with his God – maybe he had just been having a private talk with himself – Girolo had never felt more outside the *famiglia*, or more prepared to meet his maker.

And now he was about to die. An act of contrition seemed to be in order, but Peter Michelangelo Girolo, who was many things, and none of them very nice, had never been a hypocrite. And he did not intend to start now.

God would, he hoped, understand.

No good running to me now, Pietro, he could hear the Man saying, no way you are going to get out of all that hell you got piled up and waiting. No way you can avoid this Good and Merciful Lord whipping your sorry ass . . .

'So,' whispered the man who had been given the job of killing him, 'I figure you walk right down past the choir practice and find a back door to Park Street.'

This figured. Even Greco would not do it in church.

'OK.' Girolo was no coward. He planned to go out head high, with dignity. Just like when Greco himself had sat there in La Cucina Napolitana, waiting for Girolo to put a .45 slug in his brain.

But those goddam ducks had gotten in the way and Girolo had spared him.

Big mistake.

'You do it in the street. I'm all set.' Girolo moved to get up but Vito Greco laid a hand on his arm, sitting him back down.

'Do what in the street?' he whispered.

Girolo felt in a hurry to get this over with. 'Whack me. Come on, let's go.'

Greco, the Seattle *capo*, whispered, annoyed. 'Nobody whacks you. Nobody whacks Peter Girolo while I'm around.' The gangster, head bowed, was whispering to the floor so nobody could lip read. 'Get outta here, meet me later . . . here,' he palmed a tiny, folded scrap of paper to Girolo, and went on, 'I owe you my life. I gotta figure a way to kill you that will leave respect for your memory and work for my conscience. Be there between nine and a quarter after. Don't make me come lookin for you.'

With that, Vito Greco rose, crossed himself and walked towards the front door.

Girolo made his way out to the back of the cathedral by a side door. He took few precautions because it was on his mind that Greco had merely wanted to spare him a few minutes of apprehension, and would have him whacked as soon as he was on unholy ground.

But the place was clean, the sky was blue, the sun was shining and Girolo walked away. No way, he considered, was he going back to his Beaver Place apartment. No way could he be seen any place at all.

No wonder good old Joey Buscetta had been unable to look him in the eye. Joey would have known the word was out, and it was only a matter of time before his boss, Don Girolo, was hit.

If whacking him was giving Vito Greco problems with his conscience, with the mobster's concept of debts of honour, mafia-style, Girolo had – he glanced at his watch – just over nine hours to work out something that would help them both.

Sebastian Tree sauntered into Pronsias Stevenson's office. He had bought himself a well-cut tweed jacket and a pair of expensive brogues. With his $218 million he planned to buy an estate on the west coast of Ireland, in addition to one of those big houses on the coastline south of San Francisco.

An aristocrat, after all, even an illegitimate one, was obliged to keep up certain appearances. And come to think of it, he had read somewhere that the very highest English noblemen, dukes and marquises, were descended from bastard offspring of their kings, in years gone by.

'Thank you, Pronsias,' he said, coolly, sitting himself comfortably on the old leather couch and crossing his legs elegantly. 'I see you have the results of our DNA tests.'

'Indeed I have,' agreed the Dublin lawyer, crossing to his seat behind the eighteenth-century partner's desk. He arranged the papers in front of him carefully, then put on his reading glasses.

Have your moment of drama, thought Tree, it isn't every day you hand over more than two hundred million dollars. He wondered how much interest it was earning, while Stevenson sorted his papers. Take your time, he thought. I have nothing else planned.

Pronsias Stevenson cleared his throat. He glanced at Sebastian Tree, noting the new tweed coat and the squeaky-new footwear.

'There is absolutely no doubt, Mr Tree, that Sir John Fitzrowan is your natural father.'

Tree nodded, gravely. Tell me something I don't know, he thought.

'The DNA test, which you have signed a document here, agreeing to accept as full and final confirmation, one way or the other . . . am I right?'

'Yes, of course.' Get on with it, you pedantic fool.

'Well, then, just as the laboratory confirms that Jack Fitzrowan is your father, so is it equally clear about Helen Costello.'

Tree could not stop a grin from spreading across his face. Here we are, it was a wonderful moment.

Pronsias Stevenson adjusted his spectacles; he had not had so much professional fun since the original reading of the Will.

'I shall read out the words of the report.' He paused, then went on, '"Comparison of twelve separate DNA strings, taken from hair, nail clippings, blood platelets and saliva swabs, certified by the Jakov Kellenberger Institute of Zurich to be from one Helen Costello, as identified by Sir John Pearce Dunmill Fitzrowan, Baronet, of 85 Mount Vernon Street, Boston, Massachusetts, shows equality with twelve similar DNA strings taken from samples of hair, saliva and blood of Mr Sebastian John Tree, of 1143 Charlestown Road, Charlestown, Massachusetts, to be . . ."' here the lawyer looked up from the laboratory report and straight into Sebastian Tree's expectant eyes, '". . . zero."'

Tree blinked.

'It goes on to conclude, Mr Tree, that from this proven accurate scientific analysis, you are the progeny of Sir John Fitzrowan and A. N. Other. But you are no relation whatsoever of the late Helen Costello.' Stevenson paused, then he said, 'Which means of course that you are not Oliver Fitzrowan. You never were, Sebastian, and you never will be.'

Oh, bliss, thought Stevenson to himself. Wait till I tell Darcy the look on his face.

'There remains,' he addressed himself to the blinking man on his leather couch, 'the matter of my fee, and of course the laboratory's bill.'

Pronsias Stevenson tugged his half-hunter watch from his waistcoat pocket. 'My word, I must dash.' He rose and crossed to the dazed Sebastian Tree. 'I'm so sorry to dash your hopes, Mr Tree.

Would you like to leave a cheque with Siobhan on your way out?'

Tree finally stopped blinking.

He slowly got to his feet and stood there, a taller and younger man than the solicitor. His face was very pale, his eyes not those of a well man, flickering with the intensity of the fevered.

'This is a fucking set-up,' he hissed. 'You smug little bastard. I've a good mind to tear your head from your dandruffy little shoulders.'

'I do not have dandruff, Mr Tree, I use a very good shampoo,' replied Stevenson. 'And I would counsel against violence, for I am versed in the skills of Tai Kwan Do.' (Second shelf on the Wolfe Tone replica bookcase, two leather-bound volumes; Martina had sent away for them in the mistaken belief Tai Kwan Do was some form of oriental flower arranging.)

This double risposte caused Tree to start blinking again. He shoved Stevenson aside and strode from the room, slamming several doors, hard, on his way to the street.

Pronsias Stevenson removed his spectacles and smiled. It looked as if Darcy might be right after all. For Stevenson had long ago ascertained that the Websters had indeed given the real Oliver away. New York City, 1957. And when his new love had whispered to him precisely where she believed the young orphan had been taken, that too matched with his own researches.

All in all a happy day, for with that twelve and a half per cent finder's fee, he and Darcy would have done extremely well from Big Jack's legacy.

Always provided Oliver was still alive.

Should he be proved to be dead, darling Darcy would be worth even more.

14

Alison Clancy felt wickedly sinful. She had joined the pizza pool. Each morning a number of junior executives and secretaries on the fourth floor would pass a piece of paper around and order lunch, which two local places sent in.

One list was the 'healthy pool', granary bread sandwiches with lettuce and chicken or tuna fish. The other was the 'pizza pool', with delicious thin crust pizzas with all the gamut of fillings that made the American pizza the king of pizzas around the world.

Well, on this day, Alison Clancy had gotten tired of sensible eating. And she sat at her desk, munching a capriciosa with extra cheese and chorizo.

She was in a very good mood, for somebody whose life had been touched by so much recent drama. Tom Hanrahan, Grace's detective husband, had called in to Zeralda, looking for Sebastian Tree, whom he wanted to interview. Alison had been tempted to tell Tom about Tree's taking out a contract on her life, but Peter Girolo had asked her to mention that to nobody.

Trust me, he had said, you will be safer if you leave this guy Tree to me.

Anyway, she had kept her own counsel. And Tom Hanrahan had mentioned, over a cup of coffee in Grace's office, that he and a detective called Jimmy Fitz had been out to Tree's Charlestown house, but Zeralda's Chief Exec had not been seen there for a few days.

Maybe the dickwad has finally decided to run for the hills, thought Alison, as she cut off another succulent slice of capriciosa.

'Can I come in . . . ?' asked Grace, softly, knocking on the open door to Alison's office.

'Be my guest,' replied Alison, waving her hand at a nearby chair.
Grace smiled. 'I see you've joined the pizza gang.'

Alison nodded, dabbing at her lips with a paper napkin.

'So, have you had time to think, Alison? About my offer?'

Alison grinned. 'Grace, I would be honoured to join the board
of Zeralda Electronics. And I would be thrilled to have a hundred
thousand dollar raise. But you do realize I can't do what Sebastian
does. Did. He is a certified accountant. I am a lawyer.' She wiped
her hands on the napkin. 'You should talk to Paul about it.'

'Oh, we have talked,' said Grace. 'In fact, bringing you on to
the board was Paul's idea.'

'Really . . . ?' Alison wondered about that. She had always felt
Paul did not like her. Disapproved of her affair with his late father.
Still, the change in him since his father's death had been steadily
obvious. And word from Technical Research was that the kid had
a terrific brain when it came to microchip design and forward
thinking.

'You would not take over the accounting minutiae – we have a
whole department for that. Malcolm Strong is extremely able; Paul
and I will have no problem promoting him to Chief Accountant.'

Malcolm Strong was half Scottish, half Argentinian, and had
come to Zeralda highly recommended by one of Big Jack's many
contacts in Washington's Department of Defense. He was certainly
a better choice to hold Zeralda's financial affairs together.

'That's a good move. So what would I do?'

'Chief Exec. Place on the board. You have been performing that
function for the last few months, anyway. Since the NASA glitch.
What do you say?'

Alison frowned. Did she really want to commit the next few
years to corporate law and running an electronics corporation, on
a global scale? Surely there must be more to life.

At which point in her deliberations, the phone rang.

'Let's ignore that,' she said to Grace. 'I'll have Wendy take my
calls.'

'Take it. Go ahead.' Grace nodded at the ringing phone. 'It
could be important.'

Alison lifted the receiver. 'Alison Clancy . . .'

The voice on the other end was familiar, she was thrown to realize she was pleased to hear it. 'Alison, you know who this is?'

Alison tried to look businesslike. 'Yes.'

'OK, listen carefully. I have some serious problems. I can't make a deal any more. The Man wants me gone. So, I'm just phoning to, uh, I guess to say thank you. OK? So, mind how you go.'

Silence.

Suddenly Alison felt apprehensive, a huge sense of loss. Peter Girolo had been the most real thing that had happened to her since Jack's death. The big mobster had a way of looking at her, a way of being quietly amused at her businesslike approach. Jack had been the same, he too had been amused when he had begun to make his interest in her, as a red-blooded male, just that bit more obvious. Nothing too unsettling, just a look. Just a glance. Just that smile.

It was just her luck to be representing a mafia *capo*, a powerful man in his own right, who reminded her, ever so slightly, of the only man she had ever loved.

'You still there?'

Alison shook herself out of her reverie. 'Sure. Listen, is there anything I can do?'

And there was that low chuckle at the other end of the line. 'You don't want to get involved.'

'Involved? I *am* involved. Why don't we meet? Just briefly, before you go. I can try to get an answer from Foley. Let me try, Peter.'

Silence.

'OK. You know that place with the skylight?' He meant Alison's own mews house, where Joseph Cranmer had forced open the skylight, on his way to murder her.

Alison nodded and said quietly, 'I think so.'

'Meet me there. One hour.'

Click. The line went dead. Alison Clancy put the receiver back on its hook, very thoughtful.

Grace just sat there, smiling knowingly.

'I knew there was a man . . .' she said, and stood up. 'You go

354

see him. It's not company policy to come between two people in love,' and with a broad grin she walked out, closing the door.

Alison threw a piece of perfectly good pizza at the shut door and announced, to the empty room, 'I am not in love, dammit!'

The thing about cops is they are more creatures of habit than the criminals they are after. The reason for this is they are not on the run.

Even then maybe they should take more care, just in case somebody is watching.

Danny Tarantola had always been careful. As the most times shot of any detective in Boston PD, he had learned the hard way that you never know the minute.

But time is crime, as they say, and every cop has his own routine. For instance, scattered around town were five payphones Danny used to talk with his informers. Snitches were like gold dust to a detective. His best snitches were tickets to a successful career and a serious reputation among his peers.

Of those five payphones, there were two that Danny used more than the others. And on this particular day, he got out of his unmarked Toyota coupé, leaving it parked on Avery Street, on the fringe of what Bostonians called the Combat Zone, on account of the nature of its streets, with vice and crime thriving, despite the efforts of the Mayor's office and the police to damp it down.

Chinatown was gradually expanding from its Beach Street hub, a few blocks south, into the Combat Zone, but it was still a rough place for the unwitting to stroll around, particularly after dark.

It was about three in the afternoon when Danny strolled up to one of his regular payphones, on Lafayette, which is in the heart of the Combat Zone.

'There he goes . . .' said Big Time, lounging on a corner with Sergeant Jeb Kingdom. Both men had gotten 'all cracked up', which was their term for dressing and carrying on like two badass crack cocaine dealers, pushers or users.

Their clothes, their attitude, Jeb's dreadlocks, Big Time's blacker than black shades and big, lime green and orange woolly hat, made them a couple you did not look at directly, unless you were looking to score. But most users in the Zone knew those two guys were cops so, by and large, they were left alone.

Maybe Danny Tarantola had noticed them as he strolled to the payphone. Maybe he did not. Either way, he would not have been surprised to see those two black detectives working their turf.

So when he made his three calls, with a pile of quarters balanced on the phone box, nothing would have been further from his mind than what was really going on, as he went about his business.

When he had finished, he scooped up the remaining quarters and walked casually back to Avery Street and his illegally parked Toyota, with its Boston Police Benevolent Fund sticker on the windshield.

Big Time and Jeb exchanged glances.

'You get it?' asked Jeb.

'Every word,' replied Big Time, and he removed the bigger than big shades, with their built-in radio receiver, tuned to a frequency which matched the illegal wire tap they had placed inside the payphone.

Thirty-one minutes later Big Time dropped a couple of microcassette tapes on the desk of Homicide Lieutenant Tom Hanrahan.

'Shut the door,' said Hanrahan.

Big Time did that. Tom Hanrahan noticed the usually cheerful detective was not smiling.

'Any technical problems?' he enquired.

'No, sir. It was like I was in the booth with him.' Big Time looked like he had been to a funeral.

'Do we, uh, have any other problems?'

Big Time looked the Lieutenant in the eye. He nodded. 'I guess so, boss . . . Fuck it.'

In the silence, they could hear a siren wail in some nearby street.

Tom Hanrahan sighed. He nodded. 'Good work. Thanks.'

Big Time moved to leave the room. As he put his hand on the doorknob, Hanrahan said, 'Just one question.'

Big Time looked back and without hesitation said, 'Oh, yes.

You got my witness statement. Jeb's too. I ain't kept my black ass clean this long to stand still for that.' And he left.

Tom Hanrahan took a tape recorder from his desk drawer and fumbled for his brand new pack of Winstons.

Alison Clancy went back to her neat little house in Willow Mews round about two in the afternoon. She filled the base of her brass and steel percolator, a gift from Jack, and let it make some coffee while she cut an Ogen melon in two, scooped out the seeds and filled the hollow with yoghurt and honey.

She carried the coffee and yoghurt-filled melon upstairs and into her study-cum-sitting room, making a mental note to tidy up a bit before her hoodlum client came round.

'Well now, that's a healthy meal,' said the familiar, deep voice and Alison's coffee leaped in the mug as she jumped in alarm.

'It's OK. I let myself in.' Girolo had appeared from the stairway to Alison's bedroom.

'No it's not OK, Mr Girolo. It is damned well not,' said Alison, her heart thumping. 'Apart from scaring me half to death, you have just committed an offence.'

And, damn him, Peter Girolo just sat down and looked at her, smiling broadly.

Finally, Alison saw the funny side.

'I suppose,' she said, 'as offences go, this will not be the one they will settle for . . .'

And they both laughed, quietly.

'So what's gone wrong?' asked Alison, straight to the point. And Peter Girolo told her about Vito Greco.

Well, to be honest, he told her just enough about Vito Greco. In fact, this is what he said: 'There is this guy, I spared his life once. Now he has been told by the people who run the show that he has to take me out.'

'Take you out where?' asked Alison.

'It means kill me.'

Alison stared at him, horrified, yoghurt dripping off her spoon. 'Kill you? You have to go to the police. I will call Foley. He'll take care of this . . .' She put her plate down and rose to go to the phone.

Girolo stepped across and placed a hand over the receiver. 'That's a bad idea,' he said.

'Why? You can't let these low-lifes scare you.'

'It's a bad idea,' replied Girolo, 'because they will kill me, they will kill the men and women protecting me, but worst of all, they will kill you.' He paused and gazed down at her. And he said, softly, 'And I would not want that.'

Alison looked confused. She stared at him, suddenly understanding that he was deadly serious. And the enormity of it all finally hit her and she burst into tears.

Peter Girolo held her in his arms, and she felt herself yielding, unresisting, her body heaving with sobs, tears of relief on her face.

'There, there,' he said, awkward, not used to comforting anyone, not having had a wife, or any sisters, or even a mother or aunt to take care of. But there was an innate decency about the man, it may have taken all those years to come to the surface, but it was there, and it was winning in his personal struggle with the darker side of Peter Michelangelo Girolo, the schooled *mafioso*.

Girolo stroked Alison's hair, and held her firmly, but tenderly, until gradually the weeping calmed, and her breath came in long, shuddering sighs, like a little child after a crying spasm.

Eventually she said, 'I'm sorry. You have had to live with this all your life . . . Please forgive me, Peter.'

The words she used were almost formal. But still she did not pull away from the strength and comfort of his arms.

Girolo found himself still stroking her hair. She smelled so good, she felt so good. He held her a little closer with his other arm and murmured, 'This is crazy. I won't be around much longer . . .'

Alison leaned back and gazed at him, her face streaked with tears. 'If that,' she said, and smiled, sniffing and wiping her face with her sleeve, 'is the best you can think of, you don't deserve to kiss me.'

And it was his turn to be completely surprised.

'Would you like me to?' he whispered, gently moving her hair off her forehead.

They were both aware of the beating of their hearts, their bodies were so close together.

Alison examined the eyes of this man, until so recently a stranger. What was it about him that made her feel so comfortable in his arms? What was it about him that made her say what she said next?

'I think I will die if you don't.'

And they kissed.

And they kissed.

The small French carriage clock chimed five.

Pale, shaded light fell into the bedroom through the muslin drapes as Alison rested her head on the muscled shoulder of the big, lean man lying naked in her bed, his arm around her, nursing her gently.

'Peter?'

'Mmmm?'

'Tell me the whole story. Vito Greco. Why and how it came about. Why you spared his life. Why he has given you some time to prepare yourself. Tell me all that . . .'

Girolo smiled. He felt more at home with this woman than he had ever felt in his life. There was something so complete about it.

'OK,' he said, casting *omerta* to the winds. 'If you give me the whole story about this guy Sebastian Tree. And why he wanted you dead so badly.'

Alison leaned over and kissed him, her body pressed against his rock-solid frame. 'OK,' she replied. 'You go first.'

About twenty minutes later Alison Clancy knew all about Vito Greco, the Byzantine politics of the mob, the Scuola in which he had been brought up, the ruthless enforcement of total loyalty and silence, and, if she had needed convincing, the certainty that Peter Girolo really wanted out.

And Peter Girolo knew all about Zeralda Electronics Inc. and Alison's confounding of Sebastian Tree's plans to sell the firm down the river.

'The guy is an asshole,' he decided. 'Where is he now?'

'Nobody knows, Peter. Maybe he's decided to cut and run.'

Girolo shook his head. 'Assholes like that never have the common sense. He'll be back.' He scratched his jaw, thoughtful. 'There's something more to all this. I mean, this man Tree has worked for years, you can bet on it, to undermine Zeralda Electronics. Which, as you describe its history, is the creation of one man, this Jack Fitzrowan character.'

Alison smiled at the thought of how Jack would have liked being thus described. 'That's true. Zeralda is Jack's baby.'

'And how did he die?'

'He had an accident. At sea.' Alison told him what had happened.

'Way to go. Way I would choose. When I reach about ninety-six. So who was on the boat with him?'

'Tom Hanrahan,' said Alison. 'He's married to Jack's daughter, Grace.'

'OK, don't tell me. Grace is now President of Zeralda, right?'

'Right.'

'And how much did she inherit?' asked Girolo. 'I presume there was a legacy.'

Alison sighed. 'Oh, yes, there most certainly was . . .' and she told Girolo all about the codicil. And Oliver.

'Did they ever find him? This missing kid?'

Alison chuckled. 'This missing kid,' she teased, leaning over him, 'would be about the same age as you.'

He smiled, and as he turned his head and looked at her, with that look which had gotten him right there into her bed – a very private place, sometimes she wondered if she had kept it too private – Alison felt a strange sense of dislocation, of . . . she was not quite sure what, like some half-remembered line of a half-forgotten tune.

'So Hanrahan was on the boat,' mused Girolo, thinking about the cop's recent visit. 'Anyone else?'

'Sebastian,' remembered Alison.

'Ah . . .'

'What does that mean?'

Girolo nuzzled her small breasts. 'Did Sebastian inherit anything?'

'Not a penny.'

'Mmm . . . love this little nipple, look, it's very excited . . .'

'Peter . . . What did you mean, "Ah . . ."?'

Girolo shrugged. 'Whatever I meant, this guy Tree is a fuckin menace. Pardon me.' He wished he had not sworn but Alison was listening, paying attention.

'Listen,' said Girolo, 'I'm going to take this meeting with Vito.'

'Are you crazy?' Alison was alarmed. 'He's going to kill you.'

'Do I look like a lamb?'

Actually, thought Alison, Girolo did not resemble any kind of a lamb.

'So trust me,' said Girolo. And he swung out of bed and headed for the bathroom.

There was something about the way he moved. On its own it was merely a coincidence, but taken with other things it was almost scary. Let's not get carried away, she thought, it's probably predictable I would go for a similar type.

Peter Girolo turned at the doorway and glanced back. 'What is it?' he said. 'You look like you've seen a ghost.'

Alison shrugged. 'You be careful tonight.'

He gazed at her, and after a long moment said, 'You sound like somebody who gives a damn.'

'So maybe I do . . .' she replied, and shuddered, because here was another man for whom death lurked in the shadows.

'Somebody walk over your grave?' enquired Girolo, smiling.

'Something like that.' Oh, God, Alison found herself thinking, don't take this one away too.

Logan International Airport. Sebastian Tree emerged from Customs and Immigration, carrying his luggage and in a thunderous mood. He was so angry the back of his neck had seized up and his temples ached.

He had not been in the slightest doubt that he was the true Oliver, the missing son of Jack Fitzrowan and Helen Costello. He felt so stupid. It had never occurred to him that, within months – it must have been a maximum of ten months – of his 'great love' producing her offspring, Fitzrowan had sired Sebastian Tree himself, by yet another in what was to be a long line of whores and Jezebels.

Now he was glad he had fixed that goddam boom.

Whunk! He could still hear the sound of it cracking open his bastard father's head.

His only regret was that he had never gotten round to confronting Big Dead Jack with the truth of their relationship.

Why?

Because the hatred would have been transparent. Whatever else Fitzrowan had been, he was no fool. An attribute which Sebastian Tree was sure he had inherited. And that fucking Dublin lawyer, up his own ass with self-satisfaction. He had not liked Sebastian, he had made that obvious. He had not wanted Sebastian Tree to be Oliver.

It occurred to Zeralda's Chief Executive right then, as he walked into the car park and opened the hood of his silver Porsche, that it would not have been beyond Pronsias Stevenson to have submitted false samples to that Dublin laboratory.

He got into the car and sat, seething, fighting to focus his rage.

OK, first things first. What was his situation, at that moment? Tak Katakura had bombed him out. Broken his word. Welshed on their deal. So he would have to be taken care of. Alison Clancy. As long as she was at Zeralda, there was no future for him there. She was building a strong case against him. So she had to go.

There was just one snag. He had already tried to have her killed, but according to Bobby Scipio, this mafia don, Peter Girolo, the boss man in Boston, was protecting her.

Fine. So Girolo had to go. And it had been clear from Tree's conversation with Scipio in LA that Girolo was under some kind of cloud. Good, he would exploit that. He was still connected. He still had good links with the mob.

The beginnings of a plan forming, Sebastian Tree started the engine and drove out from Logan International towards the Callahan Tunnel under Boston harbour. Gradually his temper subsided.

Oh, yes, he had gotten out of worse situations than this. He could see clearly now, with Girolo out of his way, Alison Clancy was dead meat.

And with Alison Clancy out of the way, Sebastian Tree felt sure he could charm Jack Fitzrowan's dumber daughter Grace Hanrahan into believing he had been the victim of a wicked character assassination plot, orchestrated by the late lamented Alison Clancy.

As this scenario took shape, Sebastian Tree let out a small whoop of pleasure and turned up his Beethoven in-car CD. He would show the world that even a reject from Jack Fitzrowan's cast of bastards was superior to any of the common rabble. But first, he would get in touch with Bobby Scipio, ask him to give him the name of one of those *cosa* boys who was out to bring down Girolo.

In a way he was probably, he decided, doing a public service.

'OK, Grace, you can get dressed now.' Dr Steve Wentworth came back into the examination room in his private surgery on Beacon Hill, not far from Mike Medevik's law practice.

Grace Hanrahan fastened her bra and slipped on her Chanel skirt and blouse, behind a green canvas changing screen. She hated visits to the doctor, even for a routine check-up. But she knew it was common sense.

When she emerged, Dr Wentworth had gone through to his oak panelled consulting room. It was well furnished with antique desk and comfortable chairs, primitive original Grandma Moses paintings on the walls and a couple of beautifully intricate model sailing boats on side tables.

Steve had been the family doctor for as long as Grace could remember. He was also a family friend and he had sailed and played golf with her father.

'Take a seat, please,' he said, businesslike, not looking up as he scanned the various notes and printouts from her ECG and blood and urine tests.

At first this professional approach had rather daunted Grace, who usually spent those minutes expecting to learn she had some terminal disease.

Finally Wentworth seemed satisfied. He put down the papers and looked up, smiling.

'Blood sugar levels normal. Healthy heart. Blood pressure fine. Liver function good. You are very well.'

'Ah.' Grace relaxed. 'That's good.'

'I want you to pop back in a month. Sylvia will make an appointment.' He gazed at her, friendly.

Grace frowned, alarmed. 'A month?'

'Just routine.' Dr Wentworth met her gaze.

'What do you mean, routine? What's wrong with me, Steve?'

'My dear girl, absolutely nothing,' he grinned broadly. 'You're pregnant, that's all.'

Silence.

'Oh my God. Oh, God.'

'Are you pleased?'

'Oh my word. Pleased? Oh, thank you, Doctor.'

Wentworth laughed gently. 'Don't thank me. Thank that Irish cop husband of yours.'

'Can I use your phone? Oh, God, I'm going to blub.'

Wentworth tugged a few tissues from the box of Kleenex on his desk and passed them over. 'Congratulations, Grace. Press nine for an outside line . . .'

Joey Buscetta had sounded fine when Girolo had phoned him from the Charles Hotel lobby in Cambridge near Harvard Square. Twenty minutes later, Girolo watched the burgundy Oldsmobile arrive at the Bennet Street entrance. He stepped on to the sidewalk as Sonny Favaro got out and opened the back door, checking out the area like the pro bodyguard he was.

Seconds later, Girolo was in the back of the automobile and being driven at a leisurely pace back to his Beaver Place apartment.

What was the reason for this change in his plans?

After walking out of the Holy Cross Cathedral, that afternoon, wholly expecting to be gunned down by Vito Greco or one of his cohorts – maybe even by the faithful (to the *famiglia*) Joey Buscetta himself – Peter Girolo had felt he had nowhere to run, nowhere to hide, and that death at Greco's hand was merely a matter of time.

He had gone to Alison's mews house because he trusted her and he needed time to stay out of sight and think. But events there had taken an unexpected turn. The growing attraction between them had suddenly ignited and those last few hours in her bed had been like magic.

They had restored his optimism and belief in his tried and tested ability to survive. But more important, that mutual exchange of confidences, when Girolo had told Alison about the workings of the *cosa nostra* and she had given him the inside story on Sebastian Tree, had lifted the veil on several things which had been troubling him.

He knew now that as long as Tree was around, Alison Clancy would not be safe. He found it strange to be so concerned for somebody else, for Peter Michelangelo Girolo had never considered another human being before himself, certainly not outside the *cosa*, in his entire life.

But now he had changed. Which was fortunate, because in the process of figuring out a way to ensure Alison would never again be under threat from Tree, Girolo had stumbled on the possibility of his own survival. It meant carrying on as normal, taking the meeting with Vito Greco, and trusting the man whose life he had once spared. Then he would see if it had been a mistake or not.

'How are things, boss?' asked Buscetta.

Girolo shrugged. What the enforcer was asking was, where you been? What you been doing?

'*Cosi-cosi*,' he replied. So-so. Which meant it's none of your goddam business.

After a few moments, as they approached Harvard Bridge over the River Charles into Boston, Girolo said, 'So Joey, any phone calls? Any news? How are things in New York City?'

The leather-faced Sicilian raised his shoulders. '*Cosi-cosi*, Don Pietro. *Cosi-cosi* . . .'

★

Nine p.m. in Mattapan. Only the brave walk the dog.

Tom Hanrahan sat beside Detective Jimmy Fitz, who was driving the blue unmarked Ford. They were both silent. Even Hanrahan's delight at the prospect of fatherhood had been dampened, for the crime scene they had just left had been pretty unpleasant, even for two seasoned Homicide cops.

The stubs of two half-smoked cigars, Cuban, in celebration, lay in the car's ashtray. Eventually, Jimmy Fitz remarked, 'Place was a fuckin abattoir . . .'

And they drove on, in silence. It had been one of those sad little murders. Kid doing her homework, older brother puts on loud music. They yell at each other. Father comes back, drunk since eleven in the morning on account of he is too fuckin idle to look for a job, lost confidence maybe, after a string of humiliating rejections. He slaps the girl, more than a few times. Her brother steps between them, for this is one time too many. Spunky kid, faces up to their 220lb drunken father.

The drunk fat guy hits son real hard, starts to kick the kid on the floor; daughter threatens him with a big knife. In the mêlée father's arm is cut; he goes apeshit, brains daughter, grabs the knife, sticks her a couple of times. Real hard, disembowelling her in the process. Son runs to bedroom, gets Daddy's .44 Smith and W. automatic, shoots him and shoots him till all thirteen slugs are in or have passed through his sister's killer. Head blown apart, entrails burst, walls, floor and windows splattered with blood, brains and shit.

Then the kid calmly calls the police. 'I think I just killed my father,' he tells the operator.

After a few moments, as they headed north on Blue Hill towards Franklin Park Zoo, Fitz began to chuckle.

Tom glanced at him. He smiled, shook his head. He knew exactly what his partner was laughing at.

'I think I just killed my father . . .' muttered the detective. And they both chortled. Just to keep sane.

'The kid gets A for observation,' said Hanrahan, wiping a tear from his eye.

The radio crackled. 'Car forty-nine, you there?'

Hanrahan lifted the radio handset. 'Sure, Annie, this is us . . .'

'You're going to get a phone call, Lieutenant. Larry Shauseau. Private and like that.'

'Thanks, Annie.'

'Oh, and Lieutenant.'

'Yeah?'

'Congratulations, I hear you got a happy event on the way.'

Hanrahan smiled. 'Thanks. We'll wet the head.'

'You bet,' said officer Annie McClintock.

Hanrahan's mobile phone rang. He replaced the radio handset and lifted the mobile. 'Hi.'

'Tom, it's Larry.'

'Go ahead.'

'D A's just been on the line. He figures you have enough for a Grand Jury. It was the tapes that did it.'

Tom Hanrahan sighed, this was a part of the job he hated. He had only done something similar once before, when he had been a young sergeant in Vice.

'Now would be a good time, you figure?'

Shauseau's answer was without hesitation. 'Now is the only time.'

Hanrahan nodded. 'On our way.'

'Call me when it's done.'

'You bet.'

The Lieutenant cut the call and dialled another number. When a voice said 'Hello?' he replied. 'We got a go. Time is now. You have a location for me?'

And when Big Time's voice told Hanrahan the answer, he switched off and said to his partner, 'Jimmy, there's something been going down, it's time for you to know.' He glanced at his watch. 'Charles Street, Beacon Hill Flat,' and leaning forward, switched on the siren and hidden strobe lights under the dash and the back window.

Vito Greco had been alone, at the appointed place. A storeroom above a warehouse near the railroad yards in East Brookline. The place was in darkness but it had a lot of high, 1950s square-paned windows and there was good moonlight.

Girolo had been there since around seven o'clock and he had made sure the Seattle *capo mafioso* arrived alone, which the guy did, having left his car on the far side of the railroad and walked across, slipping through a gap in the wood fence like a kid playing hooky.

Peter Girolo had watched from the roof as Greco made his own prudent examination of the place, then made his own way back into the storeroom.

'I wondered if you would come,' said Greco. 'Then I hear you are still around, doing business as usual.'

Girolo shrugged. 'You can't run from the mob, Vito. You can't hide, we both know that.'

Greco offered him a cigarette; he declined.

'So,' said Greco, 'this is a bad business, Peter. What the hell did you do to piss them off like this?'

Peter Girolo shook his head. 'I don't know, Vito, and that's the truth. They want me to go to war with the Russians. I want to get our business running smooth first. The Russian war, when it comes, will be like the fuckin Alamo, Gettysburg and Khe San rolled into one. We're going to have Feds crawling all over us, good men will go down, shot or indicted. Where is the profit?'

Vito Greco nodded, understanding the argument; he had his own problems in Seattle, trying to stop the man in Florence, four floors under the earth, living like a mad cardinal, from forcing him too to go to war with the commies.

'They heard you been talking with the Feds,' he muttered, glancing away. Almost apologetic.

Girolo's heart went cold. 'Say what?' he asked.

Greco shrugged. 'Some guy, some asshole, works in some broad's office. Friend of a made fellow, minor wiseguy in LA, Bobby Scipio, you heard of him?'

Girolo said no he had never heard of Bobby Scipio.

'Anyway, this asshole passes Scipio details of phone calls this broad makes to the Feds, and to Justice, in Boston and Washington.'

Girolo looked more puzzled than he felt, perspiration trickled down the small of his back. 'What does that have to do with me?'

Greco looked embarrassed. 'You been seeing the broad, without telling a soul. You were seen meeting her at the back of the Aquarium. She drives you away, like a furtive kinda thing. You know, like . . . furtive.'

'Oh, Alison . . .' said Girolo, really relaxed, as if, what a stupid mistake, this was only Alison.

Greco, who was sharp as a whip, suddenly switched his gaze to meet Girolo's. 'Yeah. Clancy. Alison Clancy. This asshole wanted her outta the way. The result is that Joe Cranmer is dead. Desmond Dekker is dead. Word is the cops think they did not kill each other the way somebody, a real pro, set it up to look like. They can't prove nothin but that's what they think. And they think, this guy Lieutenant Hanrahan, he thinks it lies at your *porta*, at your door.'

'I have a thing going with Alison Clancy,' said Girolo, quite open about it. 'I put the word out she is not to be harmed by some dipshit outside the family running around looking for a hit-man.'

Greco had not taken his eyes off Girolo.

'Did you waste these two made fellows?' he asked.

Girolo shook his head. 'No.'

Greco studied him for a long time, then relaxed. 'I believe you. And the Feds?'

'I am using Alison to try to get to a Federal Attorney. Name of Foley. I figure he can be bought. She uses her office to communicate. The man is nearly ours. Two hundred big ones a year. They pay those people shit.'

Greco digested all this.

Then he announced, 'You know, Peter, I think I believe you.' He spread his arms apologetically. 'But I gotta kill you. They want you dead. The council voted, three to one against. You are the walking dead.'

Vito Greco walked, agitated, to the window and gazed across the deserted yard to the railroad track. 'I'm sorry, man. I owe you. Why did it have to be me?'

Girolo watched Greco carefully, his senses tuned taut, listening for the footfall, the crunch of an automobile tyre, the squeak of a door – any sound which would signal his last moments had come.

But there was only the barking of some distant dogs. They did that, they barked at the moon. He remembered from Sicily.

Vito Greco turned and faced him. 'What can we do?'

'Are you in a hurry?' asked Girolo. 'Are they in a hurry for this?'

Greco hunched his shoulders, spread his hands. 'We got a day or two. They know I have to set it up. You know what it's like . . . They always want it yesterday.'

This was one pro killer to another. Bitching about the job.

'Sure thing,' said Peter Girolo, then, casually, making conversation, he said, 'Vito, what you need is to kill me, so that the entire family knows you did it. You get Boston as a reward. Next step New York . . .'

Greco made a face, as if to say, please, you overestimate me.

'But at the same time, you are a man of respect, a man of great honour, I have known men like you in the old country.'

Vito Greco was not displeased by this flattery.

'I spared your life. And you want to spare mine. Even if we both have to defy the *cosa*.'

Greco nodded, he was clearly racked with this dilemma.

Girolo put a hand on the *capo*'s shoulder. 'It's OK, *te absolvo*. There's nothing for it. You're going to have to kill me.'

Greco stared as him, his eyes were moist. 'Don Pietro, I just don't know if I can.'

Peter Girolo smiled. 'Of course you can, my good and honourable friend. Let me give you a few hints, technical details. At least I should die in a manner of my own choice. *D'accordo?*'

Vito Greco stared at the taller man, he gripped both Girolo's shoulders and kissed him on each cheek. '*Si*,' he said, '*d'accordo*.'

They embraced. Girolo stepped back and crossed to the window, gazing out at the moonlit yard bathed in grey-blue light, like a graveyard.

'OK,' he said. 'Here is what I suggest, *mi amico* . . .'

Across the city in South Boston, at the Hanrahans' Farragut Road house, Darcy had just phoned Grace from Dublin saying she had momentous news. And Grace had said she too had some news.

'But you go first,' Grace said.

'No, you go first,' replied her sister. It had been like that since they were kids.

'Well,' said Grace, 'I have been given information which identifies Oliver. That's the first thing.'

'Who is he?' enquired Darcy, who sounded more relaxed about this bombshell than Grace had expected.

'Wait for it, are you sitting down?'

'No, I'm hanging from the chandelier shouting "Tarzan".'

'Very funny. Darcy, it's the CEO at Zeralda. Sebastian Tree. He's a horrible man, this is the person who has been trying to ruin us.'

Pause. She thought she could hear Darcy chuckling, '. . . Darcy?'

'He's been over here. In Dublin. He came to see Pronsias. DNA test. The works.'

Grace felt very flat, even her good news had been dampened by the revelation Tree was Jack's long lost love child, and due to inherit hundreds of millions. Millions that Zeralda could have used to keep pace with an expanding global market.

'It doesn't seem fair, does it?' she declared.

Then Darcy had told her, chapter and verse, as repeated to her by Pronsias, the story of Sebastian Tree's claim being thrown out, although he was indeed an illegitimate son of their daddy's. And his outraged reaction.

'". . . I'll have you know, I use only the very best shampoos," says Pronsias, bless him.' Darcy was laughing. 'Anyway, after huffing and puffing, the schmuck has gone back to Boston. And you have to fire him, if you have not already done so.'

'Darcy,' said Grace – her sister did not understand corporate affairs, never had – 'he can sue us for one point four million dollars if I do that. You should see his contract.'

Darcy, business head or not, was as practical as ever. 'Can Zeralda afford it?'

'Well . . .' Grace had considered that, talked it through with Paul and with Alison Clancy, 'there are a hundred better ways to spend that kind of money. Paul is working on an R&D project that could treble our five-year projection. The laboratory boys say he is an absolute wiz. Advanced lateral thinker, Nick Bedrosian says. He even compared him to a young Bill Gates.'

Bedrosian was Zeralda's senior Research and Development scientist. Big Jack had poached him from a Rockefeller project at NASA.

'Hmm . . .' replied Darcy, 'I think getting rid of Sebastian is the best place for one point four million dollars right now. Next news?'

Grace told her sister she was pregnant. Darcy sounded delighted. In fact, all things considered, Darcy sounded less like the spiky, cynical half-sister than Grace could remember. Tom's secret nickname for her was Cruella de Ville.

After asking all about how Grace felt and did she want a girl or a boy, and what if it was twins?, Darcy said, quietly, that she too had some more news.

'Come on, Sis, out with it,' said Grace.

'I'm leaving Edward.'

Grace was astonished. 'But why?'

After a silence, Darcy merely replied, 'Bored, dear. Terribly, terribly bored . . .'

Grace was stuck for words. 'How has poor Edward taken it?'

Slight pause, then Darcy said, 'He doesn't actually know yet. Not just at the precise moment. Grace, there is something else.'

'Oh, Lord, I don't know if I'm ready for more,' groaned Grace, but secretly she was enjoying her first good gossip with her sister since their daddy had died. 'You'd better go on.'

'I know where Oliver was taken to. After New York.'

Grace sighed. 'Oh, not the Websters. Paul has been down that dead end. Apparently their real name was Ross and they went back to Ireland.'

But Darcy said no, Paul was wrong about that. The Websters were never Irish, they were Italian. And old man Webster owned a laundromat at the wrong end of Madison Avenue. 'It was not Ross, Grace. It was Rossi. The Rossis is what Paul heard. Naturally, he took that to be the plural of Ross, a Scottish-Irish name. But all the time it was Rossi.'

'My God, you traced them,' breathed Grace. 'And what happened to Oliver? Is he still alive?'

'They gave him away.' Darcy told Grace what old Giovanni Webster had told her. And she said that Pronsias Stevenson agreed this was the likeliest route yet to finding their half-brother, the son of Jack Fitzrowan and Helen Costello.

'Or at least,' she went on, 'finding what has become of him. If he is alive or not. I'm flying down there today.' And she mentioned her destination.

'Oh, Darcy, be careful.'

Darcy laughed. 'It's OK, I'll have a good man with me.'

'And who is he? Am I allowed to know?' enquired Grace, intrigued.

'It's Pronsias, Grace. Pronsias Stevenson. We've kind of, um . . . we get on really well. And do you know what?'

'Darcy,' smiled her sister, 'you never cease to amaze me. What?'

'He can speak the language fluently. Learned it from one of those book and tape courses.'

Paul Fitzrowan was at home in his atrium study, working and thinking from time to time about Grace's astonishing revelation that Sebastian Tree was in fact their half-brother, the long lost Oliver. The alarming ramifications of that did not seem to have sunk in for Grace, but he guessed she was now too excited about her pregnancy to dwell on it.

He was quietly excited, for with his SR Microchip Project he had almost perfected a computer program which updated itself when subsidiary paths were themselves altered, provided the alterations were complementary to the main program's function.

His next task, and one that would put Zeralda Electronics several years ahead of its rivals, including the Katakura Corporation of Japan, would be to reverse the process, so that those minor programs would automatically update themselves to complement a more sophisticated master program. If successful, this would save electronics users huge fortunes in microchip replacement costs and at the same time more than quadruple Zeralda's profit over the next few years, as the Boeings, McDonnell Douglases and Sanyos of this world seized the opportunity to save tens of millions, in the long term. He had been using the mathematics of the human body's DNA strings, and his aim was to perfect a microchip capable of rejuvenating itself, in the same way that many human cells are programmed to do.

When the phone rang, he was tempted to leave it to the answer tape, but on impulse he picked up the receiver and learned from Grace that Sebastian Tree was not, after all, the elusive Oliver.

He was amused but not surprised to hear about Darcy and Pronsias Stevenson, for hadn't he seen them so cosy in Dublin just a few weeks back?

Then Grace said, 'So how is the project?'

Paul pushed a hand through his hair, the way his father used to, staring at his computer screen. 'Nearly there.'

'Do you really think you can do it?'

'No.'

'Aw, Paulie, I'm so sorry . . .'

Paul Fitzrowan smiled. 'But with the help of Nick Bedrosian I'm damned *sure* we can.'

He heard a delighted sound at the other end of the phone.

'Listen,' said his sister, 'can we have dinner tonight? You busy?'

'Come round here, Grace. Bring the cop.'

'The cop is working. I'll be there in an hour. Pizza is fine.'

'Pizza my ass,' remarked Paul. 'Bonita will make us something great.'

'I'm not sure if me and the little stranger are up to cordon bleu.'

Paul smiled. 'I was thinking of cheeseburgers and fries. With root beer. Home made ice-cream, the way Bridget used to make it. She gave me the recipe.'

'I'll be right there.'

There is an old established delicatessen on Charles Street, at the foot of Beacon Hill, which local people call The Flat, closer to

Longfellow Bridge and the River Charles than Starbucks Coffee house and De Luca's, which were at the more fashionable, Mount Vernon Street end.

'This is kind of a gay area, right?' decided Jimmy Fitz as he turned into Charles. 'I mean, no kids, no women with pushchairs . . .'

Tom Hanrahan gazed through the windshield. 'Come on, man, it's late for kids.'

'Yeah, it's the same at noon, Lieutenant.' He slowed the Ford as they cruised past Big Time and Jeb's vehicle, not their usual Chevvy, but a dark green Plymouth sedan.

Hanrahan spoke into his mobile. He had not used the police radio band since this operation had started, about a half-hour before. 'OK all set . . . ?'

Sergeant Detective Jeb Kingdom answered. 'I got five kids from the Academy, holding position. Everything's set.'

Hanrahan scrunched up his face, a trick he had devised for releasing tension. 'OK, I go in with Jim. You two are right behind. The young people stand fast.'

'You got it.'

Hanrahan switched off as Fitz stopped, double parked, a few doors away from the delicatessen.

Both men checked their Glock automatic pistols, then climbed out from the car and strolled towards the little deli, its windows cramped with Italian cheeses, sausages, fresh vegetables, pastas, coffees and olives and so on.

Behind them, Big Time and Jeb Kingdom got out of the Plymouth and strolled along behind the Lieutenant and Fitz. A wonderful mixture of coffee and cheese and smoked ham aromas lingered in the air as they approached the deli and pushed open the door.

'*Ciao*, Thomas,' smiled a pretty, olive-skinned girl as Hanrahan entered.

'*Ciao*, Sofia,' nodded Hanrahan. 'Is he upstairs?'

'*Si*,' replied Sofia Tarantola, 'my brother is cooking supper for Mamma. Good news about Signora Hanrahan.'

'Yeah, it's great.' Tom Hanrahan pushed past a couple of

customers, Armani jeans, designer T-shirts, and opened a door at the back. He and Fitz went up a narrow flight of stairs.

Sofia beamed as Big Time and Jeb came in, the bell over the door jangling again.

'Hey what is this?' she joked. 'A police convention?'

Jeb just smiled, without much enthusiasm, and leaned his back against the door.

Upstairs, was Mrs Tarantola's apartment. The main room was a kitchen and dining area. Danny Tarantola stood at the cooking top, chopping chives into a pasta sauce he was making inside a big pot, blackened from much use.

'Smells good,' said Jimmy Fitz. 'Where's Mamma?'

'Hi, guys, grab a beer. We always got enough for our friends.'

'Where's Mamma?' asked Tom Hanrahan.

'She taking a nap. I wake her up when the food is on the table. She works hard, ain't getting any younger. You know.'

Hanrahan nodded. 'Sure.'

He and Jimmy stood there, Fitz moving towards the bedroom door and casually checking inside, where old Mrs Tarantola lay snoring gently on top of the bed.

'Beer's in the ice box, guys.' Tarantola waved a hand at the fridge.

'Danny, turn the heat down, I want you to hear something,' said Hanrahan.

'Ahh . . .' Danny the Wop nodded, turned the gas down and shifting the big pot off the flame, said, 'Work. You shoulda said. Gentlemen, it's only one night off a week, can't you guys do anything without me?' He grinned, wiped his hands and enquired, 'What can I do for you?'

Hanrahan and Fitz had both noticed, first thing, really, that Tarantola's gun and waist holster rig were on top of a sideboard. And Fitz was closer to it than Danny Tarantola.

Tom Hanrahan took a small tape recorder from his pocket and laid it on the table, set for a family supper. Bottle of Chianti, jug of water. Fresh baked bread.

He switched it on, not taking his eyes off Tarantola as the tape played. Apart from the first seven words, the whole exchange was in Sicilian dialect.

It went like this:

'Who's this?'

'You know who this is.'

'Gimme the chief.'

'He ain't around.'

'Listen you piece of shit, this is a man you are talking to. *Capisce?*'

'Here he comes. [*less distinct*] Tommy, it's the cop.'

[*another voice comes on*] 'This is Tommy Riccobono, who is this?'

'It's DT.'

'Hey, Danny, how's it goin?'

'Why did you take care of Alberto?'

'The guy was a snitch, he had it comin.'

'It was too soon. They will put that with the girl in NYC.'

'What girl?'

'Come on, Tommy, the lawyer.'

'The lawyer? Fuck them. I told them to wait a few weeks.'

'It makes me nervous. A good cop would put two and two, you know what I'm sayin?'

'Relax, we will go cool for a while.'

'You better.'

'So. What else you got?'

'Bits and pieces. I'll drop it off.'

'Usual place? Dodgers gonna win Saturday?'

'Usual place. I figure the Yankees.'

'Yeah. So. Take it easy.'

'Yeah.'

Click. Dial tone.

Tom Hanrahan, grim-faced, switched the machine off. 'I have the transcript. You want to read it?'

Danny Tarantola had gone grey. He sat down, loosening his necktie, which had been loose already.

After a long moment, punctuated only by faint sounds of his mother's snoring in the next room, he began to weep.

Tom Hanrahan and Jimmy Fitz just stood there, unmoved.

Tarantola had visibly shrunk. He put his head in his hands and cried like a baby.

Jeb Kingdom's rock-solid black head appeared at the top of the stairs from the shop. He took in the scene and was right there to catch Tarantola's gun and holster rig when Fitz gently threw it to him.

Big Time squeezed past Jeb and softly walked to stand behind Tarantola. It was like they were all at a wake, only the dead man was still alive, but broken.

'Daniel Alfreddo Tarantola,' said Lieutenant Tom Hanrahan, 'I am arresting you for corruption and as an accessory after the fact, in the cases of the unlawful homicides of one Alberto Sanzo and Miss Jennifer Puzzo, attorney at law. You do not need to say anything at this stage and you are warned that anything you do say can be used in evidence at your trial. You are entitled to an attorney . . .'

So that was that.

Danny Tarantola had been on the take from the *cosa*. For how long was anybody's guess. Maybe after the fifth time he got shot. A man can take only so much, he asks himself, what's it all about?

Most men find the right answer. But Danny had strayed.

The business of taking the sobbing man out of Tarantola's Famous Delicatessen in handcuffs, with hysterical mother and sister in train, was not something Tom Hanrahan ever wanted to repeat.

Needless to say, Millicent Dunne was there with her cameraman. Hanrahan had felt he owed her that, for being so mean to her at the Sanzo killing crime scene.

15

Vito Greco received a message by word of mouth. Unlike the unlucky Danny Tarantola, he did not trust the phone, not even so-called secure digital systems. The messenger had travelled north from the mafia stronghold in Rhode Island with a communication from Albert Genovese, *consigliere* to the *capo di tutti capi*, in his Colorado desert prison.

There is a civilian called Sebastian Tree, went the message, who badly wants Peter Girolo dead. It is important that he does not get in the way of your more serious business of carrying out the *famiglia*'s instruction to whack Girolo.

Greco understood this to mean, terminate the asshole Tree, before he does something embarrassing. Girolo is our hit, nobody else's.

Sebastian Tree, reflected Greco. If ever a man had written his own ticket . . . He decided to take a look at the guy. And so it was that about ten the next morning, when Sebastian Tree jogged out from his Charlestown house, immaculate in white running shorts, UCLA athlete's jersey, Reebok training shoes and blue cotton sports socks, shades and a Sony Walkman on his Ralph Lauren Polo waist belt, Vito Greco sat in a Bell Telephone Company van, observing this fly in the *cosa* ointment.

And as he watched, using hi-power, self-focusing binoculars, Greco was struck by a certain similarity from the back, to his primary target, the man to whom he owed his life.

Sure, Tree was tall and fair haired, and Peter Girolo had thick, wavy black hair. Sure Tree had the typical West Coast, honey tanned complexion of a spoiled, Californian WASP, while Girolo was darker skinned, as befits the true Sicilian. But from a distance, if Greco had been on the look-out for a Peter Girolo who had gone to ground, maybe disguising his appearance – as well he might have done, with the mob after him – this guy Tree would have merited a second glance. On account of that first-glimpse similarity.

Vito Greco smiled to himself. Maybe he could use that vague likeness to advantage, before taking care of Tree permanently.

Sebastian Tree got back to his place, perspiring and with that feeling of well-being of the permanently fit. He had just run a shower and stripped off, when a lean, tough looking man walked into his bathroom.

'What the hell is this?' demanded Tree, pulling a towel round his waist.

Vito Greco's gaze would have reduced Medusa herself to a quivering wreck. He stood there, silent, till Tree turned off the shower and said, more respectfully, 'What are you doing in my house?'

'Mutual friends sent me,' replied Greco. 'I ain't got long. Finish your ablutions and get dressed. You got cranberry juice?'

'I'm sorry?' asked Tree, thinking was this a password, like Mr Apple, whose death he had read about in the papers.

'Cranberry juice. It's a fruit drink. I'm thirsty.'

'Oh. Sure. Sure, it's in the ice box.'

Five minutes later, the two men sat on the verandah at the back of Tree's house, Greco with his carton of cranberry juice and Tree with a glass of tap water, ice and lemon.

'So,' said Vito Greco, 'you don't like our Peter Girolo . . .'

'I just think he's a rat,' replied Tree. 'He's talking to the Feds. He is a liability to your . . . business.'

Greco seemed to think about this for a long time. Then he said, 'OK. Sebastian, you are not made, you know what that means? Made? You know what I mean by made?'

Tree nodded. 'Yes. I know.'

'OK,' went on Greco, 'but the family says I can trust you. Can I trust you?'

'With your life,' answered Sebastian Tree, almost too promptly.

Greco did that thing with his lips, like Humphrey Bogart,

inverting them against his dry gums so that he looked like he had no lips, for a moment. 'It would be your life, Sebastian. Not mine.'

He looked at Tree, then smiled, a smile so full of charm that teams of old ladies would have given him their life savings to take care of.

'You can trust me,' replied Tree, matching the hoodlum's mask of honesty.

'OK. I am the man who is to whack him. You understand?'

Oh, bliss, thought Sebastian Tree, this is the happiest day of my life. With Girolo gone, the way is clear. Next will be the Clancy bitch, then everything will be fine again. Plus, the mafia trusts me. There will be many opportunities to exploit that little bonus.

'I understand,' he said, mature, reliable, holding Greco's gaze.

'But it is not that simple.' Vito Greco paused, watching Tree take this in. 'Peter Girolo is a *capo mafioso*; he is held in respect, all over America, in my business. It would be like the Baseball Commission putting a lifetime suspension on Joe Torre. So I have to put Girolo in a bad light. I have to arrange a small *commedia*, a piece of theatre . . .'

Sebastian Tree understood. 'You have to kill his reputation, before you kill him.'

'*Bravo!*' exclaimed Greco. 'Exactly like that.'

This appealed to Tree. It was precisely how he would have preferred to have dealt with his father, Jack Fitzrowan, father of all his misfortunes.

'And how can I help? You would not be telling me this if you did not want my . . . involvement.'

'Ah . . .' Vito Greco beamed, 'you understand *omerta*, you could be a made man after this. After this favour I am gonna ask of you.'

And so he told Sebastian Tree of his plan. When he had finished, Tree stared at him in wonder.

'It's immaculate,' Sebastian declared. 'Brilliant.'

'You will help?' asked the man who had been given the order to kill Girolo.

'When do we start?'

'Today. I will have everything we need by noon.'

'It's inspired,' enthused Sebastian Tree. 'I can see how they gave you the contract.'

Vito Greco smiled thinly. 'You are too kind.'

'You seem preoccupied, Alison,' said Grace Hanrahan as Zeralda's Legal Exec entered her office.

'I'm fine,' replied Alison. 'I hear Paul and Nick Bedrosian are getting close to success.'

Grace stood at the bookcase, thumbing through a volume on patent law. She shook her head and passed the book to Alison. 'What am I doing? This is your territory. Alison, I've been thinking,' she crossed to her desk and sat on the edge, 'being pregnant has made things clearer.' She lifted the wooden plaque with GRACE HANRAHAN — PRESIDENT on it. 'I don't want to be President of Zeralda. I want to be a wife and mother.'

Alison grinned. 'I don't blame you, Grace . . . Go for it.' Grace stood up and they hugged, laughing. Grace said, 'I intend to. Now tell me I have gone out of my mind, but I think I have found the perfect person to step into my shoes.'

They sat down, Alison thoughtful. Then she looked up. 'Paul?' she said.

Grace looked anxious. 'What do you think?'

'It's bold, Grace. It's imaginative. And . . . I think Paul will be a terrific President.'

'Not too young?'

'He has grown by the day since Jack died.'

'Not too . . . irresponsible?'

'Not any more.'

Grace sighed with relief, then relaxed. 'What a weight off my mind. You are a real friend, Alison.'

'So are you. Do you want a boy or a girl?'

Grace smiled broadly. 'I really don't mind. There is something else I need to talk to you about. Darcy wants us to fire Sebastian Tree. Whatever it costs us, in terms of money.'

382

Thank God, thought Alison, and she replied, 'I think she's right.'

'There is more. Come on, let's sit over here.' Grace led the way to the two easy chairs and couch, in a corner of the big office. As she sat down, Alison could not help remembering this was where she had made love with Jack for the very last time. She crossed her legs and listened as Grace told her about Sebastian Tree's visit to Dublin and his claim to be Oliver Fitzrowan.

'Of all the nerve!' exclaimed Alison. 'I told you the man was deranged.'

But Grace went on to relate how the DNA tests had proved Sebastian Tree was indeed Jack's illegitimate son, but not the child of Helen Costello. Then she paused and said, 'But we believe we are close to tracing the real Oliver Fitzrowan.'

Alison waited. There was no sound in the room except for the sedate ticking of the Thomas Mudge carriage clock on Jack's bookcase.

'He was adopted by a couple called Webster, sure enough. Italian immigrants who had changed their name to make life easier for them in the States.'

Alison agreed this was an old story.

'They returned,' continued Grace, 'to New York with the infant Oliver and a Mexican wet-nurse. Everything was hunky dory until Mrs Webster became pregnant and had her own baby. This often happens after an adoption. Maybe because the pressure is off both partners.

'Anyway, with a new child, and money suddenly tight, the Websters sell the child to another Italian couple, the Rossis. And after two more years, the Rossis go home – to Italy. Darcy has done a wonderful detective job, and she has the family's address, at least the village they returned to in 1957. She is on her way there right now, with Pronsias Stevenson, my family's Dublin lawyer. Apparently he speaks Italian.'

Alison stared at Grace.

'Are you OK?' asked Grace.

'Where, exactly, in Italy?' asked Alison.

Grace shrugged. 'Sicily. It's a small village way up in the hills.

Apparently the couple who adopted him came from an old family of Sicilian nobles.'

Alison sat there thinking, it can't be. Get a hold of yourself. It cannot possibly be.

And yet, the way she had felt such an annoying, inexplicable, attraction to Peter Girolo. That look he had, ducking his head and gazing at her so . . . amused, but approachable. The walk, from the back.

'Are you all right, Alison?' asked Grace.

'Sure. Somebody just walked over my grave, as they say.' Alison stood up. 'I think Paul will make a terrific President. You will have to help him settle in. Anything I can do, just ask. As for Sebastian Tree, of course you must get rid of him. My advice, as your brand new Chief Executive elect is, bar him from the premises. Alert Security not to allow him past the gate.'

Grace was delighted. 'You'll take the job? Oh, Alison, that's just marvellous . . .'

Alison smiled and she walked to the door, then paused and said, 'I would really like to know about Oliver. Would you let me know when Darcy has found out?'

Grace said of course she would and Alison went to her office where she cancelled all appointments and drove back to Willow Mews, where she had a number of urgent things to do. She thanked God she had not thrown her underwear and bath towels into the washing machine.

Sometimes, thought Alison, it was fortunate she was less than perfect with the housework.

First thing she did when she got home was to look up the phone directory, business pages, under L for Laboratory.

Joey Buscetta grinned, a fearsome sight. The last sight more than a few unfortunates had ever seen, as he held out the keys.

'What's this?' asked Peter Girolo, gazing at the Jaguar XK-8 convertible parked in front of his Beaver Place apartment.

'You remember Vito, boss? Vito Greco?' enquired the mob's New York enforcer.

'How could I forget?' replied Girolo.

'He sends you this as a present. From him to you,' said Buscetta, and he handed over an envelope, along with the keys.

Girolo opened the envelope, inside was a note,

> *Grazie per mia vita.* Seattle is doing fine. This is for my life, please accept it in a spirit of friendship and the closing of any bad blood between us. Life is too short.

Girolo looked cynical. He met Buscetta's smiling gaze. 'What do you think, Joey?'

Buscetta shrugged. 'Word is he's been goin around saying how that was a hell of a thing you did. Not whacking him when you had every right. How if it had been him, he woulda whacked you, boss. But they say he got religion afterwards. Always going to the church,' here Buscetta, the Torquemada of the New York mob, crossed himself instinctively, and went on, 'lighting a candle and so on. Don Vito, no question, holds you in high esteem.'

Good speech, thought Girolo. He wondered how long it had taken Joey to memorize it. And 'esteem'; he doubted if Buscetta had ever heard the word before.

'Well, that is handsome,' he said, and handed the keys back to Buscetta. 'Come on, let's go.'

'Go, boss?' Buscetta looked alarmed.

'Sure,' replied Girolo, 'let's take it for a spin. You always wanted to drive one of these, I heard you telling Sonny Favaro.'

With the look of a doomed man, Joey Buscetta unlocked the door of the Jaguar convertible gingerly. Nothing happened. He climbed inside as Girolo went round to the passenger side, unbuttoned his grey wool Giorgio Armani jacket and joined him.

Soon heads were turning in North Boston as the sleek, ice-blue car cruised, top down, powerful engine grumbling potently, through the streets.

'Wow,' said Girolo, 'this is more like it . . .'

More like the bad old days, he thought to himself, unbuttoning his navy silk shirt and loosening the yellow Hermès necktie, with its neat design of hundreds of tiny, pale blue elephants. More like the bad old days when Tommy Riccobono and that creep Bontate were strutting their stuff all over town, with their Porsches and Mercedes and Harley Davidson motor-cycles.

But heads did turn. And the good residents of North Boston's Little Italy community said to each other, why look, there goes the local mafia don, doesn't he look fine in his new sports car?

Then Girolo told Buscetta to take him to the Marriott Long Wharf Hotel, park the new car in the underground garage there, then return to the North Boston 'office', that room above La Cucina Napolitana, to check the weekly receipts of local under-bosses, whose bagmen would be coming in and out throughout that afternoon, with cash from the mob's whorehouses, numbers games, loan sharks, casinos, escort agencies, massage callouts, nar-cotics concessions and robbery.

Buscetta did as he was told, taking one of the two cars they kept in the Marriott garage, and driving himself back, relieved not to have been blown sky high, for he was aware, although he hid it like the pro he was, that it was Vito Greco who had been tasked with killing Girolo.

But he was well aware it would not be long before he would be told to arrange Don Pietro's funeral. It would, of course, be a grand affair, befitting a man of such rank.

Another man looking forward to Peter Girolo's funeral was Sebastian Tree.

Vito Greco looked on approvingly as the former CEO of Zeralda Electronics ran a comb through his newly dyed black hair, cut shorter and re-styled with the aid of a hair drier and gel.

Greco handed Tree an expensive, well-cut grey wool coat, by Giorgio Armani, and a yellow and pale blue Hermès necktie. Tree swiftly tied the necktie, looping it with practised skill. It looked good with the navy blue silk shirt.

'He's wearing it loose at the neck,' said Greco, 'top button undone.'

Sebastian Tree stood back from the mirror and shrugged on the wool jacket. 'What do you think?'

After a moment, Vito Greco said, 'Uncanny. It's like . . . it's like him. So let's go.'

As they walked across the underground garage towards the brand new Jaguar XK-8, Greco slipped a brown paper bag to Sebastian Tree. It was reassuringly heavy.

'You don't have to shoot anybody,' said Greco. 'You would maybe miss. There's a guy at a window, across the street, he'll do the shooting. He will not miss.'

'Made man,' said Tree.

Greco nodded. 'You understand good, my friend. Just slow at the intersection, point at the target, *Bang!* Your piece fires blanks. Then hit the gas and drive away, not too fast.' Greco chuckled. 'You do not want a speeding ticket.'

Tree felt very calm. Part of him liked the role of mafia crime boss, about to blow away an old crippled man who had cheated on his numbers returns. Sure it was a shame the old guy had to die. But good order and discipline had to be maintained.

And the other part of him, the more rational part, could see that the resulting public outrage and heavy police activity would give the mob's ruling council an excuse to justify the whacking of Peter Girolo.

Sebastian Tree climbed into the Jaguar and started the engine. It sounded good, though he felt maybe he preferred the Porsche.

'OK,' he said. 'All set.'

'You know what to do?' asked Greco.

'Mister, I have a degree in accountancy from UCLA. I have already killed one man in cold blood. You will be proud of me. Take my word for it.'

'Everything you say, it's what I want to hear,' said Greco. '*Arrivederci* . . .'

As he watched the sports car growl out of the garage, tyres squealing on the asphalt, Vito Greco felt a certain satisfaction.

Satisfaction and relief, for Peter Girolo would very soon be dead, and his own contract would be fulfilled.

As it happens, Joey Buscetta himself was taking a stroll in North Boston. Joey had a sweet tooth, and there was a general store in

Hanover Street, near the Thunderbird Gift Shop, a place that sold, of all things in the middle of Little Italy, American Indian artefacts.

So when the ice-blue Jaguar XK-8 grumbled past, with his boss at the wheel, Buscetta stopped and admired the car, amazed that it was still in one piece, for he had fully expected it to do to Don Girolo what Don Girolo and he had arranged for the unfortunate Sal Spatola, he of the unfinished haircut.

As he watched, the Jaguar slowed down on the corner of Hanover and Prince, just across from Paul Revere's alleged house. He saw Girolo look around as if lost, for a moment, then the boss stretched his arm to point at old Blind Giovanni, who was not in fact blind but had a couple of amputated legs, on account of he had smoked about ninety cigarettes a day since he was ten years old, which was about seventy years ago, give or take.

And to Buscetta's astonishment, he realized Don Pietro was pointing a piece, some kind of pistol, at the old cripple.

Had he gone crazy?

Inside the Jaguar, Sebastian Tree watched with a strange excitement as the old man noticed a gun was being aimed at him by the *capo mafioso* of his neighbourhood. He realized he was actually looking forward to seeing the man and his wheelchair being blasted by the gunman hidden in a building behind him.

Meeting the ancient's terrified eyes, Tree grinned and squeezed the trigger. He wondered if blanks were always so incredibly loud . . .

'There is so little left,' remarked Barry Maguire, the police pathologist, to Tom Hanrahan at the crime scene, 'that I will have to rely on scrapings and a DNA test. The man was to all intents and purposes, vaporized. There are crumb sized pieces of him all over town. And yet, nobody else was hurt. Very damn professional . . .'

'DNA?' enquired Hanrahan. 'How do you find a match?'

'All major criminals,' replied Maguire, 'are required to have blood tests during their first year in the joint.' He smiled. 'The medic at Marion was a roomie of mine. Class of seventy-five . . .'

Big Time ducked under the POLICE – CRIME SCENE tapes and

approached Lieutenant Tom Hanrahan. 'We got a dozen witnesses, Lieutenant, it was Peter Girolo OK.'

In a comfortable prison cell, with its own sitting room and television set, the *capo di tutti capi* sat four floors underground, munching his lobster thermidor and watching CNN, with its report of the gangland slaying of Boston crime boss, Peter Michelangelo Girolo.

There was a knock at the door.

'Come in,' said the don.

An orderly entered and respectfully handed him a mobile phone, then left.

Gotti put the phone to his ear. 'I'm having my supper,' he said.

And on the other end of the line, Joey Buscetta's voice said, in Sicilian dialect, 'He's gone. I saw it myself.'

John Gotti smiled. '*Eccellente,*' he replied, and switching the phone off, returned to his lobster.

In Alison Clancy's Willow Mews house, Peter Girolo sat watching the same programme. He had changed out of the navy blue silk shirt and grey jacket at the Marriott, and he had made his way to Mount Vernon Street by taxi, disguised as a middle-aged pastor, with grey hair and bad teeth.

Alison's own telephone rang, twice. Then after a pause, began to ring again. Girolo lifted the receiver and listened, not saying a word.

'You are dead,' said the voice of Vito Greco. 'You better stay that way . . . The debt is paid.'

Click.

And thus it was, on that day in August, that Peter Michelangelo Girolo died, as violently as he had lived.

Downstairs, he heard the front door open and he listened as Alison rushed upstairs, her feet stumbling and he was there to catch her as she came into the room, face wet with tears. He held her very tight, and smoothed her hair tenderly.

It was then that he knew he had chosen the right woman. For Alison Clancy did not faint clean away. Nor did she reel back thinking she had seen a ghost. Instead, she pulled away and started to beat her fists against his head and forearms, as he ducked and fended off the blows.

'You bastard! You bloody bastard!!' she gasped, and the more he began to laugh, the angrier she got, until finally, she burst into tears again, but this time they were tears of relief.

And then they kissed . . .

Later, the telephone rang, and when Alison answered, it was the MIT Genetics Laboratory.

'Miss Clancy,' a competent sounding young woman said, 'we have the results of the DNA test. Would you like me to fax them to you?'

Darcy Fitzrowan and her lover, Pronsias Stevenson, were driven from the Mazzaro family's mountain estate, on the slopes above Caltagirone, by Alfreddo the Sicilian driver from the Catania Sheraton, in an air-conditioned Alfa Romeo sedan.

Pronsias's Italian had proved adequate for the occasion, and the seventy-five-year-old Contessa di Mazzaro di Rossi, a handsome woman, spoke perfect English with a slight American accent.

On the journey into the mountains, Pronsias Stevenson had conversed in lively fashion with Alfreddo, but on the way down, both he and Darcy were silent, deep in thought.

In fact they did not discuss their conversation with the contessa until later that evening, on the Zeralda Lear Jet, as it climbed steeply into a smoke blue and fire-streaked evening sky, after taking off from Catania's Fontana Rossa airport.

And even then, it was in hushed tones.

Paul Fitzrowan and Nick Bedrosian, an enormous bear of a man, close to retirement, emerged from the Research and Development lab on the seventh floor with broad grins. Bedrosian wiped a kerchief across his perspiring neck and the two men shook hands warmly.

'I'm going to the commissary, I need fuel,' said the big computer scientist. 'Paul, you are a pleasure to work with.'

Paul left the elevator at the fourth floor and went directly to his sister's office. Grace was at her desk, reading a document from Stevenson, Stevenson & Malahide in which Pronsias Stevenson reported formally and in detail the claim by Sebastian Tree to be the missing Oliver, and provided copies of the laboratory report, along with DNA graphs and mathematical notes, which confirmed that Tree was indeed the son of Jack Fitzrowan and proved conclusively he was no relation of Helen Costello.

The moment she looked up and saw her brother's beaming face she knew it was good news.

'Don't tell me,' she said, 'you have done it?'

Paul nodded. 'Nick and I have perfected the self-updating microchip. We have just run a sample five-year program and it works. It actually rejuvenates itself. Clever little thing.'

Grace darted round the desk and hugged him. They began to laugh.

'Paul, this puts Zeralda way out in front . . .' Grace stared at him, pushing a strand of hair from her brother's forehead. 'You are a genius.'

Paul shrugged, embarrassed. 'I just remembered some stuff Dad taught me. Years ago. He had all kinds of ideas for keeping in front of the pack.'

'But you remembered . . .' Grace moved around the room, almost waltzing with happiness and triumph.

After a moment's hesitation, Paul shook his head. 'That is not entirely accurate. I found some of Dad's notebooks, and other stuff, in his private safe. At Mount Vernon Street.'

'What other stuff?'

'Oh, just personal stuff. Photographs of Mom, Darcy's mother, like that.'

Grace was not a Fitzrowan for nothing. She glanced at him. 'Oliver? Anything about Oliver?'

Paul smiled. 'No. But photos of Helen Costello. Lock of her hair, very private stuff . . . it's all there, come and see for yourself. Any time.'

Paul had ducked his head and he was looking at her very much the way their father used to. Grace shook her head and apologized. 'Paulie, I didn't mean anything, just opened my mouth. Listen, take a seat, we need to get Alison on to the patent formalities straight away.' She sat down and gazed at him. 'And there is something else we need to discuss. You might not think you are ready for this . . .'

And Grace told Paul she was stepping down as President of Zeralda, but would remain an equal shareholder with Paul and Darcy. She told Paul she had discussed her successor with Alison and with Malcolm Strong, the Chief Accountant. And with Nick Bedrosian. They all agreed that Paul would make a wonderful chairman, even though he would only be twenty-six next birthday.

Grace sat back, watching her brother. 'So what do you say? You probably need time to think.'

Paul scratched his jaw, then ran a hand through his hair. He shrugged. 'Hell, why not? I was a lousy rock musician.'

They laughed. Grace pulled a bottle of champagne from an ice box beneath the bookcase and found two glasses.

'Just one thing, Sis,' said Paul.

'What's that?'

'Do you have a can of Guinness in there? I can't stand champagne.'

Alison was at the same time tremendously happy, being in love, and deeply anxious, for her man was in danger every second of the day until he could get out of the USA to the safety of his Caribbean island.

It had been wonderful, lying in his arms all night, listening to his plans for the bar – change nothing – and the deep-water cruiser of his dreams.

Peter had told her more about his childhood, given by his parents to the Scuola Mafiosa when he was only seven.

'They have a saying, in Sicily, when that happens,' Girolo had whispered, cradling her head in his arms, '*Prendere da un fulmine*, to be taken by lightning.'

Every few years, the best born, the brightest. In the dark she could sense he was smiling, that was how close they had gotten in a couple of days. 'I guess that was me. "Sent for by God" is another euphemism – it means the false Jesuits of the *cosa nostra* have taken that child.'

And Alison had shuddered and wondered out loud how he could ever break away from a society with such tentacles.

'Death,' Peter had replied. 'Only through death. So it is fortunate indeed, that I am dead.'

Peter had told her he had a false passport, and about four million dollars to grubstake his new life with a new identity. He needed to lie low for a few days, and planned to get out of Boston on the day of his funeral, at which every major *mafioso* in the USA would be present. And the Feds and Boston PD's Major Cases and Intel units would have all leave cancelled with every man and woman observing and recording the multitude of illustrious hoodlum mourners.

So it would be a good day to get out of town, unnoticed, provided he kept away from the cemetery.

She had not mentioned the DNA test, for it seemed premature. In any case, she was probably fooling herself. Why on earth, how on earth, could a mafia gangster from Sicily be any relation of Jack Fitzrowan's?

The buzzer in her outer office went and Wendy, her secretary, appeared at the door. 'Mrs Hanrahan says would you give her a minute? She did not ask for any files.'

Alison nodded. 'Sure thing.' She stood up, checked her lipstick and hair, and started to go, then paused and lifted the faxed MIT Genetics Lab report, which gave Peter Girolo's DNA chart, and went along the corridor to the President's office.

Grace and Paul welcomed her and she accepted a glass of champagne, noting with fond memories that Big Jack's son also preferred Guinness to the bubbly stuff.

Grace told Alison that Paul had agreed to be the new President of Zeralda Electronics Inc., and after congratulating him, and drinking a toast to his success, Alison learned about the successful creation of a microchip self-rejuvenation program.

'Paul, that's wonderful,' said Alison. 'I have the patent documents all set up and ready for filing. We should do that today, if not sooner.'

Paul smiled, for that had been one of Jack Fitzrowan's favourite expressions.

Alison had just decided that this would be a bad time to mention that she might have a contender for the Oliver legacy, when she noticed Pronsias Stevenson's report on Sebastian Tree's failed attempt lying on Grace's desk.

More important, there in black and white were printouts of the DNA strings of Jack Fitzrowan and Helen Costello, the comparison of which had proved comprehensively that Sebastian was no relation of Helen Costello and was therefore not Oliver Fitzrowan.

Grace saw Alison looking at the documents and said Alison should take them and lock them in her own safe.

After explaining to Paul the procedure for accepting his sister's resignation as President, Alison said they would require Darcy's vote in favour of Paul as Zeralda's new boss.

At which moment the telephone rang and Diana told Grace she had Darcy on the line.

Grace listened quietly, at first seeming elated, then disappointed, and finally, perhaps, relieved.

'OK, Darcy,' she said. 'Well done, both of you. I'll have a car meet you at the airport.'

When she had said her goodbyes, Grace replaced the receiver and turned to Paul and Alison Clancy. 'Darcy is in the Lear Jet right now, en route to Boston from Sicily. They stopped over at Cork, on the south coast of Ireland. Pronsias has returned to Dublin, he doesn't feel so well, and Darcy took off again at ten this morning their time, so she should be with us soon.'

Alison stared at Grace Hanrahan. 'What did she say? Have they found him . . . ?'

Grace shook her head. 'They found the family who adopted him. Oliver was adopted twice, you see. And a very good family, too, the woman's a contessa. Mazarro di Rossi. But it's a tragic story . . . the child Oliver was killed by a lightning bolt. God sent for him, when he was just seven years old. Poor little mite.'

Alison's heart was pounding.

'A lightning bolt?'

Grace nodded. 'That's what Darcy was told. So it looks as if our hunt for poor Oliver is over. In a way, I'm relieved. And not just for the money.'

'Well, I'm not relieved,' said Paul, with some feeling. He shoved a hand through his hair and paced around the room. Just like Jack, just, thought Alison to herself, like Peter Girolo.

'I wanted to meet him. To touch him. My brother, for God's sake. Dad loved Oliver's mother. I feel so damn close to him.' He drained his Guinness and stared at them both. 'And I shall tell you something. I *know* Oliver is still alive. I can feel it!' And he banged a hand on his chest. 'I can feel it in my guts.'

'That's your heart, dear,' said Grace impishly. 'Your guts are lower down.'

Paul glared at her. 'I know,' he said, more gently, 'that my brother is alive. Don't ask me how.'

Alison went across the room to Paul, stood on tiptoe and kissed him on the cheek. Then she said excuse me and, turning, left the room, collecting the Dublin laboratory DNA comparisons on the way.

Tom Hanrahan had never seen less of a human being on a mortuary table. He resisted making some macabre wisecrack about steak tartare but the police pathologist Barry Maguire did it for him.

'What do you want with it?' asked Maguire. 'Lemon or black pepper?'

'Very droll,' responded Hanrahan. 'The Department still need a positive ID. Before we can close the file.'

'Do you recognize this man?' enquired Maguire drily as he tested something unspeakable, mixed with scraps of fabric with drops from various pipettes of chemical fluid. 'This has been a nice shirt, look at that . . .' he indicated a computer screen on a trolley beside the mortuary table.

The various colour bars moved around, like some avant-garde artwork, and printed on the screen the words:

SILK 100% NATURAL DYE A-RHESUS POSITIVE RDX/TNT/GEL

'You don't get many silk shirts with their own blood group *and* traces of high explosive,' remarked Maguire.

'So, you can't sign off on this one?' Hanrahan asked. 'You can't tell, Barry, from these bits and pieces, who the dead man was.' He shrugged. 'I guess I'll just have to cite multiple witness statements.'

Barry Maguire turned and fixed Tom Hanrahan with a cool, if injured, gaze. 'Of course I can. There's more than enough here for a DNA comparison. Look . . .'

And the pathologist hit a number of keys on the computer keyboard.

On to the screen appeared the following:

P. M. GIROLO 40046174	JOHN DOE DECEASED
Blood Group: A-Rhesus Positive	Blood Group: A-Rhesus Postive
DNA Master String:	DNA Master String:
o	o
0	0
0	o
0	0
@	@
~	~
~	~
-|	-|
@	o
\	^
^	\
~	~
~	~
0	0
@	@^
o	o
|	|
^	^
0	^

Tom Hanrahan examined the two columns. 'So what does this tell us? They ain't the same. Not exactly.'

'Do you know the mathematical probability of a man with this DNA string being in a car belonging to a man with this DNA string, when only one man was seen by witnesses to have been in the car at the time of the explosion?'

'Doc, what are you trying to say? So far you could be speaking Persian.'

'Well, the word impossible springs to mind. Peter Girolo was seen in the car, which had an open top. Bang! Peter Girolo is blown, literally, into small bite-size morsels. Along with his silk shirt, which witnesses also saw him wearing.'

'So how do you explain the discrepancies?'

Maguire shrugged. 'Unless the guy has a twin brother, this is Peter Girolo . . .' he swept an arm across the mess of raw meat on the marble slab.

Lieutenant Tom Hanrahan considered this. Then he asked, 'So will you sign the papers?'

Maguire smiled. 'Why the hell not? I have a game of golf at six,' and he switched off the machine and reached for his pen, at which moment, Peter Michelangelo Girolo became officially dead.

Paul was in the attic study at 85 Mount Vernon Street, working on a research project he had been keeping to himself. Mainly because it was probably not entirely legal.

He had found a way into the Katakura Corporation of Japan's most confidential financial planning and trading prognosis for the next five years. And it interested him greatly, for Katakura was in serious financial trouble unless they came up with the Holy Grail of the electronics industry, the theoretically possible but as yet unsolved program to create microchips that would update and adapt to their surroundings.

Unsolved, grinned Paul Fitzrowan, until today.

The phone rang. It was Alison Clancy; she sounded excited. 'Paul, are you busy?'

'Never too busy for you, Alison,' he said, and the young Sir Paul had a way of conveying he actually meant it.

'Would you come down the hill to my place? It's quite important.'

'Alison . . . can it wait till tomorrow?' asked Paul, gazing at the fascinating information unfolding on his screen.

'It'll be gone by tomorrow. It really will be worth your while, Paul.'

Paul sighed. He switched off his computer and said, 'I'll be right there.' He stood up, stretched and reached for his leather zip-up jacket.

Alison Clancy opened the door to 25 Willow Mews. Paul smiled shyly, he had never been inside.

'Come in,' said Alison, and she closed the door after him, locking it and putting on the chain.

She led the way upstairs and into her sitting room, which was two rooms made into one, with exposed brick, white plaster and American colonial and Indian rugs and furniture.

A man sat with his back to the door. He did not look round as Paul and Alison entered. Paul looked at the man and to Alison, not quite sure what was going on.

'Paul,' said Alison, 'this is a DNA printout.' She smiled. 'I know you are something of an expert in such things . . .'

Paul took the sheaves of data and studied them. And as he did so, he glanced at the mystery man in the rocking chair. Finally, hands very slightly trembling, Paul gave the papers back to Alison, who seemed to be both smiling and shedding a tear at the same time.

She nodded at the unspoken question in his anxious eyes. 'Yes, Paul,' she whispered. 'This your brother, Oliver . . .'

And Oliver Fitzrowan, formerly Peter Michelangelo Girolo, climbed to his feet and turned to face his brother Paul.

The two men stared at each other. Tears streamed down Paul's face. They moved towards each other and at the same moment, threw their arms around each other and hugged for an eternity.

And Peter Girolo cried like a child.

★

Five days later, on the day that the nation's television news channels carried live coverage of the funeral of *capo mafioso* Peter Girolo, attended by legendary figures in the organized crime calendar, watched tensely by every available detective in Boston PD, and every available Federal agent, Girolo slipped out of town, quietly and unnoticed.

With him was the woman he loved.

In the President's office, on the fourth floor of Zeralda Electronics Inc., the new President, Sir Paul Fitzrowan, sat in an easy chair, with his two sisters sitting facing him. He wore a grey suit by Huntsman of Savile Row, and a sober necktie.

It was, as Darcy had whispered to Grace, 'kind of scary'.

Paul thanked them for electing him President of Zeralda and outlined the huge future ahead, with Zeralda's self-updating microchip patent confirmed. 'We also owe a debt of gratitude to Darcy, for her sterling detective work in proving, once and for all, with Pronsias Stevenson present as witness, that the elusive Oliver, Dad's love child and the subject of that codicil, is well and truly dead, deceased, and how shall I put it? No longer in the land of the living . . .'

His sisters smiled.

'Accordingly, after taking legal advice from both American and Irish experts in legacy litigation, I instructed Mike Medevik to issue an international summons for the return of Zeralda's two hundred and seven million dollars from the estate of our late father.'

As Darcy and Grace reacted to this, Darcy with predictable cold fury, Paul went over to his father's desk, above which now hung a framed portrait of Jack Fitzrowan sitting in the New York Yacht Club, and produced a faxed letter from Stevenson, Stevenson & Malahide.

'This is from Mr Justice Malahide,' announced Paul, 'on behalf of poor Pronsias who, as we all know, is in bed at our Dublin town house, suffering from exhaustion.' In an expressionless aside, Paul turned to Darcy and enquired gently, 'I trust he is being well cared for?' before continuing, 'And the good judge, being senior partner of our family law firm, accepts my revised argument and agrees that

Dad did in fact misappropriate the McDonnell Douglas two hundred and seven million. I have indicated that the return of the money to Zeralda's Turks and Caicos Islands account will be the end of the matter, along of course, with any interest which has accrued.'

'Well, I just think that is the limit, Paul Fitzrowan. How can you sleep having robbed your sisters blind like this?' Darcy was almost in tears, so great was her rage.

'Well, now,' said Paul, 'just hear me out.' He came back and sat down, offering more tea from a silver Georgian teapot, but both women ignored the gesture. 'It seems to me that neither of you ladies has any great desire to take part in the day-to-day running of Zeralda Electronics.' He smiled patiently and waited for a protest. There was only grim silence. 'Therefore, I propose to buy you out.'

If grim silence had been the precursor to this bombshell, what could only be described as deadly stillness, ominous in both ladies' lack of sound or movement, followed.

Undaunted, Sir Paul went on. 'I propose a payment, to be made out of off-shore transfers and tax-sheltered – that is, free of any tax burden – to each of you, of fifty million dollars . . .'

Suddenly both women perked up.

'. . . With an annual share of Zeralda's net profits which I predict will give each of you about ten million a year.'

The frost had thawed and Darcy poured two cups of tea for herself and her sister.

'What,' enquired Paul Fitzrowan, 'do you say?'

Grace smiled, then began to laugh, quietly. 'Paul Fitzrowan, you certainly are your father's son . . .'

Paul turned to Darcy. 'Darcy?'

Darcy nodded. 'That'll do me. Good luck to you, boy.'

And so it was that the Fitzrowan legacy was finally resolved.

As he ushered his sisters from the building, into the Zeralda Bentley, Paul felt it prudent to keep to himself the news that he was just about to make a take-over bid for the Katakura Corporation of Japan.

It was to prove timely and successful.

★

In the evening of that same day, Tom Hanrahan and Grace sat in their well-equipped kitchen eating a chicken she had roasted. Tom was getting back earlier these days, taking care his wife did not overdo it in those early weeks of her pregnancy.

'You're very happy today,' she remarked, squeezing his hand.

'Hey, I'm a father to be, ain't I? Aren't I?' Tom corrected himself.

'Bullshit,' replied his wife, glancing at the man she knew so well, 'I bet you had a nice little murder.'

Tom sipped his Budweiser. 'As a matter of fact, there was a homicide today. Old lady, nice neighbourhood. She told her daughter she was fed up with some food ritual, you know, Thursday mozzarella and tomatoes, Monday veal and broccoli.' He waved the bottle, a contented man, happy in his job. 'So daughter hits her with a steak tenderizer. One hundred and twenty-four times . . .'

Something about this rang a bell, plus Tom looked far too smug. 'What,' asked Grace, 'is her name?'

Tom smiled, in a manner he believed was enigmatic. 'The perp? As a matter of fact, you might know her. She works at Zeralda. Her name is Schofield. Amy Schofield . . .'

Postscript

When Peter Girolo and Alison Clancy arrived in their Caribbean island, not far from the coast of Venezuela, things had not turned out so well.

Girolo had obtained his passport and new identity without any trouble, for that was his profession and he had made those arrangements long before. But when he went to a number of private accounts, buried expertly in various permutations of anonymity, the *cosa* had gotten there before him. The only reason nobody had been hanging around to embarrass him with gunfire and worse was because, as far as the *cosa nostra* was concerned, Peter Girolo was dead as the Dead Sea Scrolls.

But the money was gone.

Alison had taken it philosophically. She still had Jack's legacy of three hundred thousand dollars, plus about sixty thousand of her own, plus the Willow Mews house would fetch about one-eighty thousand, after her mortgage was settled. So they were not destitute.

Still, the fast, deep-sea cruiser was out, for the time being. And since crime was no longer an option, it probably would be for ever. But when they arrived at the little bar restaurant on the cove, Alison just gasped, it was so perfect.

Peter's partner, Dean Arthur, was a friendly, smiling, competent and big-hearted man in his mid thirties. His South American wife, Lucita, was slender and beautiful, maybe a couple of years younger than Dean, and Alison took to her at once.

'Come on, guys, let me show you to your quarters,' said Dean, with that big grin which Alison was to know so well, and he and Lucita led them to a wooden bungalow on the dunes, overlooking a breathtaking view of the palm-fringed cove and the sea and neighbouring islands.

Somewhere a reggae band was playing, and the stillness and peace and warmth of the evening plucked at Alison's heart.

'Oh, Dean, Lucita,' she said as she inspected the spotless bungalow, with fresh flowers in vases and crisp bed linen, 'you have gone to so much trouble.'

'Dean's been so excited, Alison,' said Lucita. 'He just can't believe his partner is finally here. We are going to have so much fun.'

Alison could not stop smiling like a fool. What the hell was Chief Executive of Zeralda compared to this? She hugged Girolo and said, 'Would you like me to stay here? Or is that too shameless for words?'

Dean and Lucita hung back, diplomatically, as Peter Girolo kissed her and said, 'I love you. I want you to stay.'

Big smiles. Huge grins. Lucita hugged Alison. Dean shook his partner by the hand.

'Oh, by the way,' said Dean, 'you guys had better come down to the dock and inspect the *Wanderer*.'

'The *Wanderer*?' asked Girolo. 'Is that your boat?'

Dean and Lucita laughed broadly. 'I wish, Mr Morgan. How I wish, man . . .'

So they climbed into Dean's beat-up Jeep and headed for the dock. There, moored among two or three ocean cruisers, was a sleek, low-freeboard, tiered-bridge, 48-footer, with twin screws and two big Cadillac marine diesel engines. It was gleaming white, with polished wood and everything a charter skipper could ask for.

'Wow,' said Girolo. 'And who is the lucky devil who owns this?'

Dean grinned and handed Girolo an envelope. 'You do, boss. Ain't she a beauty?'

Frowning, Peter Girolo opened the envelope. Inside were keys to the *Wanderer*, owner's documents and a letter which read:

> Dear Oliver,
>   When you told me about the boat of your dreams, I guessed your former friends would find a way to clean you out. There is no way these days to hide a bank account.

So here is a present from your kid brother. Enjoy.

Also, you will find a number in the box Dean is about to give you. There are a few million bucks in that account, in Zeralda's name, in the Turks and Caicos, just a day away in the *Wanderer*.

Our father would have wanted this.

He would also want you to have what is in the box. I think you will know what to do with it.

It has made my life mean something, meeting you. You will always be in my thoughts.

Your loving brother,

And it was signed Paul.

Girolo swallowed, tough guy that he was, and brushed a piece of grit from his eye.

'There is also this,' said Dean, handing a small package to Girolo. And as Peter Girolo untied the string, which was fixed with sealing wax, Dean and Lucita retreated, saying they would be in the dockside bar.

Alison read the letter while Girolo opened the parcel. Inside was a box with something wrapped in a piece of paper: it was a gold wedding ring.

Written on the paper was an account number, as promised, and Paul had scrawled:

I found this ring in Dad's safe. He had kept it since he was nineteen, to put on your mother's finger. When he flew to Zurich, they were secretly married, just before she passed away. So you're not such a bastard after all. Keep it for your woman, when you know she is the right one. Dad would like that.

The note was signed with Paul's initial.

Peter Girolo looked into the eyes of Alison Clancy. Gently, he took her hand, and slipped the ring with which Jack Fitzrowan had wed Helen Costello on to the third finger, left hand, of the woman he loved.

And on another part of the sparsely populated island, Tommy Riccobono and his wife arrived by private plane, with two bodyguards, for a couple of weeks away from it all, after the drama of the Boston turf war.

The mobster gazed around contentedly and sighed, his arm draped across his wife's shoulders.

'Honey,' he said, 'one of these days, let us hire a boat and do some deep-sea fishing . . .'